Heaven's Gate

Book One of the Haven Series

By

Christopher R. Paniccia

Gridiron Publishing

Heaven's Gate: Book One of the Haven Series

Printed in the United States of America

First Printing: December 2017

ISBN:

For all those who keep us safe each day,

Those who stand on the wall,

Those who have given everything,

Thank you!

3

Chapter 1

The echo of the last shot from the twenty-one-gun salute rang still in Peter's ears. Sunlight glaring in his shielded eyes caused the tears already forming to roll down his cheeks. He stood staring at the closed casket of his grandfather, holding back the rushing emotions of his loss. With lips quivering, he reached forward and placed his hands on the smooth, polished surface. The casket was cool to the touch and he looked down to see his reflection mirrored back at him.

Peter Sullivan didn't notice the soldier standing in front of him holding the folded American flag. He was startled and came instinctively to attention with his hands out to receive the precious artifact. The embroidered cloth felt soft against his skin and he brought the flag up to his chest, holding it protectively. The soldier stepped back and snapped up a quick salute before returning to formation. Peter watched as the soldier stood at attention. He was mesmerized as the soldiers moved in unison and walked out of the cemetery.

He stood oblivious to the countless parade of people walking by him offering condolences. Within minutes, he stood alone with the flag still clutched to his chest with the brisk wind biting at his tear-stained cheeks. The wind still howling in his ears, he turned his attention to the lone casket before him. Peter took a few unsteady steps toward the body of his grandfather. He knelt on one knee and placed his right hand on the casket with his head looking downward.

Tears fell freely to the soft grass where he knelt. His voice barely above a whisper, he began, "Papa, I feel so alone! You were the only one in the entire family who could understand me. I'm lost without you! I hope you're watching football comfortably wherever you are. I'll make sure no one messes with your man cave and I'll take care of my mom. I promise!"

Peter looked down at the grass through blurry eyes. Using his hand to wipe his eyes, he didn't feel the light touch of his mother's hand on his shoulder. She knelt beside her son and grasped his left hand with her warm, soft hand. He turned his head slightly to see his mom with sadness in her eyes. The thought never occurred to Peter that his mother just lost her father. His mom carefully pulled him to a standing position and engulfed her son in a warm embrace. Peter could feel his mother letting loose her emotions and along with her son, they stood together, letting the tears flow freely.

For what seemed like hours, Peter and his mother held one another with the entire world running amuck around them. It wasn't until his mother peered around for a moment and noticed the darkness setting in around them. She released her son and held him at arm's length, stating, "We must go, Peter. It's getting dark! I really don't like driving in the dark!"

Peter nodded his head. He knew full well to what his mother was referring. Peter's father died in a car accident at night and ever since, Mom refused to drive at night if she could help it. He was very young when the accident occurred and could barely recall what his father looked like. His mother liked to tell him he looked just like his father and looking at various photos around their home, he couldn't disagree with her assessment.

His mother already was walking toward the waiting limo. Peter turned to follow his mother, but his legs wouldn't work. He turned to look at his grandfather's casket and rushed to it, and lay on top trying to hug his grandfather one last time. Once more, tears came streaming from his eyes, causing little puddles on top of the casket. He felt a huge gust of wind blow over him and a chill ran down his spine.

Peter stood as the wind picked up and he now felt cold. He looked down one last time at his grandfather and whispered, "I love you, Papa!"

As if in response, the wind howled, and he could have sworn he heard a voice in the wind reply, "You're the next in line. Your destiny awaits!"

He shook his head and looked around quickly to see who might have spoken to him. Darkness threatened to surround him, but no one could have spoken. He ran to the limo and entered just behind his mother, quickly closing the door behind him. Once in the comfort of the enclosed interior of the car, he stared out the window trying to locate anyone outside that may have addressed him. With no one in view, he watched as the limo pulled away.

Peter climbed to the back of the limo and peered out the window to catch one final glimpse of his grandfather. The lone casket stood in the oncoming darkness alone. This didn't make Peter feel any better having to leave his grandfather alone even though his mother explained to him that his grandfather was no longer really there. As the limo turned the corner, he lost sight of the casket and the tears began anew.

His mother asked him to sit as they prepared to get on the highway and he reluctantly complied. The plush leather seat felt soft against his neck. The seat engulfed him, and he turned his attention to the brightness of the cabin's interior. Polished wood greeted him everywhere and a warm light highlighted the mirrored glass. He was used to driving in small, efficient vehicles as that was all his mother could afford. This vehicle in which he now traveled was the most luxurious his eyes had ever seen. If not for the occasion, Peter probably would have been yelled at for playing with everything. He didn't have the motivation to touch anything and once again lay back in the seat.

He let his eyes close with the image of his grandfather's casket still in his mind. Thoughts of trips, weekends, and general time spent with his grandfather danced through his mind. One particular trip came to mind and he smiled. Their trip to New Hampshire was a most memorable one as the entire family went. Though they visited many attractions during their stay, the trip to a set of caverns made him smile.

The rugged terrain that's New Hampshire made for a challenging outing. Everyone was dressed accordingly and wore hiking boots. A long, winding trail brought them to a huge ravine with tall walls of stone threatening to close them in a trap. At the bottom of the trail, the temperature dipped by at least ten degrees. Members of his family, soaked in sweat due to the hot summer air, now shivered.

Before them, a large opening in the stone wall beckoned them further and the family pushed cautiously forward. A blast of cold air met them as they entered the dark, damp cavern. With flashlights in hand, they followed the guide deeper into the cavern. The guide deftly led them through the maze of passageways until they stood at the edge of a large spilt in the stone wall. Using their flashlights, they looked into the cavity only to see a sheet of sheer ice. The entire group was amazed to see this large sheet of ice in the middle of the hot, New Hampshire summer.

Peter and his grandfather stepped forward and placed their hands onto the ice. Peter felt a surge of electricity flow into his hand and seep through his body. He glanced at his grandfather with a quizzical look on his face and the older family member just nodded. He recalled in his mind other incidents when he and his grandfather shared the same moment in time.

The connection to his grandfather bordered on magical. Whenever he spent time with the man, Peter felt closer than he ever thought possible.

As if another jolt of electricity coursed through him, he jumped up to see his mother telling him they needed to go. He stared at his mother despite swearing he could see a glowing image of his grandfather next to her, waving for him to leave the vehicle. He blinked a few times and shook his head, trying to clear up the images before him. Another quick glance revealed just his mom's warm, smiling face. Peter thrust himself forward toward the door and exited the beautiful limo. He paused for a moment to look back at the sleek lines of the long vehicle. With one final touch of the hood, he turned and walked toward his waiting home.

Chapter 2

Peter sat on his bed staring at his astronaut posters that covered his walls. Often times, he spoke with his grandfather about his wish to travel the heavens. His grandfather would always put a warm hand on his shoulder and tell him to make it happen. Since he could remember, Peter felt the tug of space calling on his heart. He watched every science fiction show he could, as well as every new discovery real scientists would publish. His fascination with the cosmos worried some in his family.

After his father's death, he immersed himself into his studies of the heavens. At first, his mother chalked it up to her son's way of grieving. She thought after a while he'd lose interest and return to a normal routine. This didn't happen, and Peter continued to study and read the newest and latest information about nebulas and black holes. He went back and studied old space missions. The posters that now plastered his wall were from many of the early space missions during the original space race of the 1960s and 1970s.

He moved his glance from poster to poster, as if trying to read the thoughts of the astronauts staring back at him. They seemed to be speaking to him and beckoning him to join their ranks. The more he learned about these brave men and women, the more he knew he'd join them someday. Many times, his grandfather would come in to wish him good night and tell him stories of the astronauts on his wall. The way he told the stories, Peter always felt he was there among the stars with these brave explorers.

One story he vividly recalled was how his grandfather described the moon landing. His grandfather went into great detail about the race to be the first man on the moon. The story ended with an American astronaut walking on the moon first. Peter could still feel the chills going down his spine just thinking about that one small step. He asked many questions of his grandfather about the mission, which the older gentleman gracefully answered. The one question that still bugged him today was, "Why had we not been back to the moon?" His grandfather offered a quick answer about nothing being there and that it was just a hunk of rock. Something in the way his grandfather dismissed this question with such a generic answer bothered Peter.

This thought stuck in his mind as he lay back on his bed, his hands tucked behind his head. His eyes were drawn to the constellations painted in glow-in-the-dark paint on his ceiling. With his mind wandering, his gaze came to rest on Cygnus. This constellation always fascinated him, and his eye was always drawn back to this set of stars. He learned over the years that many ancient astronaut theories revolved around this constellation, as well as Orion the Hunter. Still staring at the constellation, he shot up, propped on his elbows, as he could see one of the stars twinkling before him!

The twinkle became more pronounced and he could see the light gaining strength. He closed his eyes and blinked them repeatedly as he saw many strange things this night. Once again, he opened his eyes to see a burning globe hovering a few feet above his bed. The power of the light threatened to blind him, and he could feel the radiating heat coming from the globe on his skin. Heat from the globe became more soothing and the brightness dimmed.

Peter's eyes widened as the globe came to rest within a foot of his now resting head. The shock of the moment now suspended as he saw an image form in the middle of the globe. At first, Peter saw his grandfather's face smiling at him, but then that image faded, making way for that of an angelic young woman. Peter sat unmoving with his head thrust into his pillow. The image of the woman gained more clarity and his breath sucked in as he took in her beauty.

Sparkling light now formed around the edges of the globe as the image seeped out of the globe, forming a more three-dimensional version of the young lady. The image now crystalized before him and showed more substance. Peter's body wouldn't respond to his commands to move as the image now looked solid. The image donned a sly smile and spoke, "Please be not afraid. I'm here on behalf of your grandfather. He'd like you to know he's at peace and is now with his loved ones. He'd also like you to know that now is your time as his came to an end. In time, you'll understand but for now, prepare yourself. Evil hunts you!"

Peter, too stunned to respond, just let his mouth hang open. This beautiful image before him warned him against some unseen evil. His face reddened as the woman continued to smile at him, but he felt as if she were looking directly into his soul. He knew he should say something and through parched lips, he began, "My grandfather? How is it you know my grandfather? Who are you and how are you here?"

The image smiled and responded, "Peter, your grandfather was much more than your grandfather and to a great many, he represented hope for humanity. My time with you is short but let me assure you. All questions will be answered in time. For now, take solace in the fact that your grandfather is safe and with loved ones. He wanted me to remind you that he loves you dearly and prepared you for this moment and what's to come. Just know he did what he could to prepare you before leaving."

Brilliant light formed around the globe but this time, it took on a dark-red tinge. The image now seemed frightened and looked quickly toward him. "Peter, you're in grave danger! You must find us and help me. Your grandfather left behind what you need but you must hurry! They're coming. I may not be able to help you further, but I'll be waiting when you arrive!"

His room now seemed to be on fire and the heat threatened to scorch him as the image faded. The globe now looked like a molten ball of fire. Inside the fire, another image formed, this time of a reptilian being. The grotesque image repulsed Peter. This didn't go unnoticed by the new image.

"Well, Peter, we finally meet. I've been searching for you for a long time. When your grandfather passed, so did his protection of you. You're now mine! Don't worry. I won't harm you much."

The reptilian figure cackled and sneered at Peter, waiting for a response. Peter couldn't bring himself to speak. He always had such vivid dreams. This entity before him was something altogether different as he could feel the hatred boiling over toward Peter. He finally looked up at the figure and gained enough courage to speak, "You seem to know me, but I have no idea who you are. As to what you want with me, you definitely have me at a loss. I'm just a plain teenager just trying to graduate high school. If you think I'm someone special, you certainly have the wrong person in mind."

Harsh laughter followed Peter's last comment. "This will be so satisfying to watch you learn why I hunt you. I'll tell you this, your family will soon cease to exist and that will be the last resistance before humanity falls. Now that you no longer have your grandfather's protection, you'll be easy prey. Try not to worry. I'll take good care of the humans!"

The globe burned brighter for a few moments before dissipating and leaving Peter in pitch black. He could still smell the burning pitch but there was no other evidence a large burning ball invaded his solitude. Peter remained on his bed, too frightened to move. As frightened as he felt at that moment, the beautiful image of the young lady filled his mind. He felt strength return to his body. He knew it was up to him to help but how could he, a regular kid, help this young lady when he knew nothing of her or her situation?

Chapter 3

Rebecca shook the singed feeling from her mind as she tried to re-establish a connection with Peter. Despite all her efforts, she couldn't reach him again. She turned with fear in her eyes and looked at her mother. Helena Beals looked caringly at her daughter and could feel her concern. Helena was a tall, strong woman with a stoic look to her. It was extremely difficult to place her years; she had the look of youth, but possessed the glow of wisdom only gained by life experience.

In her wisdom, she knew of the encroaching danger to her family. Her people warded the danger to humanity for generations but now the danger took on a new level with their enemy's discovery of Peter. His grandfather, through the years, used all at his disposal to protect his grandson. The earth's natural magnetic fields provided a great grid of energy to be used by those who knew how to manipulate it and Peter's grandfather was a master of this science.

Helena looked at her daughter with great concern. There was nothing she wouldn't do for her or her people, but options were now few. The impending doom was something that always threatened to consume them and followed them long ago to this beautiful planet. When Helena's ancestors reached this planet, they thought they could create a wonderful life. They soon found their past continued to haunt them and they were forced to literally go underground. The combination of the earth's elements and magnetic fields allowed them to hide from their enemies for a time.

Their protection lasted for millennia however, as the natural progression of humans on the surface reached the point of helpfulness, their enemies made use of the humans. Helena's people agreed the native population should be allowed to grow to a point where they could grasp what they could share with the humans. They watched as the earth's population grew and naturally progressed toward a more advanced people. They weren't the only ones watching the growth of humanity. Their enemies kept close tabs on this blooming species as well.

The reptilian people were the most ruthless enemy in the entire universe. Their lust for power was legendary across the cosmos and was only matched by their cruelty. Any species standing in their way was quickly identified and turned into slaves or destroyed. Human beings were an exception to their debauchery. In the case of humans, the reptilian people found a kinship as they viewed this species from afar, watching them grow in their own savagery. They even went as far as to strategically place more advanced weapons in their hands as they developed.

As the humans developed into a more advanced race, Helena's people could no longer stand on the sidelines while the reptilian people manipulated them. In spite of the humans' taste for violence, Helena's people chose to see their love of nature, animals, and each other. These two competing entities vied for control of the planet with the human race caught in the middle. During World War II, it became apparent to both factions that the human race was ready to take the next leap in technology and evolution. The reptilian people stepped up their efforts to influence the outcome with Helena's people countering so the humans could determine their own outcome.

The use of technology in World War II advanced the humans further than at any other point in their history, or so they thought. History was full of events that became influenced by outside forces. Competing entities made things very difficult on the overall development of the human race. Helena's people fought hard to stop the evil influences of the reptilian people.

Now, she faced, once again, a decision that would affect all races. She'd now need to look at military alternatives, the one thing her people despised. They chose this planet because of its sheer beauty, peacefulness, and a native population much like that of their own planet.

She stood now in front of her daughter with the fate of an entire planet in her hands. Her daughter's eyes showed as blazing globes trying to perceive what her mother thought at that moment. This young lady was extremely talented, but still had yet to discover the many gifts that would make her the powerful force she'd become. Rebecca offered a prideful smile back at her mother, who reached out to touch her daughter's cheek gently.

There was so much she needed to tell her daughter and she hoped she'd have the time to share it all before it was too late. With Peter's protection all but gone, Helena needed to find a way to bring the young man to safety. In normal times, this wouldn't be such an issue but with Peter's grandfather passing, his lack of protection left him at the mercy of the reptilian people. As if her daughter now knew what she was thinking, she lifted her eyes to let her mother know she was there for her. The two ladies clasped hands and then took each other in a warm embrace. They'd need all this love and warmth during the dark days to come.

Chapter 4

Peter stood transfixed, still hoping the events of the last few minutes were nothing more than his imagination running away with him. The burnt smell still hung in the air as a soft knock came on his bedroom door. At first, he was nervous to open the door, scared of what might await him. Another knock came and this time he could hear his mother's voice coming through the door. Her soothing voice brought him to his senses as he reached for the door knob.

He carefully opened the door and was rudely greeted by the light. As his eyes grew more accustomed to it, his mother's silhouette became a more solid figure. For a moment, the aura surrounding his mother's figure sparkled in a purple haze. His mother's bright smile broke the silence and she walked into the room without a word. She strode over and took a seat on his bed, patting a place next to her, indicating to Peter it was time to talk.

Peter sat next to his mother and looked into her mesmerizing eyes. With a quizzical look on her face, she sniffed the air. Her once smiling face became a mixture of rage and uncertainty. She, now with a very serious look on her face, began, "Peter, why do I smell smoke? In your grief, do you find it necessary to smoke?'

He sat straight up on his bed in a full panic and looked at his mother. "Mom, I don't smoke! You know that!"

In a panic, he looked around his room hoping to find something that might bail him out of his current situation. His eyes came to rest on a couple candles on his dresser from a few days ago when the lights went out. His heart settled back in his chest and he turned to his mom. "Mom, I just lit a few candles, that's all. It calmed me down being in the dark thinking of Grandpa. I didn't want to turn the lights on and I just wanted to rest."

His mother's face softened and her smile returned. "Peter, I'm sorry! I keep forgetting how difficult this has been for both of us. We couldn't talk much during this whole ordeal. Please know you can talk to me any time you wish. You spent a great deal of time with your grandfather and you two were thick as thieves. We lost a big part of our family and our hearts today. Just remember we still have each other and he'll always be with us in our hearts. No one can ever replace your grandfather and he'll be missed dearly. The time you spent with him will only prepare you for things to come."

This last statement hung in the air as he looked into his mother's eyes, which were now terribly sad. He reached across the bed and embraced his mother, engulfing her with a bear hug. The two held one another for a few moments before Peter backed away and held his mother at arm's length. He was going to ask her about her last comment about things to come but thought better and remained quiet. They looked at one another but neither seemed ready to continue the conversation.

At last, his mother spoke, "Peter, things will change now, and I want you to know I'll be here for you no matter what. Just promise me nothing will come between us."

He looked at his mother. "Mom, what are you talking about? Nothing will ever come between us. I just can't believe he's gone! He seemed so full of life, as if he'd live forever. I understand no one lives forever, but he didn't seem as if he was ready to go."

His mother moved within a few inches of him. "Peter, we never know when it's our time. All we can do is do the best we can with the time we're given. Be happy with the fact your grandfather did just that. He exuded life and lived every day as though it were his last. One thing is for certain, he lived for you! A night didn't go by where he didn't speak to me of how proud he was of you. He really wanted you to have everything and be happy with your life."

Peter looked at his mother. "Mom, I love him and will remember him every day. As much as I love him, the amount of love I have for you is second to none. Don't worry, Mom. I'll be here for you too. We'll have to look after each other now."

His mother walked out into the hallway and as she was about to shut the door, she paused. "Peter, you're absolutely right. We'll have to look after one another. Don't worry, my love. I'll always watch out for you."

She closed the door behind her and whispered under her breath, "You don't know how much we'll have to look after one another now."

Meanwhile, Peter watched his mother leave his room but couldn't help but wonder what his mother was talking about. They were always a team and looked after one another, but something in the way his mom spoke to him worried him. Was his mother worried about him as a young man without a father figure? He didn't even remember his dad except for small memories here and there. His grandfather was there for everything. That had to be it; she was just worried for him. He lay back down on his bed and closed his eyes. He opened one eye just to make sure no other globes hovered above him and then fell asleep.

Chapter 5

Peter's dreams took a strange turn this night. Tonight brought his dreams to a new level of realism. He felt the pull of an invisible force in his dream. The force urged him to follow. He saw his grandfather seated at his desk in the den, hunched over something in front of him. The figure looked up from the papers and peered into Peter's eyes with a bright smile.

He could feel the warmth coming from his grandfather's gaze and tried to move forward. His feet seemed glued to the floor and he remained stuck in his current position. The figure of his grandfather leaned back slightly in his chair and rubbed his chin. He looked at his grandson and mouthed the words, "Now is your time."

Peter stood in bewilderment, trying to understand what that statement could mean. He looked toward the desk and his grandfather was gone. Peter scanned the room to find his family member with no luck. The light now in the room faded and the last ray lay on the desktop itself to reveal a stack of old letters and journals. He couldn't make out any of the writing, but he could see they were ancient and fragile.

As the light faded to darkness, Peter could feel panic well up inside him. He turned to go back in the direction from which he came and found nothing. The darkness surrounded him, and he couldn't tell where the exit was any longer. He tried his feet and to his great relief, he was free to move. Carefully, he inched forward with his hands outstretched in the direction he thought to be the door. Slowly, he made his way back to the door until he could feel the wood of the doorframe against his hand. Using the doorframe, he let his hand glide over the wood until he grasped the knob of the door.

Peter opened the door and prepared to walk out. As he stepped into the bright light, something warned him not to continue. His foot still midstride and eyes now focusing, he almost fell forward into an inferno. He could feel the cringing heat rising to meet him and he quickly backed into the protection of the doorway. The heat from the flames threatened to explode into the room in which Peter stood.

He could make out some movement through the flames and brought his eyes into focus. The waves of heat and smoke made it difficult to see the images, but he could make out two people struggling to escape the flames. Peter watched as the larger of the two figures reached out and practically threw the smaller person on their back. In the roaring flames, he could hear the larger person reassuring the smaller person they'd be safe. He couldn't take his eyes off this epic struggle for survival as he watched the two pick their way through the raging fire.

When the two figures made it to the door, the larger of the two suddenly spun as if he needed to get something important. He reached behind him and put the smaller person down safely outside the door. The larger figure then ran back into the blaze with the smaller person screaming not to go. Peter could see the larger person didn't have much time as the room was now totally engulfed in flames. The figure scrambled to what remained of a desk and rifled through a draw, pulling from it some letters with a journal.

With materials in hand, the man raced in the direction of the door. Just as he reached the doorway, the roof above him collapsed, pinning him in the doorway. The little boy frantically yanked at the man's arms, trying to pull him to safety. Peter could see the tears streaming down the boy's face as he watched the flames move to the man's pant legs. The man never screamed or cried yet reached forward, placing the letters and journal in the boy's hands. The boy took the precious

21

materials and looked down at the man now on fire with fear in his eyes.

The older man looked at the young man and smiled. "It's okay. What you hold in your hand is more important than I! Make sure no one ever gets their hands on that except members of your family. Those documents will save humanity and you're the key. I know none of this makes sense to you now, but someday you'll understand. Our family is the gatekeeper and someday you'll help mankind find their way. Go, my boy! Go to your destiny! Now is your time."

By now, the man was completely engulfed in flames and the boy threw himself on the floor. The older man waved him on and the boy slowly backed away. He turned to run and stopped to turn at the burning man. At this point, the man on the ground glowed and then disappeared in a white ball of light. The boy looked shocked but turned and ran out the door, grasping the sorely won materials. Peter stood unable to breathe as he watched these two people fight for their lives.

All at once, the doorway he stood in transformed back into the door he recognized. He looked around afraid to touch anything for fear of burning himself. The doorframe was now cool to the touch and he inspected the hallway for any dangers. When he was certain nothing unusual was in the hall, he stepped forward at a slow pace. Something in the back of his mind told him to go to his grandfather's office. He made his way through the house until he stood in the doorway of the office, but stopped short of entering the room.

Anytime his grandfather was working, he wasn't allowed to enter. He recalled one time when he didn't get permission to enter and his grandfather reprimanded him abruptly. His grandfather gave him a lecture about respecting others, especially when they were working. Peter's grandfather was a writer and many times Peter couldn't tell if he was working or just thinking. The grandfather just told him anytime he was in the office, he was working. This made the office a special sanctuary and a special place to Peter. Anytime his grandfather invited in the office, he felt very special.

As he grew older, his grandfather allowed him more access to the office, especially when he was working on a writing assignment for school. His grandfather noticed his affinity for writing and genuinely wanted him to use the office to work. Peter recalled the day he finished a large writing project and asked his grandfather to read it before he brought it to school. His grandfather beamed the entire time and when finished, he practically leaped across the desk to give Peter a hug. His encouragement of Peter's writing allowed him to fill journals, especially with his favorite subject, ancient aliens.

Since he could remember, the ancient alien's theory intrigued Peter. He watched any show, read any journal, and talked to any author about his own ideas. The kids at school always came to him if they had any questions about aliens. He didn't mind and shared his knowledge openly. This pleased his grandfather who first turned him on to astronomy. He provided Peter with his first telescope and star charts explaining the constellations. When Peter came home with his first spaceship toy from the store, he thought his grandfather would just explode with excitement.

Looking at the hallowed ground that was his grandfather's office, he cautiously entered and sat in the soft leather chair behind the desk. He let his hands work their way across the finely polished, smooth wood. He felt he knew every inch of this desk by now as he grew up there. The wood was a deep-amber color and glowed in the early sunlight seeping through the window. Peter could see various papers littering the top of the desk, which wasn't unusual. His grandfather was constantly coming up with ideas for his new books. Nothing seemed out of place, but Peter didn't want to disturb anything.

He sat back in the chair and opened a few drawers to see nothing new again as he was aware of each item in the drawers. The office now stood in a crisp light from the sun and had a warm feel to it, which always made Peter feel welcome. He let his eyes scan the rows upon rows of books of the bookshelves. Peter couldn't help but smile as he came to the section of his grandfather's own books. The pride he felt at that moment washed over him and he pushed himself to his feet. With big strides, he brought himself to the shelf that held the precious books.

Peter looked at the titles, remembering each and the time they were published. There were quite a few that he particularly was fond of and read often. As he worked his way through the titles, his eyes came to rest on a large volume of an unknown work. At first, he didn't want to touch the book, but it seemed out of place. The volume was much larger than the rest and Peter couldn't place it in his memory. He thought he knew every piece his grandfather wrote. Peter let curiosity get the best of him and he reached forth, taking out the volume. It was heavy, and he knew something wasn't right. It wasn't an actual book and as he opened it to reveal its contents, he gasped and nearly dropped them. With his hands shaking, he looked at the contents. The volume contained the ancient letters and journal seen in his dreams. Something made him glance at the side of the volume at the title. It read, "Haven."

Chapter 6

Michelle Sullivan moved away from her son's door and walked back down the hallway toward the kitchen. With the burnt smell still in her nostrils, she stopped midstride and thought about the smell. It wasn't that of a cigarette but more of a chemical smell. She turned slightly looking back in the direction of her son's room before continuing her journey into the kitchen. She grabbed the spoon still leaned up against the bowl she was mixing before going to see Peter.

As she moved the spoon through the mixture, trying to get out the lumps, she suddenly dropped the spoon into the mix. Panic rose, and she could feel her face become red. She was about to run back to her son but met a resistance that kept her in place. That odor, she recalled where she last smelt that horrible stench. On a crisp fall evening, she came home from the store with a new costume, carrying multiple bags and Peter on her hip. Her husband had chosen to stay home that evening to fix the leaking kitchen sink.

Halloween quickly crept up on the couple and this was Peter's first time he'd be going trick or treating that he'd recall. His mother purchased an Army man costume for her son to honor her father. Peter's father was a great handyman and always seemed to be fixing something in the house. The young couple bought their first home and loved it, but it required a lot of upkeep. So, the fact that he was repairing something else wasn't a surprise.

She knew from the moment she opened the door something was terribly wrong. When she opened the door, she received the wave of burnt wood, plastic, and flesh. She rushed in the door and spun to place her son in the corner of the living room behind the couch. Peter, still very young, thought nothing of this and looked longingly at his mother as she walked away. Michelle cautiously walked toward the rancid smell, only to be met by the closed door of her father's office.

Reaching out, testing the knob for heat, she just barely grazed the knob. When she was sure there was no heat, she twisted the knob to open the door. A few inches at first until a full blast of the smell threatened to overtake her. Even with the smell, her fear for her husband overcame everything and she threw the door open to reveal the charred body of her husband. She stood in shock over the body of her deceased husband with hands on her head as she released a primal scream that would wake the dead.

At first, she couldn't move as she viewed what remained of her husband. She was about to kneel by his side when she heard the whimpering behind her. The fear returned, and she spun to meet the fearful eyes of her son looking at his now dead father. Without another word, she scooped up her small child and ran from the room of death. To this day, neither one would talk about that night, but that smell was now back, and Michelle feared for her son's life. Yet something kept her from rushing back into the room. She did remember the look of surprise on her son's face when she entered, but there was no look of fear.

Her mind went back to the night she found her husband. Jerry Sullivan, Peter's grandfather, came home just after her discovery and called the police. The ensuing investigation created more questions than answers and to this day, the cause of death was still unanswered. In the end, the death was ruled an accident. Joseph was a great member of the community and really had no enemies. The closest anyone could figure, he accidentally burnt himself. Unfortunately, Jerry neither smoked nor used fire for anything except in the fireplace. Being a very mild evening, a fire wasn't needed for warmth. With no real reason for his death, Michelle still wondered what really happened to her husband.

Peter's grandfather kept very silent about the whole matter, but stood behind his daughter and helped raise his grandson. Sometimes, she could see the guilt in her father's stare as he looked at Peter growing up. She knew her father had nothing to do with her husband's death, but she could also tell he knew much more than he'd let on. One day, she confronted him on the matter and it was the one time she could recall her father growing angry with her.

He threw back his chair and looked as though he'd fly across the desk at her. Rage filled his eyes and his lips were perched tight. It took only a few moments for him to see the fear in his daughter's eyes and he plopped back down in his chair with his face thrusted into his hands. He just broke down and sobbed openly in front of her. She knew not what to do and stood transfixed before her broken father. Jerry stopped and looked up at his daughter. "It's my fault your husband is gone! It was up to me to protect this family and I failed! Trust me, it will never happen again."

She stared at her father. "Dad, what are you talking about? Joseph was quite capable of taking care of himself. He was a very large and strong man. I'm sure it was an accident and none of us could do anything to prevent this."

Jerry looked at her with red, puffy eyes. "My girl, you don't understand; it has always been my duty to protect my family and I've done a wonderful job until now. I let my gaze slip for only a moment and it cost you your husband. Can you ever forgive me?"

With a pained expression on her face, she replied, "Dad, you had nothing to do with Joseph's death! It was an accident and I don't want to hear any more!"

Her father reached across the desk and placed his hand gently on hers. "You're right, my dear. It's just I feel responsible for every member of my family. I'm so sorry I wasn't here sooner. I always feel as though I could have done something to prevent this tragedy. I'll double my efforts to protect you and your son. That you can count on!"

She returned a prideful look. "Dad, you always protect us, and I do count on you."

Michelle recalled leaving the office that night feeling her father knew more than he'd said, but she also knew he had nothing to do with her husband's death. Jerry would die himself rather than allow any member of his family to be hurt, a trait he developed in World War II. She was always so proud of her father's service to his country. He talked little of his time in the Army but mentioned some about being an eighteen-year-old paratrooper being dropped onto the Normandy countryside.

No, she knew he'd protect his family with every ounce of his being. One thing that always picked at the back of her brain was, as a sci-fi writer, he seemed to have a wealth of knowledge about things most people would never think of. The interesting part about this was his appetite for the Germans' use of technology during the war. He wrote quite frequently about the Nazis and their race to develop their war machine. He explained to his daughter that if the Germans weren't so greedy and decided to fight a war on two fronts, they may be speaking German today. He told her how close they were to developing space weapons that would've turned the tide in their favor, but because of their greed, the allies could put an end to their reign before their plans could be implemented.

The love of technology and space exploration brought her son and his grandfather together. The two seemed to be made from the same cloth and she watched as they grew even closer after her husband's death. One thing concerned her though; her father never left the house again without being with them. He even walked Peter to school every day and then drove him to high school. She could see him starting to slow down and age creeping up on him, but he wouldn't let Peter see it. He was always there night and day for the young man. He made sure he got all the vintage posters. He made contacts and asked as many of the living astronauts to sign the posters as possible.

Peter kept these prized possessions with great reverence and looked at them frequently each day. Michelle would catch her father talking to her son about the cosmos and what he'd find there. She was sure many grandfathers had similar conversations with their grandchildren, but the matter-of-fact manner in which he spoke to Peter surprised her, as if he was explaining to her son as if he had actually visited these places. There were many times growing up that she thought her father knew more than he let on but to her, he was just Dad.

Now, both her leading men were gone, and her soon-to-be man was at a loss without either of his father figures. She was missing something, and she picked up her spoon out of the batter. She wiped it off and stirred, sure she was over-reacting due to the loss of her father. Michelle knew she needed to be strong for her son. Little did she know what type of strength she'd need in the future to help her son achieve his goals. Goals that had yet to reveal themselves.

Chapter 7

Peter stirred in his bed tangled in his sheets; he fought to release himself from his captive. Once free from the evil sheets, he peered through half-open eyes, trying to make out his surroundings. He shot up, half-expecting to see another burning globe. The events of the last evening fresh in his memory, including the burning globe, the beautiful young lady, and the reptilian intruder. His thoughts shot to his grandfather's desk where the contents of the volume of Haven stood awaiting his attention.

Last evening, he found the volume and looked quickly inside to see some ancient letters and a dilapidated leather-bound journal. Though interested, he thought it was a book and with the night so late, the events of the day exhausted him. He decided a good night's rest was called for and he could investigate further in the morning. His dreams were filled with a myriad of people—his grandfather, his mother, and unexpectedly, his father. He didn't dream of his father often and was shocked his image was so vivid. The more surprising images in his mind were those of his grandfather sitting at his desk with the contents of the volume scattered on the desk.

Once more, Peter held the contents of the volume in his hand and without thinking, walked straight to his grandfather's office. He didn't know why, but he didn't want anyone entering, and closed the door and locking it. When safely in his grandfather's leather chair, he gingerly took the precious contents of the box out and placed them carefully on the desk. The paper was dry and brittle, but he very carefully handled the papers.

With all the papers spread out on the desk, he inspected them carefully. What was before him was astounding. There was much he couldn't understand since it was written in German, but what he could seemed to be notes regarding the paperwork by long-forgotten allied soldiers. The English version of the notes outlined the ally's investigation into a secret Nazi military base south of Argentina. Peter froze. He remembered his grandfather telling him how many Nazi military officials escaped to Argentina after the war.

Peter always wondered why so many Nazis fled to this South American country. As he continued to rummage through the papers, his hand rested on a stack of fragile-looking letters. Shifting the papers a bit to reveal more of the letters, he couldn't believe his eyes. Reaching forth, he gingerly lifted one of the browning envelopes and read the address line. His brow started to sweat though the room was quite cool, and he couldn't understand why these letters would be in a pile of Nazi military paperwork.

The postmark screamed out at him and he blinked quite a few times to make sure he was correct in his reading of the marked envelope. He read aloud, "South Pole Naval Station." A million questions came to mind, but he had to read the letter. The ancient paper seemed as though it would crumble in his hand, so he took out his phone and photographed the letter before he read any further in case something happened. Reading, he became enthralled by its contents. The letter was written as one friend would write to another, but the subject seemed off. Peter continued to read and did a double take as he learned who it was from. He reached out and just brushed ever so slightly the signature at the bottom of the letter—his grandfather—addressed to a man by the name of Alex Collins.

Peter held the letter out in front of him and read it several more times, hoping not to miss anything. Each time he read the letter, he shook his head. His grandfather never told him he visited the South Pole, one of the remotest locations on the planet. The letter itself didn't make him take special note; the sketches and drawings in the margins of the letters caught his attention. If Peter wasn't mistaken, these markings were some type of rune or language.

He knew many types of picture-based languages and was fascinated by the Sumerian and Egyptian languages. These pictographs were foreign to him and he took many pictures on his phone. Peter couldn't help but open each of the other letters, all which were addressed to this Alex person. The number of runes and diagrams puzzled Peter and he made sure to take a photo of each one. Peter also read the letters multiple times, hoping to find something he may have missed. Each letter talked about mundane things, such as the coldness of the base as well as the remoteness of everything. His grandfather wrote about the strict and structured days on the base.

Peter felt as though he were there with his grandfather and could feel the cold seeping into his body. One thing kept popping out at him as he read the letters over and over—they seemed to have a pattern to them. Every letter seemed to be the exact same length and the same rhythm to its writing. He viewed the letters a few more times before picking up the brittle leather-bound journal.

As he inspected the outside of the journal, he noticed more of the same symbols or runes on the leather cover. There were no words, only these symbols. He eagerly opened the journal only to be disappointed as the beginning page was full of symbols. He frantically but carefully turned the other pages, only to reveal more symbols on each page. His frustration almost boiled over as the journal was useless to him. He was about to shut the journal when he viewed the last page. There right in front of him was a symbol of what looked to be a cross with what one would describe as a starburst behind it.

Peter shot straight up out of the chair and scanned the room. He knew of this symbol and had seen it before, but couldn't place it right now. He walked around the office, hoping to jog his memory of where he may have seen this symbol and how to locate it. The shelves of books only blended together and were no help in his search. He grew frustrated but couldn't remember and went back to the journal. Without thinking, he photographed each page of the journal. When finished, he reverently placed all the papers and journal into the volume box. He was about to place the volume back on the shelf, but something held his hand. He chose to take the book with him and he opened the door to leave. When he tried to take the box out of the room, he found something wouldn't let him move past the door. He put his hand out to see what was stopping him, but it met nothing blocking him.

Peter stood perplexed as he tried to move forward, only to be repelled. He couldn't understand what was happening. Without thinking, he placed the box down on the chair near the door and tried to leave the room. This time, to his great surprise, he walked into the hallway unmolested. Peter peered back into the room at the volume and walked back in, grabbing it from the chair. Once again, he tried to take the precious volume from the room without success.

Without hesitation, he returned the book to its original place on the shelf and walked back to the door. He walked out into the hallway without trouble. The strangeness of the encounter still fresh in his mind, he saw his mother in the kitchen and walked toward her. When safely in the kitchen, he leaned on the island in the kitchen and looked questioningly at his mother.

He began, "Mom, did you know Papa went to Antarctica?"

His mother stopped what she was doing and looked at her son as if she had no clue. "No, when did he tell you that? I don't remember him ever telling me that. He never talked about his duties, adventures, or what he did. I mean, he'd mention a few things here and there but never in great detail. I always got the impression he was uncomfortable speaking about such things with me. Why do you ask?"

He looked at his mother, trying to figure if she were telling the truth. One look at her and he could tell she was on the level. Peter smiled. "It's nothing, Mom. I just found an old letter he wrote to a friend back home while he was in Antarctica. It's just a regular letter, but still the fact that he was there's unbelievable!"

Michelle eyed her son. "A friend here? Who was it?"

Peter, not thinking, blurted out, "Someone named Alex Collins."

His mother choked and then cleared her throat. "Are you sure?"

He replied, "That's the name on the letter. Does that ring a bell?"

Michelle straightened herself. "It isn't really that big a deal but that was your grandfather's best friend during and after the war. He went missing some years ago and it really affected your grandfather. Keep those letters safe. Alex meant a lot to your grandfather."

"Trust me, Mom. I'll keep them safe!"

Chapter 8

High Commander Zosa, the all-powerful leader of the reptilian people, released a throaty laugh as the connection to the boy faded. He knew with utmost certainty now the boy's grandfather was out of the picture. His conquest of humanity was all but assured. Plans for the ultimate assault on the humans were now in their final stages and he knew they lacked the strength along with the ability to offer any real resistance. After years of planning, the commander felt it would be too easy to overrun the humans. The boy's grandfather had been the linchpin and his power alone sheltered the unsuspecting human race.

The commander thought back to the millennia of his exile and cackled this time, looking at the multitude of floating globes before him. Each globe contained various images of human cities and their hubs of government. He couldn't help but feel a huge sense of pride as he saw the many conflicts going on this very moment around Earth. Commander Zosa couldn't feel bad for them, but he wasn't sure what would be left for his warriors after all these conflicts came to a head. He was more than sure humanity would do most of the work itself, and there would be little resistance when his army came forth from the darkness.

For much of recorded human history, the reptilian people were behind every conflict upon Earth's surface. They manipulated the humans from the cover of their exiled prison in the deep caves of the earth. Long before the humans walked upright did the reptilian people inhabit this outpost as a launching point for other worldly plans for domination. Due to their very nature, they preferred the cover and coolness of the earth's many caves and underground structures. Little did they realize, their arch enemy, the Zarillion, already lived on the surface of the planet in the southernmost part.

Commander Zosa thought back to the lessons he was taught about how the coldness of the Zarillion base caused all kinds of havoc with the reptilian instruments. Originally, the reptilians took little interest in the fledgling human race, but as they quickly evolved, things changed. The humans had a great capacity to learn and as the reptilian people watched, they also saw they could be extremely brutal and cold in their nature. This brutality fascinated the reptilian people as they were viewed around the universe as the most ruthless race possible.

He continued to watch many of the conflicts and the devastation, along with loss of life with a smile on his face. The commander watched these people for century upon century while manipulating them from the shadows. His face turned to rage thinking of his enemy and the fact they entrapped his race underground using the very magnetic and energy fields that cover the earth's surface. The Zarillion used these fields to create what amounted to a force field that kept the reptilian people at bay underground. Though they couldn't physically cause harm to the humans, they used their telepathic powers to influence events on the surface. He smiled as he thought how susceptible the humans were to suggestion. It was too easy... almost.

This all changed with the death of the boy's grandfather. Commander Zosa was positive the grandfather didn't pass on the secret of the force field to the boy. Even though the grandfather lived multiple lives of men, he still ended up succumbing to aging as anything on the surface did. The one thing the Zarillion didn't count on was their force field helping stall time for the reptilian people below the surface. Once the reptilian people learned this, it was a waiting game for them.

Though births among the reptilian people were rare, they never died of natural causes, where their surface-bound counterparts slowly withered away.

The once booming Zarillion population was now only a remnant of a once great civilization. The reptilian's revenge would be complete very soon as the commander's scouts reported small cracks in the force field already. It would only be a matter of time until the reptilian people would flood the surface and wipe the humans off the face of the earth. When the destruction of the humans was complete, they'd then turn their attention to the annihilation of their arch enemy. The reptilian people would be free once again to rule over this planet and any other they saw fit.

Once more, his gaze went back to the globes showing the destruction before him, and the sight gave him a feeling of warmth. Watching these people destroy themselves was the only source of entertainment he and his warrior race had to enjoy. Soon, they'd be no more and Zosa and his people would again repopulate this planet in their image. He thought, as did the reptilian scientists, that once back on the surface, they could find the nutrients to have healthy children once again.

After a few moments of gloating, he looked down at his computer screen and waved his hand over the top, causing it to come to life. Another image came into focus on the screen of a humanoid figure. As the figure became more solid on the screen, Commander Zosa took in the uniformed man before him. Though his race's hatred for the humans knew no bounds, they were very helpful. A century ago, the reptilian people chose to try to speed up the process of ridding the planet of the humans. They contacted a people the humans called Germans and manipulated an already brewing large conflict. The conflict became known as World War I. The reptilian people watched with immense pride as the human people came close to destroying themselves, only to have their enemies intervene on the humans' behalf to thwart the reptilian plans.

The commander looked at the figure on the screen and the stoic, confident way the man stood. This human thought way too much of himself and really knew not how close he was to destruction. Still, Commander Zosa could appreciate the complete arrogance this human possessed. Arrogance seemed to be a trait most revered by the reptilian people who saw themselves without an equal as a race. That very thought crossed the commander's mind as he thought back to what would become World War II. The reptilian people threw their combined powers the way of the German Nazi Party. They, along with the rest of the Nazi party, saw every other race as inferior and pursued domination accordingly.

One thing the reptilian people couldn't foresee was the combined strength of a people fighting for freedom. This, combined with the overall arrogance of the reptilian and Nazi people, caused them to make huge mistakes in strategy that caused their complete downfall. The commander's face contorted with rage thinking of how this inferior race of humans outsmarted him. He used this defeat to fuel the last sixty-plus years with nothing in his mind but the overall destruction of the human race.

He couldn't help but cackle silently at the fact that soon the tables would turn on this unsuspecting human. The commander had the complete trust of this imbecile and used that to his great advantage. The world outside lay oblivious as to their direct danger and went about their daily lives without the slightest idea of their closeness to destruction.

With one more flippant look at the screen, he turned and strode quickly to the exit, vowing to string this man up and make him beg for mercy before gutting him like a pig. A determined look on his face, he took the corner quickly and made for the elevator to go to his bunker near the surface. He stopped and yelled some orders to a subordinate about sending a message to the human leader to meet him by the bunker. The commander didn't stop for an answer but continued without a hitch in his step as he made for the elevator.

Safely in the elevator alone, he let out a howl of rage and smashed the wall with his fist. He paused a moment to look at his reflection in the polished metal wall. Other than the scaled skin and hidden small tail, he resembled the humans he so despised. Even his face looked as though he could pass for a human except when he'd open his mouth and show his razor-sharp teeth. Teeth he hoped to use on the necks of these unsuspecting humans. His scaled skin was barely noticeable in places not covered by clothing. Clothing on his native planet was never needed since the climate was extremely hot. Here on this planet, his people used the inherent thermal heat to survive, but still many times it felt very cold to them.

The slightly distorted image of himself showed the rage still in his face. He stopped for a moment to compose himself and stood up at his full height nearing seven feet. To the humans, he was quite imposing with his corded muscles and stone-like jaw. This pleased him as the elevator came to a stop and the door opened, letting him out to a blast of cold air rushing into the small chamber. He shivered and shook his head as he hated coming to the cold surface of his current prison. As he stepped out of the elevator, he wrapped his heavy coat around himself hoping for more warmth. The air became colder with every step forward, but he pushed on until he came to the control room of the bunker.

As the commander entered the bunker, everyone stopped and stood at attention until he told them to sit down. Commander Zosa whisked his way right to the edge of the bunker and without hesitation, punched a number code on the keypad before him. With a sharp cracking noise, the wall before him split apart. The wall moved ever so slowly, and the sound of scraping rock filled the air as the two pieces of the semi-circle wall moved to the side. Once the wall opened before him, he could feel an even sharper blast of cold air come screaming through the small horizontal openings. He walked forward, shielding his eyes against the brightness seeping in through the openings, and blinked repeatedly to focus his eyes.

Once again, he laid his eyes on the stoic figure of the German leader and stilled his rage to speak to this puny man. Snow and wind whistled through the stone window, but he could see the human peering at him through the slit. It took a moment for both parties to see one another through the hole in the rock, which was always a tension-filled meeting as each loathed the other beyond belief. The German because he and his people blamed the fall of the Third Reich on the reptilian people. The commander because he hated the fact he was required to make of use of this fool to ensure his plans.

Both leaders eyed one another, fighting back the urge to reach into the hole in the rock and pull each out by the neck, while strangling the other. For a moment, neither spoke but eyed one another with suspicion and hatred. The German broke the silence, "Commander Zosa, what a pleasant surprise. I didn't think you'd come yourself. I always deal with your lackeys. This must be quite important for you to grace me with your presence. I hope I'll exceed your expectations."

The commander bit back his retort, "Yes, Colonel Whilhelm, I so enjoy our little chats. Let's keep this short and to the point as I have pressing matters elsewhere. I trust everything is progressing nicely from your end?"

Colonel Whilhelm raised an eyebrow before responding, "Commander, everything you requested is indeed in place. We just await your final approval and the assistance you promised us. We've been preparing this assault for much of the last fifty years in hopes of making the world pay for its treason. Trust me, Commander. The Fourth Reich will indeed last a thousand years, and you'll have your planet. All we ask is that you allow us to rule over what's left of the human race. With your help, we could achieve our wishes of a master race."

Commander Zosa pulled back for a moment from the hole. He despised this imp, but he knew all along that he'd have to spare a large number of humans to do his people's bidding. He was well aware of the colonel's wishes and actually wouldn't mind granting his wish. Ruling over the leftover humans would be a mundane task, one that none of his people would relish in the least bit. He carefully thought of a proper response and poked his head back into the hole. "Colonel, you need not worry about your legacy and you'll be secure in your place among the humans. Just bear in mind, you live at my grace and mine alone! As long as you please me, you shall not fear for your Reich. Also, keep in mind there may be not much left for you to rule."

The colonel's eyes shot up. "Commander, you assured us that infrastructure of this world would remain! You also said we could rule the people as we see fit, in your image of course."

He let this last comment go and responded in kind, "Colonel, understand when our plan is complete, there will be little left in the way of human life on this planet. Yes, the infrastructure may be intact but with the drastic reduction in human life we've planned, you may be forced to begin anew with our governmental structure. Yes, you'll rule but at our discretion and only as we allow it. Understand this, Colonel, you'll be a conquered species and we'll only put up with you to a point. As long as you please us, you'll be allowed to live!"

Colonel Whilhelm kept his fury in check as he calmed his face and added, "Commander, that's all we can ask at this point. It may be that when you're free, you'll prefer to stay underground, in a much different location of course. I know we've discussed this before but there are much nicer places on this planet for you to reside. I'm sure when you're free, the outer planet won't suit you and you'll need us to keep the planet in order. I guarantee when you're free, more of your enemies will be alerted to your presence on this planet. We'll be your first line of defense."

As much as it pained him to admit it, the colonel was exactly right and sometimes he could almost stomach this man. Maybe if they weren't imprisoned because of the man, he might have taken to this being. The colonel certainly was the type of soldier he respected and in his way, he followed the commander's instructions very well. As far as a tactician, the colonel was flawless in his execution of the commander's strategy. He had to agree with the Germans' assessment of the outer world situation, and he knew they'd need these slaves to rebuild their empire.

He peered into the hole. "Colonel, it's true we have need of you, but don't forget you rule at my grace and my grace only goes so far. I'm a hard master but as soldiers go, you've proven yourself worthy. I'll grant you a certain amount of freedom to rule. I hope you won't disappoint me. The last subordinate to disappoint me I believe is being tortured. Just be ready. We're about to spring the most complete assault this planet has ever seen. Our enemy is weakened beyond repair and they no longer have the power or strength to keep us imprisoned or at bay. This world will be crushed under our boots! Prepare our coming!" he colonel, out of habit, bolted to attention. "Sir! It will be done as you command!"

Chapter 9

Peter rose quickly the next day and said no more to his mother about the precious letters. He dressed and grabbed his bicycle from the garage. Without so much as a goodbye, he rode down the driveway and jumped the sidewalk, landing with a jolt on the road in front of his house. The road ahead of him looked much longer to him at this moment and he beared down on the handlebars, riding as fast as the bike would take him. As he reached his destination, he swerved into the driveway so fast he thought he might crash into the bike rack. With his bike hastily thrown into the rack, he bolted for the doorway.

The librarian eyed Peter suspiciously as he briskly walked by her and ran up the stairs to the computers. Something told Peter last night that he shouldn't use his computer at home. After his little visitation, he thought it much more secure to use someone else's computer. His hands visibly shook as they approached the keyboard. Being a history buff, he knew much about World War II and the Nazi crusade for world domination. The letters he reviewed last night confirmed a lot of what he already knew, that for some reason the Nazis were awfully interested in Argentina.

As the computer screen jumped to life, he couldn't wait to begin his research. His cell phone vibrated next to him and he glanced down to see his mother's number pop up. He shook his head—he had totally forgotten to tell her where he was going. He knew he'd get scolded, but he just sent a quick text about going to the library and turned his phone off. His gaze returned to the screen as he set up a search of Antarctica and the Nazis. So much material popped up, he found it hard to know where to begin. He refined his search and focused on the South Pole.

He was astounded to find out there were now over thirty-eight full-time bases in Antarctica manned by fifty-two different countries. He peered at the computer screen in awe as article after article appeared before his eyes on the subject. This was shocking to him as he was always taught the South Pole was a desolate wasteland. He thought seriously for a moment to himself. *There's no way that many countries are there studying the cold or the effects of Global Warming!*

Peter pulled up a map of Antarctica and looked at the locations of the bases. This completely baffled him as many of the bases surrounded one main base, that of the Germans. He stared at the German base, noticing the sheer size of the base. It took up a great deal of the land of Antarctica. Peter stood for a moment, not sure what to do next. He was quite aware that during World War II, the Germans created bases all over the world and saw themselves as a modern day Roman Empire. They even promised everyone their Reich would last a thousand years, much like that of the Romans.

What baffled him was why the Germans would waste time on a place full of ice and snow. The land itself was buried under in some cases a mile of ice and snow, being of no use to the Germans. He sat back down and continued to read all he could about the bases and their locations. The more he learned the more questions he kept writing down in his own journal. With pen in hand, he looked down briefly at some of the writing he scrawled down last night while looking at the ancient journal. The symbol of the starburst cross stood out to him. This caused him much grief last night as he couldn't locate the symbol elsewhere. As he was scrolling through some articles on the computer, he stopped at one very quickly when he saw what he was looking for.

In front of him, popping off the screen in bright color, was the very symbol that alluded him. He blinked several times to make sure he wasn't seeing things. The cross on the screen was in an article that spoke of an ancient legend of a civilization with its origins in Antarctica. He jumped up from the computer and paced back and forth. With his hand rubbing his chin, he blurted out, "Ancient civilization! That's it! That's why they were there. The Germans were obsessed with the supernatural, aliens, and ancient legends. They spent so much time trying to find religious artifacts, they lost focus on the rest of the war."

He spun around and buried his face back into the computer images before him. The pages scrolled by at an alarming rate and he stopped barely with enough time to print an occasional article that talked about the German base or the ancient civilization in Antarctica. Just by sheer accident, he looked at his watch, only to realize he spent four hours already researching and promised his mom to help her with the housework today. This being a Saturday, his mom always tried to clean up for the week, so they could relax on Sunday.

As he shut his computer down, he happened to peer across the room to see a person sitting in a chair reading a newspaper. Now this wasn't out of the ordinary, especially in a library, but how the person was dressed was. This being a Saturday, few businessmen would be here reading the newspaper in the library, but this man was dressed in a crisp, black suit. Peter cautiously picked up his journal, along with his new articles, and turned to leave.

Without thinking, he hastily walked toward the entrance and veered quickly behind a large bookcase. The library seemed so vast at that moment and it threatened to swallow him whole. He tried to sink into the bookshelf he leaned against and he could feel his heart in his throat. Without moving a muscle, he kept a close watch on the corner of the bookcase. Within a few seconds, a figure in black went quickly by his bookcase. Too scared to move, he forced himself to peel his body from the bookcase. He inched his way to the corner and cautiously peered around it only to see the man in black walk toward the exit.

He was tempted to follow but decided against this course of action, and waited a few more minutes before leaving the library. Once outside, he kept looking around, nervously expecting to be surrounded at any minute by a whole squad of men in black suits. To his great surprise, nothing happened as he hopped back on his bike and started for home. Everything seemed to be going smoothly but as he approached his house, he noticed an odd-looking van parked across the street. He quickly caused his bike to duck down the street before his and came around the back of his house. He threw his bike over the fence and hopped over himself. Without being noticed, he snuck over to the gate that was partially hidden by a large bush in the backyard. From his guarded position, he could safely view the van.

Peter sat watching the van for quite some time, but he felt the phone in his pocket and remembered he shut it off a long time ago. He quickly turned the phone on; it burnt up with texts from his mom reminding him about the cleaning. He was about to go in the house when he noticed another car pull up behind the van. A man dressed in a black suit got out and knocked on the back door of the van. The door opened and the man in the suit spoke briefly to someone Peter couldn't see inside the van. The man in the suit quickly shut the door but before he could, Peter got a glance inside the van. He noticed computer equipment inside.

When the man got back in his car and drove away, Peter knew he should go in the house to alert his mother, but he was frozen with fear. The events of the last few days crept into his mind—the dreams, his grandfather's death, the globe, and the ancient journal all caused him to bolt into the house. As he made for the back door, he didn't notice the van leave. Once inside, his mother questioned him about his absence and he offered a lame excuse about a school assignment due on Monday. Whether his mother actually bought this sad excuse, she didn't say, and she seemed so genuinely glad to see him, nothing more was said.

He shot a glance out the window and noticed the van now gone from view. Without hesitation, he dove into helping his mother clean the house. The manual labor kept his mind busy and his anxiety in check. With the two of them together, the house was cleaned top to bottom in no time. When his mother was satisfied, she had pity on her son and dismissed him for the rest of the evening. He leaned in and gave his mother a kiss, which she gladly accepted with pride.

Peter ran upstairs with his research in hand and grabbed a few other relevant items from his room before making his way downstairs. Once safely inside his grandfather's office, he closed the door behind him and went straight to the bookshelf and took down the precious box. His hands clutched the box with reverence as he placed it before him on the desk. He carefully lifted the lid, so he could pull out the contents. When the journal and letters were in front of him, along with all his research, he scoured his notes to help him make heads or tails of what was before him.

Chapter 10

Papers were carefully strewn on the top of the warm wood desk. Peter scanned the entirety of vast information before him and wondered if he could determine anything with it. Notes from the library still in hand, he placed them gingerly on top of the fragile papers. His fingers flipped through the pages and found the ones with the maps on them. He let his fingers trace slowly the outline of the continent of Antarctica. The land mass was extremely vast, and Peter couldn't help but think about what could lay beneath the cold exterior. With a flip of a few papers, he found the map of the various military bases that littered the surface of the frozen continent.

Peter still couldn't understand why so many bases and scientists would be interested in such a bleak, desolate place. He paused. "Unless there's something there. Someone is looking for something."

He picked up his notes and put them into a neat pile on the floor. The papers that remained on his grandfather's desk actually fit the décor of the office, old and well worn. The light from the desk lamp fell onto the brittle paper and for the first time, Peter could see the grains of the ancient paper. With the warm light, he carefully sifted through the papers and took out a few that seemed to describe land areas, but yet not part of an actual map. After a few minutes of taking in every detail of these papers, he grew frustrated and pushed himself back in the chair with his hands raised to the ceiling.

Without a key of some sort or someone who recognized the language on the papers before him, they were no better than ancient napkins. He let himself come forward and looked over to the journal. The leatherwork on the journal showed ornate detail despite its age; the journal itself was a true piece of art. Reaching across the desk, he lifted the precious journal, laying it carefully in front of him. The cross with the starburst taunted him. He let his fingers run along the embossed features of the cross.

Peter's fingers felt the dry surface of the journal and he followed the lines of the cross. At first, he didn't notice anything out of the ordinary accept for the depth and crispness of the lines making up the cross. He thought through the years the lines might lose their shape and depth. He continued to run his fingers along the starburst pattern and once again, he was amazed at how detailed the pattern still remained. Still something made him renew his fingers' investigation of the symbol.

Upon a second investigation, he noticed a pattern in certain raised areas of the cross and the starburst pattern. At first, he was quite puzzled, but he kept running his fingers over the patterns and then out of instinct, he used just his highly sensitive fingertips. He knew what the pattern was but couldn't believe what he was feeling. As a young man, his grandfather chose to introduce him to braille. Peter just laughed aloud as he recalled his grandfather telling him it might come in handy one day.

After studying braille with his grandfather, he spent an entire summer writing letters in braille to his friends. He quickly found his friends lost interest in the alphabet; it meant a lot of work to decipher the words. Though his friends didn't appreciate the language like he did, he continued to use it with his mom. After that summer, anytime he wanted to leave his mother a message he didn't want anyone to read, he'd write in braille. His grandfather showed immense pride that his grandson knew this rare language.

He let his fingertips guide him over the symbol and he deciphered words. At first, his hand shot back as though burnt. He sat straight up and for some reason, looked around the office. Darkness crept in through the windows and he knew not how long he had been looking at the journal. He couldn't believe his fingers. They slowly found the symbol and he read the message.

After several reads, he knew this was no coincidence. He took out his notebook and found a blank page. Just for good measure, he read the message before writing it down onto the paper. As his hands wrote the message, he couldn't help the shaking of his hands. The shocking nature of the message had him dumbfounded. Even with the message written on the page, he read it several times to make sure it said what he thought it did. Still unable to bring himself to believe the message, he stood and moved back from the desk.

The stark-white paper stood in great contrast to the darker, worn papers and leather of the journal. The message he just completed jumped off the page and grabbed him. He felt the palms of his hands sweating and his heart raced. He turned away from the desk, blinked his eyes, and then looked back, hoping something would change. To his great dismay, the message still read the same.

"Grandson, you're now the keeper of a profound knowledge. In time, you'll understand its value and only you will be able to use it. I wish I could be there to teach you, but my time has come and gone. There are larger forces trying to gain this knowledge. You must never give in. You're strong and bright like the stars above you. Let the stars be your guide. Know that I'm with you always and we'll meet again."

Peter, still standing, was now in a cold sweat. How could this be the message and what was his grandfather talking about.

He was just a teenager, what possible profound knowledge could he have? Without thinking, he looked down at the desk covered in ancient papers and the precious journal. He couldn't help but wonder what else awaited him in these ancient items.

He found himself sitting in the chair and he couldn't help but try to find if there was more to the message on the cover of the journal. After a few minutes, he was satisfied the message was complete and he didn't miss any information. When he lifted the notebook to look at the message, he kept coming back to the line about the stars. He and his grandfather were avid stargazers. They spent many nights viewing and discussing the constellations. His grandfather told him many a time that man was made to travel the stars and in the not-too-near future, he'd have the technology to travel the cosmos.

Growing up, Peter didn't think much of what his grandfather said to him with regard to the stars and space travel, but for some reason, his grandfather's wisdom came through. Still he felt the closeness of his grandfather reaching across planes of existence in that moment to touch his heart. He broke down and allowed the pain in his heart to come out. Sobbing at his grandfather's desk, he wished for just one more day with the man that always seemed to be there when he needed him.

The stars, what could that mean?

The thought of stars rattling around in his head, he chose to continue to look in the journal for any other clues to this tricky mystery. The pages of the journal said little to him as he tried to make out any detail that might give him an idea as to what it said. Out of sheer curiosity, he tried to feel with his fingertips to see if there was any more braille writing. He was disappointed to find the pages just smooth and brittle.

His eyes were barely open when he inspected the last page of the journal, hoping beyond hope a clue would be found. He closed the journal carefully and knew he could do no more tonight. Sitting in the chair, he couldn't bring himself to move despite the heavy exhaustion he felt in his bones. The events of the last week weighed heavy on him at this moment. Peter carefully gathered all the items from the desk and ever so slightly placed them into the box.

Peter walked over to the bookshelf and placed the box back into place, not willing to test the doorway tonight. With the box safely on the shelf, he just rested his hand on it for a moment. He felt he shouldn't leave, but he could barely stand, and he knew he could do no more tonight. With one last look behind him at the now dark office, he turned to leave. Once outside the office, he almost felt the air brush by his face, refreshing him a bit.

On his way to the stairs, he noticed his mother in the kitchen reading something. She glanced up at him with a genuine smile. "Peter, you look wiped! Get some sleep, my love!"

He smiled weakly. "Mom, trust me, tonight I'm going to sleep like a baby. An earthquake couldn't wake me up tonight! Good night, Mom."

Chapter 11

His feet felt leaden as he struggled up the last step to turn toward his bedroom. He could see the door to his bedroom slightly ajar, but something was off. At first, he just thought it was because he was so exhausted. The closer he came to the door, the strangeness strengthened. Peter placed his hand on the door to push it open, but stopped short when he suddenly saw a faint light coming from the darkened room. Bringing his head closer to the half-open door, he peered into the room cautiously.

To his great surprise, another glowing globe stood in the middle of his room, waiting for him. He felt a draw to its power and quickly entered the room, shutting the door fast behind him without another thought. At first, it just looked like a smaller version of the sun he saw every day, and the closer he came the warmer he felt. Without thinking, he raised his hands to grasp the globe and as he was about to close his fingers, he pulled them away at the last minute.

The image of the beautiful girl appeared in the globe. Her golden hair cascaded down her shoulders and flared out to her arms. Eyes of ice blue pierced his heart as he stood captivated by this creature. His heart beat quickly in his chest and he dared not move a muscle for fear she might leave him. Peter watched as her full lips opened, mouthing words, but he couldn't take his eyes off her gaze. She smiled brightly at him but then wrinkled her brow and gave him a more serious look.

As if waking from a dream, he snapped to attention, standing straight, looking at the beautiful image before him. Once again, she mouthed words and this time, he shook his head. He paid close attention and drew closer to the globe. The young lady's face grew more concerned and she looked sympathetically at Peter. He couldn't help but feel his face redden and feel warm as if he was in trouble.

The woman spoke, "Peter, I'm sorry to disturb you and I can see you're exhausted. Know this, our enemy is now on your doorstep and you must leave! If you stay, you and your mother are in grave danger. The enemy cares little for your mother; she's of little value to them except to harm you. You, on the other hand, are the key to our survival. I can say very little as I'm already putting both of us in even more danger by revealing myself to you. Peter, please leave now. Take your knowledge with you and make your way to the frozen continent. I'll be waiting. We have much to discuss."

Peter felt a little impatient. "Honestly, I have no idea what's going on other than everything I thought I knew about my grandfather was a lie!"

She now had a sad look on her face. "You have every right to feel this way and I wish I could answer your questions, but for now, just know I'll do what I can to answer them when the time is right. Now, you must leave and make your way south. They won't expect you to make the trip. As we speak, they may even be in your neighborhood."

She looked back over her shoulder and with a look of panic, she turned to lock eyes with Peter. "They're here! Go now! Get out of here!"

He looked around and then heard the knocking on the front door. Peter spun back to the globe. "I cannot leave my mother!"

She gently waved her hand. "Your mother is safe for now; they cannot touch her, but I cannot do the same for you. Peter, you must leave now and don't let them get their hands on your grandfather's things. Go now and if you need me, just talk to me in your mind. I'll hear you as we're connected. Hurry, Peter, I'll look after your mother!"

Peter couldn't believe his legs were already thrusting him out the door. As he made his way to the stairs, the banging on the door became louder and more pronounced. He was glad the front door was solid wood as he whisked by on his way to his grandfather's office. He nearly jumped out of his skin though as he heard it splinter as a heavy blow rocked the wooden door. He hastened his steps and flew into the office, throwing the door shut. He could still hear the smashing blows behind him as he reached for the box on the bookshelf.

With nimble hands, he held the box in one hand and swiped the notebook with all his notes from the desk. Peter held the precious items close to his chest and grasped the door knob, opening the door only to see people making their way toward him. He instinctively slammed the door and locked it, retreating to his grandfather's desk. Outside the windows, he saw flashlights now beaming in through the windows and behind the beams, he could make out armed figures. He desperately looked around the room as he heard pounding on the office door.

The door held fast, but each blow produced more rubble falling from around the doorframe. He looked at the frame and wondered how long it would last. Suddenly, he heard the smash of broken glass and knew he had to leave as a canister of gas hit the rug. A pinkish smoke came from the canister and Peter knew he had to go, but where? He was trapped. A quick look of the office gave him little hope as the only exit was still being smashed to bits. Just by chance, he looked at the large bookcases and saw the smoke being drawn into the shelves as if there was a window sucking it out.

Peter frantically pushed and pulled on the bookcase in hopes it would budge, but it stood frozen on the wall. Sweat now poured down his cheek and he wiped his brow with his sleeve. Out of the corner of his eye, he noticed an ancient book of constellations on the shelf. For some reason, this seemed to be out of place. Most of the astronomy books were in Peter's room and Grandfather made sure he had as much of this information as he could. Without thinking, he reached for the book and pulled it from the shelf. Once the book was removed, he peered to where the book once sat and to his great surprise, he saw a symbol on the wooden bookcase—the sunburst symbol. Peter stood shocked but was quickly brought to reality as a pungent smell invaded his nostrils, making him cough.

Holding his breath, he reached in and pushed on the symbol. To his relief, he heard a click as the bookcase moved away from the wall. Peter saw the tunnel open before him and didn't wait for the bookcase to open all the way. As he moved into the tunnel, he heard the door explode behind him. He spun around to find a way to close the bookcase. Luckily, the answer was on the wall to his right and he saw a control panel. On the panel, he saw a red button and thrust his hand out, pushing it quickly. Smoke now filled the office and he could see shadowy figures rushing toward him. The bookcase took forever to close and he felt paralyzed, unable to move.

An arm reached into the space now left by the closing bookcase, trying to grab him. He pushed at the arm and even kicked it against the wall. A wail came from the figure and the arm disappeared. The bookcase closed with another click. Without waiting to find out what would happen next, he flew down the tunnel, holding the box and his notes like a prized football running back would hold the pigskin.

The tunnel was dimly lit but he could see his way. He could only go in one direction. He moved quickly through the tunnel and he soon saw it was no longer made of brick, but cut out of solid rock. The air inside the tunnel was now more humid and stagnant. He moved as fast as he could and after a few minutes, the tunnel once again changed, and he saw what looked to be an old mining tunnel, now propped up with large wooden beams.

Peter kept looking back, expecting to see the shadowy figures following him. He listened for a moment and he could hear pounding coming from behind him, telling him they weren't yet in the tunnel. He knew it would be only a matter of time until they got in. With a quick glance up the tunnel, he forced himself onward. He made his way through the now mostly dirt tunnel and panicked when the wall stopped right in front of him. He was trapped, and he frantically looked around the small cavern. To his view, the walls just looked like sheer dirt with no openings.

He now heard voices coming toward him. From their angry shouts, he could tell he didn't want to be anywhere near this room when they arrived. He put his hands on his head and just happened to look up to see once again the sunburst symbol. Without hesitation, he reached up and placed his hand on the symbol. At first, he didn't think anything would happen, but then he felt a great warmth emanate from his hand. The symbol, and his hand, now glowed as if they were one. He felt power flowing through him and the symbol now pushed into the ceiling, now splitting apart with dirt and dust coming from above, falling to the ground.

A large hole with a ladder stood above him and he jumped up to grab it. The first try, he fell flat on his back with a dust cloud going into the air. On the next try, he backed up a few steps and ran before he jumped. This time, he grabbed a hold of the lowest rung on the ladder. He pulled himself up to the next rung, only to have someone warp their hand around his ankle, threatening to pull him back into the hole. Peter kicked swiftly down with his free foot and found the arm of his assailant. The man let go and he scrambled up the ladder. As if on cue, the ladder led to another smaller room with a small wooden door.

He could hear someone quickly moving up the ladder and he didn't want to be here when the man made it to the top. Peter gripped the knob of the door and threw it open. He felt the rush of fresh air run into the tunnel. Peter thrust himself out into the night. Gasping for air, lying on his back, he spun himself around and jumped to his feet. Looking around him, he was surprised to see the tunnel came out in the roots of a huge tree. He couldn't help but laugh as his grandfather would always bring him to this grove and this particular tree to tell him stories about the stars.

His thoughts swiftly turned back to his pursuers and he searched for a way to block the entrance. Off to the left, he saw a large branch he could use to brace the door shut. He wedged one end against the door and the other end into the ground. He also rolled a large rock over and leaned it on the branch for extra support. It wouldn't last forever but it might just give him a chance to escape. Without a moment to lose, he heard the pounding on the wooden door. His brace held, and he turned running into the night.

Chapter 12

Rebecca flew around the corner and raced toward the huge ornately carved, wooden council doors. The guards, too astonished to stop her, just flung open the door for her. She almost skidded into the room and the council, sitting around a large round, stone table jerked their heads up to see the intruder. Andrew Olin, the elected leader of the Zarillion people, rolled his eyes in fury at the lack of decorum coming from this young member of the gentry. Ceremony and pageantry were always followed when addressing or meeting with the council. Rebecca was what one might call a rebel and always tested the lengths of the council's patience.

Helena, Rebecca's mother, held up a hand toward Andrew, motioning that she'd address this behavior. She took a hold of Rebecca's arm and escorted her off to a corner of the room, away from earshot of the others. Helena could tell by the panic in her daughter's eyes, something serious was the cause of this visit. She placed her hands gently on her daughter's shoulders. "Tell me!"

Rebecca sucked in the air swiftly, trying to get enough air to string enough words together to speak to her mother. It took a moment for the words to come out and they threatened to just spill out of her mouth in gibberish. Her face red and perspiration beading on her forehead, she gripped her mother's arms. With a terrific effort, she blurted out, "They've breached Peter's grandfather's defenses and attacked Peter's home!"

Helena spun her daughter around. "Are you sure? We were sure the defenses would hold until we could offer safe passage for Peter and his mother!"

Rebecca, with an extremely panicked look on her face, continued, "Mother, I saw it! They practically blew his house apart. I could hide his mother and put her into suspended animation, but Peter is an altogether different matter. Peter isn't subject to my power and he just barely escaped with his life. He's in great danger, Mother, and he's all alone with no one to help him! We must do something. If they capture him, our society falls! His fate and ours are one."

Rebecca's mother led her daughter to the round table, practically dragging her behind. Once again, Andrew looked up with disdain but as soon as he saw the determination in Helena's face, he stopped talking. Helena, a tall, stoic woman stood shoulder to shoulder with the leader of her race and spoke in his ear quickly. Andrew's face crunched up and he spoke, "My friends, we have some extremely distressing news that must be addressed. Rebecca, please tell us what you know. Make sure not to leave anything out, even if you think it minor."

Rebecca relayed the events of the evening to the wide-eyed council. Her conviction won over the skeptical elders and they looked fondly upon her when she finished her tale. Even Andrew, who having dealt with her interruptions quite frequently, couldn't help but smile inwardly at the young lady before him quickly becoming a woman. He stood, placing his arms straight on the table, and looked with a serious gaze at his colleagues. Andrew backed away from the table and turned for a moment, contemplating how he might address the council. He turned back to the table and began, "Ladies and gentlemen, we've come to the greatest moment perhaps in our history! What we decide here today will decide the fate of an entire planet."

Andrew let that statement sink in for a moment before beginning again, "Our time of hiding in the shadows must end. We've helped from cover for long enough. I'm afraid if we do things as we've always done, the human race will fall. If the humans fall, it will only be a matter of time before we're overcome. Our hope of Peter being taught by his grandfather has failed. We must find this young man and help him get here safely. He's the key to saving both peoples and he's our mission right now!"

The council sat with looks of pain and concern as they viewed their leader before them. A very tall, radiant woman stood in her place and turned to the council. The strong woman standing ready to speak was none other than Holly Cheric, the second in line to Andrew. Although Andrew was officially the leader, nothing was done without Holly's say so. Her long, flowing, blonde hair seemed to be on fire as she faced her friends. "Andrew is right! This young man holds the key to more than just his grandfather's knowledge, but if omens are correct, he's the one that will reconnect us to our fathers."

She stood to her full height and looked to tower over the two other standing council members. Her voice came out with tremendous power, "It's time to fight! Fight for our lives, fight for the humans' lives, and fight for this planet. This may not be our home world, but it certainly is our home and I don't know about you, but I'm sick of hiding! We've hid for far too long and told ourselves that we shouldn't interfere. I think we can stop kidding ourselves; the humans have paid the price for our vanity. It's high time we repaid the debt in full!"

The room exploded as everyone spoke at once. Rebecca noticed one member of the council remained in his seat. Michael Gentry was their financial leader. He was the shrewdest man Rebecca ever laid eyes on, and she also knew him to be the most mysterious. While his colleagues were talking, arguing, and planning, he remained silent.

After a few minutes, the conversation toned down a bit and eyes noticed Michael still sitting. Holly turned and glared at the silent council member. Anyone would melt under that gaze, but Michael seemed unfazed. He calmly stood, using the chair to steady himself. Michael Gentry was a slight man with little meat on his bones. Even though their society could cure most ailments, Michael's situation baffled doctors. His muscle structure simply didn't develop correctly and even with protein therapy, they couldn't strengthen his body. What he lacked on the outside, however, he more than made up for inside.

The council was aware that Michael was sharp as a tack and as ruthless as they came. He thought little of others' feelings when rendering his opinions, or decisions for that matter. Holding the back of his chair with his knuckles white with the strain of steadying himself, he looked carefully at the council. His brow raised as he spoke, "Friends, friends, let us not speak in haste. This young man is important, but I think your assessment of our plight may be a little premature. Might I remind you of our dominance over this planet for eons!"

This brought a hot glance from Holly who didn't allow Michael to finish his thought. She strode to within a few inches of the frail council member. "Michael, you know as well as I do that the humans have insulated us from all dangers and we own them our very lives! We remain here in our protective bunker and tell ourselves it's because we don't want to interfere. In actuality, we're allowed to live in relative peace while the wars rage outside our doors. No, Michael, we won't hide any longer!"

It was Michael's turn to get heated. "Holly, you know as well as I do, if we interfere with the humans, we destroy what we've built here. They have no idea they live among other beings and that alone might destroy them. I know some are aligned with the reptilian people but unfortunately, we have

62

little control over that situation. All we could do was minimize the impact of that alliance.

"Also, you must realize that all the humans' confrontations allow us to remain hidden. If their population is in check, we remain safe. Unfortunately, it's necessary for our own survival. We've been over this a million times; if we were discovered and they realized what has been going on under their noses, it would have devastating consequences! No, Holly, we must be vigilant and not break containment!"

Holly looked at her council members. "This council can choose to sit on their hands, but they'll do it without my vote! I've watched for far too long as these people have sacrificed themselves, all so we can live here by ourselves. These people have every right to live as we do with the full benefits of our knowledge. We talk about not interfering but that's what we've been doing since these people first inhabited this planet. No more will I stand by and do nothing!"

She moved next to Helena and Rebecca, reaching out to grab their hands. She called to the council, "I stand with Helena, Rebecca, and the human people! Who is with me?"

Andrew stood with a frightened look on his face. On many occasions, the council became heated, but it was usually about minute things. He looked around at the animated faces of the elders and he knew he had to act fast or lose control of the entire council. He spoke in a calm, loud tone, "My friends, please sit so we can find the right solution for everyone. As a council, we've always worked for the best for everyone. I know if we take some time to discuss this rationally, we'll come to an agreement we all will be proud of."

In spite of the anger in the room, the council still had a great deal of respect for Andrew and they all took their seats. Michael smiled inwardly as he seemed to have his way with the council. Helena and Holly sat with their still red faces. Helena motioned for Rebecca to have a seat left empty by Ryan's absence. Ryan Giles was in charge of defense of the city. At this moment, Holly realized Ryan was missing.

Holly looked right at Andrew. "Andrew, where is Ryan? He never misses a council meeting."

Once again, Andrew felt panic grow inside. "Holly, he's checking something at the west entrance. He said he'd be late, but he promised he'd be here. I'm sure he'll arrive any minute. You know how he likes these meetings."

It was Holly's turn to look panicked as she had heard rumblings of attacks on the west entrance, but they always amounted to nothing. She turned to Andrew with a stern look. "The west entrance is under attack?"

Andrew flinched. "Holly, it's nothing! You know every once and a while, the humans who work with the reptilian people attempt a breach. It's nothing more than another attempt to probe our defenses. Ryan always has our city well defended. Any minute, he'll walk through that door and tell us another attempt was repelled. Now, please, can we get back to the matter at hand and decide what our next move will be? As we've already stated, this decision affects everyone!"

At that moment, the council chamber doors flew open and in ran a large muscular man with a flat top haircut. He wore a full uniform, which was now torn and full of dirt with a mixture of blood. All the council members stood in shock at once. The man stood at the edge of the stone table at attention as if ready to report to the council. He saluted Andrew. "My liege, they broke through the defenses of the west entrance! We managed to gain control and we sealed off that entrance. I've never seen anything like that before! They sent thousands against our small detachment, the only thing that saved us is the entrance is so narrow, their numbers accounted for little."

Hs stood stone faced and addressed the council, "It's time! The enemy marches on us!"

Chapter 13

Colonel Whilhelm stood stories above his troops on a large, metal grate and looked down with a large smile on his face. His life's work stood before him at attention, waiting for his orders. The rows of uniformed soldiers with their weapons ready was an unnerving sight. Several thousand strong, this force had been put together for one reason, to destroy the Zarillion's west entrance. The colonel knew if they could breach the west entrance, then the rest of the city would fall. His reptilian counterparts always encouraged exploratory missions for years, probing for weaknesses in the defenses of the city.

After years with waves of attacks on various known entrances, it was finally determined the one weakness was indeed the west entrance. According to their sources, if they could enter the city from that entrance, they could fan out into the city very easily. The other entrances weren't only well defended but they were such that an invading army would have little luck getting large numbers into the city. The colonel had to give it to his enemy, they created a sound defensive city.

Even the west entrance was well defended, but it was this entrance that allowed almost instant access to the city. He knew their numbers would be a problem at first, but they'd just overwhelm the defenses and take the entrance. He glanced down at the notes scrawled all over the map of the region. It was surprising to see all the high and low areas as well as the differences in terrain. Most looking at this area would just see a barren ice land. He knew better and went over the plan in his head. The colonel took one more look at his proud troops and knew this was the day they broke through the defenses and took hold of the city. He looked to his right as another soldier drew closer to him.

As the soldier approached, he could see the outline at first, but then the image strengthened as the light hit his second in command. Captain Hans Borman was an ancestor of a very important family during WWII and worked his way up the ranks fast. His actions, not his heritage, earned him prestige in the colonel's eyes. To the colonel, men of action were worthy of praise and not those born into a position. The captain happened to be both, a man of action with a worthy pedigree. Colonel Whilhelm looked at the man with immense pride as he watched this young man grow from small boy into the devastating soldier he now became.

Captain Borman stopped in front of the colonel coming to attention and saluting. "Colonel, the men are ready and await your orders! The soldiers of the Fourth Reich are ready to take their place in history. Sir, I've selectively chosen these men and they won't disappoint you. The mission will be a remarkable success and the city will be yours!"

Colonel Whilhelm snapped back a salute and looked at his second. "Captain, I have every confidence in your abilities, but this is a daunting task. We've been probing for weaknesses for a long time but now time grows short. Our benefactors grow impatient and it's time to show results. This isn't just about success, but survival, and if we allow our enemies to survive, then our survival is in danger. No, Captain, this is about more than just breaching an entrance."

The captain once again snapped a salute. "My Colonel, we won't fail! Our strategy is sound, and our numbers will overwhelm their meager forces. Our prior missions at least taught us that they don't expect large numbers coming against this entrance. That, sir, is where they made a huge miscalculation. We'll keep wave after wave coming at them until we sweep them away. All we need is a small window of opportunity and this entrance will fall. Once we have the entrance, we'll send word to follow up with the rest of your force. This day, my Colonel, you'll be standing in their council chambers with them all on their knees!"

The colonel smiled at the thought of seeing the frightened looks of the council members as they looked at him from their knees. He could imagine their smug, tear-stained faces and the petrified looks while begging for mercy. He'd enjoy personally escorting these arrogant people to their deaths. His reptilian allies fought the Zarillion across the universe and would stand for nothing but sheer obliteration. He turned to give a quick inspection of the magnificent sight of all his soldiers ready to do his bidding and raised his hands before speaking.

Though he didn't use a microphone, his voice carried over the vast distance with little difficulty. The ceiling magnified his voice and it boomed out before him, "Soldiers of the Fourth Reich you've been called to fulfill a long-standing vision of our forefathers. You stand on the edge of history! It will be your combined might that will win the day and your victory will make way for our rule as should have been generations ago! The path is clear, and the enemy awaits. You, the Reich's finest will drive our enemies into such holes, they'll never emerge again."

The soldiers released a roar that shook the building and the colonel stood in proud envy. He recalled a time long ago when he was asked to fight for the fatherland and his pride gave him great strength. He knew the strength of the soldiers before him and didn't doubt for one second today would be the day for total victory. The colonel looked down at the hooting soldiers and watched them work their way into a fury. He knew he could say little else to push them over the edge, so he stood at attention and snapped a salute to his troops.

The room came to a hush as they stood at attention and saluted him back with great reverence. When the colonel moved his hand down to his side, he shouted down to the soldiers, "For the Fatherland!"

Every soldier erupted into shouts, "The Fatherland!" Officers called their troops into formation and walked to the already opening bunker door. As the door opened, the freezing blast of cold air struck the soldiers and forced them to put on their goggles to protect their eyes, along with specially designed scarves. Colonel Whilhelm watched with delight as row after row of his finest fighters walked to meet their destiny. Despite his advanced age, he wished to be joining those fine soldiers in their quest for glory.

As the final soldiers walked past the open door, he could just barely make out the last rows from the howling winds kicking up snow. Though it hadn't snowed in days, it resembled a blizzard with the sheer amount of snow flying in the air. When the bunker door clicked shut, the heat normalized. One thing he still couldn't stand here was the unbearable weather. The only thing keeping him sane was his frequent trips to the more temperate climate in Argentina. He stayed at the large base there as often as possible. Now with things moving quickly toward a conclusion, he was forced to stay in this hostile climate more than he wished.

He turned swiftly to the right and made his way to the elevator, so as not to miss any of the action. The colonel intended to watch the entire incursion from the warm confines of this protective bunker. The elevator dropped him off at his floor and he walked briskly to his command center. Computers

69

and bright lights greeted him, along with the buzzing of people working furiously to have everything ready for the colonel.

Without stopping to talk to anyone, he sat and pulled himself close to the keyboard on the desk before him. The computer screen jumped to life and he watched as the first troops began their descent into the ravine leading to the west entrance. At first, nothing looked out of the ordinary and he watched his troops march unmolested toward victory.

Instantly, the snow turned red as lights flashed and his troops returned fire into the hillside. He watched in horror as his troops scattered and then tried to reform. They stood no chance as the enemy held the high ground and blended into the snow-covered hillside. With nothing to shoot at, they just shot into an area without success. These first troops were sitting ducks, dispatching quickly. With the ravine running red with blood, he could see one man standing tall among all—Captain Borman.

The captain rallied his troops and brought them back to the beginning of the ravine. Rather than retreat, the colonel saw the unfazed man barking out orders. It became apparent what the captain's strategy was; he would attack the enemy's fortifications in the hills. Using heat-signature vision, his soldiers quickly found the enemy and attacked them where they stood. The scene resembled ants climbing all over a large dirt pile. The colonel breathed and felt much better. Captain Borman led his troops toward the entrance but this time, with the recovered high ground secured.

Once within seeing distance of the entrance, the captain allowed scouts to test the defenses of the entrance. The scouts returned quickly, telling their officers nothing had changed since the last time they checked the entrance. Waving his arms, the captain motioned his troops to come to the door with large sacks, which looked like large, white blankets and the soldiers came forth carrying their heavy bundles. These soldiers took positions at the very edge of the ravine within an eye's view of the entrance and then set the bundles on tripods. Once on the tripods, the soldiers pulled off the blankets to reveal a large weapon.

The weapons looked similar to large machine guns but had no visible moveable parts. A young person could look quickly at the weapon and think it nothing but a toy. These were no mere toys and they proved their worth as they emitted a large orange ray shooting straight for the mountainside. Each ray slammed into the rock and sent exploding debris flying into the air. Wave after wave of orange blasts struck the entrance until the captain waved his hands. As the smoke and dust settled, the devastation was quite apparent. What was once a beautiful rock mountainside, was now a seared, blasted, and jagged mess. Through the now blasted hole in the side of the mountain, the colonel could see a large doorway.

With one move of his hand, the captain gave the order to resume the assault. This time, the rays pounded into the metal doors and they seemed to be little fazed by the weapons. The soldiers in charge of the weapons could see this and made changes to their weapons' controls and renewed their attack. Now the rays were a bright-red color and they struck the metal, getting sucked right in. The colonel could see these magnificent weapons now melted the metal.

His excitement heightened as he watched the rays cut through the doors like a knife through butter. In minutes, the doors collapsed with smoke pluming into the air. Out of the smoke came their enemy fully armed and ready to defend their home. The battle that took place in that ravine would later be told as one of the bloodiest in the region's history. Thousands of soldiers gave their lives in the snow and ice that day.

The defenders swarmed from covered positions, working their way around their attackers and then sent a wave of soldiers like a spear right down the middle. This effectively split the captain's forces. He watched in horror as the defending forces swirled around his troops like a whirlpool. The Zarillion only attacked the outside edge and then moved clockwise while moving in slightly. This tactic was brilliant as the members of the Fourth Reich were cut off from escape and their movement highly restricted. Though doomed from the get go, the German troops fought with terrific resolve and refused to give up.

The battle raged for hours as the Germans tried to break through the swirling defenders. Colonel Whilhelm, distraught by what he viewed to be an easy victory, could only watch in horror as his prized troops were decimated. He leaned forward and pushed a button on the control panel before him. Shouting into the microphone, he barked orders to release the remainder of his troops. Knowing he might lose all his troops, he ordered they just breach the defenders and allow his battered troops to return the base. The colonel told his officers in no uncertain terms, they weren't to advance on the enemy and this was in fact a rescue mission.

Colonel Whilhelm smashed his hands on the console and watched the rest of his troops leave. He couldn't afford any more losses. The reptilian people locked in their earthen prison could offer technology and strategy, but he needed soldiers. His thought was to breach the city before the reptilian people escaped. He knew once they were released, they'd have very little use for the people of the Fourth Reich. If the colonel could capture the city, he'd have the refuge he needed to ward off these disgusting creatures. His gaze returned to the computer screen as he watched his troops march toward their comrades in need.

As the large column of soldiers approached the battle, the colonel could see that it wasn't a moment too soon. The Zarillion forces were methodically working their way to the center of the German soldiers and it wouldn't be long before they were beyond help. The colonel couldn't believe such a large force could move in unison and as coordinated as these forces. From his point of view, it looked like a buzz saw moving quickly through a soft piece of wood. The defenders would engage the first attacker and then move a few steps to the right, but it seemed mechanical with their movements being highly rehearsed.

The remaining German forces slammed into the outlying Zarillion troops, attempting to form a breach in the circular wall the defenders created. At first, the colonel could see this having little effect as the defenders just turned and fought back to back. He stood in awe as the defenders now looked as if they were moving in two different directions. The inner soldiers still moved in their clockwise direction, but the outer layer of soldiers now moved

 in the opposite direction. The colonel just looked mystified as the soldiers just looked like large gears and his troops were getting chewed up and spat out.

At first, the colonel's troops almost bounced off the circular pattern the defenders fought in, but the sheer numbers finally penetrated the outer circle. He could see the circle lose its shape as his troops advanced through the small breach. Then he saw something unexpected as the Zarillion troops fell back and let the German troops surge forward. The colonel got on the microphone and yelled at his officers, telling them not to take the bait. His orders fell on deaf ears as his troops marched forward. He knew it would be a matter of minutes before his entire army would be surrounded.

Without a second thought, he ordered his attack helicopters into the air in defense of his threatened force. He couldn't believe his officers would get caught with their pants down like this. The colonel could only shake his head as his forces flooded into the void created by the defending troops backing up. His orders were quite specific and if carried out, a large bulk of his force could be saved. As it stood, he'd be lucky if any of them made it back alive. All he could do at this point was watch his beloved soldiers face their deaths with honor.

Chapter 14

Peter could hardly breathe with snot bubbles protruding from his nose. Thoughts raced through his head about his grandfather, his mother, and what was happening to him. His life to this point was very ordinary and nothing really happened to him. Even with his mind full of panic, he could also feel a surge of excitement as he ran through the night. His legs carried him quickly through the darkness and he flew around the corner of a familiar neighborhood. His friend Jake Andrews lived a few houses down and he turned himself in the direction of his best friend's home.

He stood for a moment looking at Jake's door before reaching forth and knocking. He didn't know what he'd tell Jake, but he knocked nonetheless. In a few minutes, a light came on from inside and a tired-eyed young man opened the door. He was the same height as Peter, but he was more rugged and muscular. For a moment, the two young men just stood in the doorway, light flooding into the night, staring at each other. Then without another word, Jake whisked Peter inside and closed the door tight, double-locking it.

Jake pushed Peter toward his room and once inside, he sat him on the bed. Peter didn't know what was going on but by the look on Jake's face, it was as though he was expecting Peter. Jake began, "It's okay, Pete! I know about it. You're safe here for the moment, but we have to move quickly."

Peter looked back at his friend with surprised eyes, which didn't go unnoticed. Jake just patted his friend on the shoulder. "Dude, you know my dad is Navy Seal! I know tons of stuff about my friends. You though are different. My dad and your grandfather were great friends. They talked all the time. I don't know everything, but my dad knew this day would come. Rest assured, he has a plan for you! So, take a moment and I'll get some water for you."

As his friend walked through the doorway going out into the hall, all he could do was stare at the back of his friend's back. *What does he know?*

Jake made it quickly back into the bedroom with a large glass of water and handed it to a still gawking Peter. Jake sat down on the bed next to him. For the next few minutes, neither spoke, trying to guess what the other knew. Peter could hear nothing in the house and was surprised Jake's mother didn't come to say hi to him. She was a fantastic lady and always took terrific care of Peter. Jake and Peter were friends as long as Peter could remember. He thought about this for a moment as he sat next to this young man who had gone through everything with him through his life.

Peter vividly remembered the time he ran into the neighborhood bully. He was walking home and as usual, reading something on ancient aliens when he walked right into the bully by accident. The other young man wasn't any bigger than Peter, but he was feared by everyone. His first act was to punch someone rather than fix the problem. Peter didn't know what hit him as he found himself on the ground with a bloody lip before he could even say sorry. He looked up to see the bully sneering at him and ready for another strike. The strike never fell as Jake grabbed the young man by the scruff of the neck, and threw him to the ground. Peter didn't even know Jake was around and he came out of nowhere.

The bully rose and faced Jake with rage in his eyes. He launched himself toward Jake, only to have him use his weight and let the bully fly to the ground. Once again, the bully rose and dusted himself off. This time, he composed himself, raising his hands for a fist fight. Jake was all too happy to accommodate the boy and raised his as well. Jake didn't wait for the other boy as he stepped forward and threw a quick combination before the other boy could react. The bully's head snapped back as Jake continued the barrage of punches to his midsection, before sending a devastating upper cut to the boy's head.

The young man's head again snapped back but this time, his eyes rolled back in his head and he fell to the ground. Jake stood over his fallen foe, ready to do battle. When he saw his foe not rising, he went to help Peter. Peter took Jake's hand and pulled himself up to see a smiling Jake. Jake was a powerful young man, but he had a heart of gold. Peter was always amazed at how Jake handled himself. He was the type of kid that should be popular and have tons of friends, but most of the time, he kept to himself. He was quite content to watch after Peter, which seemed to be quite often.

Peter looked at his friend on the bed next to him. "Jake, I'm in trouble, man! I mean real trouble!"

Jake just smiled. "I know, dude! I know!"

Peter looked perplexed. "What do you mean, you know?"

Jake just glanced at him. "Pete, did you forget how close my dad and your grandfather were? Your grandfather told my dad everything!"

Peter was still not convinced. "Everything. What do you mean, everything?"

Jake stood and turned to face his friend with a serious look. He put his hand on his chin as if trying to think of how to explain things to his longtime friend. Then he looked at his friend with genuine sympathy. "Pete, you're my best friend and

I'll always be there for you. I must tell you that first. Now, don't freak out when I tell you all this; it may be a lot to take.

"Dude, I've known you're a special person from the first time you and I played together in the sandbox. I remember playing with a truck in the sand and you made the sand blow off the truck without using your mouth. In the many years I've been your friend, I've seen many of these events even though you may not know about them. You always get this look of absolute concentration on your face and then something amazing happens. Pete, things move for you! It's as if things are at your command. Your grandfather explained it to my dad as you can manipulate magnetic fields. He told my dad it's more common than people realize but the issue is people who could do this aren't trained and lose the ability. My dad told me it's like someone that speaks another language during their childhood but then doesn't speak it anymore. When that happens, the language leaves you and you cannot speak it anymore.

"Pete, you have this ability and your grandfather was just beginning to teach you before he died. Do you remember all the puzzles and problem-solving strategies he taught you?"

Peter stood straight up and shot a glance at Jake. "What the heck are you talking about? I'm just a regular kid! I mean yes, my grandfather taught me many things. That isn't unusual for a grandfather to share knowledge with his grandchild. He knew I loved puzzles and solving math problems. There's nothing weird about that except to the kids at school that think I'm a space nerd. Jake, I know someday I'll end up in space as an astronaut but that has been the dream of many young people for a long time!"

Jake stood with him and turned to his friend putting his hands on Peter's arms, "Pete, don't worry, it's okay. I know this is messed up and you're still coming to terms with all that's going on in your head right now. You're safe for the moment, but we're going to have to move quickly. It's only a matter of time before these idiots come looking for you here. After all, I'm your best friend."

Peter couldn't help looking at his friend with a quizzical look. "You said you know what's going on? How do you know about them coming to my home after me? There's no way you could know that! Jake, my mom is still there by herself! Who knows what they'll do to her. I must get her. The young lady in the orb said she'd be fine. Jake, I just left her behind."

His friend swung him around and looked directly in his eyes. "What young lady? What orb? Dude, sit down and tell me everything from the beginning. Hurry, and don't forget anything. I want to hear every detail."

He had sweat dripping from his brow now leaking into his eyes as he didn't realize how much energy he exerted just to get to Jake's house. His eyes stung from the salty sweat now invading his eyes. Blinking furiously, he wiped his arm across his face. Peter sat down quick and with a great look of worry, he began his story.

Jake listened to every word and didn't interrupt Peter once. His eyebrows shot up a few times and he looked like he wanted to stop Peter, but he relented. When his friend was done with his tale, Jake lay back on the bed with his hands on his head. His face held a look of shock as he just lay there saying nothing. Jake remained in his position but stuck his hands in the air as if he had a million questions. With one fluid motion, he sprung up to a seated position and bounced up to his feet. He turned to his friend and motioned him up.

Without another word, he reached out and grabbed Peter by the arm, practically dragging him out of the bedroom. He whisked Peter to the cellar door and proceeded down to the basement. Peter followed as quickly as he could and almost tripped on the bottom stair. He stumbled and pulled free from Jake's grasp. When he righted himself, he started forward, coming close to the back of his friend. The two young men came to a screeching halt in front of what looked to be a sheer, concrete wall.

Peter reached up and spun his friend around. "What are we going to do, go through a concrete wall?"

His friend just smirked and reached up above him, pushing on a knothole in the beam above their heads. The concrete wall slowly moved forward. It looked to Peter as though the entire wall moved. He peered around the wall and saw a doorway leading into a tunnel. Jake again grabbed him and forced him in front of him through the doorway.

Once both young men were safe inside, Jake reached up to the ceiling and pressed another knothole, shutting the concrete wall. Jake then stopped and smiled at his friend. "Cool, right? My dad built that a long time ago after your grandfather told him to prepare himself to protect his family. I know that's a story for another day, but your grandfather was a lot more than he seemed. My dad highly respected your grandfather and that means a lot coming from my father. Being a Navy Seal, he's a hard man and respect is something earned in his mind.

"Peter, make no mistake about this, your grandfather was a very important person. I know he spent his life preparing for something very big. My father didn't speak of anything to me, but he was always with your grandfather. I always tried to get my dad to give me more information, but he always told me that it was better I didn't know too much."

As Peter stopped at the end of the hallway, he could see another steel door standing before him. He looked to the right-hand side of the door to see a control panel. Jake brushed by him and punched in a code, and the door swung in to reveal another room. Jake strode into the room with Peter following close behind. The door automatically shut and locked behind them.

Jake looked around him and raised his hands. "Pete, welcome to our command center!"

Chapter 15

Peter stood in awe, looking around the modern smooth and shiny walls of the command center. His eyes darted around the room from computer screens, to weapons hanging on the walls, to food supplies on countless shelves, shocking him. He spent a great deal of time in Jake's house and had no idea any of this existed. It was quite an overwhelming sight and he almost lost his breath. Leaning heavily on a stainless-steel chair, he pushed himself downward.

Shaking his head, he viewed Jake from the corner of his eye and saw that his friend was already working at a computer station off to the right. He turned to see Jake punching in something on the keyboard and then the computer screen leaped to life. Peter was even more surprised when the image of Jake's dad came over the computer screen. He couldn't help but shake his head; he knew Jake's dad was deployed overseas so how could Jake get in touch with him that fast?

Sitting down, looking at the image of his father, Jake looked up and spoke, "Dad, it's happening! Peter's house was invaded, and they came for him. He's here safe but you and I both know that won't last for long. We must get Peter out of here and we must do it soon! Sir, what are your orders?"

The image of Derek Andrews, Navy Seal, took over the screen. Peter was always intimidated by the man who at any moment, looked ready to snap someone in half. He stood a stoic muscular figure before the screen and responded, "Boys, first, let me say I'm glad you're both safe. Jake is right though; we must get you both out of there right away. Jake, give me a little bit to secure you safe passage to my site. For the moment, you'll be safe, and I have men in the area. I'll send a squad to watch the base. Just stand by the computer and wait for my response."

Jake stood and added, "You can count on me, Dad! Peter will be well taken care of!"

Jake's father looked at his son with immense pride. "I know, son, I know. Boys, listen to me. You must get yourselves ready for a long trip. Jake, show Peter what he needs. You'll both be coming south so dress and pack for cold temperatures. Once you have all your things together, make sure to arm yourselves. Peter, I know this may make you uncomfortable, but you'll need protection."

Peter looked at Jake's dad. "Thank you, sir! Yes, firearms always make me nervous, but I think you're right. Those men broke through every defense my grandfather had set up in a matter of seconds. I have little doubt they'll use deadly force on me. Don't worry, Mr. Andrews. I'll be prepared. Sir, my mother is still in the house. What should I do?"

The usually hard face of Jake's father showed now great concern. "What do you mean your mom is still in the house?"

Peter told Mr. Andrews the entire story and added the young lady with her orb. At this, the Navy Seal smiled cunningly. "Yes, our friends, the watchers. They've been watching over humanity for a long time but now something of great evil is coming our way and we need to be ready. All right, boys, get yourselves ready. Peter, don't worry about your mom. If I know these watchers as I think I do, your mom is quite safe. I'll have a friend of mine at the police station check on her. I'll let you know when next we talk."

He looked as if he were about to sign off but then looked up. "Peter, please tell me you have your grandfather's papers!"

At this, Peter almost gasped. "Yes, sir. I have my grandfather's papers and they're safe! I'll keep them safe until I see you. Do you have any idea what they are and what I should do with them?"

Mr. Andrews looked at Peter. "Your grandfather and I were great friends but even friends keep secrets. He did tell me a great deal about himself and these watchers I've described, but he really didn't divulge anything about his papers. He did ask me quite a bit to check on you in recent months to make sure you were safe. I could tell something wasn't right, but he wouldn't tell me any more. The work he did was quite secretive, and he shared only what he thought was important to you."

Without looking up, Peter added, "Are you telling me something bad happened to my grandfather? That his death wasn't natural as everyone tells me."

Again, Mr. Andrews looked at Peter. "I'm not positive but I do find it amazing that a man of your grandfather's stature and vitality just suddenly dies. Peter, I promise you this. I've been looking into your grandfather's death since it happened, and I won't rest if I find out something sinister is going on. Your grandfather was my good friend and taught me much. I assure you if something is amiss, I'll avenge him."

Jake stood next to Peter and patted his shoulder. "Don't worry, Dad; he has me! No one will mess with him without going through me. Just hurry and get us out of here. I have a sinking feeling we won't be safe here for long."

The image on the screen nodded his head. "I hear you, my boy. I'll have you out of there in no time, just sit tight. I need to make a few contacts but then we'll get you out of there. Let me check on Peter's mom first. All right, you guys. Get ready and stand by the computer. Good luck, gentlemen!"

Jake touched the screen. "Thank you, Dad, I mean, sir!"

The screen went black and Jake stood next to Peter. The two still were looking at the screen, almost hoping Mr. Andrews would come back. After a few minutes, nothing happened, and Jake moved over to some large backpacks leaning against the wall. He motioned Peter to come over and gave him directions for things he'd need. Peter couldn't help but think he was in a store as Jake opened another door and walked inside. The room held supplies of all kinds on multiple shelves. Both boys went quickly and filled their backpacks.

Jake kept throwing items at Peter so quickly that he couldn't keep pace and got hit in the head for his efforts. Peter gave Jake an angry look, only to see him laughing. He couldn't decide whether to pound on his friend or just laugh so he continued to pack. It wasn't long before their packs were filled to the brim and items were popping out of the top. Jake secured his pack and propped it up against the wall. Peter looked at the sheer size of the pack as it was as big as Jake.

When both young men were finished, they grabbed an extra water and sat on the floor to refresh themselves. With both leaning against the coolness of the smooth brushed steel wall, they enjoyed a precious quiet moment. Peter laid his head against the wall and looked up to the ceiling. He couldn't help but wonder what would happen to him now. He lived a pretty ordinary life and considered himself a very level-headed person, but this fiasco was anything but ordinary. Leaning slightly forward, he turned and looked at his friend.

Jake sat with his eyes closed and looked to be asleep, but Peter knew better. He was sure to be planning their next move. Jake, always the planner, was amazing at thinking three steps ahead of anyone else. He labeled himself as a big picture man. Most people would be worried right now, not Jake; he always looked down the road at what he'd be doing years from now. This was a great source of frustration to many teachers at school. At times, it seemed that Jake wasn't focused, which couldn't be farther from the truth. He was thinking of how the subject would help him down the road. To someone who didn't know Jake, he'd look as if he were daydreaming.

Jake was one of the most serious people Peter knew. He always knew what he was doing and calculated every risk. He was always ready to act and didn't let his analysis of a situation stop him from completing his task. This always astonished Peter who always seemed to think too much about something and never seemed to act.

His friend Jake was definitely a natural-born leader and he marveled at how many people gravitated to his friend. A perfect blend of strength, leadership, and friendship, Jake surely could do everything in Peter's eyes. He never saw Jake come across a situation he couldn't handle. Many years ago, Jake was faced with a group problem in class and he could have just taken control of the situation, but he allowed the group to work as a team. When it came time to present in front of the class, every member of the group was scared to death to speak but Jake. He stood in front of his class without even looking at his notes and gave a perfect presentation. Peter still could hear the class clapping for such a terrific presentation.

Peter knew how lucky he was to have Jake on his side, but something was still itching at the back of his mind. Jake said he knew a lot about what was going on with Peter, but didn't elaborate on any information. He sat for a minute and thought about confronting his friend, but thought better of it since his friend sat right beside him. How could anyone wish him harm and sit by him through this whole ordeal. Without another thought, he reached over and clasped his friend's hand, shaking it.

Jake returned the handshake with a genuine smile and playfully punched his friend in the shoulder. Peter winced in pain because even a playful punch from Jake was powerful. He managed a weak smile as Jake just laughed. "Wimp!" Jake continued to laugh. "Dude, don't worry! My dad has a plan. Trust me, you always think I have a plan. My dad is like a computer. I swear he's always playing chess with life. He'll have us out of here in no time. I wouldn't be surprised if he sends a squad to get us under cover of night. We'd be in and out of here before anyone knew what was going on. We'd be ghost's men. Seriously, we'd be gone like a fart in the wind!"

It was Peter's turn to laugh. It seemed Jake could always have a sense of humor even in the tensest of situations. Here they were locked in a panic room and Jake was making jokes. Peter just looked at his friend with confidence; he never knew Jake to be wrong in these situations. He thought back to a hike he took with Jake and his father in the spring. Peter tried to keep up with the two athletes in front of him and tripped, falling off the side of the trail, only to end up on a ledge ten feet below. Jake came back with some strong vines to pull him up with.

The fact that he could pull Peter up wasn't the surprising part. Jake knew what vine to use and where to find it in a split second. Peter definitely counted on Jake to be his guardian angel over the years and here, he was here to save him. He couldn't help but feel a little ashamed he never could do anything for Jake. His friend never said anything to the contrary. There up against that wall at that moment, he made a pact with himself that someday he'd pay Jake back with every fiber of his being.

The two young men once again let themselves lay back against the wall and relaxed. Both holding to their own thoughts, they said no more to one another. Weariness overtook them as they both drifted off to sleep. Peter thought of his mother and what would become of her. Jake thought of what plan his dad had in store for them. During their sleep, they had their heads fall against each other, deep in an exhausted sleep.

Chapter 16

Ryan Giles, General of the Zarillion forces watched in horror as the heavy steel doors before him melted away to nothingness. The doors were made of a high-temperature alloy metal much stronger than normal steel. Whatever his enemy was using cut through the metal with alarming speed. Smoke was fast filling up the hallway, but his force stood fast, waiting for the doors to give way before rushing out to slaughter these invaders. General Giles knew his forces were stronger and more highly trained than their human counterparts. To the general, it almost seemed unfair... almost.

Time after time, these human soldiers poked and prodded different entrances, hoping to find a weakness. Up to this point, the general was quite confident these soldiers would find nothing. One thing they could always count on was the reptilian people assisting these soldiers. Through the years, both peoples leaked out tiny amounts of technology in the hopes that each would gain an advantage over the other. Things seemed to be speeding up in recent years. The humans were definitely taking advantage of the technology, becoming quite handy.

The rancid smoke poured into his nose, causing him to cough. He pushed a button on the side of his ear and a helmet formed around his head. The general gave the order for the troops to comply and they did without question. The helmets also had heat seeking as well as night vision capability. They all returned to their military posture, waiting to attack. The doors then fell away with a rush of cold air whooshing in before them.

The general raised his hand and moved it forward. His entire force in one swift movement flew into the breach headlong to meet their enemies. As instructed, the general's troops paid little attention to those who just opened the doors and went into their circular formation. He smiled as he watched the flawless execution of his own strategy. His troops fluidly seethed around the advancing enemy and began their circular movement around the attackers. The enemy had no idea what to do with such a strategy as they were always taught to fight those in front of them. What kept them out of sorts was the fact they were constantly fighting another soldier.

Every time the enemy went to strike, they seemed to be flailing at thin air only to have another attacker come at them from another angle. The confusion and chaos caused by this strategy became evident early on in the campaign as the humans quickly became furious losing their formations. As the general watched his troops take apart this large force, he couldn't help but have a great swell of pride at their execution.

His mood changed quickly as he looked up to see even more soldiers coming over the embankments. Within minutes, his small force of supremely trained fighters became engulfed by sheer numbers. If he didn't act swiftly, his force would become overwhelmed. Without a moment's hesitation, he raised the communicator on his wrist and barked a code for his officers. In an instant, the entire phalanx shifted and feigned a breach down the middle, drawing in the human attackers.

The general watched with pleasure as his strategy worked to perfection. The humans were easily duped and swarmed into the void. He could see they realized too late the drastic error in strategy and tried to retreat, only to be punished severely for their mistake. With unwavering military bearing, the general maintained a stoic face but inside, he felt distraught at this unnecessary loss of life. He knew what it was like to be caught in a buzz saw such as what was before him.

Early in his career as a bright, up-and-coming officer, he faced a similar situation, nearly losing his entire regiment. His superiors were so upset at him they stripped him of rank and threw him into the brig for six months. This lesson still stung as he watched the human forces being decimated. The once pristine white embankments now ran red with the blood of the human attackers. Bodies were strewn everywhere as he saw his forces slowly making their way inward, threatening to squeeze the life out of the remaining soldiers left in the middle.

With his eyes still peeled on the dreadful sight of the humans' demise, he was so engrossed with his victory that he heard the helicopters too late. The enemy helicopters came swooping in and sent missile after missile into the general's forces. The buzz saw stopped and he saw the resolve of the remaining human troops as they saw hope, redoubling their efforts to fight their way to safety. He definitely respected all soldiers, but he gained a great deal of respect for his enemy that day. Not one man gave up and fought with everything they were for their cause. The general indeed trained his soldiers the same way and enjoyed the challenge of fighting a worthy opponent.

Although expected, he didn't think the enemy would use their attack helicopters in this case as they were customarily struck down due to issues with the harsh Antarctic weather. It seemed to the general that the enemy rectified the helicopter's weaknesses as they screamed in and out of the troops. His troops returned fire with handheld launchers, but the helicopters moved side to side as well as up and down, allowing them to avoid being hit with the missiles. As the helicopters came around for another strike in a V-formation, he once again raised his hand and spoke a code into his communicator. His forces broke formation and worked their way back toward the entrance.

Smoke rising in the air from the explosions and steam from the dissipated ice made a natural screen for his retreating troops. His soldiers, without panic, moved swiftly into the entrance as other soldiers appeared with larger missile launchers. The missiles sailed through the air toward their targets and exploded before impact, leaving the helicopters unscathed. The general shook his head with confusion. "They don't have that technology yet?"

He spoke into the communicator telling his officers to get inside quickly. They complied and moved swiftly inside the confines of the mountain. He thought everyone was safely inside when he saw a small group of soldiers pinned between the enemy and the attack helicopters. With all his soldiers now safely inside, he looked at the small attachment with him and said nothing but moved forward to assist his trapped force. With speed unexpected in soldiers, his small force intercepted the enemy soldiers slamming into them in traditional fashion.

Close, hand-to-hand combat ensued as the surrounding area was still thick with smoke and ice particles. The general rose to the occasion, ramming into an advancing soldier, dipping his shoulder, slightly sending the soldier flying over his shoulder. He rose up with fire in his eyes as now with the taste of battle in his mouth, he sought out the next enemy to defeat. Another soldier with a shaved head and arms too big for his uniform stood a foot away from him. Without a sound, both men ran at one another with weapons raised.

The general's close quarters weapon of choice was a laser-sharp curved knife which he could hold in any position and be lethal. With quick steps, he ducked under the soldier's heavy blow and sliced the man's side. The soldier hardly noticed the wound and swung a backhanded fist connecting with the general's head. His head snapped back, and he felt dizzy.

Shaking his head, he blinked his eyes to regain focus before the next blow connected.

He didn't have to wait long for the follow-up blow as he felt a large fist pummel his chest. At first, he stood stunned, unable to breathe, and went to one knee. His eyes full of the residue of the smoke, he searched hard to see his attacker. The next blow came out of the smoke and he saw it just in time to avoid another heavy hit to his head. This time, he sprung low, knowing he wouldn't defeat a man this size and strong going toe to toe. The general struck hard and swift at the man's knee, buckling it from the side. He heard the snap and watched as the huge soldier folded over and came crashing to the ground, howling in pain.

With his chest still aching and struggling for breath, he scanned the area to see his next move. Assessing the situation, he could see that most of his missing men were now moving into the mountain. His second in command grabbed him by the arm. "Sir, we must move!"

As if stuck in a dream, he failed to move as a large chunk of ice and rock fell, smashing into the ground just before him. The impact rippled through his body, bringing him to his senses. He followed his soldiers into the doorway. As the last man entered, the general ordered it shut. He turned to take one last look to see no enemy soldiers were following. He could see the last remnants of the enemy moving back into the ravine.

As he was about to turn back to go with his men, he caught movement out of the corner of his eye. The flash of steel was common to the general in his line of work, so he responded with a flash of his own steel. The knife was still in his hands and he swung quickly to meet the oncoming knife. The clash of the two blades brought instant sparks flying into the air. The general quickly saw the seriousness of his situation as he deflected another blow and positioned himself back to the wall to avoid a surprise attack. Quickly glancing left and then right, he saw he stood alone against a small group of the enemy that managed to sneak into the still open doors.

The doors were now closed so the soldiers must know their plight was dire, but they refused to back down. They slowly surrounded the general and the four men smirked as they moved closer to their prey. With his back leaning on the wall, he positioned one leg against the wall to thrust himself forward. He didn't wait for the other soldiers to make a move and launched himself into the man directly in front of him with his blade out. The unsuspecting man had a look of sheer shock as the blade entered his body just below the heart. With a quick turn and thrust upward, the general ended the man's life.

Bloody knife in one hand and the other ready to grab a hold of another soldier, he saw the original soldier advance toward him. The two met, blades scraping once again in midair. He knew he had met his match with a blade. Undaunted, the general walked the knife's dance with this talented soldier. The other soldiers, having too much respect for the two combatants, stayed their hand for the moment.

Once again, the two knifemasters struck at one another almost move for move. After a few more passes, both men stopped midstride and just glared at one another through grime-soaked faces. The other uncertain soldiers looked at one another and were ready to move forward when they heard voices coming back up the tunnel. Now with grit in the eyes, they were ready to spring into action. The general now knew he'd have no choice but to face them all.

As the voices came closer though, the men's faces changed from confident to uncertain. He looked over his shoulder to find quite a compliment of his own men now behind him. The first man went to advance on the cornered soldiers but the general raised his hand for them to stop. He turned to the soldiers. "You've fought bravely and with honor; there's nothing more honorable in life. Except perhaps a death in battle!"

At this the other knife master understood. "Sir, what would you have us do?"

The general knew the nobility of this man before him. "Soldier I'd have you live to see another fight! What's your name?"

"Sir, my name is Lars, weapons specialist"

The general responded, "Lars, you're perhaps the best I've seen. I look forward to our next meeting!"

He stood for a moment taking in the soldier. The man, even in his tattered uniform, looked every bit the soldier. His shoulders were back with a straight back. The general could see his military bearing in the way the man stood. He even smiled as the man took out an oiled rag and wiped down his knife. When the weapon was sparkling again, he slid it home into a beautiful leather sheath. The man then looked directly at the general awaiting the next move.

The general turned to his men. "They aren't to be touched! Escort them out. If anyone touches them, they'll deal with me!"

The men just nodded their heads in understanding as the general turned to leave. He took a few steps up the tunnel before he heard the soldier speak, "Sir!"

He turned slightly to look at the soldier and saw a determined look on his face.

Lars waited a moment before speaking, "Sir, the next time we meet, it will be to the end!"

The general winked at the man and nodded, leaving the answer unsaid. He then turned and walked briskly up the tunnel toward the council chambers.

Chapter 17

Both young men awoke with a start as if being pulled by an unseen hand. Jake placed a quick hand on Peter's shoulder. "Dude, how long have we been asleep?"

Peter, with a panicked look in his eye, turned to his friend. "I have no idea! Do you have a watch? What time is it?"

Jake popped up to his feet and strode over to the computer monitor on the wall. He glanced at the time. "Not too long! It's still nighttime."

Peter, now on his feet, moved over next to his friend. "Jake, what do we do now?"

As if awaiting the answer, the computer screen came to life and the image of a man appeared. To Peter's great relief as the image became clearer, he could see it was Jake's dad. Jake brushed by his friend to stand in front of the screen to address his father.

Jake quickly spit out, "Dad, what now? Please tell me we aren't stuck here?"

Jake's father responded quickly, "Son, listen to me carefully! This is a mess. I don't know exactly what's going on but there are many government agencies involved and Peter is at the center of everything. I do have a plan, but we have to tread lightly here as our movements will be found out more quickly than we'd like at this point."

Jake's father laid out a plan of escape that saw the two boys on an Army transport as part of a convoy leaving the state on maneuvers for the weekend. The boys would be picked up in a non-descript car, of all things a minivan, and transported to a truck depot just off the highway where the convoy was refueling. Once in the transport, Jake's father felt they'd be safe until they arrived at the base.

Jake's dad already arranged for the boys to be placed in military custody for their own safety. They wouldn't be prisoners, but their movements would be restricted until he could arrive. He told the boys he wouldn't be going with them initially in the hopes anyone following him would be thrown off the scent. The military man assured the boys they'd be safe at the base or at this point, safe as possible. If everything went according to plan, he'd be with the boys a day or two after their arrival.

Once he laid the plan before the boys, he let it soak in a bit before making an alternative plan with them. Both boys weren't happy to hear this plan. That would mean something happened to Jake's father and they'd be on their own. Always the planner though, he wanted the boys to be ready for anything. The alternative plan required the young men to make their way to the commander of the base and follow his directions.

Jake's father told them both their ultimate goal was to hop aboard a military flight that would land in Argentina before taking a cargo ship to their final destination. He gave them in-depth instructions about what supplies to pack and how to get them from the quartermaster. Jake assured his father they'd do as instructed, and he could count on him to keep Peter safe. His father responded, telling his son how proud he was of him and knew he'd be the perfect bodyguard for Peter.

When everything was in place, Jake's dad signed off telling the boys to be cautious and pay attention to everything around them. Both young men assured him them would do as asked and thanked him for his help. The military man wisely responded not to thank him yet, not until they were safely all together.

Once the screen went black, Jake looked at his friend. "Well, man, we're in for one hell of an adventure. You ready?"

Peter turned to face his best friend and looked into his smiling face that exuded confidence. "Jake, how are you so calm? I'm completely freaking out right now! You look like you're getting ready to go to summer camp. Dude, we may never be back! This could be the last time we see our homes or our families. Aren't you the least bit concerned?"

Jake smiled. "Pete, listen, I've known you your whole life and I always knew you were destined for greatness. Man, I'm just riding your coat tails. You still don't have any idea how important you are, do you? Let me tell you something before we're all done. You're going to be the one full of confidence and with much more power than I. I'll tell you this though, you won't go through it alone. I'm here for you!"

Peter, at first, could say nothing. Again, Jake was talking in code as if he knew much more than he let on. This cryptic talk bothered him. He felt out of the loop and he didn't like surprises. He wanted to punch his friend for his secrecy, but knew it wasn't because he was just keeping anything from him. Knowing Jake's dad and his relationship with his grandfather, he knew this was the plan all along. Peter decided they could have their secrets for the moment but soon he'd demand the truth. Right now, he just wanted to get out of this panic room and get to a more secure location.

He looked at his friend with a warm smile. "Power, you say! That could be helpful. Let's get out of here. Your dad told us to be ready to go in fifteen minutes. We have the gear needed for the moment, so we just wait for the signal. Do you really think we need all this stuff though? I mean, it looks like when your dad gets deployed. I feel like a turtle who has his house on his back."

Jake laughed. "Dude, that's funny. I used to say that same thing to my dad when he'd leave. I'd always tell him he looked like a turtle. Sure, it looks like a lot of stuff but unfortunately, we have no idea how long we'll be gone. Trust me all this stuff can come in handy. Anyway, don't worry about that right now. That's great news about your mom being safe!"

Peter winced at the mention of his mother. A part of him still wanted to go back for her but he also knew if he returned she'd be in great danger. Jake's dad told the boys Peter's mom was now resting comfortably at one of Jake's friend's houses. Jake's dad sent a couple of his men to gather her. She was a little shaken about having her house broken into, but she couldn't remember anything else. Peter was relieved to know she was safe and didn't want to put her in further danger.

With school vacation coming up, Jake's dad came up with some story about taking the boys on a little military trip. Peter's mom knew it would be good for Peter to get away for a bit and didn't complain too much about her son going. Peter still couldn't help but feel he was leaving his mother in danger but at the same time, he trusted Jake's father implicitly.

The two young men slung the huge duffle bags onto their backs. Both slightly bent over trying to adjust to the weight of the equipment on their backs. It took a moment, but both straightened out and stood tall. An outside observer would only see two young soldiers preparing to be deployed. Jake looked to his friend. "You look every bit the part, my friend!"

Peter just offered a hearty laugh. "Are you kidding me! I feel like a fish out of water. You're the one who looks the part. Honestly, dude, you were made for this stuff. It's in your blood.

Your dad is so proud of you! Although I have to admit, it feels pretty cool to have all this equipment."

It was Jake's turn to laugh. "See, that's the spirit. I'll make you a military man one way or another."

Peter eyed him with suspicion. "Something tells me that would make you quite happy but I'm not the military type. At least not the fighter you are. I have to admit I love the strategy of the battles, but the loss of life grieves me to the core. No one should have to lose their life for another person's cause."

Jake turned with a serious look. "I hear you but unfortunately the world doesn't work that way. I do hope someday people will look beyond their own desires though and think of the greater good of mankind. People are so busy living their own lives, they forget that even their small actions have greater consequences."

Peter smirked. "You, my friend, always surprise me by your thoughtfulness and your deep thinking. I know many people misjudge you and think you rather simple."

His friend just cackled. "My dad is always telling me to keep everything close to the vest and not let anyone really get to know you. Outside the family that is."

Peter smacked him on the shoulder. "Let's get out of here."

Chapter 18

The military transport was filled with soldiers and the boys were stuffed between two large men cleaning their side arms. Peter looked around at the faces of the surrounding soldiers and noticed the seriousness in their faces. Jake's father mentioned maneuvers, but these men looked to be preparing for combat. Even Jake who spent a great deal of time in the presence of these men seemed a little uneasy.

Peter took a moment to listen to some of the conversations taking place around him. These men were bound to the base and then were actually going on a mission. The men spoke to each other in guarded tones and looked questioningly at the young men. He could tell they weren't trying to say too much in front of them. Jake nodded, telling him to let it go. Peter sat back, leaning his head on the back of the military vehicle.

Rattling down the highway, Peter's head constantly bumped forward but he was so tired, this didn't bother him. He could barely hear the soldiers making their final preparations as they neared the base. Within minutes, he saw those eyes, those piercing blue eyes peering into his soul. Once more, the image of the beautiful young lady came into his head.

Peter couldn't move as the image of the young woman crystalized before him. At first, she seemed to be just comfortable watching him. Peter couldn't help but notice the strong, athletic arms of the young lady and could tell she wasn't as soft as she seemed. He looked at her height and saw she was slightly taller than he and had a slender, athletic build. As she walked toward him, he could see she was dressed in a sheer, white dress with a slit to the side of one leg, revealing one of her well-defined, muscular legs. Peter couldn't help but think this creature, although beautiful, was also very dangerous.

She came to within a few feet of where he stood and stopped with her hands on her hips, as if waiting for something important from Peter. He felt as if a force was pulling him toward her and found himself somehow now within a few inches of her face. He could feel his face getting hot and didn't want to look directly into her eyes. An unseen hand lifted his head upward until he could only see those big, beautiful, blue eyes.

He was now mesmerized by the true-blue nature of her eyes and could now smell a hint of what Peter thought was a pine tree. Peter couldn't help himself and his breathing quickened as he now was within an inch of her luscious lips. He could almost feel a surge of electricity go through him as his lips pasted just over hers. In that moment, she held him at arm's length and spoke, "I can tell you're going to be nothing but trouble!"

Peter shook his head as if coming out of a dream and looked ahead to see this fetching creature before him smiling warmly in his direction. He looked at her and noticed her attire had changed to a military uniform. At first, he didn't know what to do. He just stood staring like a typical teenage boy.

She just laughed. "I thought this might be less distracting. I really have to talk to you. Things are happening right now that shouldn't be and once again, I'm forced to warn you and help if I can. Evil surrounds you at every turn right now! You must be careful with whom you trust. Jake is in grave danger as well, so please look after him. You're both extremely important to us and we cannot afford anything to happen to you."

Once again, Peter shook his head. "I know but what can we do about it? Jake's dad gave us instructions, but we really still have no idea what's going on. He just told us to get to the base and he'll meet us there."

A sad look came over her face. "Peter, I hope Jake's dad will be there for you but if by some chance he cannot make it, you must follow his instructions and make it to me. I'll tell you more as you get closer. Trust me, I wish I could help you more but I'm as much a prisoner as you are at the moment. Trust me, though; that won't always be the case. You and I together will bring our enemies to their knees."

Peter once again couldn't ask the million questions circling in his head at the moment. "I'll make it to you and I'll take care of Jake!"

She smiled and reached out to touch his face with the side of her hand, but it just went right through his skin, telling him she wasn't actually there. He backed up slightly and wanted so much to reach back for her but held fast. Peter looked at her and realized that her hair was now slightly behind one ear. He peered quickly at her ear and noticed it had a slight point to it on top. He wanted to ask but held his tongue.

Once more, she smiled. "All questions will be answered in time. I know this is all more than most could ever handle. I assure you, if there was any way I could be with you in person right now, I would. As for now, be safe and look after each other. I'll be your guide. Now wake, hurry, trouble is coming! Peter, wake up! Wake up!"

He felt his body shaking and his eyes sprung open. Jake stood over him with a panicked look on his face. He was grasping Peter and trying to pull him up. He screamed, "Dude, get up. We have to get out of here!"

Peter shot up and for the first time, saw the carnage before him. Soldiers jumped out of the back of the transport and he heard shouting with gunfire going off around him. He still had his backpack on and Jake tugged him out the back of the transport. Both boys jumped on the ground and scrambled to follow the soldiers. They fell in behind the soldiers and for the first time, realized they were without weapons.

The soldiers in front of them, with weapons drawn, moved forward quickly, looking both ways. Peter could see the base they were making for about a half mile off in the distance. Also, the soldiers steadily worked their way toward the cover of trees just off to their right. Following the soldiers without question, they hid behind the trees and the soldiers peered out to take notice of their situation.

A large soldier told them to stay behind the trees and not come out until told to do so. The large soldier peered out behind his tree and whispered a few orders to his fellow soldiers. Another taller, slimmer soldier jumped up and went out into the open with his weapon before him. Peter did as told, staying behind the tree but heard the gunfire and the cry from the man as he was hit. The large soldier swore and looked around only to see three soldiers with him. He snuck over to Peter and Jake. "Listen, you two, you have to get to the base! Run and don't stop. They're expecting you. We'll cover for you. Now get going!"

Peter stood unmoving with Jake not ready to go anywhere. The soldier gritted his teeth. "Get going now!"

Jake grabbed his friend and pushed him forward. Both boys didn't look back but could hear the gunfire and the cries of the dying. They ran as fast as they could and quickly left the protective cover of the trees. He looked quickly next to him. Jake did the same and waved him on as they could see the base once again. Peter then lagged behind as the weight of the equipment now hampered his strides. Jake fell back and practically pulled his friend forward.

As they could now see the gate of the base, they then heard voices yelling at them from behind telling them to stop or they'd shoot. Both didn't look back and continued forward until they were within sight of the soldiers guarding the gate. As they ran to the nearest soldier, gunfire once again rang out and the soldier next to Jake went down. Now other armed soldiers came to the gate, returning fire. A few soldiers grabbed Jake and Peter, whisking them through the gate and surrounding them with a human shield. The soldiers pushed them forward without another word until they were inside a bunker.

Peter could hear the weapons being discharged behind him and others shouting behind him. As the door to the bunker closed behind them, they could hear the repeated hits from gunfire rounds striking the outside of the bunker. The soldiers pushed them forward, still surrounding them and led them down into the bowels of the bunker. Within minutes, they were brought into a large computer room resembling a control room.

Jake ran forward and was now in quick conversation with another soldier dressed in Air Force blues. Peter could tell right away Jake was familiar with this young lady. Jake spoke furiously and with great animation. The young lady smiled at Jake and brought him in for a hug before releasing him. They both talked and then looked Peter's way. Jake went over to his friend. "We're safe for the moment, but this base isn't really equipped to ward off a sustained attack. Jess, a friend of my dad, just told me this base is mainly for analysis."

Peter realized he still had his backpack on and let it fall off his shoulders, crashing to the ground. The weight lifted from his shoulders and he stood straight up, moving over to his friend. He looked around him and realized Jake was right. This wasn't a base that could repel a coordinated attack for any length of time. At the moment, that didn't matter as long as they remained tucked in the bunker.

The young officer came to rest just before Peter. "Well, Peter, it's nice to meet you! I wish it were under better circumstances. We'll make your stay as comfortable and safe as we may. Just be aware that you may be asked to move at a moment's notice. Be sure to keep your equipment within arm's distance at all times. We may not be a base that can survive a long attack, but we'll protect you as best we can."

Peter looked at the officer. "Thank you, I cannot begin to apologize enough for putting you and all these people in danger."

She smiled. "Peter, you need not worry about us as we're all highly trained. It's true we aren't a combat base but we all have a great deal of combat experience. Trust me, we already have a call out to the local National Guard and they'll be here in less than an hour. I also have alerted my superiors and they'll be calling back within minutes. We'll have an extraction plan in place for you momentarily and you'll be safe!"

Jake stood next to them. "Peter, just be ready to move but in the meantime, let's get something to eat. I could eat a horse right now! Jess, where is the mess?"

Jess laughed. "Typical guy, first thought is of food. Don't worry, guys, the mess is right next door and the food is actually pretty good. By all means, get something to eat. When you return, I'll give you your orders."

Jake grabbed Peter. "Let's go, dude! Who knows when we'll eat again."

Peter couldn't help but look worried at that comment.

Jake noticed. "Don't worry, man. I'm just kidding. It's just something my dad says. When you're on a mission, you just cannot take meals for granted. No worries, I'm sure we'll have plenty of food."

Chapter 19

General Ryan Giles, supreme leader of the Zarillion forces, stood with sweat pouring down his face, waiting for his orders. Andrew stood frozen in thought as if afraid to respond to the news the humans finally were really at their doorstep. During the last eighty years, Andrew and the council successfully kept their society a secret from the advancing humans. For a millennium, they were careful not to alert the humans to their presence but as the humans advanced in technology, the more they explored.

Throughout the history of the humans, there were always the whispers of a hidden society of people. Natural curiosity caused the humans to search for this mythical land. The issue arose that during the last three thousand years, the earth's poles shifted slightly causing the polar caps to shift as well. What was once a plush area the Zarillion lived now was a desolate ice land. So, the whispers of a paradise among the humans became only a memory to the Zarillion people.

To make matters worse, the reptilian people were within a whisker of escaping their earthly prison. Andrew stood staring at the council members before him, knowing the next sentence he uttered would define his rule. The council members looked to their leader with nervous glances while Holly moved to his right-hand side. Andrew began, "Our society always viewed this planet as our home, but because we arrived during a time when the indigenous population wasn't ready for our technology, we decided to let them grow on their own. Little did we know we were betrayed and followed by the greatest evil the cosmos has ever known!"

He paused to let that sink in. "We're at a great precipice and one wrong move could destroy two peoples and an entire planet! We know these barbaric reptilians all too well and we were too slow to act on our home planet, causing our near extinction. The humans cannot pay the price for our cowardice. If we finished off our enemy when we had the chance, many lives would've been saved. Our love of all life was nearly our downfall and since then, we've become a warlike people just as our enemies!"

He looked at General Giles with a sympathetic smile. Once more, he rose to his full height and looked every bit the leader he should. His lips pursed, and he slammed his fist down on the table with such force, the large table shuddered. All the council members stood back knowing this behavior was quite out of character for their calm, cool, and collected ruler. Andrew's face was now splotched with red and his eyes could no longer hide his rage. He strode over to his general and put his hands on the man's shoulders. Andrew, extremely tall for his people, towered over his general.

He glared at the man with a serious expression. "General, make us ready! We're prepared for this contingency, but we always thought this day would never come. Our over-confidence may be our undoing. We thought their prison would hold but now they'll be unleashed onto the world of men. The humans will pay the ultimate price and we'll be next. The time has come to stand and take back our home! The time also has come where our secrecy can no longer be guaranteed. I just pray we aren't too late. My goal of keeping our society together, while allowing the world outside to grow on its own, will no longer suffice."

Andrew patted the man on his shoulders. "Go, my friend! Do what you must to get that young man here safely.

That's priority one. When he's here safely, we'll begin his training."

Chapter 20

Colonel Whilhelm stood at attention, facing the screen with his entire body taut, waiting for punishment. The enraged image before him of the reptilian High Commander Zosa was cause for alarm in even the stoutest heart. His dry throat caused him to swallow frequently as he awaited his fate. The colonel bore witness many times the punishment for failure. In this moment, all he could do was stand with pride and dignity. He could almost feel the heat coming off the reptilian's body oozing through the screen, threatening to burn him whole.

High Commander Zosa wanted to vaporize this insignificant being before him, but knew all too well that if his campaign was to be successful, they needed the humans. He struggled to control the rage building within him and couldn't even speak for fear of sending out energy that might destroy the colonel. It took a few moments for him to calm his storm before proceeding. Still he needed to instill fear in this man to make sure this never happened again. Once the reptilian people were free and controlled the surface, he'd take care of this military man, maybe make him his personal slave.

The colonel opened the dialogue, "Your Excellency, I know and understand your reasoning behind not advancing our technology too much but in this case, we are unprepared to face their own technology to breach the entrance!"

Commander Zosa rebuffed him, "Colonel, to me, this sounds of another excuse as to why you cannot complete the small tasks I ask of you."

As if stung by the tendrils of a jellyfish, the colonel straightened even more, and it was his turn to become angry. In all the years he served under the commander, he was never given the whole story. In a conflict where intelligence was absolutely critical, the commander never gave the colonel enough information to do the job properly. His own agenda of ruling the world of men seemed much more important but now with the decimation of his force, his tactics warranted a change.

The colonel glared at the screen. "Commander, over the years, have I not served you with distinction and honor?"

High Commander Zosa with a smirk retorted, "Colonel, if this is what you call distinction, then I respond, no!"

With a bark, the colonel came back, "From day one, sir, you've played a game with me! Each time I ask for assistance or proper intelligence, you hold back. I'm a fighter and will fight to my last but in a conflict such as this, we're at a huge disadvantage not having all the information we can. You knew about the buzz saw technique they employ but once again failed to divulge that information. You sit there in judgement of myself and my troops, yet you sit comfortable in your own bunker away from the fight."

With a quick gesture, he sent the colonel flying through the air and into the back wall. He hit with terrific impact and the wind expelled from his lungs, leaving him gasping for breath. The commander laughed. "You, Colonel, are insignificant and can be easily replaced. I may not kill you where you stand just yet, but I promise you when I'm released from my prison, I'll teach you some manners. As for your request for more intelligence, the tactic employed by our enemies today is an ancient technique. To my knowledge, it hasn't been used since your kind became involved."

The colonel struggled to his feet, brushing himself off. "The fact is, Commander, with your extended lives, you think small details like that aren't important. I assure you, sir, in the field against an already superior foe in terms of technology, we need the same advantages!"

Commander Zosa seemed to expand to an even larger form on the screen. "Colonel, it won't be long until we can meet face to face. I'll then provide you with the tools that will offer us ultimate victory. In the meantime, you'll need to prepare your main army for an all-out assault. We're quite sure after your little skirmish today, you were at the right entrance to breach. In spite of the loss of your men, you came within inches of taking the entrance. I'm confident despite my rage, you're still the man for the job."

With a salute, the colonel once again stood tall. "Sir, what's our next mission?"

The commander stood with a serious look on his face. "I need you to capture someone for me."

A quizzical look came over the colonel's face. "Sir?"

High Commander Zosa looked amused. "Not what you were expecting, Colonel? For now, we won't send any more engagements toward our enemies. We'll make them think we're coming and send a few air attacks on the entrance just to keep them off the scent. No, for now, we need to focus our energy on the capture of a dangerous enemy who could topple us all and we need him on our side. If we can convince him our cause is just, it will forever turn the balance of power in our favor."

Again, the colonel looked confused. "Sir, forgive my ignorance but how can the capture of one individual have such an impact?"

With a smug look, the commander began, "This individual is unknowing of his power. We could destroy his mentor before his training began. Now he's wandering around with no sense of direction or real help. If we could gain a hold of him and bring him into the fold, we would be unstoppable. Just think, Colonel, when you started working with us, all the things you've accomplished toward your goal. We're almost where we want to be, and this is the last piece of the puzzle."

Colonel Whilhelm stroked his chin. "Commander, what is it you'd have me do?"

A broad sinister smile came across the commander's face. "Colonel, I'd have you unleash hell, but for now, I'll accept the capture of this individual. This is a delicate operation as he already is being helped by our enemy as we speak. They think they could grant him safe passage to their stronghold but, Colonel, you and I both know that won't happen. You're to dispatch men to bring this young man in."

The colonel did a double take. "Young man?"

The commander continued, "Yes, Colonel, a young man. He's what you'd call a teenager. Do not let that fool you in the least. He's a formidable foe and will grow in power as he gets closer to our enemies. No, he's the not the feeble person he seems. Once he figures out what he can do, we may all be in trouble. Our power is great but if he joins forces with the Zarillion, they may have the power to keep us imprisoned or even exile us."

For the first time, Colonel Whilhelm sensed some uneasiness in the commander's voice. "Commander, what exactly can this young man do? Especially if he's unaware of any power he may have. That should be to our advantage. We can capture him before he becomes aware of anything he could do to us. Just in case, what types of things can he use his powers for?"

Commander Zosa took a moment before responding, "Colonel, this young man has what you'd call powerful magic.

We, however, know it as science. He has the ability to manipulate matter and use the planet's magnetic forces in such a way that he can do almost anything he can dream up."

Colonel Whilhelm didn't seem impressed. "Commander, we ourselves work with individuals that can use similar forces. What makes this one so special?"

With a flourish of his hand, an image of the earth came to view in front of the colonel. The military man could easily make out the various magnetic fields that covered the planet. The commander spoke, "Yes, Colonel, I know you're familiar with some of the work we do with magnetic fields but what you know only scrapes the surface. Before we destroyed this young man's mentor, the only reason his mentor didn't destroy us was he kept trying to keep his protégé away from us. He alluded us for years and it was only by accident we found him. His friends gave away his location. Once we could pinpoint the location, we could lock in and destroy the target."

The colonel once again looked confused. "Sir, then why is the boy not with us already?"

An upset look came to the commander's face. "He had help from our enemies! They'll all pay. Now get your men ready. I want this boy found and brought before me! Now go!"

The colonel saluted and turned quickly, walking with a great purpose toward the door.

Chapter 21

Rubbing the sleep from his eyes, he propped himself up on his elbow to see where he was situated. The events of the last twenty-four hours still swimming around his head, he looked around the room. First, he noticed the concrete walls with their porous look to them. The gray added to the dull nature and feel to the entire room. Looking down to see his bedding, he smiled at the green coarse Army blanket that still sat on his lap.

Pushing himself up to a seated position, he looked around the room. He was so exhausted that he was asleep before his head hit the pillow. The soft glow from the fluorescent lights above didn't hurt his eyes but seemed to give everything a dull haze. At first, the room seemed too enclosed upon him but as his eyes became more accustomed to the light, he searched for Jake.

He frantically rose to his feet only to realize he was standing in his underwear. Looking down at his half-naked self, he couldn't recall stripping his other clothes last night before retiring. Turning quickly to search the room, he couldn't locate Jake. To his right stood a small metal folding chair with his clothes thrown onto it. He couldn't help but laugh as he took the room in. It reminded him of a jail cell and all that was missing was a single commode in the corner.

With quick, shaking hands, he pulled on his pants and threw his shirt on. He plopped himself back on the bed to lace up his shoes. At this point, he noticed the stale air in the room. He wondered about the last time someone used this room. Once his shoes were tight, he bounced off the bed and scrambled for the door. He knew he needed to find Jake and fast.

As he reached for the door handle, it flew open and in swished Jake, nearly running Peter over. He stopped abruptly before his friend. "Well, sleeping beauty, it's about time you got up! We need to get going. They allowed us to stay the night but just like they said last night, they cannot withstand an attack. Right now, our attackers are still at bay, but something tells me they're just waiting for reinforcements. Come with me. We need to get some more supplies. They'll also brief us on what's happening around us and what our next course of action should be."

Peter shook his head as if still trying to wake. "Jake, I don't even remember going to bed."

Jake smiled. "Dude, you were out on your feet. I even had to help with your clothes because you would just sleep in them. My dad always says to take the clothes off and let them air out. I put you to bed and stayed up for a little while, trying to find out what was going on. The folks that attacked us haven't advanced at all, but remain steadfast where they were last night, making camp. The soldiers here have great surveillance, but they sent a couple scouts out last night to see if they could get any intel from their camp."

He looked cautiously at his friend. "Jake, is that wise to send people out there? I mean, if they get captured, they could be forced to give up information about us, or worse."

Jake patted him on the shoulder. "Don't worry, man. They all came back and are reporting to the base commander right now. Come with me. Let's get you something to eat and then go see the commander."

Peter and Jake made their way to the mess and grabbed trays, quickly moving through the line and eating as they went. They hardly sat down as they practically threw food down their throats. Both young men threw their trash away and placed their trays on top of the barrels. They then scrambled out the door and nearly ran to the commander's office.

The base commander waited for them and smiled warmly as the boys stood before him. The boys must have looked a mess; the commander shook his head as if they were recruits. He sat assessing the two young men for a moment. With a quick movement, he rose from his seat and walked over to a large screen. Grainy images of the outside of the base came into focus.

Both young men looked at the images with great interest, trying to determine the extent of the danger in which they were now involved. They quickly discovered the encampment just off the base's property line. Their attackers seemed comfortable right where they were and felt no need to get any closer at the moment. Peter couldn't help but think this was the calm before the storm and he knew they needed to leave.

He blurted out, "Commander, thank you for your help but we really need to leave! Every second we're here endangers your men. We'll just get our stuff and go, that way you're no longer in danger."

The commander looked at him with pity. "Son, don't you worry about us! We're a lot stronger than we look. You're safe at the moment, but you're right, we do have to get you out of here ASAP. I'm just waiting for my second in command to get here and then you'll be on your way."

Jake and Peter took a seat at the behest of the commander and they listened to him talk about the work being done at the base. He told them about the analyst work they did. According to the commander, this base was all about crunching data and occasionally re-tasking a satellite to view some important target. The commander enjoyed the quiet nature of the base and seemed a little put off that his structure was thrown off. He was gracious, but the boys could tell he'd be glad to get back to normalcy.

As the young men listened to the commander's purpose at the base, they couldn't help but think how important all the information they gathered here would be to the military. Jake knew information was vital to the military's mission. His dad would always tell him they couldn't have enough information during an op. This made Peter smile. Jake was always asking questions, trying to gain an advantage in any situation.

Peter remembered a time during history class when they were talking about World War II and Jake was like a pit bull with questions. The teacher at first was grateful for the interest, but his good nature quickly became sour when Jake pressed his advantage to gain more knowledge. The teacher misunderstood Jake's thirst and gave him detention for disrupting the class, only to have his dad come in with full uniform. As soon as the teacher saw his father, he apologized and released Jake.

Instead of getting mad, Jake's father sat with the teacher and explained how his son was a searcher of knowledge. He told the teacher of the military history books that lined his walls where usually a young man his age wanted to play sports. He explained how Jake knew more about military tactics than most of the soldiers in his father's unit. The teacher was amazed and from that day on, he brought anything he could find on military history for Jake. Jake and the teacher became tight and Jake repaid him for his kindness one day on the way home when a bully was picking on the teacher's son.

Jake saw the bigger boys pushing this smaller, meek boy and came to his aide. Three larger boys surrounded the young man and took turns pushing him until he landed on the ground. The frightened boy naturally cried, which spurred the bullies on more. They grabbed at the boy's clothes, trying to pull him back up, and his backpack. This caused the strap to get caught under the young man's chin, choking him.

Jake ran through the older boys, tackling one, and releasing their hold on the backpack. The young boy looked gratefully at Jake and grabbed his things, running home. Jake was a good-sized kid with great muscle structure, but he was still growing. These boys he faced were older and one was much larger. The three boys circled Jake with hatred in their eyes. Their prey was now long gone, but they could still take care of this intruder.

One of the older boys seemed to be the leader and nodded to the others to attack. Jake saw this and awaited the strike. The two other boys attacked Jake at once. With a quick rush forward, he met the two attackers head on with a close line for each boy. He ran through each, leaving them on the ground writhing in pain. The leader was now furious and came screaming toward Jake with fists raised. Jake ducked to the side and landed a punch to the boy's midsection. The boy bent over in pain, not knowing what to do next.

Jake turned to see the other two now up again and in rage at their leader being hurt. Both young men swung at Jake at the same time. Jake was too fast for them and ducked out of the way. He watched as the two attackers struck each other in the face. Jake learned early on in his training to let other's momentum help in his own defense. Both boys went down in a heap, grabbing at their faces. Again, Jake saw the leader back on his feet standing tall. He remained in his stance and moved in on Jake more cautiously this time.

Jake and the bully squared off facing one another, measuring each as they moved around in a circle. Jake could tell this boy was a seasoned fighter by the way he bent his knees and moved gracefully on his toes. The two other boys knew better than to attack while their leader was engaged, and watched as backup. The two combatants moved in on one another and exchanged blows. The first few blows just glanced off each other's defenses and they both backed up to reassess the situation.

After a few more exchanges, the boys just looked at one another and knew it would be a stalemate at best. The bully stopped and did something surprising—he extended his hand to Jake. He took the boy's hand and made peace. While speaking to the boys, Jake found out that the teacher was in the habit of giving these boys detention. Jake knew how difficult the teacher could be and explained that to the boys. He told the boys he'd talk to the teacher on their behalf, but they'd need to leave the son alone. The boys agreed and they all became fast friends.

This thought brought Peter back to the current situation of listening to the commander. He looked up at the man droning on and just politely nodded. Jake saw his loss of attention and interjected on behalf of his friend. "Commander, tell me about your second in command. What can we expect from this soldier?"

The commander sat up straighter in his chair and they could see the pride swell up in his face as he became ready to talk about his second. He smiled. "Boys, you'll never meet a finer soldier, except for your father of course. William Pace is one of those rare soldiers that has a perfect blend of soldier with the compassion of a saint. Jake, you'll get along with him. He's always asking questions. He's just like you, constantly looking for information and some reason things happen.

"Due to his constant thirst for knowledge, Captain Pace specializes in advanced weaponry. The captain is here with me working on some new ideas for our satellites. I cannot get more into it, but you've seen some of our work here with the satellites. Captain Pace is an invaluable resource for this base. He's, however, a true soldier and really wasn't meant to be stuck on a base analyzing data. I envy him being able to go with you. You may not believe this but there was a time not long ago when I'd be going with you. Unfortunately, that's the price one pays for a command. My wants and needs are no longer my own but are used for the greater good. We'll, however, assist you on the ground here in any way we can. You can count on that!"

Chapter 22

A stocky officer in full dress uniform stood in the doorway. Captain William Pace filled the entire doorway and despite the uniform, looked ready for action. His hair was freshly cut and cropped tightly to his head. The choice of a flat top couldn't have been more perfect for this soldier. His chest threatened to burst out of his tightly tailored shirt and the multitude of ribbons protruded for all to see. The boys could tell right away why the commander was so fond of the captain. He exuded confidence, intelligence, and strength.

The commander noticed his second in command and waved him in quickly. The young men found themselves staring at all the ribbons on the captain's chest which covered an entire pocket. They also took in the captain's entire uniform seemed to be devoid of any wrinkle and he looked as though he just stepped out of a dry cleaner.

Captain William Pace, Army Advanced Weapons Specialist, stood at attention with his heels clicked together and saluted his superior. The commander stood briskly and saluted back with a snap. With formalities exchanged, the captain then smiled and broke military bearing telling the commander it was great to see him again. He then turned to the boys and offered a hand to each one.

Peter couldn't believe the size of the man's hands as they engulfed his own, dwarfing it. He thought the man could easily crush his hand, but the shake was firm but genuine. Captain Pace shook Jake's hand but then as though he were already a member of his unit, slapping him on the back, telling him he couldn't wait to meet his dad. Jake chose not to say anything, but he was certainly nervous that his dad wasn't already here with them. The captain told the boys he heard all about Jake's dad, but it always seemed as though they passed each other without meeting.

Everyone now sat before the commander waiting for orders. The boys couldn't help but keep looking at the captain's freshly pressed uniform in admiration. This wasn't lost on the commander. "Boys, did I not tell you! This is by far one of the finest soldiers I know!"

Captain Pace smiled. "Sir, it's only because I have fantastic leaders that I can become a great soldier, along with the terrific men and women I serve with!"

The commander nodded. "Captain, that may be true, but you're more than many see. I'll leave it at that. I have to say, Captain, we're in grave need of your help. Jake's father should already be here, and we've heard nothing about his whereabouts."

He looked sympathetic at Jake. "I'm sorry, son. I'm sure he's fine but we cannot wait. My orders are quite clear—give you the support, counsel, and supplies you need while sending you quickly on your way. You know the grave urgency in your mission. I don't to claim to know everything about it, but it's plain that speed is key."

Peter and Jake looked at one another and knew the commander was right. They couldn't wait for Jake's father.

Jake turned to the commander. "Sir, we understand. Tell us what you need us to do. I know my father told me the same thing, that I wasn't to wait for him. I know my dad will catch up with us when he can, but I cannot help but be confused about what might be keeping him. My father is never late for anything."

Captain Pace put a supportive hand on his shoulder. "Worry not, I'm sure he was just asked to finish an op that cannot be put off. I know he'll meet us on the road. Let us get ourselves ready to leave."

He turned to the commander. "Sir, the attackers remain a safe distance from the base and seem content to wait us out. I have the National Guard just over the ridge waiting for my orders. Do you want them here to help with security?"

The commander peered at the captain. "Delay that order, Captain. There's no sense in causing a confrontation if we can help it. There are a lot of sensitive items and equipment here. I'd prefer not to have my base leveled to the ground."

He rose from his chair. "Focus on securing everything these boys need and I'll brief you on the escape route."

Peter looked up. "Sir, escape route? Aren't we going the way we came?"

The commander responded, "Peter, that may well be the case but there's more than one way out of this base. Captain Pace and I'll come up with the best plan. In the meantime, you boys get your things ready to go. I'll send Captain Pace to you when we're finished here. Be ready to move within the next hour. When we go, it will be quick."

Both boys looked at each other and stood thanking the men for their help. They made their way out of the room and walked down the hallway at a quick pace. Peter knew they had to hurry. Something told him they weren't as secure as the commander seemed to think. Jake led the way and they went to their bunks to get ready.

Captain Pace waited for the boys to leave and turned to his commander. "Sir, Jake's father is MIA! No one has seen or heard anything from him. I spoke to his commander and they're quite concerned. Nothing like this ever happens when it comes to Jake's dad. He's the consummate soldier. I'm afraid something terrible is happening and we cannot wait. I must get these boys out of here. These parasites at our doorstep are up to something, I know it."

He looked up from the desk and the commander added, "Listen, Bill, you're right. Something crazy is going on here and I don't claim to know what. All I know is that these two boys are critical to national security. Both these boys seem to be terrific but for the life of me I have no idea what makes them special. They're typical teenage boys. They also don't seem to be carrying anything ultra-important."

The captain paced across the room. "You're right, sir. They're cool kids but nothing out of the ordinary. Something isn't right here but I assure you. I'll protect them with my life if need be. What are my orders, sir?"

After a brief pause, the commander spoke, "Captain, it's imperative these boys get safe passage to Argentina. There, you'll be given new instructions, but you have to get them there safely. From everything I've been told, these boys are the key to some great secret."

"Argentina," cried the captain. "What the heck are they going to do in Argentina? Hide out like some war criminal."

The commander laughed. "Honestly, Bill, I wish I knew but this is even above my pay grade. Just get them there safely. I tell you, Bill, this will be your greatest task! Just the sheer urgency by my superiors tells me this is no joke. No, my friend, this is no babysitting assignment. You're protecting a national asset here. Go get yourself ready, Captain. We're going underground, or I should say you are. I'll cut a path for you, my old friend. These jerks won't know what hit them. They think us just a bunch of computer nerds. We'll show them."

Captain Pace looked sternly at his commander. "They're waiting for something. Why not come in and grab the boys? They know this isn't a combat base. The only thing I can think is they're afraid of hurting the boys and if they wait until we move them, they could grab them easier."

With a brief nod, the commander spoke, "Whatever they're waiting for, they're going to be surprised when the National Guard goes to pay them a visit as a diplomatic mission while you slip out the back. There's no way they have the intel about our secondary exit. You and I are the only ones that know about it. You'll be long gone before they catch on to what's happening. That will give you a great head start."

The captain stood and saluted. "Thank you, sir! I won't let you down!"

The commander smiled. "You've never let me down and I don't expect you to now either."

Chapter 23

General Giles, still full of grime and dried blood, walked quickly back to his quarters. Holly joined him from behind, who darted in front of him, stopping him in his tracks. The general looked up into her azure eyes and waited. Holly looked as if she wanted to reach out to him but then backed away. She remained paused, looking at the military man before her with uncertainty crossing her face. Both stood unmoving for a moment before Holly broke the silence, "Ryan, we have to get those young men here safely!"

With a hand held up, the general began, "I know but it's a little more difficult than just going to pick them up. This last breach attempt was the most successful yet and our enemies continue to provide the humans with more and more technology. I'm afraid soon our borders will no longer be safe, and our enemies will be free soon. Holly, we'll be fighting a war on two fronts. That's the easiest way for defeat."

Holly looked critically at the general. "We've known this all for quite some time, but you and I both know that none of that will matter if those two boys perish!"

The general looked worried. "I know, and I agree with everything you're saying. It's just that we're really in the greatest danger now that any of us can recall. The slightest mistake could destroy not only our home but that of the humans. This all could happen under my watch. I'm sorry, Holly, but I'm very distracted right now by my responsibility toward the races. I cannot make one wrong move without ultimate consequences."

With sympathy in her eyes, she reached out and grabbed his hand. "Ryan, you're the finest soldier that our race has ever known. Our safety is always in good hands with you at the helm and I fear not that you'll make the right decisions, you always do. Have faith in your abilities as we have ultimate faith in you. I know whatever you decide, we'll be well taken care of."

The general forced an uncomfortable smile. "Holly, you know how I feel about our people and about the freedom of all races. I'll make sure we're all looked after. It's just a bit much right now. I knew this day would come but you never really are prepared for something like this. I just need a moment to think of how we can get those boys and keep our own borders safe long enough to get them back here. See, Holly, I'm sure I can get them here safely but what happens if here is no longer safe. Then what happens?"

Holly closed her hand around his. "We'll fight together. It's time for us to rise. We've stood in the shadows for far too long, telling ourselves it was for the good of mankind but honestly, I think we liked having the humans deflect everything. I for one think it's payback time. We chose to live here and this planet in turn grants us a great life but at what cost, secrecy?"

General Giles lifted her hand and kissed it. "Holly, you're always gracious and supportive, Thank you! I'll be sure not to disappoint. Now if you'll excuse me, I have preparations to make. I'll be leaving as soon as possible to gather these boys. The difficult decision remains as to whom to take along to ensure these boys will come along with me. I cannot very well tell them, Hi, you need to come with me and the fate of the world hangs in the balance."

Holly laughed. "Yes, that's quite the story and a couple of young men may like it, but they may not altogether believe it.

How many do you think you should take? Is it a big company or a small quick force?"

The general smiled. "I'd love to take a large force with me, but you know as well as I that would draw too much unwanted attention. No, I must bring a small company with me and depend upon stealth. This group needs to be specialized with a wide range of qualities."

Holly turned to him. "Who will you bring?"

He turned back to her. "I'll bring a couple of my warriors and a few people I believe can help the boys. Would you care to come? I could always use your diplomatic skills along the way. There's no doubt this will be a very diplomatic trip. I'd also appreciate any suggestion you could offer as I value your opinion greatly."

Holly flashed a sly smile. "You, sir, just want me to be with you, is that it?"

With a brilliant smile, he clasped her hand softly. "I want you with me always! There isn't a moment I spend on this earth that I don't want you by my side. When this ordeal is finished, we'll announce our plans to the world but for now, let us keep things as is."

She reached over and embraced him in a large hug. "You're right but I cannot help but imagine what it would be like to live a regular life. What would we do if we weren't always protecting the world? Would we have a little house on the water? Would there be little children running around getting into mischief? Would we host holiday celebrations? Worse yet, would we have regular jobs?"

At this, he laughed. "Holly, there's no way you could do a regular job. You're a born leader, plain and simple. Although, I do agree if we win, things will change for us. These two boys will be a changing of the guard. Peter is just starting to figure out what he can do. I can feel it when his power rises in him. You'll have to take on his training. Without his grandfather's tutelage, he's lost and scared."

Holly looked worried. "I feel his conflict. He shouldn't have to go through this alone! You're right, I need to accompany you. He'll need guidance if he's to make it here safely. Besides, I need to stretch my legs. I'm much too restless here and need a little adventure. I also need to keep an eye on my investment!"

With that, she grasped his hand tightly. "I'll never let you go!"

The general blushed. "I'd hope not. I know Peter will be in good hands with you, but I'm very concerned for Jake. There has been no word from his father and no one can locate him. He's a magnificent soldier but we should find him. Again, both of these boys have no idea what's going on and they're out there alone."

Holly gripped his hand that much harder. "They aren't alone! We'll guide them. Let us get ready. Speed is of the essence and those boys need our help. I can be ready to leave within the hour. I'll alert the council of our plans."

General Giles stopped her. "No, my love, don't tell anyone. I feel we just need to leave unannounced. Something tells me that the fewer people know about our movements, the better off those boys will be. I continue to get an uneasy feeling our plans are finding their way into unfriendly hands. At this time, let us gather our small force and be gone with no fanfare."

She donned a sly smile. "Yes, stealth mode would be best. I leave the military strategy to you, My Lord."

The general smiled back. "Yes, My Lady. It's just during the last few councils I can see things are much more contentious than ever before. It's as if there's another agenda at play here. This makes me very nervous. I know in a balanced society such as ours, there will always be different views, but this is unlike anything else we've faced before. I wouldn't sound paranoid, but my gut tells me our enemies are close to our council."

Holly's face became serious. "Ryan, if you feel this way, maybe we shouldn't leave our city undefended. Should we send others to retrieve the boys?"

Ryan turned to her with fire in his eyes. "No, these boys are the key to everything! If they perish, we all burn. No, my life, this is our mission. There are standing orders and the city is in good hands. It's those two boys that are in the most danger. We cannot wait another minute. I'll round up those soldiers I have in mind and meet you at the south entrance in one hour."

He leaned over and kissed her lips gently. As he backed slowly away, their lips pulled away from each other with great resistance. They both stood for a moment as the electricity between them dissipated. As their hands unclasped and fell to their sides, they couldn't force themselves to leave.

Holly broke the silence. "One hour! No more!"

Both nodded and turned bolting in opposite directions.

Chapter 24

Rebecca watched Holly rush into her quarters and knew it was time. Holly would never reveal to Rebecca what was really taking place and blocked her thoughts well. Rebecca, even without the use of her mentor's thoughts, knew something was about to take place. She followed Holly a lot now for fear of being left behind. There was too much at stake for the elders to announce her too young to assist.

Crouching behind the wall, she tried to guess what would happen next. Straining to see in the dim nighttime light, she watched as another figure made its way to Holly's door. The figure stood tall but slightly bent and angular. Rebecca's mind went to thoughts of Michael, the financial advisor to the city. He was always trying to get Holly's attention. Rebecca laughed inside as she thought of persistence of this man. Michael, for as long as Rebecca could remember, was always trying to carry favor with Holly with no success.

She watched as the door opened a crack and there was a quick conversation as the door closed just as fast. When Michael turned to leave, Rebecca could see even in the shadows he was quite upset. The man's robes flew behind him as he sprinted away, cursing under his breath. Something told Rebecca she should follow the man but as she moved in that direction, she felt the pull toward Holly's door. Without another thought, she took up residence back behind the wall.

When the door opened, Holly peered cautiously around before coming completely into the hallway. Rebecca noticed that Holly carried a large pack on her back. This was surprising as Rebecca never knew Holly to be the adventurous type. Holly took off in the direction of the armory. Without another thought,

Rebecca followed, holding to the shadows. Carefully moving against the wall, hoping not to run into anyone she knew, Rebecca kept her distance.

Holly moved through the hallways swiftly without once looking back. Her strides were long and smooth. The distance between Rebecca and Holly grew and Rebecca decided to risk someone seeing her, so she could maintain a closer view. The light in this part of the city shown extremely bright, and Rebecca could see Holly's reddened face and a look of sheer determination on her face. Without any word between them, Rebecca knew she was going after the two young men. Rebecca knew all too well the mind of her lady.

Rebecca looked at her own attire and knew she wasn't ready to travel. Looking around quickly, she tried to determine where she was in the city. Her thoughts raced to her home and she weighed whether she should risk grabbing her things and return, or just to continue her vigil following Holly. She watched as Holly reached the armory. What was surprising to Rebecca was the soldier didn't even flinch when Holly entered. Rebecca knew Holly's standing was high in the city, but one would expect at least a quick inquiry as to the nature of the visit.

Rebecca saw her opportunity and ran full speed down the hall toward her own home. If she hurried, she could easily make it back to the armory in a few minutes. As she ran around the corner, she ran headlong into the chest of an unknown man. The two crashed to the ground. Rebecca bounced up only to see the seething face of Michael Gentry, the city's financial wizard. Rebecca, now on her feet, looked to Michael as he rose to his full height. Even with the slight bend in his spine, he still towered over Rebecca. She could see the clear agitation in his lined face. He composed himself and brushed the dirt from his hands before glaring at Rebecca.

He began, "Miss Rebecca, what are you doing out at this hour and why would you be in this part of the city?"

For her part, Rebecca actually got along with Michael as she loved finances. She even spent time asking him questions and visiting his office. That all stopped when Rebecca came closer to becoming a woman. She caught him looking at her many times while she was in the finance office, learning lessons from others. These looks made her blush and feel uncomfortable. The looks were now of longing and envy. The more time she spent in the office the worse the looks became as Michael would see to her education. One day, he put his hand on her shoulder and she recoiled from him. He saw her reaction and apologized right away but the damage had been done.

After that day, her visits to the finance office were few and far between. He even came to her home and tried to make amends, stating she was such a great student, he found himself very proud of her. Rebecca accepted his apology, but she still didn't spend much time in the finance office from that time on. During other encounters after that, she saw Michael's sad face when he looked at her as if she caused him some type of hurt. When she didn't return to the finance office, the hurt looks became looks of hatred. Their last interaction was very heated as she was no longer a little girl.

Rebecca got tired of the looks in her direction and she confronted Michael in true young person fashion. This confrontation took place in front of other elders and embarrassed Michael a great deal. At the end of the meeting, Michael looked as if he'd twist her neck in two. Rebecca didn't back down and told him to move on. Michael composed himself and refused to be dragged into her little game. Holly stepped in and separated the two combatants, but she saw what transpired and inquired from Rebecca details. Holly understood as she knew Michael always seemed to have a young, smitten girl by his side.

She saw the powerful man use these girls and discard them. The fact that Rebecca refused his advances must have infuriated him.

From that time on, however, Holly took it upon herself to protect Rebecca. Not that she needed all that much protection. Rebecca was the most powerful sorceress in the city, even if she didn't know this herself. Rebecca was quite unpolished and knew little of the power she possessed. Holly hoped she could teach Rebecca and Peter to use their powers together. Rebecca didn't know this, but Peter was more important to her than just an infatuation. Holly taught her little things to satisfy her thirst for the power but ever since this situation with Peter arose, Rebecca's power grew exponentially. Holly knew if she didn't teach her to control the power, they'd all be in trouble.

The two still stood staring at one another, neither wanting to give in. Rebecca spoke first, "My Lord, forgive my clumsiness! I found myself daydreaming and out far too late. I was hurrying back home so I wouldn't get in trouble. I'm so sorry for running into you like that. It was truly all my fault and I feel terrible!"

This took the man by surprise. His face twisted from anger to confusion. "Rebecca, no, pardon me. I also was hurrying and not paying attention to where I was going. Please accept my apology." He looked genuinely sorry. "Rebecca, I know I ruined our relationship and I'm very upset by that. I let the fact you're now a stunningly beautiful woman get in the way of our friendship. I think that's what makes me more upset than anything else. I'm always with pretty ladies, but you're different. You're bold, intelligent, and beautiful. Your strength is envious. I just thought maybe you'd see me as more than just a teacher, but I should have realized my relationship as your teacher was most important." Michael stood before her and she could feel his icy stare melt. "Rebecca, I know now that I was so wrong! I hope someday you can forgive me."

His words were so powerful, she almost leaned in to him for a hug. At the last minute, she pulled away and his words lost their power. She stood straight up and gazed at the man. He was quite tall and angular, but she could see the girls appeal to him. He wasn't a bad-looking man and he was quite charming. Rebecca thought about this for a moment, too charming went through her mind. With a quick nod of her head, she brought herself back into focus.

She stepped back. "My Lord, I really must go. I'm so late! I could have handled the situation in a much more lady-like fashion. I too am sorry for embarrassing you in front of the elders. I have much to learn about diplomacy. I really did value your lessons and was very upset when I could no longer learn. To me, you'll always be my teacher and out of respect, I could never see you as anything other than that."

Michael was taken aback, and he couldn't find the words. He shook his head. "Yes, I know now the parameters of our relationship and again, my apologies for trying to take it in another direction. Please know that I value you as a student and miss our discussions. I also understand the damage I caused you and I hope someday to remedy that situation. Yes, you need to get home before you get in trouble. I'll cover for you, if need be. Good night, Rebecca."

Rebecca looked quickly and saw a sad look in his eyes. "My Lord, it's just my responsibilities are different now. Someday I could return to my lessons. Thank you for the kind offer. I'll take it under advisement. Good night."

She walked briskly away and refused to look back. She turned the corner and bolted to her house at full speed, not stopping until in her home. Rebecca flew up the stairs only to come face to face with a mound of clothing she still didn't put away and nearly crashed right into the wall trying to avoid the mound. Without stopping, she fell to her belly with a grunt and reached under her bed for her pack. She yanked it out and stood, throwing it onto her back. Ready to run out the door, she caught sight of herself in the mirror. She laughed aloud as she looked at her reflection.

She stood looking at herself in her formal robes. These garments were unsuitable for travel. She reached over and shut the door quickly, stripping her robes. With little time to lose, she dressed and slung the pack on her back. Nearly ripping the door off its hinges, she ran out the door and nearly leaped down the stairs. She could hear her mother milling around in the kitchen but chose not to say anything.

As she came closer to the door, she heard her mother's voice, "Rebecca, is that you?"

She turned swiftly. "Yes, Mom, it's me. I just came downstairs to get something. I'm tired. I'm going to bed early, good night."

From the kitchen, she heard, "Okay, have a good night. I'll see you in the morning. I'm just preparing something for dinner tomorrow. Your dad is in the workshop. We'll see you in the morning."

Rebecca answered, "Okay, Mom! See you tomorrow."

Without a sound, she remained stationary in the hall waiting to see if her mom would come in. Listening for a moment, she could hear the sounds of her mother working on the meal. When she felt comfortable to leave, she crept to the door and ever so carefully opened it. Without a sound, she closed the door behind her and made her way back toward the armory. After a minute though, she turned and looked back toward her home. She felt bad about leaving her parents this way, but there would be no way they would consent to her traveling anywhere right now. Her parents were well aware of the strife outside their city. Tensions were high, and all travel was restricted.

She also could see Peter's panicked face when he knew his house was being invaded. This quickly put her back on track and once again, she ran full speed back to the armory. She arrived just in time as she could see Holly leaving with what looked to be a large staff and a long sword slung over her shoulder. Rebecca thought this odd as they had many more technologically advanced and smaller weapons at their disposal. Rebecca also knew Holly needed none of these weapons—she was the weapon.

Holly was also a very powerful sorceress and Rebecca spent time learning from her now. This was really the reason she spent less and less time with Michael. Besides the way Michael became interested in her, she was much more interested in her own power. Growing up, she knew something was a little different about her. Several times, she made things move across the room at night in her bedroom. When she was older, Holly showed her a few things but now that she was older, these little parlor tricks weren't enough, and she wanted to know the full potential of her power.

Holly was always very gracious with her teaching, but Rebecca knew she was holding back on teaching her real magic. Rebecca didn't mind all that much, but she grew more restless as the situation around her city became more dire. Without a doubt, Rebecca knew she could help more than people allowed her to around the city. She knew she was young but felt as though she were being treated as a child.

Once more, she shadowed Holly, moving from shadow to shadow and trying to stay out of sight. Rebecca now recognized the area they were traveling. Rebecca knew this to be what was called the south entrance. This was a secret entrance used very rarely for military purposes. Rebecca only knew this because General Giles caught her with several other young people playing near here and were scolded for it heavily. Holly described the entrance for her and she stayed far from it after that.

Holly quickened her pace and Rebecca nearly ran to keep up. As they came closer to the entrance, Rebecca saw another figure following Holly. It was hard to see the person following her, but another look revealed Michael's tall, angular body. From her vantage point, Rebecca could see a weapon now in Michael's hand and he sped up his advance. The unsuspecting Holly continued walking toward the entrance. Rebecca couldn't stand by and do nothing. Without hesitation, she ran forward and was about the jump on the man from behind, when she felt rage and power build within herself.

Unthinking, she unleashed a wave of power toward Michael, lifting him off the ground and sending him hurdling through the air into a stone wall. Michael crashed into the wall with amazing force and Rebecca thought she killed him for a moment until she saw him move slightly. The commotion alerted Holly who now spun to see what transpired. With her guard up, she released the sword from its sheath was stunning grace and power. Rebecca looked at Holly in awe; this wasn't Holly the politician she saw before her, it was a dangerous warrior.

Rebecca came forward from the shadows to see the shock on Holly's face. For a moment, neither spoke. Rebecca looked toward the downed Michael. Holly now moved over to see the fallen man and then looked to Rebecca for answers. Rebecca just pointed to the ground near the fallen man. There on the ground was a firearm. Holly looked toward the man with rage in her eyes. She bent down and picked up the weapon, placing it into her belt.

Again, Holly glanced at Rebecca with a questioning look. "Rebecca, what in the world are you doing here right now?"

Rebecca looked at her. "Holly, I followed you and saw Michael following you, ready to attack you."

Holly looked at the man on the ground starting to come around. "Yes, I can see that! Rebecca, you must return home now. We'll talk about this when I return. I'll alert the authorities about Michael. Go home, child."

Rebecca raised her voice, "I'm no longer a child and if I weren't here, he'd have hurt you!"

Holly's face softened. "I'm grateful for your assistance but where I now go, you cannot follow."

At that moment, another figure appeared out of the shadows. Both ladies turned in defensive stances to meet the new threat. The ladies crouched slightly, ready to pounce. The figure moved into the light to reveal his true self. Holly let out a sigh of relief and strode forward to meet the new figure. Rebecca could now see the new figure was General Giles. He came forward to address the ladies.

Both ladies at once said, "General, we have trouble!"

The general looked at the now recovering man. He went over and picked the confused man up by the scruff of the neck. The bewildered man looked into the general's hard, steely eyes. Both men stared at one another for a moment. Then the general propped him up in front of him.

General Giles poked the man in the chest, nearly knocking him down again. "Michael, what's the meaning of this? An attack on a senior member of the council is punishable by death! You have exactly thirty seconds to explain before I carry out the sentence myself right here."

Michael's usual confident demeanor was now replaced with sheer terror as he looked into the general's stone-cold face.

The general took out his sidearm and pointed it at the elder. "Michael, start talking!"

At first, he wouldn't say anything and looked around as if he were waiting for something. When the general advanced on him and put the weapon under his chin, he began to speak.

Michael shook a little. "General Giles, with all due respect, I owe you nothing. I'm a senior member of the council and I don't have to explain myself to you."

This angered the general even more and he grabbed the man by the collar and lifted him straight in the air. "You fool! I too am a senior member of the council and in case you don't remember, when someone on the council is assaulted, it's my job to protect them by any means necessary. You'll pay for this, Michael. I could end you right here without trial and I'd be within my rights to do so!"

The general turned to Holly and Rebecca. "Let's go! We can wait no longer."

He threw cuffs to Holly. "Bind his hands, he's coming with us. It's too dangerous to leave him behind."

Chapter 25

Peter couldn't believe what was going on before him as chunks of rock and dust flew by his head. The explosions rocked the base around him. The smoke and dust were heavy in the air. He brought his shirt up to cover his nose and mouth, guarding him temporarily from the stench. Quickly, he moved forward to stay with his friends as they fled. Peter could barely see Captain Pace in front of him, but Jake remained on his right. Both boys struggled to keep up with the finely tuned soldier.

Through the smoke and dust, Peter could make out the outline of a door. Jake waved them on and they quickened their pace to catch up. Out of breath, the boys looked to the military man for guidance. Suddenly, as the captain was about to speak, gunfire broke the silence. They swung to see flashes through the smoke. The captain put the boys behind him and turned his own firearm toward the skirmish. Peter and Jake crouched behind the large man but couldn't help but peek around him.

A figure came running out of the smoke, weapon pointed at the trio. Captain Pace squeezed off two rounds, dropping the man where he stood. He put one hand out to tell the boys to continue backing up toward the door. Again, they heard weapons being discharged and this time, several soldiers came rushing through the smoke. The captain almost fired but recognized one of his own soldiers just in time to avoid a horrible mistake. The captain's men reached their leader and then turned to form a protective shield around the captain's charges. Captain Pace turned quickly and punched a code into the keypad by the door. When nothing happened, he tried repeatedly with little success.

One of the men looked at the keypad before taking out an electric screwdriver. The soldier swiftly took the keypad panel off and hotwired the mechanism. The door opened as more shots were fired in their direction. Bullets struck the wall, sending pieces of concrete everywhere. Captain Pace rushed the boys through the door, pushing them in front of him. The captain's soldiers returned fire into the building smoke. Once through the door, they ran into a well-lit hallway that seemed to go on for miles.

They all continued their flight, when a great explosion rocked the entire hallway, sending them sprawling onto the floor. Quickly to their feet, they all turned to the end of the tunnel only to see it completely destroyed. Again, the captain pushed them forward down the endless hallway. Peter looked around and besides the captain, they now had eight other soldiers with them to aid in their escape. The small group ran down the hallway at top speed.

Coming to an abrupt stop at a large bunker door, the captain strode forward and again punched a code. This time without delay, the large door cracked open and swung open slowly. When the door was open enough to squeeze through, they slipped out into the immense cavern. Light softly peered in from an opening at the far end of the cavern. The captain turned and shut the bunker door. When finished, he motioned them to follow him. Without question, they followed closely behind until they came to a small outcropping of rock resembling a small cave. The captain went inside, and they stuck close behind. Once inside, he told them to sit and he grabbed a lantern from the corner, lighting it.

When the light was strong enough, the boys noticed the small cave was more of a supply closet. Everything from food, to clothes, to munitions, and even reading material could be found in the cave. The remaining soldiers fanned out and grabbed what supplies they could carry. Captain Pace came over to have a good look at the boys before nodding his head and joining the other soldiers gathering supplies.

After the soldiers gathered what they could, they took places on the ground to check their weapons. Captain Pace again came over to the boys and this time sat on the ground next to them. Peter waited for the captain to speak but it looked as though he were still assessing the entire situation. Again, he looked the boys over and smiled. He reached out and patted each one on the shoulder.

He smiled again before speaking, "Well now, that was interesting?"

The boys both gave him a quizzical look.

He again nodded. "I guess they were done waiting! That was a very quick, coordinated attack. It's a good thing we were already moving you out before the attack began. By the looks of that destroyed tunnel, we won't be pursued from that direction, but it won't take them long to figure out where we exited. We'll take a few minutes to regroup but then we must be on our way. We have a ship standing by a few miles from here and we need to make it there as quick as possible before our pursuers catch up. Boys, grab a quick bite and drink. After you're done, double check your own supplies and gather what you need. The ship we're going on is a cargo transport rather than a military vessel to throw off our scent."

Peter sat up straight. "Captain Pace, I'm sorry about the loss of your men! That battle back there was intense and your men protected us with their lives. I'll be forever grateful."

The captain again patted Peter on the back. "You're a good man! I'm beginning to see what all the fuss is about. Don't you worry yourself, young man. As a soldier, we all know the risks and gladly fight for the freedom of others. I do have to say though, when the dust does settle, I believe there will be fewer casualties than you expect. Our attackers were on a mission to capture. Yes, they engaged but you could tell they were being careful not to harm you boys. No, I don't think you have to worry. I'm sure we lost fewer than you think."

Again, Peter looked at the captain. "Still, sir, I cannot help but wonder again why all this trouble over a few boys? Jake will be a terrific soldier himself but me, I'm just a normal kid. From what I gather, my grandfather was a person of interest but not me. I'm a nobody."

That last comment sat in the air a moment before the captain responded, "Peter, first, you're a very special young man and I can already see great leadership skills in you! Also, you let others lead when you should, rather than questioning everything. That, my dear boy, is a very noble quality which again tells me what type of leader you'll one day be. Yes, I know from your perspective, things seem odd, but I'm used to judging people and you aren't at all who you seem to be. Your humble nature will serve you well throughout your lifetime and when it's your turn to lead, it will be your greatest trait."

The captain spoke with such conviction that Peter really didn't know what to say. He just nodded a look of thanks in the direction of the captain. Jake stood and walked to Peter, looking fondly at his friend. He stopped and held out a hand to help his friend to his feet. Peter gladly took it. Both boys looked at one another before gathering all their things.

Captain Pace couldn't help but feel a sense of pride as he looked at the two friends covering each other's backs. The more he learned about the two young men, the easier it became to watch over them. Peter was right though, his outward appearance would suggest just a regular, every day young man trying to find his way in the world. At closer look, however, something just below the surface told the captain this young man held the key to something very powerful. As a military leader, he was used to dealing with those who were in great positions of power. This boy, though he didn't know it yet, showed qualities of some of the most powerful individuals the captain had come across.

He watched as the two boys gathered up everything and readied once again for travel. What amazed him was the willingness to go on. Both these young men knew not what awaited them, but yet they used a great sense of duty to prepare themselves to go on. Some of the captain's own troops didn't have that sense of duty. He again smiled thinking about what type of soldiers these two would make.

Once the small troop was slightly rested and resupplied, they followed their leader out into the larger cavern. With little conversation, they all fell in behind the captain as he led them from the darkness. At first, the light stung their eyes but after a few moments, they easily focused on their surroundings. The terrain remained rocky but just in front of them stood a lush grove of trees. This would offer great cover and the captain led them at a quick pace into the wood. As they jogged through the wood, the smell of trees and vegetation invaded their nostrils. This was a much-welcome fragrance after dealing with the sulfur smell of gunfire.

Everyone welcomed the cover of the canopy of leaves above them. The fresh air brushed against their cheeks as they rushed through the woods to their next destination. The size of the woods surprised them. After running for thirty minutes straight, they took a brief break. Again, the captain checked in on his young charges only to find them slightly winded. He just shook his head thinking how nice it must be to be young. The small squad took more water and food but then went right back to their trek.

This time the captain asked two of his squad to double back and check to see if they were being followed. In the meantime, he led the rest of the squad forward at a reduced pace. At their slower pace, they could see more of the wood. The overhead canopy kept the sun from beating down upon them, but they could feel the air getting warmer, telling them the day was getting on. They continued forward and only stopped briefly as the two soldiers returned to update the captain on their surroundings. According to the soldiers, they could see no one following them and the coast seemed clear.

Again, the captain had them jog through the trees until they came to the edge of the wood. He stopped them just inside the tree line and searched the open ground before them. When he deemed it safe, he led them from the protection of the trees. Once in the open, the heat seemed to rise, and the sun beat down upon them mercilessly. The captain assured them they'd be to the ship just after dark, but they needed to hurry as he still didn't trust the lack of pursuit.

Without further delay, they continued moving forward quickly. The rest of the journey was very uneventful with the group welcoming the damp sea air and the sun setting in the distance. Now that the sun was gone, the breeze now changed to a cold, crisp, nighttime air. They all quickly put on jackets and continued toward the dock where their ship awaited. Just outside the marina, the captain took everyone to a higher location atop some containers to get an extended view of the area. They all lay on their stomachs scanning the area. The area seemed to be very quiet. It was too quiet for the captain. The docks were always busy with ships coming and going at all hours; no, something wasn't right.

The captain's answer came as they saw a group of soldiers stealthily moving into position around the entrance to the docks. Looking at their ship though, there seemed to be no activity but further down the docks stood a large naval vessel. They could see some movement around the outer edges of the dock, just out of sight of the vessel. It seemed as though their plan was working, and their enemies planned to attack them at the naval vessel. Surprise was on their side, but they still needed to make it undetected to their own ship.

With the sound of seagulls and buoy bells, they could hopefully slip in without being heard. The captain deftly worked his way down the containers, which were away from the entrance and offered great cover from the waiting soldiers. Once on the dock, the small band crept from shadow to shadow until within a few feet of the ship. Taking one last look around, the captain motioned for them to follow.

Each member followed their leader quickly up the gangplank onto the huge container ship. Once aboard, the captain again checked to see if they were followed. When he was satisfied they were safely aboard, he pushed them onward. He led his group to a side door. To this point, they didn't meet any crew, which Peter thought quite odd considering they were about to depart. Everyone followed the captain into the belly of the large ship, no questions asked

Chapter 26

As the small band hustled to stow their gear in the small metal room with hammocks hanging in the corners, they looked at their meager accommodations. Everyone in the room looked forward to some much-needed rest. The captain went from man to man, checking on health and supplies. When satisfied with their status, the captain took time to get the boys settled. Both young men, despite being very tired, were in great spirits talking softly to one another when the captain arrived.

He sat with them for a moment. "Boys, we've done well to get this far but we must remain on our toes. We aren't out of the woods yet. When we're to sea safely, then we may talk a little more freely. For now, we'll keep our communication brief and get ready for the first watch. Normally, you'd be expected to keep watch as well but the men agree that tonight, you need your rest. Trust me, you'll have your turn at watch as our journey is long and dangerous."

The boys looked at the captain and understood the logic. Both boys had hardly gotten any rest or sleep over the past week. They just nodded and went back to preparing their area for sleep. Peter took out one of the letters from his grandfather, but the captain thrust his hand out, telling him not here and to put it away. Peter did as he was told and just hopped into his hammock with a blanket. Jake was right next to him and they both watched the soldiers who were already to turn in as well. Many of them were still cleaning their weapons. They both looked at each other with a sigh of relief that they made it this far and a slight glimmer of hope they'd make their destination.

While they made ready to turn in, the crew of the vessel now came to life as more lights came on and the passengers could hear moving about and preparing for departure. It became apparent the captain signaled the other captain somehow but they boys didn't recall him speaking with anyone. The boys then felt the vessel jolt a little, knowing they were pulling away from the dock. This made everyone feel more comfortable as they could now hear the hum of the engines grow louder. Each soldier was now ready for a much-needed rest and those who took first watch, took their places.

While the ship was about to get underway and the crew bustled to make ready to leave, no one noticed a shadowy figure climb over the railing on the ship. When the figure was safely on the deck, he quickly untied his rope, letting it fall into the sea. Without a sound, he slithered back into the shadows, undetected by any crew member. Sticking to the shadows, he worked his way around the deck until he slid into an open hatch. With the darkness covering him, he melted into the belly of the ship.

Down below, the members of the captain's squad already put the finishing touches on their day and looked forward to the journey ahead. The captain himself now lay in his own bunk while the last few finishing touches on preparations for the following day were gone over in his head. With one last look to check on the boys, he finished his thoughts and lay his head down. He rested his hands behind his head and assessed the day. His men performed well and achieved their mission to get the boys safely to the ship. Of course, he knew full well this was only the beginning and they'd encounter many other dangers along the way. For now, he took comfort in the fact the boys were still with him and safe!

Peter and Jake lay on their sides talking softly while the other soldiers readied themselves for sleep. Peter propped himself up a little and smiled, looking around quickly. He saw the captain finally resting. The sight encouraged him as he let a sigh out. His breath became more even, and he scanned the room again. Peter noticed the room now became quiet and they could hear the hum of the ship's engine fully engaged as they headed out to sea.

Peter peered over at Jake. "Man, that was a crazy day! I'm so tired but I can't get to sleep. I'm so wound up. I just want to know what's going to happen next. I told the captain I'm a normal person but what normal person gets to run from danger to danger the way we are right now? I'm just in shock over this whole thing. I sure hope my mom is okay. That girl told me she's okay but am I to trust her?"

Jake chuckled. "That was your first mistake, trusting a young lady!"

Peter glared at Jake. "Wait a minute, I didn't say I listened. There's something about her that tells me she speaks the truth. Jake, it's as if I've known her my whole life! When she speaks to me, I cannot take my eyes off her. It's as if she were staring right into my soul. The weird part is I don't mind. I find myself hoping she'll contact me again at night. Last night, I got worried that something would happen to her!"

Jake's face became serious. "Peter, this is bad. You have it bad!"

Peter got nervous. "What? What's bad?"

Jake's face softened. "Man, you're in love! There's no other explanation."

Peter looked shocked. "Jake, it can't be love. I've never even met the girl. I mean we could meet and she might not even like me."

Jake laughed. "You said it yourself that you feel like she's known you your whole life. When you feel that way toward someone, I doubt meeting them would spoil it."

Both young men laughed and lay back, looking to the ceiling. Deep in thought, they didn't speak for a long while. The groaning sound of the engine came through the metal walls. Listening to its rhythmic sound caused both boys' eyes to droop and close. Peter's last thought before falling into a sound sleep was of his mother by herself. A pang of guilt once again hit him, but he was too tired to face it this night. Sleep again took him, and he drifted off.

The warm feeling surrounded him as his eyes opened to see the molten globe hovering just above his hammock. The beautiful image of the girl came into view as he came awake. He carefully placed his feet on the floor and peered around the room to see if anyone else was awake. The room was dark, and Peter couldn't see anyone stirring. The image of the girl didn't speak but motioned him to follow. Without question, he followed the floating globe through the hallways and onto the deck of the large ship. He shuttered as the misty, cold air struck his face. The mysterious globe led him to another room just off the deck and inside, he saw crates from floor to the ceiling.

Even without looking in the crates, he knew they were weapons of some kind. The girl said nothing but let the scene wash over him. Peter wondered where these were headed. This many weapons couldn't be good. He knew their situation was more dire than he imagined. Something huge was about to happen and he was stuck smack in the middle.

The image in the globe led him to the other side of the room and motioned him to sit. He found a lone crate and sat, looking at the soft image of the beautiful girl with admiration. This look wasn't lost on the girl and she returned a similar smile.

Peter felt the electricity in their stare. He knew he must see her soon. His heart couldn't take being away from her. He was very conflicted in his head as he never even really noticed young ladies to this point. Most times, he was either with his grandfather or Jake. Noticing young ladies never really came up until now. Once more, he turned to take in the image of this angelic face looking back at him.

When she spoke, he felt the magnetism pull him closer. "Peter, things are in motion right now that will determine the fate of the world. I want you to know we're doing all we can to bring you to us safely. As a matter of fact, there's a rescue mission underway and they should reach you soon. In the meantime, keep your eyes open; the vessel you're on serves two masters. The owners of the vessel are playing both sides of the fence, so be very careful."

Peter looked back at her and could say nothing. Each time he tried to speak to her, his throat became dry and he'd croak out a few words. The only words that came out now were, "I will."

She looked at him with a beaming smile. "Peter, it won't always be this way. I know communicating this way is unnerving but soon you'll talk to me face to face. Please take care of Jake."

He glared at her with a serious look. "No need to worry about that! I'll never let anything happen to Jake. He isn't just my best friend, but he's more like my brother than anything else."

The glowing image warmly smiled, making him blush. "That's one of the things I admire about you the most, your loyalty to friends and family. That trait will serve you well in this world and others."

This last comment made him shake his head a moment. This world and others. What was she talking about? He couldn't help but keep his eyes glued to hers and she turned away for a moment. When she returned his glance, she smiled but didn't speak. He waited while he could see her struggling with what to say next. Peter knew the feeling and waited for her to find the words.

Once again, she smiled. "Peter, yes, I too have some difficulty finding the words when speaking to you. There's so much I want to tell you, but this isn't the time or the place. I promise one day I'll tell you all. Please don't get mad. I know how hard it is to just put blind trust in people. I won't lead you astray."

He felt a pang of sorrow. "I really am not mad. There's just so much going on right now, I don't know which end is up. I just seem to run from danger into more danger now. My life was so plain and ordinary, and now it seems like something from an action movie. I just wish my grandfather was here to guide me."

Her face now looked sad. "Yes, Peter, your grandfather was a great man. Trust me, we all miss him. You're right, things might be much different if your grandfather was still alive. The one thing we can do now is continue his work and make him proud."

Peter couldn't help but think about what she was talking about. Once again, he was seriously confused that so many people seemed to know his grandfather. To him, his grandfather was an immensely important person, but he was learning there was much more to the man he thought he knew so well. His thoughts went back to the journal and then back to the gaze of the young lady.

She looked at him. "Yes, Peter, the journal is the key to a lot of things! You've only scratched the surface. Keep it safe and never let it out of your sight. It's imperative you get that journal and yourself safely to us. I'm sorry to say that once again my time with you is short. It takes a lot of energy to communicate this way, but it was worth it to see you again."

He felt his cheeks get red at that last statement. Peter smiled. "Trust me, the feeling is mutual. It's a great pleasure to see you, always! I'll do as you say and keep the journal safe. I look forward to our first meeting. I pray it won't be much longer."

The young lady's face turned a little red now. "I pray it won't be much longer as well!"

She motioned him to follow her and she led him back to the doorway of his quarters. "Wake Jake and tell him what I showed you. Make sure the soldiers know and have them on the alert."

He smiled. "I will. Thank you for looking after me. Maybe someday I could repay the kindness."

She smiled. "You, Peter, have a heart of gold and I know you'll help us all before the end."

As her image faded, her face became panicked. "Peter, hurry. Wake everyone! They're coming! Hurry!"

The image disappeared, and he rushed into the room. Without hesitation, he woke Jake and ran around rousing the soldiers. Peter could hear yelling as the door to their quarters flew open and in rushed men brandishing weapons. At first, it was difficult to see the men as not all the lights were on. In the dim light, Peter could see his own soldiers pointing their own weapons at the intruders. At first, it seemed time stood still and neither group wanted to engage one another but a large, barrel-chested man came forward with a shotgun pointed at the captain who didn't take too kindly to the threat.

The captain strode forward, leading with an upper cut, dropping the man where he stood. The room then erupted into gunfire, shouting, and chaos. Jake and Peter dove behind some crates in the corner of the room, peering out to see what was taking place. Even in the chaos, Peter remembered the girl's warning not to let the journal out of his sight. He looked out from behind the crate toward his bunk. His large backpack lay on the floor undisturbed.

He ran from his protective crate and slid to the ground just in front of his backpack. Peter grabbed the pack and turned to go back to his crate when a large sailor lifted him off the ground. The man's face was covered in grime, but he was large and strong. The man glared at him and walked toward the exit with Peter firmly in hand. He struggled to break the sailor's grip with no luck. He looked around the room for the captain and saw him engaged with another man in hand-to-hand combat.

As they moved toward the door, Peter felt a jolt as his captor was struck in the side by something. Peter went sprawling onto the floor, still clutching his pack. He swung around to see Jake pulling to his feet. Both boys now faced the large, grime-covered man. In the light, they both could make out the corded muscles bulging beneath his shirt. The man looked at the smaller boys and smirked before lunging toward Jake. Jake cut under his grasp and ran to the right to lead the man away from Peter. Instead of chasing Jake, the man turned toward Peter and stalked forward after the young man.

He never got close to Peter as Jake came forward and hit the man in the back with a pipe, sending him to the ground. Within moments, the man was back on his feet and clicked open a knife, growling while he strode forward. Pipe still in hand, Jake stood in front of Peter and waited for the attack. The man swung the knife and Jake deflected the blow with the pipe. Again, the man swung the knife quickly, this time catching Jake's sleeve, slicing through the material but just missing the skin. Jake brought the pipe around and hit the man on the side of the face. Both boys heard the sound of the pipe crack into his skull. At first, the man staggered but then righted himself and renewed the attack.

Both boys looked at one another and stood their ground when he came for them. Peter could see blood streaming down the side of the man's face. Jake noticed his wound affected him as he came forward more cautiously. Knife clutched in his hand, he came at the boys once again and received the same welcome, with a pipe to other side of his head. This time, the attacker lay on the ground unmoving and the boys marched toward the rest of the fighting soldiers. Peter looked around the room and noticed there were no firearms being used. Everyone in the room were locked in hand-to-hand combat as if ancient soldiers defending their last.

Peter did recall they all entered brandishing weapons, but it seemed everyone involved didn't want the discharge for one reason or another. Peter and Jake made for the captain who stood yelling orders. When they stood in front of the captain, they could see a nasty cut above his left eye still oozing blood. He caught sight of the boys and protectively pushed them behind him. Another attacker lunged at the captain, receiving a kick to the sternum for his effort. The captain motioned them to follow him and shouted for his men to rally to him.

The captain's soldiers now formed a protective ring around the captain and the boys. Peter could see around him, and the attacking force was mostly dispatched. Figures could be seen sprawled on the floor, some moving with others in heaps.

The captain's force remained mostly intact with a few minor injuries. Following the captain, the boys now found themselves working their way through the bowels of the ship until they all stood on the control deck of the vessel. The captain practically ran over the captain of the vessel and lifted him up, slamming him into the wall.

The ship's captain could hardly breathe with his face turning red. When released, he fell to the floor, rubbing his neck. Then with an angry glare, he stood looking at the intruding captain. He angrily shouted, "How dare you to come on to my bridge and handle me this way!"

"That's Captain Pace to you, scum!" shouted the captain.

Captain Pace moved threateningly back toward the man, only to have him cower back against the wall. The rest of the man's crew seemed nervous to attempt anything against these trained soldiers. The vessel's captain relented and stood with a defeated look on his face. He walked cautiously to a viewer and pointed to it quickly. Everyone turned their heads to look at the screen. They could see an outline of what looked to be a submarine. Captain Pace swung around, grabbing the other captain.

He growled, "What's that, captain?"

The vessel's captain croaked, "That captain is your doom! They're here for the boy and they aren't leaving without him!"

Captain Pace looked directly at Peter. "I won't let them take you." He turned to his team. "We have to get to a defendable position. We'll go back quickly and grab what we can. Captain, where is the best position on the ship?"

The other captain responded, "It depends, there are many places within the ship, but you could be trapped. In the

160

bow of the ship, you could see anyone coming and be defended from the backside."

Captain Pace smiled. "The bow might work as we'd need to move quickly and not be blocked off."

He looked at his soldiers and pointed to two near him. "Tie all these men up and put them in the mess, locking the doors. We don't need them alerting the intruders to our plans."

The soldiers did as asked, and the captain along with his team ran to the elevators. Cramming as many as they could, they all went back to their quarters to grab what they could. When equipped, the boys followed the soldiers into the elevator. They were soon standing on the deck of the large ship, pelted with wind and mist. The weather was now very crisp with a cold bite to it. The captain led them to the front of the ship but told them not to pin themselves in just yet.

Peter could see various soldiers setting up positions behind barrels and large sacks of materials with weapons drawn. Once the captain was comfortable with their position, he ordered some of his soldiers to shoot out all the lights, so the enemy couldn't see them. After the soldiers did this, the darkness that enveloped them was eerie. Peter could just barely see Jake on this moonless night. Jake reached out and patted him on the shoulder. The captain came over to check on them but said nothing and moved back over to his soldiers.

All that could be heard was the whistle of the wind and Peter shuddered as the cold blast went right up his back. As he struggled to keep warm, he strained to see through the darkness. They all waited anxiously in the silent darkness. Within minutes, they could hear shouts from below, alerting them that the ship had been breached. The captain didn't have enough soldiers to prevent this so his best play was to defend a good position. All they could do was wait.

Chapter 27

Bright sun rays invaded their sensitive eyes, forcing them to blink rapidly until they could make out images. Being a race that was used to artificial light caused them to halt their journey for the moment to gain their senses and sight back. General Ryan Giles was first to regain his bearings being more used to the light as he visited the surface from time to time. He scanned the area to make sure they weren't followed and then looked to the horizon to see if anything obstructed their journey. When satisfied they were safe, he bent down to check on the ladies recovering their eyesight.

Rebecca stood next to the general and viewed the open area before them. She looked to the horizon and could see nothing but a white land of rolling hills and mountains. The air was crisp and clear. She let the cold air fill her lungs and felt more alive than she had in many years. Excitement gripped her as she always wanted to visit the surface and help those struggling here. With a quick glance at the general, she could see Holly was now at his side and for a brief moment, Rebecca thought she saw her hand release his.

She couldn't put into words the glorious sight before her eyes. This unblemished land stood as a white blanket covering everything within sight. They stood unmoving, taking in the beautiful scene, until the general broke the silence. He clasped both ladies' hands and smiled. He led them up to the top of the hill on which they now stood. Just below them, they now saw what looked like another cavern.

He smiled. "Come on, we have to get out of here. It won't be long before our enemies become aware of our movements. They know we rarely come out into the open, so they'll be ready to intercept us quickly. Follow me. I have transportation for us."

He led them rapidly down the slope of the hill toward the cavern. Once inside, they could see a large door barring their entrance. The general went to the side of the door and called out commands forcing the door to open. Inside, they could see various vehicles and the general ran to a large one with tracks instead of tires. He climbed up and motioned the girls to do the same. They followed his lead and placed their prisoner in the back, still bound and gagged. Michael just looked at them in sheer hatred.

Once moving, the vehicle moved over the open terrain smoothly and quickly. Rebecca was amazed at the speed with which the vehicle traveled. Inside the vehicle wasn't very attractive—seats, a few cabinets, and windows all around which allowed for a nearly 360-degree view. The control panels were very simple as well and the general sat in the driver's seat holding a steering wheel.

Without further delay, they made their way forward through the desolate snow and ice-covered land. The general explained to them they needed to make it to their warm water port to reach their submarine that would take them to the mainland. Rebecca watched in awe as they continued to fly by hills and mountains but nothing else. The land was devoid of life. This made her very sad as her home was always warm, heated by the earth itself. Her comfortable existence caused her to view the desolation with pity. She thought back to the many times she took things for granted in her safe and comfortable life.

The general alerted them that their trip would take several hours but he didn't see anyone following them or anyone ahead of them. He told them to take a rest and he'd let them know when they arrived. Holly refused to rest and never took her eyes off Michael. Rebecca, however, sat back in her seat and let her eyes close. Her thoughts once again drifted back to Peter. She could see his soft face and a warmth came over her body. In her mind, he lay on a hammock talking to Jake.

A shiver went down her spine as she saw soldiers swarming over the vessel the boys were now on. She brought her thoughts once again to Peter and contacted him. The danger was strong each time she contacted him for both Rebecca and Peter alike. It was like Rebecca sent up a flare saying to their enemies, "Here we are!"

Rebecca talked briefly to Peter and warned him of the impending attack. When she was done with her communication, she shot up and told the general what transpired. He assured her they'd get the boys here safely. This didn't make her feel any better as her nerves continued to get the better of her. Holly placed her hand on Rebecca's and smiled softly.

She looked at her and nodded. "I know, my dear! It's difficult to be away from someone you care about."

This shocked Rebecca. "I don't know why I feel this way. I've never even met him! How can I feel this way about someone I don't even know?"

Holly laughed. "That, my dear, is the eternal question. Why do we have feelings for those we do? If you could answer that, then you may very well control the universe. No, there's no answer to that yet, but I'll tell you this. The heart is rarely wrong."

This last statement stuck in her head for a moment. She thought all the time about Peter and found herself checking in on him all the time. She watched the way he treated his mother and the people around him. He was the most genuine person she had ever seen. She laughed at his awkwardness but smiled at his graciousness. Still, he knew not who he really was and what great things he'd achieve. This made her a little sad. Once the responsibility coming his way was heaped upon him, would he remain the same humble person?

Rebecca went back to viewing the open terrain flashing by her and thought about what she might do when they finally did meet. Would they hug, shake, or would Peter just grab her and kiss her? She let her mind guide her and could imagine him grabbing her gently and kissing her softly. Just as this thought entered her head, she sensed the danger.

She shouted to the general that danger was imminent and told him from what direction to expect the threat. The general assured her he had them already on his screen. Three vehicles similar in nature to theirs now came onto the screen on the dash. The general checked to make sure it was only three. He cursed his luck as he maneuvered the vehicle around obstacles. They were getting close to their destination and the land was becoming more broken. This would slow them down.

He moved the vehicle forward at a great speed and drove skillfully around the impending landscape. The chasing vehicles caught up quickly but were careful in the rougher terrain. The general spotted a large hill and drove the vehicle straight up to the top. When he was on top of the hill, he spotted a sheer edge and drove to it, letting the back tracks rest near the edge. He waited for his pursuers to attack and checked his weapons.

The first vehicle breached the top of the hill and the general unloaded his weapons directly at the oncoming vehicle. The enemy vehicle didn't stand a chance and was hit rapidly with weapons from the general's vehicle. Smoke and fire engulfed the attacking vehicle and stopped in its tracks. Through the black smoke appeared the other two vehicles spread out, one on the right and one on the left. The attacking vehicles returned fire as the general unleashed everything he had on his attackers.

Blasts rifled through the thin walls of the general's vehicle and he knew he couldn't take much of this punishment. He screamed at the ladies to get below. They did as instructed, and climbed below in a small compartment under the main cabin. This compartment was made of a larger gauge metal and provided some protection. Above, they could hear the vehicle taking several different hits. Holly heard the cursing of the general above and her own worry took over.

Above, the general blasted away the remaining attackers. The vehicle to the left was just barely fighting back. He concentrated his fire on the wounded vehicle. He was successful, and a large blast went into the air as he struck the fuel cell, causing a huge explosion. Then he felt the blast rip through the front of his own vehicle and through his arm. The pain shot through his body and he couldn't grip the controls. With his remaining good arm, he tried to move the vehicle to face the last attacker, but the controls were dead. He could only watch as the oncoming vehicle approached to finish them off.

He yelled down to the ladies and told them to get out. They moved over to a trap door below and jumped out onto the frozen land. They dragged their prisoner behind and moved away from the now unmoving vehicle. Holly moved them over to a small outcropping and they hid behind the ice. Rebecca could see the general's twisted face as he fought pain, trying to finish off the remaining attacker. He was very upset but remained focused on his enemy.

Rebecca could see the general was a sitting duck in great danger. The remaining enemy vehicle rammed into the general, threatening to push him off the edge. It backed up for another pass and she came out from her hiding place. She could hear Holly screaming at her to get under cover. Rebecca strode forward, hands thrust by her sides and she could feel her insides growing in anger as she approached two combatants. Energy grew in her as she now stood directly in front of the oncoming vehicle and raised her right hand. The energy built up within her was then released, crashing into the attacking vehicle. She then moved her hand and slowly motioned it to the edge of the hill. The large vehicle slid toward the edge. Rebecca could see the pilot trying to move the vehicle without success. When it went over, Rebecca fell to the ground exhausted. Holly came running over to check on her and propped her to her feet. At first, Rebecca could barely stand but after a few moments, feeling came back into her legs. She could see the rage and concern in Holly's eyes. She just held herself up and asked how the general was doing. They all went to the general, still in the wounded vehicle and found him binding his own injury on his arm.

Holly looked at the dark blood-soaked bandage and took it off. She examined the wound and gave the general a piece of cloth and told him to bite down. Holly then unleashed a glowing energy into the gash as it steamed at first but then closed, leaving the wound completely healed, at least from the outside. She told him that was the best she could do right now but when they got to safety, she could complete the healing. Holly warned that her solution was only temporary, and it could open up again if he wasn't careful.

The general looked at her with thanks and clasped her hand warmly. Holly then turned her angry look toward Rebecca. Rebecca winced but then returned the look back at Holly. Both women glared at one another and then it seemed they came to an understanding. They then placed a hand on each other's shoulder and sat down.

Holly started, "Rebecca, I know you felt there was no other way, but you still don't know what your powers can do. You need training. You could have killed us all! I know you want to help but without your training being complete, there are just too many unknowns. It has taken me many lifetimes of humans to learn about my own powers and I still get nervous sometimes."

Rebecca nodded. "I understand, I really do but you cannot expect me to do nothing! He'd have been killed. I had to do something!"

Holly placed a hand on her shoulder. "Yes, my dear, you certainly did something! There isn't one person from our race I've ever known that could do what you just did. That's what makes me nervous. As your teacher, sometimes I feel I cannot teach you all you need to know about your powers. Much of what you can do is well beyond what anyone has been able to do, ever!"

Rebecca sat without responding. She knew Holly to be right. Ever since she was young, she could do things that no one else could do. Each of her classmates had certain powers and could do very useful things with them but many times when Rebecca tried to do the same things, the power would take over. Her lack of control over her power caused much debate in the council; they all knew not how to control it. Holly was chosen as her mentor because her own power rivaled Rebecca's on the surface. Holly soon found that Rebecca held a power that only scratched the surface.

Holly took the young lady under her wing and taught her many things about using her substantial power. The one issue that remained for Rebecca was control. When she stayed calm, she could control her power very well. If she got flustered or angered in any way, her power took on a life of its own. She recalled a time when one of her classmates challenged her to a competition and Holly warned her not to engage. The classmate made fun of Rebecca and that sent her into a rage and she pummeled the girl, flying into the back wall, nearly breaking her in two. The girl's parents wanted Rebecca arrested.

Holly convinced the council to allow Rebecca to study with her alone. Rebecca was close to womanhood and would be independent soon anyway, so the council relented. Holly trained her as best she could and along the way, they became close, more like mother and daughter. Rebecca respected Holly and wanted to make her proud. She worked very hard to control her power, but it still took over sometimes. When she saw the general hurt, the energy she felt was unlike any other she had felt to this point. She didn't tell Holly, but the power was getting stronger.

The thought of the power becoming uncontrollable frightened Rebecca, but she said nothing to Holly. There were times though that she'd look at Holly and it was as though she knew what Rebecca was thinking before she said anything. She knew they could communicate with one another without voices, but she didn't know if Holly could read her mind. She learned much from Holly and enjoyed her company; no others seemed to understand her. Her former classmates always jeered her when they saw her. Rebecca knew she could squash them like bugs but chose to let it go.

The two ladies looked at their prisoner who now wore a surprised expression on his face. The ladies weren't impressed and left him gagged. Holly especially enjoyed Michael being unable to speak. In council, he was always a pompous fool and never stopped talking. Many on the council would take their turn to speak just so they didn't have to listen to Michael ramble on about the finances of the city. It's true that the city never stood so well financially, thanks in large part to Michael, but the methods were very questionable.

Holly knew for years that Michael was into other endeavors that helped the financial landscape of the city, but she also suspected he was dealing with some quite unsavory characters but could never prove anything. Here he sat, unable to speak and once again a thorn in her side. She'd have laughed if the situation were different. Michael just looked to the two of them hoping they might ungag him.

General Giles alerted them that the vehicle needed a few minor repairs, but it could get them to their destination as long as they left soon. He assured them they didn't want to be caught out here when the sun went down. This was the Antarctic's summer, which saw some temperatures get above fifty during the day, but at night, it would be a different story. He hurried them back into the vehicle and soon they were under way.

They could hear the whistle of the wind through the broken panes of glass and the vehicle ran quite rough now, but they still made good time. Their vehicle stopped on a ridge within view of the dock which housed a sleek submarine that looked more like a spaceship. General Giles spoke into a communication device on his wrist and ordered the craft ready for departure within the hour. The general then parked the vehicle up on the ridge out of view and they all walked down to the dock.

The general led Michael in front of him and pushed him forward. Some soldiers met them who took control of Michael and after conferencing with the general, led him away. They then found themselves being led onto a platform and walked across to the waiting submarine. Once inside, they were brought to small, but comfortable, quarters. They were instructed to wash up now; once they were under way, they'd have to wait until next port to use the water. The sub was there getting repaired and not ready for a trip, but under the circumstances, it would be ready to take them where they needed to be.

After a briefing, the general learned they'd go to a United States Antarctic Base and finish repairs before traveling north. They assured the general it wouldn't hinder their travel schedule, but they needed a few parts that weren't at this location. The general thanked the men and settled down in his quarters. As he was about to get into his small shower, there banged on his door. He threw a towel on and opened the door. A red-faced soldier stood before the general.

The general questioned him, "What is it, son?"

The soldier winced. "Sir, Michael has escaped."

General Giles jaw tightened. "How?"

The soldier's face grew red again. "It's my fault, sir. I undid his restraints, so I could cuff him to his bunk, and then he struck me and escaped. He looked so feeble I didn't think he could overpower me."

The general shook his head. "Son, he's very devious. Where did he go?"

The soldier explained, "Sir, we followed him off the sub. He disappeared into the night."

General Giles commanded, "There's nothing more we can do about it now. I cannot stay and capture him again. Alert the city and have our troops on the lookout for him. Have him detained and kept from the council. I'll deal with him when I return."

Chapter 28

The shadowy figure came over the screen talking fast as if the hounds of hell were after him. He blurted out, "The general is on the move! They're taking a submarine from the coast and going after the boys."

High Commander Zosa growled at the screen, "You were supposed to keep them in the city!"

Again, the figure's voice came quickly, "Commander, I did what I could, but things are in motion right now that I as one man cannot control. I have very few in the city willing to go against the council."

The commander pondered this response, "I have to say it has been rather helpful having an inside man. I want you to go back to the city and continue your work. You need to recruit others. The time has come to rip the city apart from the inside out. We're on the verge of penetrating the city from the outside, but a city rotting from the inside, now that's just divine."

The last statement made the figure shiver, but he nodded and was gone. Commander Zosa sat looking at the screen for a moment before lifting his huge-scaled frame to his full height. One of his subordinates came over and whispered something in his ear. The commander nodded and dismissed him quickly. Traveling quickly through the myriad of hallways, he came to his private quarters and before entering out of habit, checked the door for signs of forced entry. When he double checked the hallway and the door, he went into his chambers.

Once inside, he set his elaborate security system and moved through the room until he stood looking at what appeared to be a blank wall. A quick glance around the room revealed a modest living space with very few comforts. The commander lived a simple military life and to him, less was more. Where others craved wealth and possessions, the commander was power drunk. He lived for a single purpose—to gather as much power as was possible in his lifetime. This focused, single-minded purpose made waves among his people. Most would be considered complacent when it came to the humans and would just assume live with them and share the planet.

The commander had much different ideas and his focus to gain power was nearly complete. Once the Zarillion fell, then too would the humans fall. The thought of all these beings under one rule, his rule caused a wide sharp-toothed grin to creep across his face. His plan moved along perfectly, except for the boys not in custody, yet everything was moving along nicely. He couldn't afford to take any chances though and moved forward, waving his hand in front of a sensor that looked exactly like a part of the wall and the entire wall opened.

The commander entered a natural rock chamber with dim lights strung on the walls. The blast of cold air hit his face and he cringed. This icy prison was the cause of much pain and suffering for him and his people. The beings responsible would pay soon. He strode forward, quickening his pace. After making his way through the maze of tunnels, he came to a solid rock wall with a single horizontal slit in the face of the rock. He peered into the opening to see Colonel Whilhelm waiting for him. Without hesitation, he snorted and growled. This little man offended every sensibility the commander possessed.

He snorted into the slit, "Colonel, please explain to me why the boys aren't here being interrogated by me right now?"

Leaning forward and glancing into the opening, the colonel responded, "Sir, our men were all over the dock but to be quite frank, the dock is huge, and we searched every vessel. The ship they made it on was a piece of junk hauling just that, junk. I thought we had them on the ship, but they alluded our capture. They're now on a submarine, making their way to Argentina. Sir, without destroying the sub, we cannot take them now, but I'll have as many men as can be spared waiting for them when they make it to Argentina."

Commander Zosa actually smiled. "Colonel, I'd like to say that would be fantastic but my faith in you continues to be tested. Have our forces in Argentina briefed and ready to intercept when the boys arrive."

Colonel Whilhelm held his tongue. "Yes, sir, it will be as you ask. Pardon my inquisitive nature, sir, but what's to be done about the escaped Zarillion?"

This brought a rage-induced pounding of the rock by the commander, "Use the technology I've supplied you with and destroy them!"

Again, the colonel maintained his military bearing. "Yes, sir! I understand; it's just that even with the technology they have use of powers, we cannot begin to comprehend and therefore know little of defending ourselves against its likes."

For a moment, the commander stopped. "Colonel, I understand your plight and I honestly wish I could send some of my troops with you, but the field that holds us here is still in place. It's weakened substantially but not yet passable for us. When we can join you, we will, but in the meantime, win the day for us and I promise you all your wishes will come true. The surface will be yours!"

Nodding, the colonel peered back. "Sir, I've always served you faithfully and it will be done as you ask. They'll be taken in Argentina and brought before you. Are there any other orders at this point?"

The commander thought for a moment, "No, Colonel, at this point, the capture of these two young men is paramount. Bring them here and I'll question them myself. I'm sure by then the field will be down enough for us to take custody of them. Go now and don't come before me again unless you have those two in chains. As for the Zarillion, you have my permission to destroy them by any means necessary. Those council members shouldn't have interfered and it will cost the council dearly to lose such important members. Once again, things continue to turn in my favor as we've tried for years to rid ourselves of those council members, only to be foiled at each turn. This time, things are working exactly as I'd hoped, and it will be a crushing blow to our enemies."

The colonel again nodded. "Thank you once again, sir, for the chance to serve you and assist in your grand design."

He stood and saluted before turning and walking briskly away. The commander watched him walk away and as much as he disliked the man, he needed to admit to himself the soldier was useful. In the commander's current situation, he needed to rely on this man and despite his missteps, the man accomplished most of what the commander required. Even the commander admitted to himself, the colonel was in a difficult position serving another race that he really knew nothing about. The colonel was like the commander in one respect—he craved power above all else.

Once the commander was safely back in the warm confines of his comfortable quarters, he sat on a chair. From his position in the chair, he called out orders and another wall moved away to reveal a large screen and computer station. He again barked orders and the screen came to life. On the screen came to view an enormous room with untold rows of military vehicles and then he clicked onto another screen, showing another housing aircraft of all kinds. He smirked as he continued to click through the screens to see his waiting military might about to be unleashed on the unsuspecting humans.

For centuries, he watched as the humans killed one another almost doing his job for him several times during the years. Of course, the humans were given incentive by himself and others, only to have his enemies stick their noses in on the behalf of the humans. This time would be much different and when he was free, he'd see to it personally that all the humans suffered untold horrors. That fool Whilhelm was only a little bug to be stepped upon. When he was finished, this entire planet would be the launching pad for the recovery of his race. Once topside, they could contact any refugees in the solar system and have them join his people on the surface.

He leaned his head back and thought of the boy for a moment. If he was anywhere near as powerful as it seemed, he could be useful. In his new world order, he'd have need of powerful allies. The boy, being young and impressionable, may be someone he could mold for his own uses. All along, he thought of nothing but destruction for this young man, but as the colonel pointed out, they'll have need of help. The boy knew little of his power and if he did teach the boy to control this power, he may use it for him.

The thought of the boy under his control amused him and he laughed heartily aloud. At that moment, an incoming message came across the screen. He sat up and answered the incoming call, only to see a frantic soldier on the screen. He shouted as if the commander couldn't hear him, "Sir, we have a big problem!"

The commander stood. "What is it, soldier? Spit it out!"

Again, the nervous soldier called back, "Sir, there has been some kind of accident!"

He screamed back, "What kind of accident!"

The soldier almost couldn't bring himself to answer when the commander felt a shudder as the walls of his chambers shook.

The soldier continued, "One of the thermal shafts went crazy and shot a heat wave into one of the armories! There are explosions everywhere!"

Again, his chambers withstood a shockwave which almost sent him sprawling. Standing his ground, he looked at the shaken soldier. He was about to scream at the soldier but calmed himself. Without another thought, he said, "What section and what is being done? This has happened before. What's the damage?"

The soldier called back, "Sir, this time is different. Where the heat struck, the weapons created a blast that set off a chain reaction!"

The screen then went black and an explosion could be heard nearby that rocked his quarters, this time sending debris crumbling from the ceiling. He just made it out of the room as the roof caved in. Continuing forward, he wormed his way through the now half-dark hallways and debris-filled tunnels. When he burst forth into the control center, he could see soldiers scurrying everywhere, trying to get the situation under control. One noticed the commander and rushed to him.

He stood at attention. "Sir, we're gathering as much information as we can right now. Things are coming in slowly. It seems as if one of the armories literally went off like a bomb and caused a chain reaction into the various other military sections."

At this news, the commander couldn't fathom losing any military advantage, but he couldn't be weakened now. Not now as his greatest military triumph was about the take place. He gathered himself and with a calm outward demeanor, he looked at the soldier.

He started, "Are the explosions over?"

The soldier glanced back. "Sir, I believe they are but like I said, things are sketchy. Communication in certain areas is down now. I sent a team down there and they did report back that most of the aircrafts and vehicles are intact, but our arsenal of weapons is all but destroyed!"

At this, the commander's eyebrow raised. "Our entire arsenal?"

The soldier flinched. "Sir, that isn't confirmed but my team is down there now as I stated, and they don't see much that's useable at this time. Keep in mind, sir, that lights are out and there are still small fires and smoke everywhere right now. Once everything is under control and we can assess the overall situation, I'll have a full report."

Commander Zosa barked, "No, soldier! You'll personally take me down there, so I can see for myself!"

A panicked look crossed the soldier's face. "Sir, I'm not even sure the explosions are over! I cannot guarantee your safety!"

The commander laughed. "I appreciate your concern for my wellbeing, but I assure you I'll be quite safe!"

With an unsure look, he agreed, "Yes, sir, follow me."

Quickly, the soldier brought the commander down to the armory and like the soldier described, things were a mess. Fires still raged, and smoke was thick, filling the lower levels. Soldiers were quickly opening vents to let the smoke escape, which brought blasts of cold air streaming in, and swirled around the commander. He swiftly made his rounds and went to personally view his prized air fleet. To his great relief, a few aircrafts were damaged but none permanently. The vehicles were in similar shape, but all the weapons were gone.

Once safely back in the control room, he barked orders for the soldiers to inventory any surviving weapons and see what could be salvaged. He wanted to know where they stood if attacked once the field came down. This now was a concern for him. He definitely still had air superiority but without armed ground troops, he could only do very little. If he was invaded when the field went down, they'd be sitting ducks. Aircrafts and vehicles would do no good in this type of attack.

All he could do now was wait for the report, but he couldn't help but think of the cause of explosions. Due to the nature of his people's need for extremely warm temperatures to maintain their bodies, they made their residence near large thermal vents coming from below the earth's surface. Now the temperatures themselves didn't really bother the reptilian people, but their equipment was another situation altogether. During the large build up for the commander's invasion of the surface, space was at a premium and therefore, weapons were put in proximity to the vents. This turned out to be a fatal flaw in the commander's grand design.

He couldn't blame anyone else and walked to his alternative quarters with a scowl on his face. Entering, he shut the door and picked up whatever wasn't nailed down and threw it at the rock walls. After nothing seemed left, he threw himself into a nearby chair. Everything the commander planned was nearly destroyed in an instant.

Chapter 29

Captain Pace braced for the impending attack with his sidearm pointed toward the darkness. Peter and Jake were crouched protectively behind a crate, the captain, and his men. The captain told them to stay down and not peer out. Peter could see the attentive glare of the captain peering into the darkness. He could hear voices approaching and then silence. Jake couldn't help but peer around the crate. He could see shadows of men approaching quickly.

Flashes and the crack of small firearms broke the silence. Bullets riddled the crate in front of them and splinters of wood flew into the air, covering them. At first, Peter thought the captain lost his nerve and wouldn't return fire. He watched as the captain silently signaled his men and they all waited. Again, a volley of bullets struck the crate and still the captain waited. Peter could hear the click of weapons out of ammo and then the captain waved his arm. The captain's men, in one smooth move, rose from their hidden positions and fired into the reloading invaders.

Peter could hear the confusion of the men trying to return fire, but the captain's men were ready for the task and took out every last man. The battle was over in a matter of minutes, but the captain waved to his men and they went back into their crouched positions behind the crates. Jake looked to the captain and with a wave of the hand, he motioned for Jake to sit back down. Again, voices could be heard but still a way off and the captain motioned to reload. His men readied themselves for the next wave and Peter could see in the dim light, a quiet confidence in the captain's demeanor.

As before, silence took the night and the captain peered out through the still hanging smoke to see the shadows approaching. His men still remained hidden, awaiting their captain's orders. This time, the rapid fire of automatic weapons rang out in the night. The crate nearly blew up in front of them, but the captain again waited. His weapon raised to his face, he prepared to return fire when automatic fire again raged, this time nothing hit the crate. Confused voices and screams could be heard in front of them. The captain rose to return fire but as he aimed, he hesitated. Once more, weapons fired into the invading men from behind their position and the captain watched as his enemy was leveled by a surprise force.

The captain motioned his men to wait, but they all stood ready with weapons pointed at the new force. In a few minutes, again the battle ended, and the captain looked quickly at his men to see if there were any casualties. He nodded as everyone was accounted for and safe. The captain returned to his post and aimed out, expecting to fight. Through the cloud created by the fire fight, he saw the sight of soldiers whisking through the smoke like ghosts through walls. The captain smiled and left his position to meet the new soldiers.

With a warm embrace, the captain nearly bear-hugged the advancing officer. Lieutenant Rhodes peeled himself from the embrace, informing the captain his distress signal was picked up and they came to his aide as quickly as possible. The captain just pounded the man on the shoulder and said nothing more. He walked quickly in the other direction with the young officer following. The lieutenant led them back down to the platform near the bottom of the large cargo ship. Walking across the large platform, Peter could see they were walking onto a large submarine. His pulse quickened, knowing he wasn't a fan of confined spaces but followed without comment.

Once aboard, they were rushed into the infirmary to make sure they were sound. The doctor checked them both and labeled them as fit for duty, which made the captain laugh. The rest of the men were also checked and beside a few minor injuries, the men were in terrific shape. When the doctor dismissed them, the captain took control of them and rushed them to their own quarters. He told them they'd be safe, and they needed to stay put for now. Captain Pace informed them once they were rested, he'd claim them and tell them about the next leg of the journey.

Both Peter and Jake sat crammed into their small bunk on the submarine, unable to move to see much of their cramped quarters. Peter was having a difficult time breathing the stale air and the claustrophobic conditions made him feel anxious. Jake didn't seem to be bothered at all and kept telling Peter they needed to explore. Peter suggested they get some rest first and then take a walk around the ship. Jake, with a disappointed look, agreed and they lay down to get some much-needed rest.

Peter stared at the metal underside of Jake's bunk. It looked unblemished except for one area in one of the top corners. Peter took a closer look and saw a date scratched into the burnished metal. It read, September 11, 2001. A date recalled by Peter as the day terrorists attacked New York, bringing down the Twin Towers. Peter knew a sailor scrawled this date on there to remind everyone aboard always that the fight for freedom never ended.

He lay back and thought of his own fight for freedom. His flight from home and his subsequent situation on the submarine would make for an interesting tale someday. Resting his head on the pillow, he could feel exhaustion set in and allowed sleep to take him. It wasn't long before the beautiful face of his mysterious young lady friend filled his thoughts. This time, he knew this was a dream. He met the young lady on a beach and they sat looking at the beauty of the last rays of the setting sun. With hands on knees, both looked deep into each other's eyes, waiting for the other to speak. Without a word, they both turned to see the last of the sun set beyond the horizon.

The stark nature of the dream startled him, so much so it rose him from his sound sleep. Silence and darkness surrounded him in the tiny compartment. The wall threatened to cave in upon him until he realized he was on the submarine, cruising toward the unknown. This fact didn't make him feel any better and he tried to even out his breathing. Listening intently, he heard the hum of the submarine's engines running smoothly. He wondered exactly where on the craft they were. The captain rushed them to their quarters so quickly, neither boy could get their bearings. He lay back with his head in his hands, looking toward his sleeping friend. Smooth, low breathing confirmed Peter's suspicions that his good friend was sound asleep.

With hands still wrapped around the back of his head, he felt himself drifting off to sleep. That's until he recognized a small ball of light appearing just off to his right. He slipped to an upright position on his bunk, bumping his head in the process. Rubbing his head, he blinked his eyes a few times to focus on the growing ball of light. Hovering within a foot of his head, Peter could easily see the beautiful, soft features of his mystery lady.

She didn't wait and spoke first, "Peter, I'm glad to see you safe. We're traveling to you as we speak and should intercept you soon. Be sure to keep your eyes open and whatever you do, don't lose sight of Jake. I only have a few seconds. This is very hard to do even on land, but under the sea, it seems almost impossible. I had to try to just let you know things will be all right."

Peter felt a soar in confidence as this stunning creature addressed him. He couldn't help but feel his cheeks becoming red and warm. Despite his awkward feelings, he felt assured that many people were looking out for his interests. Trying to come up with a response, he stumbled over his words.

He began, "I'm not so comfortable under the water myself. I'm not a fan of confined spaces."

She smiled. "I'm not a fan either but I'll give you a hint. I'm traveling toward you in a similar craft."

Peter sat up quickly and again bumped his head. "You're in a submarine too?"

Her smile continued, "Yes, my sub is a little different from yours, but most of the inner workings are similar. We've already been in contact with the captain and will meet you very soon. Peter, I must go! Please look after yourself."

And just like that, she vanished into a wisp of smoke in the dark air. No matter how many times he saw the glowing ball, it still made him uneasy as to whether he actually saw what took place before him. The young lady seemed to be always warning him of imminent danger and he wondered what type of trouble they could get in the submarine.

Chapter 30

Explosions rocked the submarine and Peter was thrown across the cabin with terrific force. His back struck the opposite wall and knocked the wind out of him. In a daze, he tried to look for Jake, but in the dark, he could see nothing. Trying to regain his breath, he used the wall to prop himself up. At first, it seemed his voice wouldn't work, and his lungs still burned from the force of hitting the wall. Using his arms, he pushed against the wall until he stood unsteady, looking into the dark. Then he heard the rustling of another person a few feet from him.

"Jake?" he croaked.

Jake answered barely above a whisper, "I'm here. Are you all right?"

Peter sucked in a breath and winced in pain. "My side hurts but I think I'll be okay, you?"

Jake now stood next to him but in the dark, it was hard to make out any features. "Pete, we have to get out of here! If something happened to the sub, we need to get to the bridge."

Peter put his hand on Jake's shoulder for support. "You're right, let's go."

They carefully crept toward the door, only to feel the blast of another explosion. This time, they could cushion the blow by bracing themselves in the doorway. Pushing forward, they made their way into the corridor. Emergency lighting showed a ghostly way as they now heard yelling and could see sailors running ahead of them. As fast as their legs could carry them, they plowed forward. The corridor filled with smoke and water was now on the floor. Both boys sloshed through the smoky wet mess.

The smoke became a dark cloud of rancid-smelling, debris-filled nightmare. Still moving through it, they covered their mouths. Coughing and tearing eyes, they finally came to the bridge. Peter's eyes searched for Captain Giles. There in the dim light, the soldier stood giving orders and maintaining an air of authority. The captain spotted them and ran over to them.

He started, "Are you two okay?"

Peter retorted, "Define okay! We're alive but what's happening?"

The captain's face became serious. "We've been attacked!"

Jake piped in, "Attacked, how does anyone know we're here?"

Captain Pace barked, "Great question. We should have been completely off the grid. We've repelled the first wave, but something tells me they aren't done. We got caught with our pants down. They have some kind of jammer and it makes it hard to find their location. Luckily, their engine makes noise, so we can track them that way, but it has cost us dearly. The captain of the vessel is trying to get us underway but right now, we're a dead stick." He looked at the boys quickly. "Listen, guys. I have to get you to the escape pods. Follow me quickly."

Without hesitation, they ran right behind the captain. Once they stood in front of the pods, the captain instructed them on how to operate the small vehicles. He told them the pods would bring them to the surface and then act as lifeboats. The boys just gawked at the captain in surprise. He gave them a radio and told them to wait for instructions as he still held out hope he could right the sub and escape. They accepted the radio and took up positions in front of the pods as instructed.

Captain Pace quickly turned to go back to the bridge, yelling over his shoulder that he'd return. Peter and Jake just looked at one another, leaning up against the wall. Peter's side hurt, forcing him to slide down the wall to the floor. Jake told him to lift his shirt, revealing an already forming ugly bruise. He knew before Jake even said, he either had a severely bruised or broken rib.

Both boys were leaning up against the wall when they felt the sub move. The captain's voice came over the radio telling them he had regained some power and they were making for the surface. He told them repairs were going well, and they should have main power back soon. Peter asked if they should go back to the bridge and the captain told them not to move.

Lights flickered, and the main lights snapped on, revealing damage everywhere. Lights hung swinging from the ceiling, ready to fall to the ground and the corridor a few feet from them was scorched from a recently extinguished fire. A huge, gaping hole stood before them. As they peered in, they saw what was left of the armory. Much of the room lay in ruins but Jake walked forward and reached for a handgun lying on the floor. Peter gave him a look but said nothing as Jake put the weapon behind him into his pants. Once again, they took up positions near their pods.

Just then, a frantic message came over the radio, "Boys, get out of here now! Hurry, we're a few miles off the coast of Argentina. Make for the coast and when there, go to the naval base just outside Buenos Aires. I already alerted the base you're on your way. If we're lucky, they'll meet you before you get to land. They're sending destroyers in the area to assist us, but we may be sunk by the time they get here. Hurry, boys! I'll meet you at the naval base. Now go!"

Jake grabbed the radio. "Yes, sir! Can you tell me the coordinates?"

Captain Pace sent Jake the coordinates and none too soon, as the radio went dead. A large explosion rocked the wounded sub and sent them once again sprawling to the ground. Both boys were on their hands and knees, looking at one another. Without a word, they scrambled to their feet and launched themselves toward their pods. When standing in front of the hatch to enter the pod, they both stopped and looked at one another. Nodding to one another, they pressed the button to open the hatch. Peter's opened with little difficulty, but Jake's hissed and sparks flew from the control panel. The door wouldn't open, and Jake pushed it again, and this time nothing happened at all.

Peter waved for Jake to come over to his pod. They both peered into the pod and knew it would be difficult to fit both of them in the small space. Both were surprised the pods weren't designed to carry more sailors.

Jake whispered, "Maybe they have larger pods somewhere else."

Peter almost laughed. "This will be fun. Listen, you take the chair and I'll try to squeeze in behind you."

Jake pushed himself into the small cockpit chair and Peter scrunched in behind him, closing the door. Jake pushed buttons on the control panel as if this was old news. The entire inside of the pod came to life and Peter noticed all the lights with words all over them. There were toggle switches of all kinds on the walls as well as small video monitors. To Peter, it resembled a spaceship more than an escape pod. Jake seemed right at home and told him to hold on.

Another large explosion struck the sub and this time, the boys knew they only had moments to escape. Jake released the escape pod and Peter could feel them fall slightly, only to be bounced up by the water. Jake took control of the pod and piloted them away from the sub. Through the small windows, they could see the dimness of the murky water they now floated in.

Without another word, Jake drove the pod forward, making for the coordinates the captain asked him to find. At first, everything seemed to be going smoothly and according to the calculations on the computer, they'd be to the base within the hour. Jake told Peter they'd make sure someone came back for the captain and crew. This made Peter feel somewhat better, but he felt terrible leaving anyone behind. Jake knew there would be many more sacrifices to get Peter to his destination, but he said nothing.

Through the murky water, they rode until they came to the surface and the bright light of the sun blinded them for a few moments. When their eyes adjusted to the light, they knew they were in big trouble. Jake tried to get the pod to respond but something else now was in control. Peter felt the engines shut down and they stood floating, looking at several ships surrounding them. Jake tried everything to bring the pod back to life without any luck and he then stared out the window.

Jake shouted, "Pete, those are Nazi warships!"

Chapter 31

Captain Pace stood on the bridge of the destroyed submarine and watched in horror as the warships surrounded his vessel. He just hoped the boys followed directions and escaped. The entire bridge was a disaster and most of the crew were already escaping in pods. He hoped the crew could dive deep enough in the pods to avoid depth charges the warships may deploy. For the moment, the warships seemed content on surrounding his vessel.

The captain did a double take as he just now viewed the standard the warships were flying. He couldn't believe it, no one had flown those colors since World War II. Right on the top of each ship, blaring in the sun, was the Nazi flag. A million things went through his head about the people who would have the gall to fly that flag in open waters. A flag which meant evil to most who would look upon it.

Here, over seven decades later, someone did have the gumption to fly that flag and it was equipped on each of the now surrounding warships. Captain Pace surveyed the horizon to see if there might be any chance for escape. In his small plane of view, there was a minor opening between two destroyers but that was the only place he might go. His vessel was so damaged he couldn't dive; also, minimal power was now at his disposal. The state of his vessel didn't give him much confidence of an escape that way.

He once again viewed the blockade before him and tried to come up with a viable option for escape. With the state of his vessel, there was little choice but to go directly at one of the destroyers. The enemy would certainly not suspect a full-frontal assault by the wounded sub. Being a fully automated sub would come in handy today as the captain went to the one remaining functioning computer keyboard, typing in a sequence of commands. In a few moments, the sub reluctantly lurched forward, beginning its last voyage.

Picking up speed, the destroyer ahead now took note and turned its guns to engage the attacking sub. The captain released two torpedoes and continued his trip into the heart of danger. Both torpedoes scored a direct hit to the bow of the destroyer, causing a massive explosion. The huge guns were no longer turning his way, so the captain pressed his advantage, sending two more torpedoes toward the huge, burning ship. Again, both found their mark and rocked the front of the grievously wounded ship.

Captain Pace felt a ray of hope but only for a moment when the wounded ship returned high-caliber, anti-aircraft fire into the hull of his submarine. With not a moment to lose, he again typed in commands into the computer and put the vessel under automated control. His last command was the self-destruct sequence and once pressed, he ran out of the room and down the corridor. As he sped down the corridor, he panicked as every escape pod was jettisoned. He looked from side to side only to see every pod gone. With a spin of his head, he thought about the boys for a moment. That was it, the boys used the smaller escape pods down below, and so his hope was to find one still intact.

Racing as fast as he could down the metal stairs, he came to an abrupt halt when his feet hit water. Looking down, he could see the lower decks were already full of water. He spun, trying to think of another way to get to a pod, but realized this was his only chance. Without a moment's hesitation, he threw his coat off and jumped into the water. Being a very strong swimmer, he knew he could hold his breath long enough; the question was would a pod still be there.

The water was surprisingly warm and clear this close to land and he didn't have difficulty finding where the pods were located. Swimming rapidly, he went from empty bay to empty bay hoping to find one pod left. He was starting to run out of breath when he saw one off to his left. Again, panic struck him as this was the pod he told Jake to take. He couldn't help but think something awful happened to the boys. There wasn't much he could do now, and he was in his own hot water at the moment. Quickly, he pushed the button to open the pod. He knew he'd have to get in quick and shut the door so not too much water would enter the pod; everything was already submerged.

Nothing happened, and the door stood fast. He quickly pressed the button again with the same result. His breath now just about gone, he looked around and saw a piece of broken pipe just below him. Picking it up, he struck the control panel and pried it out to reveal a few wires. The captain grabbed two wires, hoping he wouldn't get electrocuted, and pulled them apart. Then without thinking, he pushed the two wires together until they touched, creating sparks in the water but it worked, as the door opened. Now he knew why Jake wasn't in this one.

Pushing his way into the half-open door, he managed to get in before the door was completely open and closed the door quickly. He looked around and was relieved to find not too much water in the pod. Leaping into the cockpit chair, he pounded on the buttons and released the pod. The pod shot downward and he made for the floor of the ocean. The pod was equipped with enough air for several hours, but he hoped not to have to wait that long. Taking the small control pad from his shirt pocket, he watched as the sub continued its journey toward the destroyer. Machine gun fire riddled the sub but to no avail, as the sub crashed into the bow of the already doomed ship.

The sub wedged itself in the cavity provided by the torpedo hits and there was nothing the ship could do. The captain watched as the submarine exploded, ripping apart what was left of the destroyer's hull. Huge plumes of smoke and fire flew into the air. The sight somehow reminded him of the grainy video he used to watch on the history shows covering WWII. Of course, the eerie similarity was even more closely related due to the fact he was now being attacked by an enemy flying the Nazi colors.

The rest of the attacking ships moved toward the land. The captain assumed they were content with the destruction of the submarine. One vessel stayed behind to pick up survivors from the wrecked destroyer. As he watched the ships leave, his mind went back to the fate of the boys. He assumed they scrunched into one pod; this one wasn't working correctly. Where were they though? Did they make it to shore? Would they make it to the base?

He took the wellbeing of the boys very seriously and a sinking feeling sat in his gut about their whereabouts. If they followed directions, they'd at least made it to shore. Jake was used to these types of adventures growing up a military kid. Peter was another story. Peter was a terrific, smart, and energetic kid but he needed to learn a lot about the way the world worked.

As he remained on the bottom of the ocean for the most opportune moment to follow the departing ships, he contemplated his next move. He needed to make it safely to the base and get some trustworthy help. It seemed to him that at every turn, his enemy knew what was happening before it actually happened. There was no way anyone knew where they'd be. A haunting thought occurred to him. Did one of the boys have a tracker on him? He nodded as that was it; someone tagged one of the boys with a tracker. In all the chaos getting the boys this far, he didn't even think to scan either boy before they came aboard the sub.

He was furious at himself for not thinking of this very important detail. As an officer, he prided himself on not missing anything and always thinking of everything. Being a detail-oriented person came in handy in situations such as this and that's why he was promoted so rapidly. His own commanding officers were amazed at how thorough Captain Pace was in every aspect of his assigned duties.

When he met Jake's father, the two became fast friends being cut from the same military cloth. After Jake's father explained his son's plight, the captain said he'd protect the two boys with his life. Of course, here he was on the bottom of the ocean and he knew not where the boys were. Turning on the pod's computer, he turned it toward the land and made way slowly, keeping as close to the ocean floor as he could. The land quickly arose, and he needed to surface soon. Keeping tabs on the other ships with radar, he kept well off to their left and they didn't seem interested in him. Their radar picked him up as a fishing vessel, being as small as it was.

Surfacing, he viewed the beach to see if any unwanted visitors would greet him. When he was sure it was safe, he popped the hatch and dove into the water, swimming toward shore. Feeling water logged and exhausted, he picked himself out of the water, walking toward the beach. With significant effort, he dragged his soaked body onto the beach and lay on the warm sand, letting the hot sun hit his wet body. He closed his eyes for a moment, thinking of what to do next when he heard movement. He opened his eyes to see guns pointed at his head.

Chapter 32

Jake frantically tried to regain control of the pod, but nothing worked. He called over his shoulder and looked around the interior of the pod until his eyes fell upon what he was looking for—the escape hatch. With a quick motion, he pointed to Peter and told him to press the button. Peter did as asked, and the hatch blew off, revealing the fresh, salt, ocean air. Both boys scrambled to the top of the pod and dove into the water. Swimming as fast as they could, they made for the beach with the waves helping them coast.

Once safely on the beach, they looked back toward the oncoming ships, only to see men in small boats following them. Without a word, Peter and Jake rose to their feet and slugged through the sand until they reached the dunes. Once on the dunes, they turned quick to see how close their pursuers were. Peter stood staring at the oncoming soldiers as they jumped out of their boats. Jake grabbed Peter and pushed him forward. They ran through the dunes until they came to a dirt road.

They could hear a car coming and dove to the ground behind some bushes. Peering out from behind the bushes, they could see a few Army jeeps working their way down the road. They remained hidden as the jeeps drove quickly past them. When the coast was clear, they jumped off the ground and followed the road in the direction of the base. Keeping just off the road, they ran for the first mile but quickly tired, slowing to a walk.

At this time, the land changed, and the dunes gave way to a much larger beach. Now they couldn't hide from view. Off to their right, they saw a group of soldiers on the beach surrounding a man lying on the sand. They could also see the dark cloud of rising smoke coming from a damaged vessel out in the water. Peter and Jake could see the five soldiers now with guns pointed at the man on the ground. The man calmly rose and allowed himself to be led along. Jake grabbed Peter's arm and pointed at the man. Both boys could see it was Captain Pace.

Captain Pace didn't see them, but they could see him. As the soldier's led him up the beach, Peter could see the calm in the captain's eyes. When they reached the waiting jeeps, the soldiers pushed the captain toward one as three of the soldiers got in. The two remaining soldiers were left to put the captain in the jeep. The captain then swung around with a huge backhanded fist and struck the first soldier, dropping him where he stood. The other soldier, totally caught off guard, received an upper cut to the face for his trouble and he went down as well.

The captain rifled through the downed soldier's pockets until he came up with keys in his hands. When the boys saw the captain fighting the soldiers, they ran full steam toward the captain. As the captain was about to get into the jeep, Jake shouted. At first, the captain did nothing until Jake shouted again.

Jake yelled, "Captain Pace, wait for us!"

The captain then turned with a huge smile on his face as the boys ran to the jeep. He waved them in as the other soldiers left in pursuit. The soldiers were too late as the captain threw the jeep into gear and sped off in the direction of the base. The other jeep was quickly in pursuit and crashed right into them, causing the captain to swerve quickly and then struggle to regain control. Again, the oncoming jeep tried to ram the captain, but this time, he was ready for them and cut the wheel sharply to the right. The attacking jeep sped past as the captain also braked, letting the other car get in front. Now, the hunter was the hunted and it was the captain's turn to do some damage.

Captain Pace floored the gas pedal and raced toward the soldier's jeep at full speed. Instead of smashing into the back, the captain came around the left side and side-swiped the jeep. This caused the soldiers' jeep to skid out of control into the beach sand and flip over several times before coming to rest on its hood. The captain didn't stop to check on the soldiers, but drove as fast as possible toward the base.

He peered back at the boys who looked jostled in the backseat, but otherwise unharmed. A slight smirk came to his face as the boys just looked at one another and grinned. The captain carefully guided them through the remainder of the road without incident. As the captain turned onto the road leading to the base, an odd look came to his face. The boys, seeing this in the mirror, questioned him.

Jake began, "What, what is it?"

The captain looked at him. "I'm not quite sure, I just have this feeling."

At that moment, an explosion on the side of the jeep caused the captain to swerve suddenly to the left. He cut the wheel as hard as he could but still, the blast hurled it into the ditch on the side of the road. The jeep hit the steep embankment and flipped over several times before landing on its roof. Both boys hung upside down, still with their seatbelts fastened. Jake was unconscious, and Peter was just barely aware of his surroundings. His ears rang, and his vision blurred as he tried to see how the captain was in front. From where Peter sat, it was difficult to see the status of the captain. To Peter, he looked knocked out and unmoving.

Out of the corner of his eye, Peter spotted movement. His head ached but he managed to turn just enough to see figures coming toward them. At first, it was hard for him to make out the approaching figures, but it soon became apparent they were soldiers. Peter panicked when he saw the uniforms; they were of the soldiers that initially attacked Captain Pace. Jake and the captain still weren't moving as Peter scrambled to undo his own seatbelt. He finally managed to unbuckle himself and fell to the ground with a thud. Again, his injured side burned with pain as he squirmed out of the window.

As he tried to get up, he was struck on the back for his efforts and hit the ground. He spat dirt from his mouth and turned himself over just in time to feel large hands grip him and haul him to his feet. Peter looked up into the face of an angry soldier. The man spoke broken English. Peter quickly tried to place the accent and to him, it sounded German. He yelled at Peter not to say a word and then struck him in the stomach to illustrate the point.

Peter doubled over and nearly puked his guts up right there on the man's shoes. He was usually a very level-headed person but something in him came to the surface. Rage generated inside him as he struggled to stand straight again. When he looked to the jeep, he could see the captain and Jake being dragged out. Both his friends were still not moving but one of soldiers gave a swift kick to the captain's lifeless body. Seeing his good friend being treated this way made him furious.

He grunted and sped toward the soldier that just kicked his friend. With speed and strength he didn't know he had, he speared the soldier in the side with both tumbling to the ground. The unsuspecting soldier lay on the ground stunned. Peter, in the meantime, was up on his feet feeling the rage and looked for his next target. He could see four soldiers creeping cautiously toward him, closing the gap with each step. Jake stirred, and Peter looked to him as another soldier grabbed him and hauled him onto his shoulder and started to walk away.

Seeing his best friend taken was too much for him to bear. Something inside him snapped and he let out a primal scream. Without thinking, he whipped his hands toward the attacking soldiers and an unseen wave of energy came forth from Peter's hands and leveled the four soldiers. All four soldiers lay on the ground in extreme pain and he stood staring at his hands. He couldn't explain what just happened. Without a moment's hesitation, he turned to see Jake being loaded into another jeep.

Peter ran forward and with the rage still built up inside him again, he raised his hands and released the energy. This time, the soldier took the brunt of the wave of energy and flew into the side of the jeep, striking it with terrific impact. As the man fell to the ground unmoving, Peter could see the outline of the man's body from the dent he caused. He could feel the energy inside him lessening and then felt weak. Struggling to stay on his feet, he made his way to Jake.

Jake was now almost fully awake and looked around at the carnage. He just looked at Peter with questions in his glance. Peter helped his friend to his feet, but Jake could see that Peter's remaining strength was all but gone. Both boys helped the captain into the enemy jeep and Jake slipped behind the wheel with a giddy look on his face. As he put the jeep into gear, a hand came in through the window and grabbed him by the throat. Jake floored the gas and took the soldier with him, dragging him on the road. The man maintained his grip on Jake's throat for a moment, but couldn't hold himself and lost his grip, falling to the road.

Now in control, Jake drove down the road toward the base's location. For the first time, the captain was awake and told them to drive forward. The gate was a quarter of a mile in front of them. As they turned the corner, they could see what the captain was speaking of. Still way off, they could see a large, steel gate. The wall surrounding the base was at least twelve feet high and made of steel as well. Whatever type of base this was, no one was getting in without permission.

As they pulled up to the large, solid-steel gate, the captain looked suspiciously at the large guard towers on either side of the gate. Jake drove forward slowly as the captain waved him to proceed. Once within a few feet of the large gate, Jake brought the jeep to a halt. The captain told him to stay in the jeep and jumped out to check with the guards. The captain called up to one of the guards in the tower, but no one came out to respond to his request. With a puzzled look, he stared back at the boys and then returned to the jeep. He leaned into the jeep and told the boys something wasn't right.

Just as the captain leaned into the cab of the jeep, the large steel door slid open. He turned just in time to see a soldier behind the gate waving him in. The captain paused but then looked behind where they were as if they still should keep going forward. He told Jake to pull into the base. Jake did as he was told, putting the jeep into gear, and drove past the open gate. Once safely inside, the gate closed behind them with an ominous clang.

They looked around and couldn't see the soldier that let them in. Once again, there seemed to be no one around. The captain looked frightful at the closed gate and ordered Jake to drive the jeep down the road leading in the other direction. Jake swiftly brought the jeep to full speed, traveling down the lone road from the gate, causing them to go further into the base. The captain told them there should be other gates they could escape through. They looked all around, waiting for someone to chase them but the base seemed deserted.

The road turned slightly to the left, following the edge of the huge, steel wall. After more than a mile, they still couldn't see another gate. All of a sudden, the base opened before them into a large airfield. Without Jake doing anything, the engine of the jeep automatically cut out and rolled to a stop just before the large hangar before them. Jake furiously tried to bring the jeep to life and when it was quite obvious the car was dead, they looked around nervously. The large hangar door opened to reveal a large force of soldiers and what looked to Peter like a spaceship inside the large building.

They were quickly surrounded with weapons pointed at their heads. Soldiers advanced on the passengers of the jeep with stone faces. The boys turned to the captain who swiveled this way and that to get a good look at their situation. If the boys weren't under his care, there would be no doubt he'd prefer to fight his way out. Looking at the boys, he told them to stand down. Now the jeep was completely surrounded, and the soldiers waited patiently for their captive's next move.

Chapter 33

Rebecca shot up screaming into the night. The lights came on and Holly rushed to her side, looking into her eyes. Tears streamed down Rebecca's face as she cried, "They've been captured! Something is keeping me from seeing Peter! I can see Jake and another man, but Peter is invisible to me! Something dreadful is happening, I know it!"

Holly communicated to General Giles, who rushed into the room a few moments later with a sidearm raised. He went to the ladies' sides with a questioning look. Holly grabbed the general's arm and turned him out the door. The general followed without hesitation. Once in the hall, she confronted the stone-faced general. He waited for her report.

Holly stood to her full height. "Peter and Jake are in our enemy's hands!"

The usually calm and calculating general lost his cool. After he put his sidearm in its holster, he punched holes in the wall. Holly did nothing to stop him and waited for his rage to subside. After a few minutes of destruction, the general turned to face Holly in a calmer manner.

He looked at her apologetically. "My Lady, forgive me!"

Holly grabbed his hands. "My heart, there's nothing to forgive, but if we don't do something, those boys will perish!"

The general gathered himself. "We'll get them back, I promise you. Was Rebecca able to tell you anything of value as to where they may be?"

Holly looked sad. "She's devastated! Her connection continues to grow each time she contacts Peter. It's the strongest connection I've ever seen! Even stronger than ours!"

He gently rubbed her hand. "I'm not sure I believe that, but it's no doubt strong. One thing is certain; if we don't find Peter soon, Rebecca's mind could be irrevocably harmed. Please talk to her some more and see if she remembers anything that may help locate the boys."

Holly released his hands and returned to Rebecca's bedside. Rebecca's face was tear stained and she looked to Holly protectively. Both women reached for one another, holding each other tight. After a warm embrace, Holly held Rebecca at arm's length and looked into her eyes. Rebecca returned her gaze and teared up again.

Holly wiped the tears away. "My dear, we'll find them and make those responsible, pay for their transgressions. First, however, I need you to tell me everything."

Rebecca sat up straight at the edge of her bed. "Holly, I'm embarrassed by my feelings, but it's almost as though I have to check on him before I can sleep now! I don't know how to describe it; he's in my thoughts always."

Holly laughed. "That's natural, my dear. You two have a very strong connection, in more ways than one. I'm sure when you meet, you could solve that riddle for one another. I can tell you all about those feelings but really, you must figure them out for yourself. Just know that what you're feeling is a very good, healthy thing. Trust in this, I'm sure Peter feels much the same."

Rebecca held Holly's hand. "Do you think he's okay?"

Holly held her hand warmly. "I have no doubt. Our enemies will want to learn about Peter. For now, he'll be safe, but we have to get him away from them. What else can you tell me?"

Rebecca smiled. "He used his power! I felt it! Holly, he has such strength but knows nothing of it. Oh, Holly, he must be scared to death! We must get him back!"

Holly stated, "Of course, dear. What else can you recall?"

Rebecca thought hard. "They're at a base of some kind with a large, steel wall surrounding it."

Holly smiled. "That's great, child. At least we can begin there. Is there anything else?"

Rebecca shook her head. "No, ma'am. I just saw them put some kind of restraint on Peter and then I felt terrible pain and woke up screaming!"

She patted Rebecca on the hand and stood, walking out the door. Two soldiers now stood on either side of the door. Holly gave them instructions to guard the door, but to let the young lady rest. She returned to the general who still waited in the hall. She reached for his hand and led him up the hall into another room. The lights automatically came on as they sat at a small metal table. Both looked across the table at one another. For a few moments, it seemed as though neither wanted to speak.

Holly broke the silence, "According to Rebecca, they have the boys on some kind of base with a large, steel wall surrounding it."

The general perked up, "Are you sure? I know that base. I always thought that was a friendly base."

Holly shook her head. "All Rebecca could recall was the wall and they put some type of restraints on Peter. These restraints caused a great deal of pain and severed Rebecca's connection with Peter!"

The general questioned with a stern look, "Restraints? That's odd. Is Rebecca going to be okay?"

Holly said, "For now, she's okay, but if we don't find them soon, she's going to drive herself crazy with worry. Honestly, Ryan, her connection to this young man is remarkable. When the two do meet, death will come swiftly to whomever tries to get between them. Just the power those two wield is enough to bring this planet to its knees. Our enemies really have no idea what's in store for them."

The general looked across the table at his love. "We'll find them. I know the base and we aren't far from there now. We'll be there within the day. I have a few other ships joining us and they'll catch up with us tomorrow. They won't risk moving them off the base yet. My love, I must leave you for a while. I'll return once plans are solidified."

Holly stood and grabbed his face, planting a genuine kiss on his lips. "You, sir, are dismissed, for now. Oh, and one other thing, Rebecca informed me that Peter used his power!"

The general stopped in his tracks. "What! If he unleashes that in the wrong situation, he could unknowingly hurt someone he cares for."

Holly nodded. "Yes, I know! We must find him. It seems our enemies have found a way to hold him for the moment, but if he figures out how to truly unleash his power, a great many people will be hurt."

He turned and strode away at a quick pace. Holly watched as he turned the corner and then went back into the room to check on Rebecca. Rebecca still sat up on her bed and seemed to be much more in control of herself. Once again, Holy sat next to her and held her hand. She looked into her eyes, telling her it would be okay.

Holly began, "My dear, I need you to do something for me and it's going to feel weird for you, but I think it will help locate the boys. Would you be willing to try?"

Rebecca's face brightened. "Holly, anything! What would you like me to do?"

Holly's face got serious. "I need to link my mind with yours. Our combined powers should be enough to get the connection back. There's however a risk of pain for both of us, since you said it was painful when the connection was broken. It's the only thing I can think of right now until we make it to the base and retrieve the boys."

Rebecca grabbed Holly's hands. "Let's do it!"

Holly looked once again into the eyes of her protégé and then closed her own, allowing her power to flow into Rebecca's mind. At first, Holly almost lost the connection right away as it was hard to control the flow of Rebecca's extremely powerful energy. Holly was used to doing this with her students, but Rebecca's power far exceeded that of anyone she worked with up to this point.

Rebecca could feel Holly's power searching her mind and allowed her teacher to enter. The probing continued, and she could tell her teacher was looking for something in particular. Holly worked quickly, and Rebecca felt little in the way of intrusion. She felt the warmth of Holly's own power surging through her. Rebecca now saw Peter's form materialize. At first, the image was blurry and grainy, but she could tell it was Peter. He seemed to be in a large building of some sort, surrounded by guards. Rebecca couldn't see Jake but still tried to keep her contact with Peter, but it kept going in and out.

The connection threatened to break, but Rebecca could feel more power from Holly being mixed with her own to keep the image strong. Seeing Peter shackled made Rebecca's emotions rise. The more upset she became the more power she could feel coming on. As more power came to the surface, the image of Peter became so strong, it was as if she stood in the room with him. She looked around to get a good look at the holding room.

Rebecca could see the room was made of porous concrete and the floors were a simple tile with fluorescent lighting that gave the room an eerie glow. She could only see Peter surrounded by four guards and couldn't locate Jake. Peter looked to be sound except for the shackles on his hands. A closer look at the handcuffs revealed to Rebecca a bluish electrical current running through the cuffs. Rebecca knew instantly this was the reason Peter could no longer use his power and why she lost the connection with him.

Again, she felt the anger rise within her and the power surge. She wanted terribly to reach out to Peter but knew if she did now, their enemies would be on to her. Once again looking at Peter, she faltered as she thought of his situation far away from home with no one but Jake with him. She was just coming to terms with responsibility that now rested on her shoulders but Peter, caught in the middle, still knew nothing of the destiny that now awaited him. Her power waned as she now felt sorrow for her captured friend and the image wavered. She tried to regain her focus, but the connection faded. As the image was about to fall away, she sent one last gasp of power through to Peter with three words, "I am coming!"

She came out of the trancelike state with a jolt and stood straight up. Holly caught her and steadied her, looking directly into her eyes. The beautiful woman held her at arm's length until she could stand on her own. Rebecca, one of the most powerful wielders of magic in thousands of years, was still very green with the knowledge and capabilities her magic brought. Holly knew if she couldn't learn to control this power, Rebecca would be in grave danger. Holly looked at her protégé and smiled. The young lady studied hard and did all that was asked of her in lessons. One problem remained, Holly knew there would come a time soon in which Rebecca would need to look to other sources for guidance as Holly's own power, as strong as it was, wouldn't be a match for Rebecca.

Rebecca, now feeling the effects of the melding wearing off, stood unaided and looked at her mentor. She smiled and reached out, touching Holly's shoulder. Holly smiled warmly back and motioned her to sit next to her. Rebecca took a seat next to Holly and tears once again pooled in her eyes. She glanced over at Holly with embarrassed eyes. Holly put her arms around the young girl and comforted her.

Holly started, "I saw most of what you saw but tell me about that power surge. I've never felt anything like that in any melding. It almost felt as if you were drawing power from a third person."

Rebecca's wet eyes looked up. "I saw him sitting there in chains, helpless with no one and I just pulled more power from somewhere. It was scary, Holly. It was almost limitless!"

Holly's eyebrows rose. "You felt that much power?"

Rebecca nodded. "It just kept coming. I was so angry, and I just kept reaching for power. He's in a type of handcuffs that generate power, which is jamming Peter's. The more I looked at his situation, the sadder I became and then the power faded."

Holly stood. "Yes, I saw those cuffs. He's being held in a concrete bunker and it's probably built very thick to shield any radio or cell service. Finding him once we're there will be difficult; that close, I dare not meld with you. Doing so would alert our enemies to our presence and we need stealth for this mission."

Rebecca's eyes moistened again. "He's all alone! I couldn't find Jake. We must get to him!"

Holly sternly spoke, "We'll get both of them and keep them safe!"

Holly sat next to Rebecca and looked at the floor. Both ladies just contemplated their next move for a moment. Holly then grabbed her hand, pulling her up. Without question, Rebecca followed Holly through the maze of the ship until they stood on the bridge. The general spun to meet Holly's eyes and he recognized the steely gaze. He strode over to her and clenched her other hand. The three stood on the bridge of the ship hand in hand and seemed to glow. Those on the bridge saw three very powerful individuals and stood in awe.

After a few moments, they released each other, and Holly told the general all they learned from the melding. The general also filled them in on how far away they were and when they expected to arrive. According to the general, they were extremely close. He then turned, giving some more orders and everyone snapped back to work. The three Zarillion once again took powerful postures on the bridge and watched the monitors.

Chapter 34

Colonel Whilhelm, seated in the cockpit of his own underwater craft, eyed his enemy's vessel with nothing but destruction in mind. The colonel's anger was at a boiling point and this day, which started out with such promise, now rose to be a disaster. After discussing strategy with High Commander Zosa, he was even more upset, as the commander wanted the capture of these rogues. This was the farthest from the commander's mind as only destruction would cleanse his pallet today. His fingers restlessly gripped the yolk which controlled the ship and he eyed the missile controls at his fingertips. With one push, his unsuspecting enemies would be no more.

He moved his thumbs into position to press the button to release sheer destruction, but then held up as the monitor before him blinked. He then saw once again the gruesome face of the high commander staring at him. He looked reluctantly at the commander and relaxed his hands. His anger now took a new target and hoped that someday he'd have the chance to come face to face with this creature. The colonel knew of his power but also knew these creatures could die. Through the years, he helped some escape into the wide world, only to die shortly afterward.

Someday, the colonel would have his day and put an end to this scourge. Right now, he needed to stay the course and secure these prisoners. He turned once again to the monitor and relaxed his tense, corded muscles. The commander seemed to be waiting. A few tense moments passed before the colonel spoke.

He began, "Yes, Commander? I'm within striking distance! Two missiles will end them!"

The commander barked, "You'll do no such thing! I need them intact! I know you don't care but those three are among the most powerful beings in the universe. If we could use their powers on our behalf, there would be no question. The human race would bow to us. I know your thirst for blood and I applaud it but in this case, a steady hand is needed. Capture them and bring them to me. You have the shackles I gave you and that will render them powerless."

The colonel clenched his teeth. "Yes, sir! I understand and will deliver them to you as requested. I have one request though. The general, may I kill him?"

Cackling, the commander laughed. "In another life, you and I would be good friends! I'll tell you this. When I'm finished with them, you may fight him to the death with my blessing. I'll even make sure his beloved Holly watches. Although I'll warn you, he's no easy foe! I've been fighting him for eons and everyone I've sent to kill him has never returned. I'd love nothing more than to have you end him and you'll get your chance."

Once again, the colonel stood gawking at the screen. As much as he hated the commander, this would happen every now and again that he would speak to him as an equal and not a subordinate. This confused him on many levels; just when his hate for the creature seemed to be at its apex, the commander would redeem himself. The colonel once again took control of the vessel and assured the commander he'd complete the mission.

He took the vessel in closer for the range of his guns and brought it around to disable the craft. This would be very difficult, but he needed to hit the propellers just right so the craft could still surface. As he pulled within range, he couldn't help but think of what the commander said about the general.

The colonel would very much like to test his medal against the general. He did indeed know the stories of the general's prowess as a warrior. The colonel did very much respect those men and looked forward to meeting such opponents.

Although one thing haunted him as he pulled within range, his enemy's own technology. The commander explained the cloaking capability of his vessel but surely his enemies had a counter to that and could locate him. To this point, there was no sense of danger but from experience, he knew they could be baiting him into a false sense of security. In spite of the danger the enemy vessel posed being much larger and more armed than his, he seemed to have surprise on his side.

Now in position for a perfect shot, he took a moment to think of the craft's ultimate destruction. If these creatures were so powerful, then they needed to be destroyed. He quickly put that out of his mind and tightened his grip around the steering mechanism, readying himself for the strike. As he was about to pull the trigger, he noticed small doors on the side of the submarine open. Without another thought, he released his guns on the propeller of the submarine.

At this range, his shots were right on with terrific effect. The propellers were all but destroyed. Just in time as the submarine countered with torpedoes of its own, homing in on the colonel's small vessel. The colonel took control and averted the first wave, thanks in part to his vessel being small and highly maneuverable. He sped up and turned his craft to run while calling his awaiting backup to assist him. The next wave, he was less lucky as one torpedo struck the side of his vessel, ripping a gaping hole in the hull of his ship. Water gushed in and the colonel didn't have any choice but to surface.

Blowing the ballast tanks, he floated to the surface when another torpedo again ravaged his ship. Without another moment to lose, he pushed the button and the whole cockpit released from the entire vessel and turned into an even smaller vessel. He turned and made for the surface, hoping the other ships would be there when he arrived. As he broke the surface through the water spray, he noticed the awaiting warships.

As he was about to turn for the protective ships, his enemy's vessel broke through the surface in front of him. Knowing the commander specifically forbade destruction of the vessel, the colonel thought himself doomed. In his small craft, he couldn't engage the enemy as there were no weapons aboard. Rather than be a sitting duck, he sped toward the enemy vessel. Just before the small craft struck the submarine, he blew the hatch and dove out into the sea water. Even from his view below the water, he could see the terrific impact the small ship caused, striking the hull of the submarine. A large explosion rocked the larger ship, sending a huge shockwave through the water, spinning the colonel over so he lost his bearings.

He struggled to make it to the surface and saw the damaged submarine was now just barely staying afloat. When he broke to the surface and sucked in a huge gulp of sea air, he could see smaller boats in the water already surrounding the crippled sub. The colonel noticed once again, doors all around the sub open, revealing a myriad of weapons. The smaller boats didn't have a chance and were dispatched quickly with the colonel diving under the water for cover.

As he bobbed his head in the waves, he saw the larger attacking ships preparing to return fire, but something stopped them. The colonel knew this was a tactical mistake as the wounded vessel knew not the plans for capture. As far as the people in the sub knew, they were to be sunk. The colonel backstroked away from the kill zone while keeping an eye on the proceedings. Once again, the wounded sub retaliated and sent missiles toward the larger ships this time. The missiles struck home, causing great damage to the closest warships. Again, the colonel marveled there was no return fire.

From behind the colonel, he heard gunfire and the bullets riddled the submarine. The sub was now showing signs of sinking as the bow was now much lower in the water and the stern came out of the water. The colonel could see the destroyed propellers. The water hissed as the damaged sub sank lower in the water. Again, the warships from the side unleashed gunfire into the wounded sub. The sub returned fire but at a smaller rate this time, and the colonel knew the sub was doomed.

A large explosion came from the sub and shot water spraying into the air. The colonel knew the crew would have to surrender or go down with the ship. A wave struck him from behind as he treaded water, causing him to be pulled under. Through the cloudy water, he saw the escape pods being jettisoned. He pulled himself up to the surface. He raised his communicator out of the water and hailed one of the ships, alerting them to the escape pods. The captain responded and sent out ships of his own to retrieve the escaping enemy.

In a few moments, another small boat picked him up. Waterlogged but otherwise unharmed, he grabbed a blanket and wrapped it around himself for warmth. The soldier gave him an update alerting him to what was taking place right now. He nodded and looked back toward the water where his escaping enemies were. He could hear some muffled explosions rising from the water but in a minute, they stopped. When aboard one of the larger ships, he stood on the bow watching the proceedings, still clinging to the blanket. Two escape pods rose from below and now floated on the surface, surrounded by smaller and larger vessels alike. The colonel could see the seething eyes of General Giles staring at him through the foggy windshield of the pod.

The look of hatred brought a smile to the colonel's face. Weapons small and large were now pointed at the two small pods. The occupants knew their plight and surrendered. The three prisoners were taken into custody without incident, which surprised the colonel as he expected quite the struggle. It appeared the general was chivalrous and wasn't willing to endanger the lives of the ladies in his care. To the colonel, this was identified and the general's weakness which he'd surely exploit.

When the prisoners were brought before a dry colonel, they stood before him with hatred in their eyes. The general looked as if he could easily break his restraints as his muscles bulged out from behind his uniform. There was no doubt in the colonel's mind that here was a formidable opponent. He said nothing and turned to assess the ladies. The older woman was extremely tall, even taller than himself and looking at her, he saw the power just emanating from her very being. The younger lady, shorter in stature but not by much, looked ready to explode. He could feel the heat and hatred coming from her very soul.

Yes, these were definitely dangerous people and everything in his head told him to do away with them right here and now. Then the commander's voice came in his head, asking if they were captured. The colonel, still very disturbed by this mode of communication, spoke into his communicator, telling the commander of their victory. The commander told them to make for the base, pick up the boys, and return them to him. Colonel Whilhelm agreed and returned to his prisoners.

One thing he intended to do was torture these prisoners. The commander expected them intact and he'd deliver them so, but he'd be sure to make them suffer first. He brought the prisoners below and sat them down in metal seats while the doors were shut tight. Lights were turned directly on the prisoners. The colonel brought another seat and placed it in front of them. He sat, appraising the situation carefully.

He spoke, "Welcome, my friends. You've led me on quite the chase but nonetheless, you're mine. I can assure you that your captivity will be painful, but you'll be brought before the commander to die."

He let that sink in as he looked at the general, who as a veteran of many campaigns, definitely knew not to say anything and looked forward with a stone face. He knew he wouldn't break the general and then he looked at the taller woman. She also sat with a stone face and he knew this wouldn't work with them. The younger girl, however, was another story. Her face was red, and the anger just continued to build in her. The colonel himself almost stopped for fear of setting her off, but he needed intel and she was his best bet.

He looked at her. "Well, my dear, you can make this easier on your friends if you'll just cooperate. I won't hurt them if you tell me what I want to know. First, you can tell me how many other vessels you have in the area and do they pose a risk to us?"

Rebecca looked up at him with red eyes. "I'll tell you nothing!"

The colonel liked her spirit. "Yes, I can see that. Maybe this will help you decide."

Behind the colonel, a large screen came to life showing a cement cell in which showed a huddled figure in the shadows. Rebecca could see the outline of Peter and shuddered. This didn't go unnoticed by the colonel. He cackled and pointed at the screen. When he motioned to the person by the screen, the soldier spoke into a communicator. Rebecca could see the shadowy figure convulse and shake.

Rebecca screamed as she watched Peter writhing on the floor of his prison, "Stop! Leave him be!"

He turned to the young lady. "That, my child is up to you!"

The colonel waved his arm and the convulsing figure stopped. He once again looked at his prisoners and he could see the general's muscles flexing. Holly's eyes were focused on the colonel but still no emotion. When he turned to the young lady, she was all but ready to tear the colonel's head off. Again, this emotion would help the colonel.

He began, "My dear, all you need to do is tell me what I want, and his pain stops."

Rebecca lunged forward, leaping from her seat, and kicked the colonel straight in the chest, sending him sprawling to the ground. Even though she was young, she was proficient in combat. Her legs were free, and she used them. She quickly kicked the colonel repeatedly in the head and then he turned while she threatened to stomp on his head. The swiftness of the attack surprised the colonel and he lay on the ground dazed as the repeated strikes came. He turned just in time to see the foot coming for his head and rolled out of the way.

He sprung to his feet and saw the guards now running toward the young lady stalking him. The general was now up, and bull-rushed the first two guards, spearing them in the midsection, causing them to fall to the ground. Holly dove past the strike of one guard and swept her leg around, catching another guard's knee. The colonel saw the chaos and tried to call on his own communicator for more reinforcements, but received a jump kick to the side of his head for his trouble by this pesky young girl.

The colonel once again found himself on the ground and this time, when he rose, he looked for blood. He reached behind him and took out a combat knife and flashed it in front of him to ward off the next attack. Just then, the door to the room opened and in poured more soldiers, this time with weapons pointed at the prisoners. The general dispatched one more soldier but then saw all the weapons pointed his way, and then stopped. Holly saw this as well and ceased her fighting. Rebecca was, however, caught in the throes of attacking the man hurting her beloved, lunged at the colonel. This time, the colonel was waiting and used her weight against her, and threw her to the ground. Rebecca rolled on the ground and couldn't stop herself as her wrists were still bound.

When she looked up, there were several weapons pointed at her. They dragged her back and threw her back in her chair. This time, several guards with weapons drawn pointed at the captives. The colonel sat and wiped some blood coming from an injured lip. He looked at the young lady who attacked him and nodded. As a soldier, he could appreciate the spunk shown by this young lady and in some cases, wished his own troops showed that much heart.

He smiled. "That, my young lady, was very well done but as you can see, there's no way out! Also, you need to be taught a lesson!"

He waved his hand and the shadowy figure once again shook. Rebecca's face became beet red and was ready to lunge. She didn't know how much he could take. She raised her hands and signaled them to stop. The colonel waved, and the convulsing stopped. He turned toward the young lady. She looked beaten, but she was so upset, she could feel her power rise again in spite of the shackles. She rose to view her enemy but before saying anything, she broke the containment field of the shackles and sent a message to Peter, telling him she was captured. She told him to find the secret entrance to the city and she'd find him there.

Rebecca was so furious the power kept coming and she stood, tearing her hands from the cuffs. She pointed her hands at the colonel and released her power, striking him in the chest. The blast of energy threw him against the back wall. The soldiers must have thought he was dead as they unloaded their weapons on Rebecca. The power surrounding Rebecca threatened to destroy everyone and everything in the room. The weapons discharged never even touched Rebecca, bouncing off the energy field now surrounding her.

For an instant, she saw a flash of Peter and he searched for her with petrified eyes, hoping she was okay. It looked as if he too broke through the shackles. In that instant, she faltered, and her energy field was disrupted as a discharged weapon struck her. The power from the weapon surged through her and every muscle fiber in her body was on fire! Her muscles were useless, and she could feel herself blacking out. The last thing she remembered was Peter's face.

Chapter 35

Peter awoke to darkness and silence. His head pounded, and he struggled to get his eyes to adjust to the darkness. After a few moments, he struggled to sit up and lean against the concrete wall of his cell. The damp, musty smell told him he was down below the base in some type of cellar. There were no windows that he could see but far above him, he noticed the outline of a light fixture.

Once upright, he looked around to see where the door was and then located it a few feet to his right. Just the smallest amount of light came into the cell from below the door. Peter sat up more and straightened his back out with his bound hands in front of him. The metal cuffs dug into his wrists and he felt dried blood from where they rubbed his wrists raw. His head hurt so much he could see little flashes of light every time he blinked.

Struggling to his feet, he approached the door and tried to look through the cracks, but he could see nothing. He then got on his hands and knees, and tried to look into the hallway from under the door. The light hurt his eyes, but he could see a little bit of it filled hallway. Just to the right of the door, he could see a pair of boots belonging to the soldier guarding him. Once back onto his feet, he went back to his bunk to regain some comfort as his head pounded.

As he closed his eyes, his thoughts went to Rebecca and where she was at this moment. He wondered if she could find him in this dungeon. Also, he hoped she was all right and not worried about him too much. Just then, he felt a jolt of energy shoot through his body and he fell off the bunk onto the floor. After the pain subsided, he remained on the ground huddled against the wall. Again, a huge surge of energy went through his body, causing him to convulse and shake on the ground.

Peter couldn't stop his body from shaking and contorting as the energy shot through him. When the energy stopped, he nearly coughed up his insides but managed to struggle back to his corner. His mind was very cloudy, and he wondered what was going on. Then he saw her. The beautiful eyes and face of an angel came to him. He almost tried to reach out and touch her. He could see her concerned look and waited for her to speak.

There was no smile but a very straightforward message this time, "Peter, I've been captured! You must make it to the hidden city and find the secret gate. I cannot help you right now, but I'll join you in the city. I'm sorry! I know I promised to meet you now, but I'll see you in the city!"

He felt his anger rise inside as the energy surged through him one more time and he bounced around on the ground for a moment before it subsided. This time, with Rebecca's image fresh in his head, he rose to his feet, this time in his full fury. Once again, he could feel a swell of energy coming up from within. He let his anger fuel him and the power swelled. When he could feel the power tingle in his hands, he thought of Rebecca and that put him over the edge. The thought of her being captured brought emotions to the surface he never knew he could feel. Without hesitation, he snapped the cuffs and they fell, sparking as they hit the floor.

Focusing on the door, he let the anger and energy flow through him and released it into the door, which exploded into thousands of pieces. He strode into the hallway, expecting to fight his way out, but he noticed the guard now on the ground with bits of the door sticking out of him. Peter stood for a moment looking at the devastation and then ran toward the exit. He flew around the corner and ran right into a guard. They both went crashing to the ground and Peter popped up and sent another blast of energy into the man, sending him across the hall. The guard went crashing into the cement and fell to the ground unmoving.

Peter was about to run again when he heard a voice. He heard it again and recognized the voice. It was Jake and the captain. He told them to back up and get away from the door. He kicked the door in and out ran his friend with the captain. Without saying another word, the captain got in front of the boys and told them to follow him.

They ran through the halls without any resistance until they came up to the upper reaches of the base. The captain dispatched of a few soldiers without a sound and they went much more slowly now. When they were on the upper most level, they stopped behind several pallets of supplies and watched from their vantage point for an escape avenue. The captain kept watch and told them as soon as they could to get to a vehicle. Peter and Jake watched through the pallets and could see various soldiers moving all kinds of supplies.

The captain saw a soldier come close to them and snuck out, knocking the soldier out, dragging him behind another pallet. He took the man's clothes and dressed as an enemy soldier. He looked at the boys and told them this was their ticket. As they watched a large truck being unloaded, the captain told them to be ready. When the truck was ready to leave, he advised the boys just to follow him and act naturally. They walked right by everyone and got in the cab of the truck. The keys were still in the ignition and the captain started the truck, putting it into gear.

No one even noticed they were in the truck as it rumbled away from the loading dock. The captain drove the truck right to the gate and waved at the guard, who didn't even question him and lifted the gate to allow him to leave. Once on the road, the boys let out a sigh of relief as the captain told them not to get too comfortable; they weren't far enough away yet.

He blurted out, "They captured Rebecca!"

Jake turned. "What? I thought she was some super being. How?"

Peter continued, "I don't know much. I was in my cell and I saw her. She said she was a prisoner and would meet me in the city."

Jake's face looked puzzled. "Pete, we have no clue where this city is, except that it's on the continent of Antarctica."

Peter cringed. "I know! I know! I really don't know how we're supposed to find it without her. I was counting on her to show me the way. The larger problem is her! Jake, I can't leave her there!"

The captain chimed in, "Absolutely not! Peter, she's there only because they want you! If you make it to Antarctica, they won't need her. This may buy us some valuable time. Seriously, Peter, I wouldn't worry; from what you tell me of her powers, I'm quite sure she can handle herself very nicely. I wouldn't be surprised if she catches up with us before we get to the continent."

Peter thought for a moment, "Captain, I cannot just leave her there!"

Once again, the captain looked up. "I know, Peter, but we cannot risk you being captured. Honestly, my mission is to see you safely to the base in Antarctica. We're very close. I'll tell you this. When I see you safely to the base, I'll put together a rescue mission and get her! I promise!"

Peter's face brightened. "Thank you, Captain!"

The captain lifted his hand to stop him. "Do not thank me yet! After what we just went through, it will be a very dangerous mission. I'll do what I can to retrieve her. That's all I can promise."

Peter acknowledged, still excited, "I know you'll get her! I know it!"

With a nod, the captain went back to driving. After that point, no one said much but watched the road ahead, expecting to be chased at any moment. Luck was with them and they saw no sign of being followed. As the miles drifted away, Peter closed his eyes and let himself rest as he could hear the hum of the engine.

His thoughts sought out Rebecca and at first, he could see nothing but darkness. He was about to give up when he caught a glimpse of a sparkling light. The light became stronger and then morphed into a grainy image just barely visible. There on the ground with her hands shackled in front of her sat Rebecca. Peter could just make her out in the shadows. The dim light just barely glinted off the cold, metal cuffs.

Peter surprised himself as usually, Rebecca contacted him, and he monitored her. She looked not to be in distress and then he noticed another figure just off to her right. If possible, this figure looked more powerful and tall. She too sat on the floor, glancing at Rebecca. Peter could tell right away this creature was related to Rebecca in some way. He looked at Rebecca with a pang of guilt that he was free, yet she still sat in the cell.

He reached out to her. "Rebecca, I'm here! I escaped, thanks to you. The captain will drop me off at the naval base and then come get you. You can break those cuffs! Use your anger, they cannot hold you!"

He heard just above a whisper, "Peter, I'm so glad you're safe! Do not worry about me. Holly and General Giles are with me. We'll take care of this from our end. You just get to the base and find the entrance to the city."

Peter's voice faltered, "I'm sorry I couldn't get you! I'll be waiting for you!" He could feel himself losing the connection. "Rebecca, where is the entrance located?" The vision wavered, and he could see Rebecca trying to answer. Rebecca disappeared before his eyes and he tried to grab hold of her. He shot forward, shouting, "No, Rebecca!"

Jake grabbed a hold of him. "Dude, it's okay! I'm right here! We're still in the truck."

Peter blinked. "Jake? I saw her. She's cuffed like I was and she's with two of her people."

The captain perked up, "Peter, I'm telling you, with their power, I'm sure they'll escape even before I get there. I wouldn't be surprised if they get to the city before you do."

Peter grew sad. "I tried to get the location of the entrance to the city but lost the connection."

Jake put his hand on his shoulder. "Don't worry man, we'll find it!"

Peter nodded and leaned back, thinking only of Rebecca. They continued their journey through the day without any inkling of being pursued. The road they were on remained devoid of people and they saw no animals. Houses were sparse and once in a while, they could see a farm off to their right near some small hills. For the first time, Peter felt the heat rising. When on the ship and submarine, the temperature was controlled. Even when they escaped and arrived on the beach, it was cooler due in part to them being soaked, but also the sea breeze. Now, Peter could see the waves of heat coming up from the paved road.

The captain kept a good pace as to not attract any attention, but the lack of cars or people made for an eerie scene with each mile passed. Into the afternoon, they stopped briefly to take refuge under a few trees to eat a meager lunch of some MREs they found in one of the soldier's packs. Luckily, there was some bottles of water also in the pack. Peter felt starved and ate quickly without savoring any of the food.

His mind wandered back to Rebecca and several times, he tried desperately to reconnect with her mind with little success. Beads of sweat grew on his brow from exerting his mind to find her. Worry overtook him, and his anxiety seemed unchecked. Jake could see his friend struggling and suggested they take a walk to clear their heads. Both boys felt the tug of their heartstrings for loved ones lost or left behind. They walked in silence for a long time, lost in their own thoughts.

Jake spoke first, "Pete, I know this whole thing is crazy but just look at where we are, man. Argentina. I mean, a few weeks ago, if you asked me about what we'd be doing for the summer, I'd have said bored off our butts! Look at us now! Seriously, we're in the midst of a grand adventure. People dream their whole lives of being involved in such an adventure. What a story this will be to tell our children. Think about it, Pete, we aren't even in college yet and we're out travelling the world. We rock, dude!"

For the first time in a long time, Peter smiled. "Jake, that's why you're my best friend, man. You see the good in everything! I hear you a hundred percent. My connection to Rebecca is unbelievable. Jake, it's as if we're one being sometimes. You and I are close. I know sometimes how you're feeling but this is much different. My need for her is unquenchable, I feel my heart breaking right now because I'm not with her. Jake, I haven't even met her in person yet! What if I disappoint her? What if after all this, she doesn't want me?"

Jake frowned. "Pete, you and I both know that isn't going to happen. Like you said, the connection you two share is amazing. I know when you two finally meet, it will be epic! What I'm worried about right now is getting you to the city safely. We're definitely in enemy territory now and it will get worse with every step we take toward the city. Pete, your destiny awaits in that city and you've heeded the call. I have no doubt in my mind that your whole life will change once you're in that city. I have a feeling all our lives will be much different."

Peter grasped Jake's shoulder. "Thank you for always being there with me. I don't know what I'd do without you. I don't deserve such a friend as you."

Jake smirked. "Yep, you definitely owe me! Trust me, I'll collect at some point. I think we better get back. It's time for the real fun to begin."

Chapter 36

Rebecca frantically tried to reconnect with Peter and couldn't find him. She searched the dark recesses of her mind for any little spark that would lead her to Peter but found nothing. Before losing him, Peter made sure he told her about the cuffs around her wrists. The cold metal didn't look like anything other than regular, steel handcuffs, but Peter was right. Ever since they put them on, her powers were muted. One of the last things Peter told her was to use her anger to break free; it would amplify her power and destroy the cuffs' hold.

Right now, finding the anger wasn't an issue. Her anger was and had been brimming just under the surface for a long while trying to get to Peter. Every time she was within sight of him, something thwarted their meeting. No, she was angry and this time, she'd use that anger. Her teacher Holly was in a cell down the hall from her and she couldn't speak to her as her powers weren't working. Holly always taught her to control her emotions when dealing with her power. Rebecca recalled a time when she was young, and Holly taught her how to transmute an object across a room.

Rebecca's focus that day was elsewhere and she struggled to move the object where Holly wanted it. Holly scolded her, and Rebecca lost her temper, sending the object hurling through the air, smashing into the opposite wall. The object was imbedded so deep into the wall, rather than take it out, they chose just to fix the wall with the object still inside. Since that moment, Holly spent a lot of time teaching Rebecca how to keep her emotions in check.

Holly was successful in teaching her protégé how to control herself but since meeting Peter, her emotions were now on overload. She let the rage take over and she could feel the power building inside her. The power grew until it hurt her not to release it. Her whole body felt on fire and every fiber crackled with energy. In her dark cell, the light around her grew and in a matter of moments, the light was so blinding it threatened to consume her. The cuffs melted away from her hands and she stepped forward, looking at the door standing in her way.

Rebecca concentrated on the large steel door preventing her from her destiny and released the blinding energy. The full force of the white light struck the door, sending it flying into the hallway. Steel blew to pieces as the door struck the stone wall and shattered. Much like the object years earlier, the door was no more. Rebecca stepped out into the dimly lit hallway only to see a startled young soldier standing in front of her, not sure what to do.

Without a second thought, she used her remaining power to hurl him into the wall. The soldier struck with great force and crumpled to the ground. She whisked by the fallen soldier and ran to Holly's door, nearly ripping it of the hinges to reveal a surprised Holly staring back at her. Rebecca tore apart Holly's restraints and gave her mentor her hand. Holly grasped it and the two went flying back into the hallway. Holly led the way to the general's cell. Once the general was released, they all made their way up through the maze of tunnels.

At first, they saw no human life but as they worked their way upward, they saw more signs of life. Offices, conference rooms, and locker rooms littered the hallways. Soon, they ran around a corner only to see men walking their way. The general grabbed them quickly and shoved them into a classroom before the oncoming soldiers could see them. Once inside, the general told them to stay out of sight for a minute as he wanted to find out more information about their prison. He slipped out, leaving the two women still holding hands. Holly watched as her love left her in search of danger.

Holly turned to Rebecca. "Tell me!"

Rebecca got a sheepish look on her face. "All that work you did with me on controlling my emotions is terrific, but this time I disobeyed your mandate, letting my power loose. Peter contacted me briefly, explaining he did much the same to break from his bonds. The cuffs were strong, but my power amplified by rage was no match. The cuffs melted away and I blew the door to pieces!"

Holly's eyes looked concerned. "That's exactly why I taught you to control your emotions. Imagine if you didn't have control! I'm glad you're safe but please know that what you just did does have consequences. How do you feel? I can still see the energy dancing in your eyes!"

She looked forward. "Holly, I feel great but I'm a little concerned with how easy it is for me to gather that much power. It's as though I'm drawing power from somewhere else."

Holly frowned. "That's because, my dear, you are! You're a conduit and you're gathering power from the very earth. You must be extremely careful using that much power. Just like anything else, you can burn out. Each time you use that much energy, you drain away some of yourself. Now you're strong, perhaps the strongest of us I've ever seen or heard of for that matter, but you aren't infallible."

Rebecca hugged her mentor. "Don't worry, I'll use it only in great need! You've taught me well and I'll always use your lessons. Still, it's quite unnerving knowing all that power is available to me. Holly, ever since I met Peter, I just have such a need to see him and be by his side. We have to get to him."

The matronly woman hugged her back. "My dear, trust me, your meeting has been preordained throughout history. Your meeting will align a great many things and put the worlds back in balance."

Rebecca looked at her mentor. "Balance? Balance what?"

Holly looked at her. "Don't worry for now. I'll explain everything when you two are together and then I can explain all instead of giving you information piecemeal. Both of you need to hear this information together."

Rebecca nodded. "Holly, let's get him!"

At that moment, the general snuck back into the classroom, wearing another uniform. He briefed them quickly and told them to stay close. He instructed them to keep their hands folded together close to their waist to mimic the look of still being bound. They walked right past several soldiers standing, have a lively conversation. Still, the general pushed them on through the hallways until they came to a well-lit and wide hallway brimming with life. He moved them forward at a constant pace as to not attract attention. All seemed to be going well when a huge soldier stepped in front of the general and backhanded him, flattening him to the ground.

Holly levitated the man, sending him smashing through a glass office door. Shards of glass flew everywhere and now soldiers came at them from every direction. The general was now up and took out his first assailant. Grabbing his side arm, he unleashed rounds into the oncoming attackers. Rebecca and Holly used their abilities to ward off wave after wave of attacks, but more soldiers kept coming. The general dropped soldier after soldier, but the ladies could see that even the seasoned general was losing ground.

Rebecca's own stamina now wavered, and she felt her own energy diminishing quickly. The hallway was riddled with writhing and unmoving bodies. There was now little room to move and still oncoming soldiers surrounded them. The general continued to fight, now hand to hand as weapons were no longer an option. It seemed for every soldier he dispatched, ten more would come forward. They were forced up against the far wall and remained surrounded.

Surrounded and almost spent, the trio stood looking at one another when they heard a shot ring out. The shot found its mark and the general hunched forward, holding his side. The wound wasn't life threatening but the general's fighting would be very limited. Holly released some energy to shield them, but nothing happened. She looked at Rebecca in dismay and without another word, she put up a shield. Too late as it turned out as another shot broke the silence, this time striking Holly in the shoulder.

Seeing her mentor bleeding caused the already exhausted Rebecca to lose her grip on control. Again, the anger and hatred seeped into her mind. She could feel the energy build, even faster this time. Rebecca let out a primal scream and released the energy, nearly blowing apart the entire complex. The blast blew through anything living or not, and blew it to pieces. Rebecca's anger wouldn't subside however, and Peter's face came to mind. Seeing Peter made her anger even worse; these people kept her from him. Again, she released the energy and even more just kept coming out, to the point where she was losing control.

At last, she could no longer hold on to the power and it subsided. When the energy got to a point where she felt in control, she could see the devastation she caused. She looked down to see both the general and Holly looking at her in sympathy. Without hesitation, Rebecca looked around her and saw nothing but the bright light of the sun scorching down on her head. The entire compound was leveled, and pieces of human flesh littered the ground. The sheer, stark reality of what she unleashed hit her all at once, along with the exhaustion she already felt.

Rebecca collapsed into Holly's arms. Holly held her tight. General Giles took her from the woman's arms and walked out into the sunlight. Once away from the devastation, he quickly found a jeep that remained unharmed. Holly looked down at Rebecca who wouldn't wake, with a look of dread on her face. She stroked the young girl's face gently.

She croaked, "Ryan, we have to get her out of here! I told her to be careful, but I think the exhaustion along with the use of that much power has left her this way. Drive fast and get us away from here quickly. We must get her back to the city! Hurry! I don't have what I need here to cure her, and she may not have much time."

Without another word, the still-bleeding general floored the gas and headed back to the coast. He knew as well as Holly, without this young girl, they were all doomed. The road flashed by as they closed in on the dock. By nightfall, they found what they were looking for—a simple boathouse. The general carried the limp girl as Holly followed. General Giles placed Rebecca into the waiting boat seat. He turned just in time to see Holly go limp and fall to the ground.

He rushed to her side. "My love! What is it?"

Holly looked up weakly. "I haven't the strength to heal myself. I can't stop the bleeding."

The general looked at the shoulder wound and for the first time, saw Holly's entire front shirt covered in blood. On the seat, he picked up a rag and stuffed it on the wound. He needed to stop the bleeding, or he would lose both of them. To his right, he saw a small Sterno stove and lit it quickly. He thrust his big field knife into the flames until it glowed red. With love in his eyes, he turned to holly and stuck a small stick in her teeth to bite on. Quickly, he placed the molten-hot blade on her precious skin, searing it to stop the bleeding.

With the bleeding stopped, he placed Holly carefully in the seat next to Rebecca. Both beautiful women sat unmoving and he jumped into the driver's seat, knowing time wasn't on his side. The engine came to life and he thrust the gear shift forward. Soon, the boat cut through the waves back toward home. Only the general hoped he'd be in time; both his charges were in grave danger.

Chapter 37

Colonel Whilhelm threw the large wooden desk out of the way and picked up a chair to bash something to tiny pieces. The colonel's office looked like a war zone, and nothing remained unscathed. Destroyed items littered the floor, broken glass protruded from the walls, and papers were strewn everywhere. Rage went unquenched as he pounded what was left of the wooden chair on his desk, causing splinters of wood to spray everywhere.

He picked up the remainder of the chair and was about to proceed with his quest to destroy everything in his path when the door opened. A subordinate peered in and was about to turn to leave when the colonel stopped. He glared at the young soldier who just disturbed his rampage with venom in his eyes. Still holding what amounted to a wooden stake, the colonel looked much like a vampire slayer, minus the blood everywhere. Tossing the stake to the ground, he straightened his uniform and composed himself.

With a smirk, he looked to the soldier. "What is it that you felt the need to disturb my playtime?"

The nervous soldier looked as if he'd be sick. "Sir, we've located them!"

A glare returned to his face. "Finding them is one thing, son! Capturing them is another! Now, I'd advise you not to step foot in here again until you can produce their wretched hides. Now go, before I decide to use you to redecorate my office; it seems I need new furniture."

The man looked as if he'd vomit. "Sir, I need your authorization to launch another submarine. They're trying to make their way back to their home. They'll be at the docks very shortly. My sources confirm they have a vessel waiting."

Rage still in his eyes he nearly spat out the words, "Capture them, boy! By any means necessary! Now leave me!"

The soldier stood at attention and saluted the colonel, who was about to rip into the young soldier but looked at his pressed uniform and polished shoes. This young man needed to learn a lot, but he took his duties seriously. Without hesitation, he snapped a salute back at the young man. The soldier released his salute and turned swiftly, leaving the colonel wincing as he seemed to see his devastated office for the first time.

Things fell off the rails quickly and the colonel stood with his hands on his hips. This alliance seemed to be great for his cause but now he questioned its merits. Sure, the reptilian people were powerful but behind their prison, it was the colonel's people who faced their enemy's wrath. He thought of the uncountable times over the years his men paid the price for the reptilian's schemes. This arrangement was definitely one sided and the colonel's only hope was once the reptilians were released, the balance of power would shift. For the colonel, his only endgame was to see the rise and survival of the Fourth Reich.

According to the high commander, the reptilian people would be free any day and things would change. Colonel Whilhelm knew his people were expendable in the reptilian grand scheme, but he'd wait for the right moment to make the commander pay. Two could play at this game and the commander would never see it coming. The colonel peered around the destroyed room and became mad at his own lack of bearing. Being the consummate soldier, he lived by the code of control and here, these reptiles have forced him to lose his bearing.

Turning swiftly, he strode out of the office, passing a lackey telling them to fix his office before he returned. The soldier saluted and ran into the office. Meanwhile, the colonel nearly ran down the hall to the command center. Once in front of the master screen, he waved to a soldier who brought up the image of the high commander. Commander Zosa, with a scowl on his scaled face, looked disappointed and gave the colonel a death stare.

The colonel, used to this approach, ignored the commander's mood. "Sir, we know where they are and will have them back within the hour!"

Rage filled the commander's face. "Colonel, my patience is wearing thin! Time and time again, you fail in the simplest tasks I assign you!"

It was the colonel's turn to be rage filled. "Everyone out!" He turned, yelling and smashing his hands on the console, "Everyone, now! Out!" The room cleared out quickly and he turned to the bane of his existence. His blood boiling, he gritted his teeth. "You, you question me while you stand behind a boundary where you don't know loss! I'm on the front line and I'm the one losing men daily for your cause. If I fail, it's because you won't provide me with what I need to go against an enemy with powers beyond my own. Stop taking your insecurities out on me and my men. This alliance is what, an alliance, no. It's my men fighting to their deaths against an enemy we aren't prepared to face. Don't talk to me about failure when you have no blood on your hands!"

Teeth and fangs flashed as the commander seemed ready to jump through the screen. "How dare you, you insubordinate little ant! You live at my grace and right now, your life is in the balance. I'd tread lightly if I were you."

The colonel laughed. "We all die, oh right; you don't, but my men do. You want to win, then provide me with the proper training and weapons to fight. This is an enemy you yourself continue to fight throughout the galaxy and they've bested you at every turn. How am I supposed to defeat an enemy you have yet to defeat?"

Rage in his eyes, the commander spat out the next words, "You may have a point. Yes, it's true you've fought to make the way for my own force. I believe the time to call home the troops is at hand. My scientists assure me the boundary will be down within days. Bring all your available troops to the compound and we'll secure our plan for invasion once the force field is no more. If you capture them this time, sedate them until I can question them. If they're sedated, they cannot use their powers and they'll be harmless."

With a nod of his head, the colonel looked up. "Sir, it shall be done as you ask. Like I said, they'll be in custody within the hour. My men have tranquilizer darts that will take down an elephant. They'll be brought before you soon."

A softening of his voice, the commander responded, "Colonel, be sure it does."

The screen went black and the colonel stood alone in silence, thinking that the commander was a hot head but still used wisdom in his decisions. This was actually a sound strategy; instead of running all over the world, preparing an invasion of the enemy's homeland should be paramount. For the colonel, it seemed as though he was always fighting on two fronts. He prepared for the assault but much of his time was taken away by all these useless decrees the commander always spouted to him. This time, the commander saw the importance of breaking the enemy where they live.

He leaned forward, pressing a button on the console, inviting everyone back into the room. Quickly addressing his staff, he updated them on the switch in strategy. There seemed to be a collective sigh of relief as everyone could now focus on one major objective. From that point on, the mood of the entire complex changed, and more energy was spent preparing for invasion. The newfound energy even inspired the colonel, but still he knew that without the right weapons, his people would be easily slaughtered as happened so often when attacking this enemy. At least it seemed as though the commander could now see his plight.

Now he sat in a chair at the console as he gave the order to pull back the troops and told them to meet him at the Antarctic base. He now leaned back in his chair and for the first time in a long time, he felt he was focused. Not being torn into so many directions allowed him to think. The only thing he wanted more than invading the enemy homeland was defeating General Giles. The colonel was a prideful soldier and to this point, the only man to beat him was the general. He knew the commander would greatly love to see the general defeated soundly. In his mind, he could see the commander's face when he brought the defeated general before him.

Although the commander would never compliment the colonel, it would be a great moment in the colonel's life to bring the general before the commander. Just the look on the commander's face would make the colonel's career complete. The colonel's career was ending, and he knew this would be his last campaign, making it so important to him. Unlike his allied reptiles, he and his kind aged quickly on the planet. He spent his life as a soldier and would see his precious Reich take back what was his people's birthright.

He spent his career watching his human kind fighting for scraps. Although he enjoyed the strategy of war, he was just like anyone else. He wanted to live his life. As a little boy, he knew the military was his calling, but he was never comfortable with taking lives or wasting lives without great purpose. His alliance with the reptiles forced him into many decisions that made him uncomfortable. Yes, he wanted to see his Reich take power, but he felt if there were a powerful ruling entity, humanity would come together under its umbrella. If he could make humanity see what he saw, then people could live together.

As he sat thinking of this pipedream, he recalled all the times he fought against warlords looking to make money and gain more power. Every time he vanquished one of these foes, another would take his place. What was needed was all humanity under one rule. Once everyone was brought into the fold, they could all just live. Humanity never really understood their power together as they all fought amongst themselves. The commander spoke to him many times about selfish human nature. The reptile people lived as a collective, sharing everything and living for each other. This was difficult for the colonel to understand as there were so many differences among the human people.

Although in principle, the colonel agreed with the commander that the humans needed to fall under one ruler. He knew what the commander was really planning. Dealing with men of power his entire career, he knew men like the commander were cruel and hideous. The commander only wanted to enslave and destroy the human race. The colonel wouldn't allow this to happen and when the time was right, he'd deprive the commander of his life. The colonel knew the possibility of aligning with his human enemies may be a possibility to vanquish the commander. He'd use them and then dispose of them as well.

He gave orders to leave a skeleton crew at this base, but the rest were to mobilize and follow him to the Antarctic base. Within the hour, he was in a vehicle heading toward the docks for another water trip. He kept his eyes on the road, thinking of catching up to the general. Sure, his people would catch the general, he'd like to see the general's face while he tortured his beloved Holly. But the girl, now that would be sweet to destroy her in front of him. Of course, his orders were to capture them alive and untainted, but he could still have a little fun first.

The road remained empty as he and his men approached the docks. Still no word on whether the general was captured as he drove quickly toward the ocean. When he was about to pull up to the submarine, his communicator broke its silence. He eagerly pushed the button and asked for an update. The voice on the other end came through and just blurted out one statement, "We got them!"

Chapter 38

Captain Pace saw Peter and Jake safely to their battleship. The captain wasn't taking any more chances as a small fleet of ships escorted them. The captain stood at the bow of the ship with the boys looking at the vast ocean before them. The three friends watched as the sun fell lower in the sky. Peter marveled at how beautiful the evening sky looked aboard this ship of power. The striking colors or reds, pinks, oranges, and yellows took his breath away. He couldn't help but think of Rebecca.

Her striking features, soft skin, and inner energy cut a lasting image in his mind. He clung to that image as the last rays of the setting sun fell behind the horizon. With the oncoming darkness, a chill ran down his spine and he came back to himself, realizing how cold it was getting on the water. Cold and dampness crept into his very soul at this point. They stood silent for a few more moments and then turned almost in unison, walking back into the large ship.

The captain led them to the mess and they sat together eating a meager meal but a well-met one at that. They sat in silence but each thinking it was quite some time since they all ate an actual meal. Once the meal was over, they sat back and just looked at one another, trying to decide what to say to one another. Peter looked around to see the last few remaining soldiers leaving. He turned to the captain and just sighed. Jake just smiled and leaned back in the chair. The captain looked calm, but the boys could tell he was still on edge.

Peter took this moment to speak up, "Captain, what next?"

The captain leaned on the table, putting his arms straight out as if to push himself up. "Boys, we have to keep vigilant. We're surrounded with a formidable force, yet our enemies will stop at nothing to ensure we don't arrive at our destination. I'm sure they won't attack this far out at sea but when we get closer to the coastline, we must be on our toes."

Jake piped in, "Captain, how long will it take us to arrive at our destination?"

Captain Pace looked toward Jake. "If we're lucky, sometime tomorrow. Now, boys, it has been a long day. I need you to get some rest. Tomorrow will be long day. Anyway, I need to check in with command. I'll drop you off at your rooms and then check in with you in the morning. Come, let's get you settled in."

The boys followed the captain and stepped into their quarters. The captain bade them good night and then vanished. Peter and Jake took in their surroundings. Peter couldn't help but feel relieved that this room was much larger than the tight quarters of the submarine. The air was fresh here and not stale, however, the room itself still had that metallic, sanitary feel to it. The same dull, grey walls made Peter feel somewhat trapped.

Jake felt much the same but being a military brat, he was used to such accommodations and just unpacked silently. He opened the metal drawers, placing his garments carefully. When the drawers looked nice and neat, he closed them all. He plopped on his bed and propped himself on his elbows, waiting for Peter to be done. Jake couldn't help but laugh to himself as he watched Peter struggle with taking his things out and placing them in the drawers. Jake was reminded that he knew Peter his whole life; he wasn't what one would call a neat freak.

Peter finally finished and lay on his own bed, looking up at the ceiling. He lay there for a moment and then pushed himself up against the wall next to the bed. Peter looked at Jake but didn't say anything. Jake could see he struggled to find the words. Jake knew this was very hard on Peter. Pete's whole life was one of very much structure and normalcy. Where Jake's life was ever evolving, thanks to his dad's military service, Peter's life was his mom and his grandfather. Now Peter didn't have either and Jake could see him struggling with that prospect.

Peter looked at his good friend. "Jake, what happens when we get to this base?"

Jake peered at Peter. "Dude, I have no clue. Honestly, I think it's going to be up to you. After all, you're the one who figured out the journal. Obviously, you're going to have to use the journal to find the city. Hopefully your girlfriend can help us with that."

Peter's cheeks reddened. "She isn't my girlfriend, yet."

Jake laughed. "Dude, are you kidding me! You guys are practically married!"

Peter looked shocked. "Jake, that's not funny, man! I haven't even met her in person. What happens if I'm a disappointment to her when she finally meets me? Jake, she's the most beautiful thing I've ever seen. Just the way she carries herself, it's as if she were a queen. I'm just plain old me, a normal guy. How am I supposed to be good enough for the likes of her?"

It was Jake's turn to be shocked. "Are you kidding me! Dude, you're anything but ordinary. Just look at what you've accomplished since this journey began. Look at where you are. No normal person would be where you are right now. No, my friend, you're just as special as she. I know you don't believe that, but I've been your friend since birth and again, I've always known you were more than meets the eye. You are very much her equal and one day you'll realize that."

Peter couldn't help but blush. "Thanks, man. That means a lot coming from you."

Jake smiled. "Dude, it's true. I know things are crazy right now, but take a moment to think about what you did to get here. Also think about your newfound power. That's amazing, my friend. You're like a super hero, man!"

Peter lay back on his bed with his hands behind his head. Looking up at the metallic ceiling, he thought of what Jake said. He indeed was much different now than when he left his shattered home. His thoughts went to his mother. He feared for her safety and wished he could make sure she was okay. The captain contacted people on Peter's behalf and he assured him she was well. He needed to know himself. He closed his eyes and thought about how he could see Rebecca. His connection to his mother must be just as strong. Without thinking, he closed his eyes and focused his energy to search for his mother.

At first, nothing happened but after a few moments, a whisky image of a woman sitting on a couch with a book came into view. As the image gained more clarity, Peter could feel peace as he viewed his mother reading. He knew this was her favorite pastime and she enjoyed a good story. His heart sang to see his mother safe and comfortable. Without thinking, he called to her, "Mom."

As if she could hear, Peter's mother looked up. "Peter?"

She looked around and then down at her book. "My son, I know you're in good hands and I know you'll find your destiny. I'll be here when you're ready. I love you, my son!"

Peter could feel tears coming to his closed eyes. "Mom, I think of you every day! I'll return to you. You have my word."

She smiled and looked down at her book. He felt a rush of love as he took one more look at his mother. Seeing her peaceful and content warmed his heart. Only if he could see his grandfather again. He decided to try his luck with Rebecca. He focused on her beautiful face. Instead of light though, he saw darkness. In the dim light, he saw three figures in a military vehicle with the general driving. In the back, he saw two figures of women.

Peter tried to focus to see more of the backseat, but the figures remained dark. From what Peter could see, both ladies weren't moving. He tried to focus in more on the smaller of the two figures. He now could see Rebecca as the general drove through a series of street lights. Rebecca looked asleep, but Peter could tell something wasn't right. The general looked back every few seconds with grave concern on his face. Peter now knew something was terribly wrong.

He then turned his view to the older woman. He saw blood all down the front of her dress. Again, the general turned. "Don't worry, my loves. I'll get you to safety."

The images went dark and Peter tried to see what was wrong with Rebecca. He couldn't see anything physically wrong with her, but he knew she was in danger. He wanted to reach out and touch her. For a few moments, he just looked at her with pity in his heart. How could he leave her like this and what could the general do? Peter made up his mind; he needed to find the city and find his love.

Peter shot up out of the trance only to see Jake holding his shoulders. He looked into Jake's eyes. "What?"

Jake looked back at him. "You were in another one of those trances but this time you were talking aloud. What's wrong with Rebecca?"

247

Peter sat up. "Something is wrong. She's unconscious and unmoving. The general is with her, but something is also wrong with the older lady. She's covered in blood. Jake, they're in danger!"

Jake looked seriously. "Then, my brother, we need to find that city. Tomorrow, we'll get to work. We'll find them. The general will get them to safety. You, my friend, need some rest. We'll figure it out tomorrow. There's nothing more you can do tonight. Also, remember your beloved is a very powerful person herself. She'll be fine."

Peter leaned forward. "I know but still, I cannot help but worry. On the bright side, I saw my mom. She's safe and comfortable."

Jake laughed. "I told you, man. People were after you, not her. She knows nothing. Not to mention the fact you're now halfway across the world. Don't worry about your mom. Just get some sleep, man. We'll get after it tomorrow."

Peter lay on the small pillow and closed his eyes. Rebecca's face took up his thoughts. He remembered the first time he saw that face in one of her glowing globes. The smell of the burning globe entered his mind. It seemed ages ago his room was invaded by images of good and evil. This made him think about that first time the reptilian figure interrupted their initial conversation. What if he could find the reptilian leader and confront him face to face. That would be something worth trying. He was too exhausted to try tonight, but he knew after some rest, he'd use his gifts to locate this enemy.

The thought of being pursued across continents and oceans alike made him extremely angry. He'd seek revenge, but it would have to wait until tomorrow as he could feel himself drifting off to sleep. This enemy he was sure wouldn't expect an attack this way. Peter knew this would give them an advantage and looked forward to surprising his enemy. This gave Peter great comfort as the sleep took him. Tomorrow, he'd become the hunter and not the hunted. Tomorrow, he'd fight back.

Chapter 39

Cutting through the waves, the small vessel sprayed water everywhere as the sea became extremely choppy. Through water-soaked eyes, General Giles kept peering over his shoulder, hoping beyond hope the two ladies would wake. To his great horror, they both remained still with their eyes closed. Using his hand to brush back his soaked hair, he tried to see anything before him. He felt he should see the coastline by now, but the dense fog of the morning still prevented him from seeing much of anything now. Looking down at the computer screen, he could tell the coast was off to his right. Without hesitation, he turned toward his destination.

Finally, through the fog, the general saw the dark outline of land. The fog gave the land an ominous feel to it and he cautiously slowed the boat in case he was walking into a trap. According to his instruments, there was nothing to fear but the general knew better and expected an attack at any moment. He took one more look at his damaged cargo and turned the boat toward the shore. Moving forward at a snail's pace, he crept ever so slowly, being careful not to race the motor for fear of giving away his position. The fog still currently hiding him from prying eyes, he intended to keep himself hidden for as long as possible.

After a few minutes, he could make out the rough, jagged edges of the coastline. Waves broke against the scattered rocks, covering them in seaweed. The general followed the rocky coastline, looking for a place to land. At first, it looked as though the rocky coast wouldn't relent but as luck would have it, he came to an opening in the rocks. A small inlet revealed a nice, sandy beach and he turned his vessel toward the sanctuary. He brought the vessel in close enough where he could put the anchor out but still wade to shore with the ladies.

Carefully lifting Rebecca, he put her across his shoulders and brought her to shore. He placed her gently on the wet sand and turned back for Holly. As he was wading out to bring her to shore, he felt something grab his leg. At first, it seemed a nudge but then something wrapped itself around his leg and pulled him under the water. Out of sheer instinct, he held his breath as the mystery creature brought him beneath the waves. He struggled to see what now grabbed at his body, but the water was extremely murky, and he could see little.

The creature dragged him further out to sea and he could feel teeth now breaking through his boots. The vice-like grip now pressed harder on the flesh of his ankle and pain accompanied the biting. Although he couldn't see anything but a large shadow of the monster attacking him, he could now see a small cloud of blood filling the water in which he now found himself. He reached quickly for his large hunting knife, taking it from its sheath. With a quick thrust, he jammed the weapon all the way to the hilt into the soft flesh of the attacking monster. The pressure on his ankle gave way and he was free. Without a moment to lose, he darted to the surface, breaking through the waves, spitting water everywhere, expelling air from his lungs. He sucked in the fresh sea air and spun around, trying to locate his attacker.

The air was still heavy with fog and dim as the sunlight failed to break through yet. This made it very difficult to see anything in the water or on the water. He noticed, however, the water breaking and the fin of a shark coming toward him. The general knew the shark wouldn't rest until he finished the hunt. He also knew the blood was an open invitation for the shark to feed. With a quick grab of breath, he ducked below the water and faced the shark head on.

Under the water, everything became even murkier and his vision was blurred even more. He could see the blurred shadow of the large shark heading straight toward him but little else. With knife in hand, he slashed out in front of him, connecting once again with the soft exterior of the shark. This time, the knife stuck into the flesh of the shark and refused to come out. The general didn't hesitate and made for the surface. His head darted through the water and he could see the boat off to the side.

Swimming as fast as he could, he made for the boat. Wearing clothes and heavy boats made swimming difficult and slowed him down, but he reached the boat just before the shark grabbed hold of him. With great difficulty, he dragged himself back aboard the boat and lay panting on the floor of the vessel for a few moments. He forced himself to sit up and noticed the trail of blood and water now covering the stark-white material of the boat's floor.

The general quickly peeled the boot off of the damaged ankle to inspect the damage. He was pleased to see a few minor puncture wounds but nothing major. In a few moments, the bleeding was under control and he dressed the wounds while placing his boot back on for support. Despite the dull pain, he felt relieved the wounds weren't more severe. Peeling himself from the deck of the ship, he moved toward Holly who still lay in her seat. Ryan Giles, fearless general, looked down at the love of his life and saw her pasty-white skin. His heart skipped a beat when he reached down to check her breathing and relief washed over him as he felt breath on his hand.

Gently he lifted her, careful not to jar her, he slipped into the water and worked his way to shore. Sloshing through the hip-deep water, he finally took his eyes off his love to see where he was walking. Fright took hold of his body as he scanned the beach for Rebecca. She was nowhere to be found. He placed Holly safely on the sand and searched for his charge.

He quickly found the area where he laid Rebecca's unmoving body. Her body's indent still was visible in the sand. What surprised him was a single set of footprints leading away from where Rebecca once lay. He turned back to see Holly still motionless in the sand. The general sat on his knees in rage at his predicament and balled his fists, punching them into the sand. Once more those that depended upon his protection were again in danger. Grinding his hands further into the sand, he forcefully rose from the ground and returned to Holly. He knew he'd have to find help for Holly and return to track Rebecca. It was easy to see that Holly's health was of grave concern. The general also knew he'd need Holly's help to retrieve Rebecca from whomever took her.

General Giles bore his love from the beach and walked through the dunes toward a road in the distance. Although Holly wasn't heavy, the general's own injury to his ankle made traveling through the sand difficult. It got into his boot and ground into his open wounds. He trudged up one dune to get a better view of the land and stood in despair at what laid before him.

As he crested the top of the dune, he expected to see the barren road before him, but instead, enemy troops stood. He watched as the troops closed in upon him with weapons drawn. The general got a sinking feeling in the pit of his stomach as he glanced down to assess his own weapons. His gun holster was empty as well as his knife sheath. With no weapons besides his bare hands, he'd fare poorly against this lot. He looked down at his helpless love and knew surrender would be the only option.

He walked calmly toward his captors but glanced around for signs of Rebecca. All the troops surrounded him quickly. He still saw nothing to indicate these men knew where Rebecca was at the moment. This puzzled him as the soldiers stopped within a foot of him. A young officer stood a few inches from him, informing him they'd be taking him into custody. The officer just wanted to know where Rebecca hid.

Again, he looked confused but gathered himself, telling the officer she was the victim of a shark attack. He offered his still bleeding ankle as evidence. The officer looked at his tattered leg and nodded with a sympathetic nod. The young man assured the general they'd do all they could for Holly and mend his own wounds. He called for a pair of young medics to accompany Holly to the truck and informed them to take extra care of the fallen woman. The general nodded a sign of thanks and proceeded to hold his arms out, expecting to be shackled.

To his surprise, the officer left him unshackled and just asked him to get into the truck swiftly. He did as asked, and another medic came along to tend to the general's own wounds. Still unaware of what was exactly happening, he gracefully took the care as his wounds were cleaned and bandaged. Out of instinct, he looked back and scanned the area for signs of Rebecca. He could see nothing, and his ruse of her demise was well received by his captors. Still, he sat in the truck, stumped by her disappearance, and he couldn't help but feel devastated by her loss.

The general sat with his head leaned back and for the first time, he felt the pain from his shark bite. His head pounded, and he could feel sweat pooling on his forehead. The young officer tried to strike up a conversation, but the general's thoughts were a million miles away. The truck he rode in was equipped with a double cab and Holly sat in the back with the medics attending to her. He peered in back to see the medics conferring with one another as to what may be wrong, but they were stumped.

Up front, the officer listened intently and assured the general that once they got to headquarters, she'd be well taken care of. The general spoke no word but glanced at the officer in understanding. The rest of the ride was quiet with the medics occasionally breaking the silence with an idea to try to revive Holly. Still, she sat unmoving and the ride dragged as the miles went by.

After an hour, the convoy pulled onto a side road and drove down a long, dirt road. The general, out of habit, looked around his surroundings for clues that may help him later. To his surprise though, there was little to see. On each side stood knee-high grass for what looked to be miles. There were no telephone poles or powerlines anywhere. Everything looked desolate and the air even seemed stale.

They rumbled down the road at a good clip for a few minutes until they came over a small hill. Once they crested the hill, the general saw a large compound before his eyes. The original buildings looked to be some type of ancient villa but just behind that stood some more modern military buildings. The officer drove them right up to the villa.

General Giles looked at the villa and compound to see if he could learn anything. The villa looked plain, made up of yellowed stone and a tiled roof, but a closer look revealed a sophisticated security system. Small, closed-circuit cameras and laser eyes marked the property. Just behind the house stood a field of solar panels and off to the right, he saw the military buildings. Some of the buildings were the easy-to-build, metal, prefabricated buildings while others were more permanent hangars.

Overall, this small compound in the middle of nowhere seemed a formidable foe for any enemy. He saw troops training in a far-off field and transports off in the distance. The one thing he didn't see were planes, despite the hangars. When the officer came to a halt in front of the villa, he asked the general to follow him. The general did as instructed, and disembarked the vehicle but wouldn't leave the side of his love as the medics brought her into the compound on a stretcher. The young officer looked a bit dismayed but followed the medics to keep an eye on the general.

Once inside, the medics brought Holly to a comfortable-looking, large room retro fitted to be a modern-day infirmary. They placed Holly carefully onto a comfortable-looking bed and called over the radio for one of the doctors to meet them swiftly. General Giles plopped himself in a chair by her bedside. Even though the officer wanted him to follow him to HQ, it became quite apparent the general wasn't leaving the fallen woman anytime soon. He thought better of trying to convince the general to follow him, but told him he'd return to check on their progress in a few minutes.

While the officer ran off to confer with his superiors, this gave the general his own time to assess his current situation. Since they were captured, there wasn't another word spoken about Rebecca. He sat up in his chair, still trying to process his charge's disappearance. Everything came back to that one set of footprints in the sand. Who knew they were there and who besides his enemy would want to take Rebecca. He was very confused by this whole ordeal and wouldn't rest until both women were home safe.

His attention returned to the beautiful but deathly white face of his love lying on the bed. Some color seemed to return to her cheeks but overall, she looked in rough shape. He reached out and placed his hands in hers, holding on gently.

Although her face looked cold, her hand still seemed warm and lively. This gave the general a ray of hope as he continued to hold her hand fondly.

It remained a mystery to the general why Holly was still out cold. He knew Holly to be one of the strongest people he ever met. Her strength oozed when others met her, and she held herself with terrific grace, along with wonderful dignity. He sat looking down at her peaceful face and he could see her breathing returning to a more normal rhythm. His own breathing slowed at this point as he continued to hold her hand.

At this point, he realized how extremely tired he was and took a moment to lay his head forward onto Holly's bed. He closed his eyes for a moment just to rest when he felt movement. His head shot up with eyes bright and looked at Holly's face. To his great surprise, she now looked at him with groggy eyes of her own. He reached forward and caressed her face, smiling warmly back at her. She returned the smile and gazed in confusion around the room. The general held her hand and assured her everything would be all right.

She looked around the room. "Ryan, where is Rebecca?"

Panic filled his eyes. "My love, she was taken."

Her eyes opened wide. "Taken? By whom?"

The general looked to her. "I have no idea! You both were in bad shape. I brought you to the coast to get help and someone took her before you and I were captured."

She looked around. "Captured?"

He winced. "Yes, my love, captured!"

She growled, "Ryan, we must find her! Everything depends on her!"

The general sat up straight. "Yes, ma'am, we'll find her! You have my word!"

Chapter 40

Jake awoke to Peter pacing around the room, waving his hands and talking frantically to himself. If not for their current situation, Jake would laugh but knowing the gravity of what Peter wrestled with, made him hold his tongue. He rose and put a hand on Peter's shoulder, who swung around and looked frantically in Jake's eyes. Jake said nothing but led him over to the bench and sat with him. Peter let himself be led and sat dejected with his head bent forward. Jake couldn't even begin to understand all that swam around in his friend's head at this very moment, but he was his man and would stand by him.

Peter's face came up with a perplexed look and looked as if he was about to speak, but nothing came out. Once again, his head bowed, and he slung forward on the bench. Jake grabbed his shoulder in comfort but couldn't bring himself to speak either. Both friends sat in silence as the magnitude of the moment and their situation washed over them. Each young man should be spending time worrying about the upcoming school year but yet here they were, halfway around the world, in the midst of a world-changing event.

Peter shot up. "I'm done feeling sorry for myself! These people will pay; they threaten my family, my world, and Rebecca! I cannot let this stand. Jake, I don't know what power is in me, but it was given to me for a reason. It's time to stand up and make those who would harm our freedom tremble in fear."

Jake stood with a bright smile. "Pete, I'd expect nothing less! I told you there's more to you than others see. I've seen it for a long time. It was always just below the surface. What's your plan?"

Peter stood tall. "Right now, what we need to do is exactly what Rebecca suggested and get our butts to the city. Once we're there, we can find out what's really going on. Also, once I'm there and not in the open, I'll make a visit to our reptilian friends."

With a pat on the back, Jake spoke, "Dude, I'm with you. We seem to be always running. It's time to make those idiots feel some pain. The only problem is right now, we're so close but yet so far away. People have been searching for a way to get to the ancient city for thousands of years."

His face twisted as Peter spoke, "All I know is the journal is the key! I'll need help to figure it out. First things first, let's talk to Captain Pace and figure out our next move."

As if on cue, the door opened and in walked the captain. "Good morning, boys. I take it you slept well?"

Peter looked at him with a raised eyebrow. "That depends on how you define slept well. Tossing and turning all night doesn't allow for a sound sleep. I do have to say it's the first night in a long while I felt safe enough to sleep at all though. So, I guess from that perspective, we slept well."

The captain laughed. "Forget I asked. Okay, guys, we have some big decisions to make today. We can hold up here for a while and determine what our enemy is up to, or we can take the fight to the enemy. What's it going to be?"

Peter shot forward. "We're taking them down!"

A sly smirk came to the captain's face. "Peter, you surprise me. I'm with you. As a military man, my first instinct is to take the fight to my enemy. We must be smart about this though. I've arranged for us to be dropped at a naval base on Antarctica. We'll be quite safe and according to my sources, it's near what researchers feel might be an entrance to the hidden city."

Peter's eyes brightened. "They know where it is?"

The captain hesitated, "They might. Remember, Peter, people have searched for a long time for this civilization. Knowing what I now know about you has given me much hope. I feel our chances are great to find the entrance and get into the city."

Jake interjected, "So, what are we waiting for? Let's go! We've waited long enough!"

Captain Pace held up his hand. "Hold tight there for a minute. I said they'd drop us off but you're still going to one of the harshest climates on the planet. We need to be prepared for such an encounter. Right now, as we speak, the crew is putting together everything we need. The proper gear and equipment is needed to survive in such harsh conditions. I'll come back in a bit to get you for briefing and training."

Peter and Jake nodded as the captain opened the door and left. They both scrambled around the room, throwing their meager possessions together so they'd be ready when the captain called upon them. Peter sat on the edge of his bed, nibbling on a protein bar while Jake still stood in the middle of the room. Nervous energy filled the room and Jake plopped on the bed next to Peter, grabbing what was left of the bar, popping it into his mouth. He got a punch to the shoulder for his trouble, but then Peter playfully grabbed him in a headlock.

Both boys were still horsing around when the captain came into the room with a serious look on his face. He informed the boys their things were prepared but now wasn't the time for play and they needed their game faces. Peter rose from the bed and straightened his mussed hair. Jake strode over and picked up both their bags, following the captain. Peter brought up the rear and grabbed his bag away from Jake. Sticking close to the captain, they didn't even pay attention to the maze of halls they strode through.

The captain deftly guided them forward and in no time, they stood in a large control room. There was a flurry of activity with people whisking this way and that. Captain Pace stopped long enough to speak briefly to another officer before waving the boys to follow him. Again, the captain quickened his pace with the boys struggling to keep up with the grizzled veteran. The hallways now became larger and doorways sparser. The captain kept his torrid pace and the boys were winded when they finally came to a halt before a large, metal door.

The captain turned to them. "Grab your gear. Put these on!"

He handed each boy a pair of boots, ski pants, and a heavy coat. They quickly put on the heavy clothing and then they were given a hat and ski googles. When they were dressed, the captain helped them sling their large military backpacks on each of their backs. When done, they both looked like proper military members, ready for an important mission. The captain looked at his newest recruits, inspecting them from head to toe and nodded proudly.

The captain then opened the large, metal door and a fast, icy blast of sea air rushed into the warm, metal hold. Both boys shuddered with the cold but followed the captain through the wind as snow flew in their faces. They were led down a ramp to another smaller, waiting vessel. As soon as they were loaded, the small boat took off quickly and in a few minutes, shivering with cold, they stood on a frozen dock.

Peter tried to look around to catch a glimpse of his surroundings, but the wind and snow blasting through the air made vision very difficult. He quickly pushed his goggles on his face and looked around him. To Peter, it looked like a scene from one of his many military video games with the ice and snow. It looked like a frozen wasteland. As much as he wanted to take in the scene, he could barely see the captain way in front of him pushing forward. He scrambled to catch up to Jake and the captain. The wind and snow pelted him as he closed the gap and finally caught up, struggling to breathe in the frozen air.

The captain was relentless and pushed them forward through the oncoming storm. Each step became more difficult and the arctic air blasted through them like needles pinching their skin everywhere. Even though only a foot in front of him, he could barely see the captain. Jake was right next to him, but Peter could see he too, was concentrating on the captain. Finally, the captain came to a halt in front of a large building that resembled a green house. He quickly threw the door open and pushed the boys inside.

Once inside, the boys took their goggles off and blinked multiple times to allow their eyes to adjust to the bright lights. Once they could focus, Peter saw multiple sets of eyes gazing back at him. It took a few moments to shake off the cold, but the boys followed the captain as he was already moving off in another direction. He directed the boys to leave their gear and follow him.

Peter dropped the huge pack to the ground and stood feeling a hundred pounds lighter. He quickly fell in line behind the captain and now in the warmth of the building, he could keep up with the military man. Captain Pace brought them to a small room with a few computers set up and a couple of researchers looking at the screens. He stopped in front of one slightly bent man gawking at his computer screen. The man continued his work and reached out to punch in something in his computer. The captain waited patiently while the man completed his task.

Once finished, the man pushed himself up and stood, extending his body to his full height. With a twist of his waist, he turned to view those who broke his solitude. As the man turned and Peter could see his face in the light, he gasped. Peter did a double take and looked at the man again.

Peter moved forward. "Grandfather?"

The man moved forward to meet Peter. "No, Peter, I'm Alex Collins. I'm not your grandfather, but I knew him well. We were great friends, some described us as best friends. Yes, many times we were mistaken for one another."

Peter once again took the man in. He was tall and lean with a mussed full head of salt and pepper hair. He couldn't help but stare at the man that resembled his grandfather in every detail. The resemblance was uncanny, and he couldn't comprehend what was happening at the moment. The captain came forward and shook the man's hand, thanking him for his assistance.

While the captain and Alex spoke, Jake took Peter to the corner of the room. "Dude, are you kidding me! That guy looks exactly like your grandfather!"

He looked at Jake. "You're telling me! Something isn't right here."

Jake calmly said, "No, don't get crazy. I mean, think about this for a minute. We're tired, hungry, and freezing. I think we need to get some grub and warm up a bit. We'll then process this a little better."

Peter smiled. "You're right, my friend. I know it has been a long journey. I know I'm starving!"

Jake slapped him on the back. "Now that's the spirit! I always think better after food. Let's just check in with the captain first."

Peter spoke up, "Captain Pace? I hate to interrupt but is there by any chance something to eat here? I'm so hungry I could eat a mammoth right now."

The captain swung around. "Peter, yes. I'm sorry. I've been so focused on getting you here, I didn't really worry about food. Of course, I'll show you to the mess and get you fed. Gentlemen, come with me."

Both boys followed the captain into another small room with a few tables and chairs cast around the room. The aroma of cooking food made them even hungrier than they already were. The captain instructed them to have a seat. Peter sat first, and Jake plopped right next to him. Jake watched as the captain disappeared behind a large counter, only to come out a few seconds later with two bowls. Steam rose from each of the bowls and Peter could tell they were fresh from the kitchen. The captain paused before them and placed one bowl in front of each of them. Without a word, they grabbed a spoon from the table and slurped the hot liquid with gusto.

The captain laughed and returned to kitchen to grab a bowl for himself. He too plopped down in a chair and dug into the steaming soup. For a few minutes, no one spoke as they eagerly ate the savory soup. Although just a simple bowl of soup, someone watching the trio would think they were enjoying a gourmet meal. When finished, they all leaned back in their chairs and laughed.

Peter broke the silence, "Who knew soup could taste so good!"

Jake laughed. "That was crazy good! What's for dessert?"

The captain leaned back in his chair. "I do have to say that did hit the spot! Don't get too excited though; meals here are very bland and straightforward. The menu is very limited due to the nature of the base, being so far from civilization. As you can tell by the weather, not too many people are signing up to come to this desolate place." Again, the captain laughed. "Welcome to the South Pole, boys!"

Peter and Jake just looked at one another. The South Pole. Not that long ago, they were home worrying about what they would do on a typical teenage day. Now, here they were in the South Pole on a mission of grave importance. Peter looked down in his bowl to make sure he didn't leave one drop and then raised his head to look at the captain. Jake followed suit and the captain could tell what they wanted.

He looked at both young men. "Peter, obviously this man Alex resembles your grandfather, but you looked like you saw a ghost. Does he really look that much like your grandfather?"

He took a moment to answer, then Peter remarked, "Captain, he looks just like him. If I didn't bury my grandfather myself, I'd think this was definitely him. It's just shocking how much they look alike. I'm sorry for such a response. I hope the man didn't think me rude."

The captain's face got serious. "No, I don't think that, but he definitely has a lot of explaining to do."

Chapter 41

As the trio was about to leave the mess, Peter's would-be grandfather joined them. He pulled up a chair and sat looking at Peter. Both Peter and the man took each other in. Neither seemed content with their last meeting and kept staring at each other. It took a few minutes of brooding before anyone spoke. The silence was deafening.

Jake spoke up, "Okay, guys, we can't just sit and gawk at each other all day!"

Peter snapped out of his trance. "Sorry, excuse me. I just cannot get over how much you look like my grandfather. We were very close, and I loved him beyond measure!"

The man's face softened. "I can see that love in your eyes. He was an extraordinary man and I'll miss him dearly."

Peter retorted, "If you missed him, how is it you never came to see him?"

The man's response surprised Peter, "I did come to see him, many times. We just would meet off the record and in places where no one would find us. Yes, I know that isn't much of an answer but that was for a good reason. Your grandfather and I needed to be very careful with our meetings and they needed to be very rare. Someday when time allows, I shall explain to you in more details our many dealings, but right now, we have more pressing matters. Do you have the journal?"

Peter shot up from the table, looking to escape this obvious trap. He snapped, "What journal?!"

The man rose, raising his hand in comfort. "It's okay, Peter! I know about the journal. Let's just say, over the years, your grandfather and I met many times just to discuss the journal. Be comforted that I'll take its secrets to my grave if necessary."

Peter calmed and sat back down. "What do you know of the journal?"

Alex folded his hands and looked back at Peter. "Everything! Well, almost everything! I do know this—it's the reason we're all here. We're looking for the entrance into the ancient city. Legend has it the ancient city we're looking for is the real cradle of life for this planet."

This response took Peter by surprise, "Cradle of life?"

The old man stood. "Yes, Peter, the cradle of life. Most scholars would tell you the area that was once known as Persia is the cradle of life, but many scientists today believe this is where our kind began."

Jake chimed in, "Our kind, what does that mean? Humans?"

The man looked at Jake. "Yes, humans, but our research indicates there are many kinds of humanoid species on this planet. We're still trying to come to grips with the fact there isn't just one kind of human."

Peter shook his head. "More than one kind of human? Aren't we all one human race?"

Again, the man responded, "In theory, yes, one human race, but just like with all animals, we're finding there are different species of humans. Some of us need to be placed in different categories. According to our research, we're just scratching the surface of all the kinds of human beings there are on this planet."

The boys just sat stunned. They were always told there was just one race, humanity. This man told them there were all kinds of different humans on the planet. They both couldn't fathom exactly what that meant to their current task. Peter couldn't help but think there was nothing he could do about the different humans. That would have to be another conversation for another day.

He spoke up. "Alex, that's cool research but let's get back to the journal. You say you think you know where the entrance is. Are you sure you know its location?"

Alex looked around and whispered, "I believe I may have located it but keep your voices low. I think there's someone here that doesn't want us to find it. Two of my assistants have gone missing and I'm sure there's foul play involved. One of the things your grandfather did tell me is that even if someone could find the entrance, they couldn't enter without the journal. Whatever you do, keep it safe and show it to no one but the captain, or myself."

At this, the captain leaned in. "You mean this base is compromised?"

The man also leaned in. "I wouldn't say compromised, but more infiltrated. I just think our enemy has their fingers in every cookie jar. It's just better to be ultra-cautious. Let's just say our enemy is looking for a way in as well, and will stop at nothing to take over the ancient city."

Again, the captain cut in, "This is disturbing news. We just narrowly escaped to this base and it would be nice to know we were safe even for one day. What's being done to flush out the perpetrator?"

Alex raised his shoulders. "At this point, not much. We aren't even sure whether what we found is the entrance or another dead end. Trust me, I've been searching for this entrance for the better part of fifty years. The only reason we feel we're close is thanks to your grandfather."

Peter turned. "My grandfather knew a lot more about this journal than I ever will. I really don't know what to do with it."

Alex offered a sly smile. "Oh, I highly doubt that. I know your grandfather spent much of your life teaching you about the journal without telling you. I bet you could do some cool things with it. Tell me I'm mistaken."

Peter sat still and quiet while he thought carefully of his next words. He thought of finding the code and figuring out how to read the journal. Alex knew more than he was letting on, but something in the back of Peter's mind screamed don't tell this man anything else. He thought back to the many times his grandfather played problem-solving games with him over the years. Peter always just thought his grandfather was quizzing him for school. Now he thought about his grandfather talking to him about secret languages and codes as a child.

He peered back at Alex. "Like I said, Alex, I'm really in the dark with this whole thing. Maybe you can work with me and teach me what you know, so I can figure it all out."

Alex laughed. "Good boy! You were indeed trained by your grandfather. Lesson taught, lesson learned. Your grandfather would be proud. Yes, my boy, we'll unlock its mysteries together. This will be fun!"

Captain Pace stood up. "Alex, I know there's much to discuss but the boys are exhausted. Would you please show them to their rooms? I'd like to talk to the commanding officer before retiring for the night myself."

Alex rose, extending his hand to the captain. "Sir, it would be my pleasure. I'd also like to thank you with all my heart for making sure the boys made it here safely. Tomorrow, you'll need to tell me the entire tale. For now, though, you're correct. The boys need some rest. Sleep easy tonight. I'll spread the word you're research interns. You'll be safe."

Alex brought them to a small room with a couple of temporary cots already laid out. The captain was assigned a cot next to the boys. Even though as an officer, he was used to better accommodations, he took one look at the cot and said no word. Once the boys placed their things in the room, the captain left them to it and went in search of the commanding officer. Alex excused himself and told them how excited he was to work with them tomorrow. Alex couldn't contain his excitement and left like a giddy schoolboy.

After Alex left, the boys sat in silence, taking in all the old man spoke to them about. Peter thought about the journal as how it might be the key to finding the entrance and getting into the city itself. For much of the journey here, he never allowed himself to think much about the actual city. To this point, his goal was to survive and make it to Antarctica. He let out a sigh of relief and lay back on his cot, looking up at the plain ceiling. His mind cleared a bit and he could feel sleep coming on.

Jake, on the other hand, was wired and paced around the room. He watched as Peter closed his eyes and drifted off to sleep. He too couldn't believe they were finally here and could solve the mystery of this hidden city. Something tugged on his mind though. Alex mentioned the missing assistants and someone else looking for the entrance. Jake couldn't help being on heightened alert at the thought of an enemy being right under their noses. Although Jake knew the captain would keep them safe, Jake couldn't help but think about Peter's information falling into the wrong hands. He knew he'd have to be vigilant while Peter worked to find a way into the city.

Jake settled on a plan in his mind as he finally succumbed to his own exhaustion and lay down on the cot. He lay back, staring up at the ceiling, thinking about the possibilities of this hidden city and the indication from Alex that there may be different types of humans on this planet. This intrigued Jake as he already knew how diverse as a people the human race could be. Was this the reason peace around the world might be so difficult to achieve? Since the dawn of man, peace always seemed just out of reach and those who craved power always held sway with the people.

Jake studied the mysteries of the universe in his mind on the cot when he heard a noise. The one light coming into the room was through the crack in the door from the hall outside. He turned onto his side and propped himself on one elbow, looking to where the noise came from. At first, Jake just assumed it might be the captain coming to bed himself but when he could see no one coming to the cot, he became suspicious. This time, he strained his ears to listen for more sounds and at first, he could hear nothing.

Thinking he was nuts, he lay back down and closed his eyes. Again, he heard a noise like heavy boots on concrete. This time, he turned onto his stomach and tried to search the dark. As he did, he could make out a shadow in the corner of the room. At first, he thought he was seeing things until he saw the shadow move forward toward the boys. Jake couldn't move as the shadow continued toward him.

Just then, the door to the room swung open and the captain came in and walked to his cot. The shadow took off toward the back of the room and snuck out a door. Jake propped himself up and alerted the captain to what just transpired. The captain told Jake not to worry and suggested he'd keep watch for the rest of the night. Tomorrow, he'd find some soldiers to shadow the boys.

Jake felt immediate relief but couldn't help but wonder who was spying on them and what were they after. He finally lay down and closed his eyes. Again, the excitement of entering the hidden city built in his thoughts. Here, he was just an ordinary young man about to find and enter an ancient civilization. Jake couldn't help but be excited for the possibility of so many unanswered questions about life being answered during this quest. He envisioned himself as Peter and Rebecca's knight as he now drifted off to sleep.

Chapter 42

Jake could feel the tugging of his arm as he groggily rose up on his cot, only to see a concerned Captain Pace. Even in the dim light, he could see the captain motioning him to follow. Stumbling out of his bed, he crept behind the captain in complete silence. He peered over his shoulder to see Peter still sleeping. He thought it odd the captain didn't wake Peter, but followed anyway. The captain now slunk along the shadows of the opposite wall, keeping close tabs on Jake.

As the two moved toward the deeply shadowed corner, Jake could sense someone watching them. The feeling rose with each step forward until the air itself felt heavy. Jake reached out and grabbed the captain's shoulder as if to stop him, but the captain just shrugged him off. Jake, never one to panic, tightened his brow and followed slightly behind. As they inched closer to the corner, Jake noticed a small light flash. To Jake, it could have been a small pen light and in the darkness, it was barely noticeable.

The captain raised his hand and with a small pen light of his own, signaled back. This made Jake stand up straight and ask himself, "What's going on?"

Within a few seconds, the captain halted his forward motion, showing a larger flashlight but covered it slightly with his hand. A soft light appeared on a strange soldier's face. The soldier stepped forward and whispered into the captain's ear for a few moments. When he finished his report, he turned and disappeared into the darkness as if he never stood before them. Through the whole sequence, Jake spoke not a word and just waited for orders.

Once again, the captain turned off the larger flashlight and grabbed Jake's arm, tugging it back in their original direction. Without a word, the captain brought Jake stealthily back to his cot, motioning him to sit. Jake did as instructed, but watched the captain like a hawk as he moved quickly to the door to the room. Captain Pace stood flattened to one side of the door as if listening for any unwelcome sound. When comfortable, the captain opened the door slowly, just a crack.

Jake saw the captain barely peering out the small opening in the doorway. He watched as the captain opened the door carefully and walked quickly into the hallway, letting the door close behind him. Jake still sat on the edge of his cot, trying to figure out the events of the past few minutes. Jake didn't have to wait too long for his answer as the captain quietly slipped back into the room and bolted the door shut. He swiftly moved to the back of the room and did the same for the back door. After making a quick sweep of the room, he bolted back to Jake and sat next to him on the cot.

Jake eagerly awaited an explanation when he noticed Peter stir. The captain waited until he was sure Peter remained asleep. He once again leaned in toward Jake. "Listen, Jake, I know things have been a little secretive lately, but after everything we've been through, I can't help but be extra cautious. Keep in mind, this is a military base doubling as a research center. Yes, there's loads of research being conducted here, but the main purpose is that of a strategic military base. The base's position on the water has a specific military significance. I'm trying to get up to speed without drawing too much attention to us."

Jake whispered, "Why? We don't want anyone to know we're here?"

"I really don't think it would be a big deal if anyone knew we were here, but after what we went through to get here, I want to be very cautious," he spoke back.

Jake nodded. "Who was that? Was that the guy we saw earlier slinking around in the dark?"

The captain smiled. "Yes, that was him. He's a soldier that formally served under me at another location. We can trust him. He was just updating me on the current events going on here at the base."

"Anything we should be surprised by?" asked Jake.

Again, the captain looked at him. "Not much. It seems quiet. They're doing a few training exercises but other than that, just scientific research."

Jake couldn't help it. "What about the old man?"

"According to my sources, the old man is legit and is a fixture here. From what I was told, Peter's grandfather and Alex were as thick as thieves back in the day."

Jake let out a sigh. "Great! That will make Peter feel a lot better. He really didn't know how to take Alex and seemed quite unnerved by the old man."

The captain nodded and gave him a few more tidbits of information about the base before telling him to turn in for the night. He alerted Jake to the fact he'd still take watch and wake him if he needed anything. Jake, too exhausted to argue, lay down and was almost asleep before his head hit the pillow. The captain looked at the young man and not for the last time, thought what a fantastic soldier Jake would become.

Without shutting his eyes, the captain also lay down on his cot, trying to process all the information the soldier just shared with him. As he told Jake, there wasn't much going on except for one small detail and that was everyone was sure Alex knew where the entrance to the city laid. During his career, he heard many rumors revolving around an ancient alien civilization based in Antarctica. Just like most military members, he chalked it up to scientists trying to make a name for themselves.

That's until he met Peter and Jake did he start to take the legends seriously. These two young men were pretty remarkable to survive their trek here. He felt proud to have these two young men with him and made a vow to see them to the end of the road. With a slight bend of his neck, he looked at Peter and couldn't believe this mild-mannered young man was here now. From the moment he met Jake, he knew the boy would be a fantastic soldier. It was Peter that totally surprised him. Peter, at first, was quite meek and timid, but this experience definitely changed the boy in a tremendous way. The captain would now consider Peter as a great candidate for officer training and he marveled at the leadership skills the boy possessed.

The overall growth in both boys was pretty amazing to the captain. In his time in the military, he was used to seeing young men molded by campaigns, but in the case of the boys, it was a trial by fire. Few young men in the boys' shoes would be this composed. He couldn't help but think about what Alex and Peter could accomplish together in the morning. If they did find the entrance to the city, could they enter?

His mind raced thinking of the possibilities. He as a military man could only think of ways to surround the boys with a wall of men to protect them against the unknown of the ancient city. That's if indeed it did exist. Tomorrow would be a day of discovery and intrigue. While Peter was working with Alex, he'd spend time working with Jake to form a military strategy in case Peter was successful. Too wound up to fall asleep, he sat up and decided to make his rounds.

He walked around the room, checking the doors and the hidden corners. When he was satisfied, he returned to the cots. Jake slept soundly but he noticed Peter tossed about. Instead of waking him, he sat and kept an eye on Peter in case he needed the captain's help. Peter moved around on the cot a little but then settled down, but the captain could see the concerned look on his face.

All at once, Peter's body straightened out and the captain could see all his muscles struggle against an unseen enemy. Sweat beaded on Peter's forehead as he saw the muscles in his arms bulge. Peter said not a word, but the captain could tell he was locked in some type of spectral fight. The captain watched as Peter's face contorted with rage and his body glowed. He was mesmerized and couldn't take his eyes off Peter. The inner struggle Peter battled was about to come to a head.

Peter then shot straight up with his fists in the air, ready to strike at the unseen enemy. The captain intercepted the boy before he lashed out. Peter swung and almost connected with the captain, who just barely ducked. He wrapped his hands around Peter and told him it was okay. At first, Peter struggled mightily, and the captain couldn't believe the boy's strength. He let go of Peter and the boy turned to him, waking up now, seeming to recognize him.

Peter's eyes blinked. "Captain? Where the heck am I?"

The captain came forward. "Peter, it's okay. We're at the military base in Antarctica."

"Yes, the base, of course! Sorry, Captain, I seem to be a little out of it right now. I must have been having a dream," stated Peter.

Captain Pace patted him on the back and told him it was okay. Being in a new place usually did that to soldiers until they acclimated to their surroundings. Peter just nodded and got up, taking a quick walk around the room before settling down on his cot. He could feel the exhaustion in his bones and lay back with his hands behind his head. A part of him wanted to spill the beans about what he just tried to accomplish, but he wasn't sure just yet how the captain would handle this type of use of his powers.

He couldn't help but think of Alex in that moment and trying to figure out his grandfather's journal. So many questions but the encounter tonight exhausted him and he could barely keep his eyes open. Turning to see Jake sleeping, he allowed sleep to come to him. Tomorrow would be an epic day. Would he find his way to the city and could he enter the city?

Chapter 43

The young officer returned to check on Holly and brought a doctor with him. After a few minutes, the doctor smiled at Holly and told her she was recovering nicely. A sigh of relief came to the general's face and he smiled warmly at Holly, still sitting comfortably in bed. The color now returned to her face and there was a warm glow about her. When the officer was comfortable with Holly's state, he excused himself and left them alone. General Giles sat on the end of Holly's bed, rubbing her hand gently.

Holly looked lovingly at the general but quickly turned her mind to Rebecca. She sent out feelers to see if she could make a connection with Rebecca. Frustration quickly took off as she couldn't find Rebecca no matter how hard she tried. Something was terribly wrong. Even if Rebecca was captured, Holly should be able to locate her and establish a connection. Holly came out of her trance to see the concern on the general's face.

Holly looked up. "I cannot find her, Ryan! I should be able to at least locate her even if she's unconscious. She's in grave danger and I cannot help her from this hospital bed. Ryan, we need to leave and now!"

The general nodded. "I agree, my love, but right now, even though we're being treated as guests, we're still prisoners. I know when healthy, you could obliterate this entire compound but Holly, you just suffered a great injury."

"I know, my love. I know," she conceded.

He looked at her. "Trust me. We'll find her and get her back safely but right now, we need to find out what's going on here. Let me do what I do. We'll make our move when the time is right."

Holly couldn't argue even though she knew they needed to find Rebecca. Trying to escape without finding out where they were and what their enemy was up to wouldn't be wise. Her head still pounded, and she knew the amount of energy expended to find Rebecca took much out of her. She lay back against the propped-up pillow with a grunt of disgust. Looking to the ceiling, she couldn't help but feel useless. As one of the leaders of her people, she was used to things working out the way she planned.

From her bed, she felt the pang of guilt rise within her as she knew Rebecca was out there somewhere by herself. She watched over the young lady her entire life, trying to prepare her for this very moment in time. Rebecca didn't know it yet, but the cosmic events bringing her and Peter together were about to take over. With fate intervening, Holly needed to find her protégé quickly to instruct her once the two met in person. To Rebecca, it just seemed to her that Peter was just an epic love. That may very well be true, but the universe also had other plans for the couple.

Holly shuddered to think that Rebecca still didn't know enough about her powers to be ready to meet Peter. From what she could figure, neither was Peter ready to meet Rebecca as he was completely new to his own powers. Holly knew the boy's grandfather and became aware of the passing of him as well. This concerned Holly as the boy needed to be prepared for his fate as well. For both to survive, they'd need all the help they could get. It was a race against time to find the two and teach them before it was too late.

She could feel the general's calloused hand holding hers and looked up. Smiling, she warmly clenched his hand. Both struggled internally with the same question. How did they get out of here and find Rebecca? Each looked at the other but sat for a moment unable to speak. The general then stood as he saw the young officer return.

He brought some food for Holly and asked the general to accompany him to the next room. When asked why, the officer informed him that his superiors would like to talk to the general. He looked back at Holly who nodded, assuring him she'd be fine. The general agreed and followed the young officer into the next room. Headquarters looked neat and well organized. People were calmly at their stations monitoring their computers while some were talking into microphones.

General Giles settled in front of a large computer screen hung on the wall. In a moment, the screen came to life and the image that came into view was recognizable. The image was of his nemesis Colonel Whilhelm. The general was used to dealing with the colonel but for some reason, this time he was offended seeing the colonel's image before him. Rather than wait for the colonel to say anything, he took the initiative.

He glared at the screen. "Colonel, you have quite the nerve holding us!"

"My dear General, you aren't a prisoner but rather my guest. How much longer you remain my guest depends upon you. I take it Holly is well?"

The general peered up. "She's doing well. I find myself in a precarious position of thanking you for your assistance."

Colonel Whilhelm smiled. "Yes, it's quite the situation. I've faced you numerous times on the battlefield and many times you've bettered me, but this is definitely a new turn of events. I don't believe Holly has ever left the confines of your vaunted city. Something important must be happening for you both to join forces and leave the city together. Care to fill me in?"

"Really there isn't much to tell. Rebecca was feeling rebellious and against our wishes, broke out of the city and got herself into trouble," he stated.

With a raised eyebrow, the colonel continued, "Yes, the lovely Rebecca. Of course, at her age, they think they know it all but my dear general we both know Rebecca leaving was a little more than a temper tantrum."

General Giles answered, "Yes, as you know, it was a little more than that, but it really comes down to her wanting to meet the young man. As you stated at her age, she thinks she knows everything."

With a nod, the colonel responded, "Speaking of the young man. I have to commend you as he continues to allude capture to this point, but I assure you he'll be in custody shortly."

Without changing his expression, he looked at the colonel. The fact that the boys still avoided capture brought him a huge ray of hope. Now, all he needed to do was get Rebecca and bring the boys into the protection of the city, so Rebecca and Peter could train together. In his many dealings with the colonel and his reptilian brethren, they never once seemed to put two and two together where it concerned Peter and Rebecca. They were aware of each other's powers but really didn't understand what will happen when they join forces. If the reptilian people really knew what Rebecca and Peter had in store for them, they'd definitely try harder to capture both together.

"Why don't you just tell me what I want to know so you can remain my guest?" said the colonel.

The general nodded. "As I already stated, Holly was quite upset by her protégé disrespecting her and she wanted to talk to her face to face about it. You know as well as I do, the boy's grandfather did much research on our civilization but even he didn't know how to enter. I know that's what you really want but the only one capable of that is me and me alone. I'll turn myself over to you if you wish, but I ask from soldier to soldier that you allow Holly safe passage back to her homeland."

The colonel's eyes shot up. "Now that's a fine offer, General, but you and I both know I cannot allow neither of you to return to your city. That would be a very poor tactical move on my part. Now that I have the vaunted general in my possession, your defenses are that much weaker."

Again, the general didn't respond but chose to think about his response. What the colonel said was true in terms of strategy. Even with the high confidence in his men, he knew the defense of the city fell to him and while here, he wasn't fulfilling his responsibilities. Leaving his homeland without his expertise bothered him but he trained each of those men and knew their meddle. Once he straightened that out in his head, he looked once again at the colonel.

"Yes, you seem to have me at a disadvantage, but you surely don't think you can overrun my forces," said the general.

"No, but having you in my possession does allow me the one thing that has alluded us and that's a way to enter your city. So, make yourself comfortable and we'll chat again soon."

The monitor went black, leaving the general steaming. He turned quickly, not saying a word to the young officer, and strode back to Holly. Right away, Holly could see the frustration in his eyes and quickly took his hand, diffusing him right away. He sat on the bed, but this time leaned in for a big hug and held her softly for a few moments.

After the embrace, he rose and looked at her. "Enough of this, how are you feeling?"

"My love, now that I'm awake, I can do anything you need me to do. I don't know for how long I could keep it up for, but my powers remain intact. What did you have in mind?"

The general eyed her. "Just follow my lead and be ready."

Without another word, they both just looked at one another, waiting for the right moment to make their move. It didn't take long for the young officer to return. He was apologetic about the discussion with the colonel but the general assured him it was a quite civil conversation. The general informed the young officer that Holly would like to take a walk outside and she was feeling much better. This brought a smile to the young man's face.

He agreed to take them outside with a few guards. This was exactly what the general counted on. The young officer called two other soldiers and Holly followed along with the general until they were outside. The villa's grounds were immaculate and well groomed. Gardens with plush plants and flowers exploded with vibrant colors. Holly could feel the energy of the beautiful nature surrounding her rejuvenating her each moment she remained.

She found a wooden bench nearest to the garden to sit and take in the pungent fragrances. The garden was teeming with life and a chipmunk came from out of nowhere and joined Holly on her lap. Holly laid her hand on her lap, so the small creature could enter her palm. The small animal sat in her palm, felt her power, and shuddered. He looked quickly at Holly and then scooted off. She felt alive and comfortable in this wonderful place. In another time, she'd feel grateful to share in this beauty but while Rebecca was missing, she couldn't let herself be swayed.

The soldiers flanked each of her sides and they didn't notice she was building her power. Using the very beautiful nature around her to help, she made the vines grow at an alarming rate. The two soldiers didn't know what happened to them until the vines wrapped around their mouths, rendering them harmless. Holly allowed the vines to confine the men without harming them. She knew they were only following orders and had no wish to hurt her.

The general's questions about the villa and the surrounding grounds occupied the young officer. He didn't even notice the missing soldiers. For that matter, few would notice the frozen soldiers stuck in the vines as they blended into the background of the garden. General Giles took his cue and grabbed the soldier's side arm swiftly and pointed it directly at the man's head. A look of panic filled the young officer's face. The general apologized and told him under other circumstances, he'd love to chat about this beautiful place. He offered an excuse that Holly was worse off than they knew, and she must return home for proper treatment.

Holly followed as they worked their way out of the garden, trying to keep from being noticed. The general informed the soldier he'd be going with them until he felt it safe to release him. The soldier was more than willing to help and in spite of his situation, he brought them right to a jeep in the front of the villa. The general could see soldiers in the guard towers, but everyone recognized the young officer, and no one questioned him. They all got into the jeep without incident.

The young officer offered them council as to the best route for escape. They actually left the base the way they came in and the officer recommended they go to the dock for safe passage home. Once at the docks, they could find an American submarine that would take them home. The general thought of taking the soldier with them, but he felt his help earned him a reprieve and he let him go. The jeep he disabled first but he knew the soldier could get transport back to base once they were on their way home.

Holly and the general boarded the submarine with little fanfare. The general checked in with the commanding officers and alerted them to their current plight. The officers assured the general they'd have little difficulty returning them to a base close enough for them to return to their home. They made their way to their quarters and turned in for the evening. Both exhausted but knowing they needed to locate Rebecca and get her safely home as well. They just held each other's hands as sleep took them.

The young officer, meanwhile, placed a small tracking device on the sub to add to the one he already slipped onto Holly's dress and walked away. He quickly found transportation back to base and hopped in, smiling the entire time. While on the way back to base, he talked into the watch on his arm. In an instant, an image appeared—Colonel Whilhelm.

The colonel looked pleased with himself. "Did they buy it?"

The young officer looked back. "Yes, sir! They have no idea."

"Good, now that you put the tracking device on them, we can follow them into the city. We don't even need them to open it for us. We'll walk right in when they do. Good work, soldier!"

Chapter 44

Rebecca's eyes felt extremely heavy as she struggled to open them enough to see what lay in front of her. The light that snuck into her head hurt and felt like a thousand needles piercing her brain. She shut her eyes and waited for the pain to subside. When she was more comfortable, she tried. This time she blinked repeatedly until her eyes became used to the light. Now that she could make out images, she realized she was in a small bed. What was surprising was the view.

Turning slightly, she could see a clear wall looking directly out into the open ocean. Now that her eyes could focus, she could see the beauty of the underwater landscape. Because of the curvature of the glass, the passing sea life seemed magnified and she could see lights off to her right. Her curiosity won out and she was intrigued as the lights came closer. Within a few minutes, she could make out small dwellings and buildings under the water. Rebecca realized she could see an underwater city.

Where was she and what was going on were the only questions popping into her head at the moment. As the small craft came to a halt in front of a large underwater building, she could feel something large grab a hold of the craft. Once the craft docked, she could feel the engines stop but still, she could see no sign of life. Lights now seemed to be everywhere in the city. Except for the fact that the city was underwater, it didn't seem all that different from her own.

The similarity in architecture and design intrigued her even more. She was anxious to speak to her host about their whereabouts. Still to this point she remained alone. With great energy, she tried to lift her legs. At first, they refused to cooperate. Again, she willed them to move and this time they responded. She swung her legs over the side of the bed but didn't trust them to hold her up since their lack of response. Rebecca hung on the edge of her bed, trying to decide what the best course of action would be. If she fell onto the floor, could she rise again?

Just as she was about to try to leave the comfort of her bed, the door to her quarters opened to reveal a person entering. Rebecca's face brightened for a moment until she got a good look at the person. At first glance, the person looked exactly like Holly, but a closer review revealed slight differences. Still, Rebecca almost greeted her as Holly. The woman saw Rebecca's response and nearly laughed. She instead walked up to Rebecca and grasped her hand gently. She held Rebecca's hand softly and smiled at her in the way a family member would.

A glance into the strange woman's eyes revealed the similar crackle of energy Rebecca's own would show before releasing her power. The dancing energy seemed warm and friendly, which made Rebecca's anxiety melt away. Now that her nerves were calmed, she felt her courage return and knew the question needed to be asked.

Rebecca paused and then asked, "Please excuse my apprehension. It's just, you remind me of someone dear to me."

Rather than scowl, again the woman smiled. "Yes, Rebecca, I'd hope I remind you of my sister Holly!"

"Your sister! How is that possible? Holly's only sister Grace perished at sea long ago!"

Again, the woman laughed. "That, my dear, is partly true. I was in fact lost at sea many years ago when you were but just a babe. I'll tell you all about it someday but right now we have little time for family reunions. We're all in grave danger. The invasion my sister feared is coming and if we're unprepared, everyone will be destroyed!"

"Okay, keep you secrets right now but tell me this, does your sister know you're alive?"

With a deep frown, Grace looked up. "No, my dear one. That's also another long story and also for another day. Rest assured though, there isn't a minute that goes by every day that I don't think of my lovely sister."

Rebecca's anger rose, and Grace looked into her eyes. With a look of understanding, Grace reached forward and rubbed her shoulders. Then the woman did something unexpected as she pulled Rebecca close to her in a full-on hug. At first, Rebecca wanted to pull away but within moments, she could once again feel her anxiety lift. Rebecca shot back, looking at her estranged aunt with questioning eyes.

Grace smiled gently. "I'm an empath. I can feel one's pain and help relieve it by taking it into myself. Part of the reason I'm here is the need to learn control of my gift. Rebecca, there will come a time in the not so distant future where rebuilding mankind will require my gifts."

Rebecca couldn't help but choke. "Rebuilding mankind?"

"My dear one, darkness is coming, and it will change the world as we know it. Even if we're victorious, nothing will ever be the same. There's so much I need to show and explain to you but for now, just know fate definitely brought you to me."

Both women sat looking into one another's eyes, trying to take measure of the other. The amount of energy bouncing back and forth between the two was enough to power the entire city. Rebecca was first to allow herself to relax and leaned back, taking in her would-be aunt. The resemblance was uncanny and there was little doubt this was her flesh and blood. She searched her aunt's thoughts and couldn't see everything, but a few memories her aunt let her.

A scene of two small girls racing after one another along a rocky path came forth into Rebecca's head. She could see both girls were mirror images of one another. The two seemed close and were genuinely having fun with one another. The entire scene changed in an instant when one girl slipped on the rocks and went over the edge. A panic-stricken Grace threw herself on the ground, looking over the edge. To her great relief, her sister Holly fell only a few feet down onto another ledge, but it was quite evident something wasn't right. Grace scrambled down to her sister to assess the damage. Holly sat scared with blood streaming from an open wound on her leg. Grace ran to her sister, comforting her. Both girls embraced, and Rebecca could see Holly's leg heal.

Holly looked at Grace with great surprise. Grace told Holly not to tell anyone; as far as everyone was concerned, she didn't have any powers. Holly couldn't understand why Grace would hide such a wonderful gift. Grace just explained most of the council just cared about powers that could help with the defense of the city. Holly told her that was nonsense and praised her for such a beautiful gift. Grace grabbed her sister and embraced her for what seemed to be forever. The vision faded and left Rebecca staring at her aunt with deep affection.

She shared with her aunt some of her own struggles as a young girl trying to come to grips with her own power. Telling her aunt about Holly training her got a rise out of Grace. Grace just nodded and listened intently without interrupting. When Rebecca finished, she stood assisted by the wall and leaned slightly for balance. Grace shot up to provide stability and took her niece's arm for support. Leading the way slowly until Rebecca's leg strength returned, she took her onto a platform leading to a much larger door. Grace didn't touch anything but sent out more energy and the door sprung to life opening.

Rebecca, now moving under her own power, followed her aunt slowly, taking in the sights of the underwater city. The lights, although not natural, offered a soft glow. She could feel a soft breeze coming from some unseen place. What really took her by surprise was how much this city resembled her own. As she continued to look, her mind told her there was no way this city wasn't built by her own people at some point.

Grace could see her mind racing and confirmed her suspicions that the founders of her own city made this one. Grace explained that long ago, something happened between the two cities and they became estranged from one another. She assured Rebecca that the two cities would be needed in the defense of humanity. Rebecca just went with the cautious explanation but knew there must be something else to the fact she never heard anything about this lost city.

Both ladies remained silent throughout the rest of their journey. Rebecca looked up in awe as they entered a huge domed area in which plants of all kinds grew. She could feel moisture in the air and cherished the freshness. The ceiling was made up of triangular pieces of metal and glass. She could once again see into the beautiful underwater scenery. Her eyes shot from plant to plant, hoping to recognize them. To her great relief, she did in fact recognize most of the plants but there were more than a few that seemed strange to her.

Grace noticed this and informed her that plants from all over grew here and yes, there were a few that didn't grow in Rebecca's city. With a wave of her hand, Grace motioned Rebecca to follow her. Before she could, Rebecca noticed a small animal scamper under her legs and into the safety of a large flowering plant. Rebecca giggled, which brought a smile to

Grace's own face. The two now walked into a long tube-like hallway made of clear glass. Again, Rebecca could see the area teeming with underwater life and off to her left, she noticed a large reef. They then entered another large domed room but this time, it looked more like a training facility.

Rebecca halted to monitor as two combatants were locked in a hand-to-hand struggle. A quick scan of the room showed training of all kinds taking place, but most seemed of the physical nature. Grace smiled and told her they'd be spending plenty of time here training, but she wanted Rebecca to see a special place. Rebecca's pace quickened with great curiosity. Grace was quite tall like Holly and moved very quickly. Rebecca maintained the pace but could feel exhaustion creeping into her muscles. They entered another large room not a moment too soon, as her legs buckled.

Grace led her to a large, soft chair and asked her to sit. She grabbed a chair of her own and joined Rebecca. Catching her breath, Rebecca let her eyes scan the room. Grace informed her this was known as the sanctuary and this was where most lessons would be taught. She noticed the great stacks of books lining the walls and comfortable lighting with warm tables to sit and learn. The room remained quiet and the air seemed unmoving as Rebecca took in the learning environment. Right now, only a few learners were seated who didn't even notice them. With a smile, she sat back in the chair and thought of how happy she could be in such a magnificent place.

Reality swarmed back into her mind. As beautiful as this lost city was, she needed to get to Peter. Her heart skipped a beat as she thought of him and her determination to find him almost overwhelmed her. Pangs of guilt swept through her as she realized her aunt could help her learn to control her power, but at the same time, she was kept away from her love. Also, the whereabouts of Holly and General Giles remained at the forefront of her mind. She couldn't leave them in their time of need. Grace could sense her apprehension and assured her they'd do all they could to help her friends. This news calmed her slightly but the uncertainty surrounding Peter's whereabouts and freedom was too much for her to bear.

Her mind searched for Peter only to see a shocking scene. He materialized in a type of battle with a reptilian creature. A closer look revealed the creature Peter was locked in combat with looked much like a human except for the blood-red eyes and huge fangs threatening to chomp on him. The two figures grappled with each other and Rebecca couldn't help but root for Peter.

Peter seemed to grow before her eyes and she noticed his own fury feeding his strength. The fight surprised the reptilian figure this human directed. After a few more minutes of wrestling and throwing each other to the ground, no one seemed to have a clear advantage. Both enemies stood stalking one another when Rebecca observed Peter's anger continuing to build. Peter then let out a wail and smashed the reptilian figure with a blast of energy. The figure went sprawling to the floor unmoving.

Peter's face peered up to see other reptilian figures rushing toward him. Rebecca almost ran to Peter until his image faded away. She stood watching the exasperated faces of the reptilian soldiers as they went to tend to their fallen comrade. The figure on the floor stirred and threw the groping hands away from him as he rose unassisted. His blood-red eyes now glowed, and the image wavered as she saw the figure now turning back to a more reptilian form.

Rage showed in his face. "How dare he challenge me! I'll see him and all he loves destroyed! Mark my words, that young man won't survive what's to come next. All of you, get back to your stations. I'll have a nice conversation with the colonel now. This little imp invaded my realm. One of you, go find my science officer and tell him to report to me. I want to know how this is possible. This boy shouldn't be able to break into this realm!"

The soldiers scrambled to comply and all saluted while practically running into one another, trying to get out of the room. Commander Zosa looked disgusted at these little stooges as they ran around. Soon, when the field was lowered for good, he'd train real soldiers, and no one would ever challenge him again. What they all needed was combat experience. Many of these soldiers would be considered fat cats with little actual combat experience. The time to push the envelope was now on the horizon and he'd have the army he needed.

Chapter 45

Peter worked up his courage all day to prepare himself for his confrontation with this dreaded enemy. As he let himself fall into a fast slumber, the image of an imprisoned Rebecca fueled his rage. As soon as his eyes closed, he searched out his enemy through the miles of open space. At first, all he could pick up was a few images of other important reptilian soldiers scrambling around, following orders of their superiors. He calmed his mind, causing him to focus more on his target. Within a few moments, another image came into view.

High Commander Zosa sat at a desk cluttered with random papers and folders everywhere. Peter could tell the commander didn't know he was being spied upon. The figure's huge shoulders painted an intimidating image. Arms hulking to the sides upon the desk the commander looked ready to spring at any threat. Scanning the room, Peter saw just one exit, a plain door at the front of the room. He swept over to the door and using his energy, locked the door silently. When satisfied that his enemy couldn't escape easily, he turned to face the reptilian being.

What shocked Peter was how much this creature resembled a regular human being. Gone were the customary scales, and the bone structure was now identical to his own. He couldn't help but catch a glimpse of the creature's eyes, which were bright red at this point. Peter found himself stepping closer as the last time his eyes were laid upon this creature, he looked much different. He couldn't help but wonder what form this creature took naturally. Was this his original form or was the entire reptilian form the norm.

At that moment, the commander rose from his chair, turning to face Peter, who was taken aback, coming face to face with his enemy. Commander Zosa was a tall, rugged man and his muscles appeared tight under his immaculate uniform. Peter said nothing at first while the commander rose to his full height, looking down slightly on him. Both figures seemed to be calculating their next move.

The commander broke the silence, "Well met, my young friend. I see your power is growing by leaps and bounds. What brings you to me now? Don't you have a damsel to rescue?"

"I'm here for you!" Peter growled.

A surprised look came across the commander's face. "So it would seem. Now that you're here, what are your intentions?"

Rather than answer, Peter could feel the rage boil over inside him and he reached for it, focusing it on the commander. His reptilian enemy seemed quite surprised as he took the first blow, unsuspecting to his midsection. Both men crashed to the floor and Peter spun, hopping up to finish off his enemy. Commander Zosa couldn't remember the last time anyone challenged him in combat. He rose to face his attacker, this time with caution.

He smirked. "My boy, you certainly have grown. I commend you on your training. It isn't often I'm challenged. You have my respect but don't think for one second your attack can stand."

Again, Peter lashed out, this time grappling with the military veteran which may have been a miscalculation. The commander easily tossed him into the wall. The air whooshed from Peter's lungs and he struggled to get to his knees. He looked up just in time to see a boot sailing toward his head.

Peter fell to the ground to avoid the large boot and used his arms to push himself back to a standing position. Again, the commander looked surprised while preparing to strike. With another kick forward, the commander caught the young man in the midsection, forcing him back a few feet.

Peter rushed forward grabbing the commander's arm while twisting at the same time. The reptilian cried in anguish and returned a blow of his own to Peter's chest. The blow glanced off his chest and Peter plowed into his enemy, causing them both to the ground. When they faced each other, both wore the scars of their battle. Peter's nose leaked blood while his nemesis showed signs of struggle with cuts and bruises on his face. It was plain to see the commander wasn't used to being challenged for supremacy.

Both combatants again circled one another, and the anger grew amongst each as the seconds passed. It was Peter's anger that brewed over first and he let his anger fuel his power. He could feel the energy rush to every part of his body before releasing it. Peter directed all his angst toward the reptilian commander. A large blast of energy travelled across the room and struck the unsuspecting commander full on in the chest. The impact sent the commander sailing across the room and left him unmoving on the floor.

Peter looked down at his shaking hands and then to his fallen enemy. He took one step forward to finish his enemy, only to see the door burst open and in flooded in other soldiers. Feeling exhaustion grip his body, he knew he couldn't face this many attackers at this moment. He decided to retreat for now, knowing he could return to finish the job at another time. Peter could feel the images waver as he felt himself returning to his sleeping body.

He shot up in his bed, shivering and panting, only to see Jake staring at him with concern. Peter's eyes needed a moment to focus and then he saw Jake more clearly. His friend was in the bed with him asking if he was all right. It took a moment to gain his bearings, but he reached up and patted Jake's shoulder to acknowledge he was all right. He rose from his cot, only to feel a shiver of cold run down his spine and for the first time, he noticed he was covered in sweat. Captain Pace steadied him and looked concerned. Peter just reassured him he was all right. He grabbed a towel hanging on a nearby rack and wiped his face.

Once the towel left his face, he turned to look at Jake who was now getting dressed. The captain told the boys he'd be right back as he wanted to check in with Alex and the officer in charge. He left briskly through the front door, leaving the two boys alone. Jake watched the captain leave before turning to address the unsaid questions hanging in the air.

He looked at Peter. "Dude, what the hell was that?"

"I told you I was done letting others dictate my fate! I just let our enemy know he isn't the only one with power."

Jake's eyebrows rose. "Really! Tell me!"

"It's simple. I used all the knowledge I've gained during this journey to send a message to our enemies. I snuck into our enemy's office and attacked him!"

"You did! How did it go?" Jake looked interested.

Peter gathered himself. "We fought, and I put him down! Not permanently as I was interrupted, but there will be another time in which I'll finish my task. Although I know I was successful only because of the element of surprise, I have a feeling our next encounter will be much bloodier!"

Both boys sat on the cot staring at one another. Jake caught Peter up on the events of the last evening. Peter was very interested in having a spy working for his trio. While waiting for the captain's return, they went back and forth, talking about what Alex could do to help them in deciphering the journal. Jake's face brightened as he wanted to see how the journal could help them just as much as Peter.

Captain Pace sauntered into the room with a large smile on his face. He crossed the room and picked up a small backpack from his own cot. He opened the backpack to check its contents and when satisfied the things he needed were there, he closed it once again. Slinging the pack onto his shoulder, he motioned the boys to follow. Peter and Jake followed suit, grabbing their own backpacks, falling in behind the captain. The captain led them into the hallway and deftly brought them to a large conference room.

Peter smiled as his eyes met those of an excited Alex, who now rose to greet his guests. The captain told Peter he would spend most of the morning with Alex looking at the journal. He went on to explain for them to see what they could do in here for now. This was a secure location. The captain further explained that if they needed anything further, they could work in the library in the afternoon. He alerted Peter that the library was a pretty open space, so they needed to secure it first before working there.

Alex thanked the captain and sent him on his way, shoving him out the door. Peter couldn't help but laugh while telling the captain he'd be fine Alex's watchful eye. With a nod, the captain left the room and waited for Jake out in the hall. Jake seemed conflicted with whom to stay but he could see Peter was already sitting at the large conference table and taking out the journal. He knew he'd be little use in this part of the journey so decided to see if he could assist the captain.

300

Chapter 46

Alex clasped Peter's hand and offered a huge smile that seemed to engulf his face. He motioned Peter to sit next to him. Peter complied and took his seat, looking at the excited old man. He sat for a moment not knowing exactly how to begin. His journey was filled with danger and evil around every corner. Something kept nagging him not to say too much to Alex, but it was so hard not to feel comfortable around the man. Alex could sense the trepidation and reached for his hand, nodding to comfort Peter.

Alex took that as his cue and he began, "Peter, I get it, trust me! This whole situation is beyond belief. Everything you grew up believing is about to change. Your view of the world and, for that matter the universe, will now change for you forever. I'm just sorry your grandfather isn't the one explaining it to you."

At the mention of his grandfather, he welled up. "My grandfather really told me nothing of this. Anything I know I actually figured out on my own and I'm woefully unprepared for all of this coming my way!"

"My boy! You've come to the right place. Together, you and I will finish your grandfather's work," said the old man.

"Alex, where do we even begin? I know nothing about this supposed ancient civilization!"

"Fear not, Peter. I know quite a bit, and something tells me you know a lot more than you think." Alex smiled.

For the next few minutes, he shared with Peter the general sense of what his work at the naval station was for the last twenty years. Peter was astonished to learn Alex all but knew where the secret entrance lay. He couldn't believe the amount of research and information the old man had at his disposal. As Alex laid out all of his own information before Peter, things made more sense.

Peter sat motionless for a few minutes, trying to process the amount of information Alex shared with him. Even still, with all this information, Alex said little about his grandfather. For someone who was supposed to be close to his grandfather, one would expect more stories. Again, Alex seemed to sense his thoughts and again smiled warmly. Alex shook his head and actually laughed.

Alex looked up at Peter. "You're just like your grandfather! The same mannerisms and facial expressions. I'd love to talk about your grandfather all day but in light of all that has transpired, I feel we may have to wait."

This seemed to make sense and Peter felt embarrassed for his trepidation toward Alex. After that, he felt more comfortable for he knew Alex to be absolutely correct when it related to his grandfather. He recalled one day his grandfather caught him trying to sneak out to play football with Jake before his homework was complete. His grandfather went on to lecture him about when it was time to work, work, but when it was time to play, play. He laughed inwardly as here was Alex basically saying the same thing.

Knowing so much was at stake, he refocused his efforts and listened as Alex laid out his plan for Peter's journal. Again, Peter was surprised to find out how much Alex knew about the journal and he even asked if Peter found the message yet. Peter didn't know what to say and just nodded. The old man continued to describe many of the conversations that took place between himself and the boy's grandfather regarding the journal.

When Alex was finished, Peter just looked stunned. He knew of the importance of the journal from the first moment he laid eyes on it. Now it was actually time to use the journal and he felt ill prepared to assist Alex. Here was this man who spent a lifetime preparing for this moment and Peter knew nothing that could help. Frustration seeped in along with anger. He stood and paced around the room. After a few moments, he stopped and leaned on his chair, looking at Alex.

He started, "Alex, this is crazy. I have no idea how to help you! The only reason I'm really here is Jake and his family knew what I was supposed to do. Me, however, I'm clueless. Without Jake and his family, I'd have been captured long ago."

"I feel for you, my boy! I really do, but let's not focus on that right now," said Alex.

He instead asked if he could see the journal. At first, Peter didn't move but he glanced around the room to make sure they were alone. When satisfied no one else could see, he reached into his backpack and produced the precious journal. At that moment, Alex's eyes sparkled as he rose, taking the journal gingerly in his hands, holding it with reverence. As soon as Peter saw how Alex handled the journal, he knew everything would be all right.

Alex carefully placed the journal down on the table and longingly ran his hand across the carefully crafted cover. Peter couldn't help but feel a small amount of jealousy rise in him as the old man handled the journal. This feeling quickly dissipated as Alex carefully handed the journal back to Peter. He instructed Peter never to let the book out of his sight or to let anyone else handle it again, including him. This surprised Peter, but he could see the serious look in Alex's eyes. He placed the journal in front of himself and he ran his own hand against the starburst cross slowly.

Without looking up, he blurted out, "Alex, what's the significance of the starburst pattern?"

The old man nonchalantly shrugged. "Don't you know? Think for a minute. Search your mind."

Peter felt frustrated, but he remembered his grandfather doing exercises of this nature with him. Rather than get mad, he sat back in his chair and cleared his mind. He let the image of the starburst flow into his mind. At first, all he could see was pure blinding light but after a few moments, the images of constellations filled his view. As his mind went to each constellation, it connected the dots and each constellation resembled one of the symbols on the journal.

He bolted up from the chair and nearly jumped out of his skin. Alex rose to comfort him, but he waved the old man off and sat back down on his own. He carefully reached into his backpack and brought forth all the letters and spread them onto the table. With kidlike excitement, he poured over all the letters, looking at the symbols. Peter leafed through the journal doing the very same. He felt a mixture of excitement and pride build up within himself. Although, a small amount of sadness crept in as a result of being unable to share this discovery with his grandfather.

At that moment, however, he just happened to look up and see Alex's face. The pride made Peter feel warm inside. Alex rose and came over to him, offering his hand. Peter also rose, meeting the old man halfway and shook his hand vigorously. The two exchanged the handshake for a few moments and then released, looking at one another. Each seemed too excited to speak just trying to capture the gravity of the moment.

Alex started first, "Well, now that you understand what we have to do, we need to get to work. Knowing what to do is great but still there remains the puzzle of putting the pieces together."

"I know but still, it's so exciting to visualize what my ancestors left for me!"

Alex smiled. "I'm excited for you!"

Peter then grabbed a legal pad from his backpack and scoured the first pages of the journal, writing each of the symbols in the exact order they appeared. Once the first page was written, he took out one of his astronomy books he managed to grab on his way out the door. With his head down, he went to work matching each of the constellations with the symbols in the book. When the first page was complete, he looked up at Alex and was at a loss. They were definitely on to something but right now, all he had was symbols matched up with constellations. He realized he still didn't have any way of reading the symbols.

He leaned back and let out a growl. "Another puzzle! Why can't they just say this is where x marks the spot and call it a day?"

Alex smiled. "Peter, it may not seem like much but what you figured out in five minutes, took me over ten years. All we need now is the key."

As if hit by lightning, Peter stood. "The key, that's me!"

"What are you talking about, Peter?"

"Everyone keeps referring to me as the key to everything. I still don't know what that means but it definitely has something to do with me," Peter said.

Once again, the two sat looking at one another, trying to figure out what to do next. Alex suggested they take a break and reconvene in the library after lunch. He told Peter he wanted to grab some more of his notes on the constellations. Peter told Alex he'd continue to read over his own notes and they'd meet up after he got a bite to eat. The old man stood up using both arms and placed a hand on Peter's shoulder with a confident look. Peter knew they were close. The look Alex gave him made him feel as though together, they could crack this code.

Peter watched as Alex strode from the room with a new spring in his step. The new energy in the old man was quite evident and this made Peter feel very good. He sat unmoving for a few minutes with all the notes and papers still strewn about the table. Then he got a cold feeling and his skin became riddled with goosebumps. He put all the papers, including the journal, in his backpack and left the room. Turning to see he wasn't followed, he shut the door behind him and proceeded down the hall toward HQ.

Practically running, he burst into HQ to find Jake and Captain Pace deep in conversation. He could tell by the seriousness of their facial expressions, something wasn't right. Without disturbing his friends, he took a seat just to the right of them. The conversation was quite animated and neither of his friends noticed him. He tried to pick up the gist of the conversation but only caught bits and pieces. He did hear something about an imminent invasion. This piqued his interest and he tried to lean closer.

Jake's face met his and all conversation screeched to a halt. Jake came over swiftly to his friend asked him for an update. Peter caught his friend up on what he and Alex discovered. Jake seemed very relieved but wouldn't reveal any of the conversation he and the captain just were involved in. Jake told him they'd talk later but said he was famished and wanted lunch. Both boys asked for permission to go to lunch and once granted, they sprinted to the mess hall.

Chapter 47

Hurrying back to his room, Alex couldn't help but feel a jolt of excitement. He spent the better part of the last ten years figuring out the runes and language. With Peter's breakthrough, he knew they'd both crack the code and enter the ancient civilization. Would they get there first? Alex was very aware of their enemy's constant attacks to break into the city. Even with all the technology to protect the civilization, Alex realized their approach was a much safer one.

When in his room, he closed the door tightly and checked to see if anyone was hiding. He then went into his closet where a metal air grate was part of the wall to allow airflow. He pried the grate loose and reached inside, taking out his notes and own journals. Once standing, he looked at the last twenty years of his life caressed in his arms. The time now approached where his work would pay off and none too soon. A pain shot down his left arm and his breathing became labored.

He sat for a moment until his heartrate slowed became more regular. When he felt better, he rose and placed all the items into the backpack. He spun around to make sure nothing of importance was left behind. Alex grabbed the door handle and walked toward the library. Quickly moving through the halls, he whisked into the library with excitement brimming over. He walked to a secluded corner of the library with plenty of tall bookshelves and no other tables nearby.

Once comfortably seated, he leaned back in his chair and stretched. With a clear head, he thought about the constellations and how they could be a language all to themselves. He was astounded how Peter figured out the connection. Now, the two needed to crack the code. They definitely could work on the language here, but Alex knew if they were to crack the code completely, they'd need to be onsite. He decided now would be the time to come clean.

Peter found him sitting quietly in the back of the library. Captain Pace wasn't kidding when he said they'd clear the library. The air was a little stale and the only sound he could hear was his own footsteps hitting the floor. The library itself wasn't the typical structure of dark wood but a more sanitary and military feel to it. The bookshelves were made of grey-covered metal and the floor a high-polished tile. The tile made Peter's footsteps echo as he tried to find Alex.

He worked his way to the back and snaked through the maze of bookshelves until he found the old man sitting at a table pouring over notes. Alex looked up with a brilliant smile and motioned him to sit. Peter pulled up a chair right next to Alex and took out his notes also. The two shared their thoughts as to what the constellations could mean. Bantering back and forth, they decided each symbol may not be a language but a code in the sense of numbers. Peter felt each constellation was a certain number and then all they needed to do was figure out the number. Alex still thought they stood for words and this left them both at a standstill.

They worked well into the afternoon, scribbling on their notebooks, trying to break the code. Alex stopped them and suggested they make their way out to the site. He told Peter if he saw the actual site and runes, they might have better luck. Peter thought this sounded like terrific advice; besides, since his arrival, he spent all his time inside. They spent about another hour reviewing and sharing one another's notes before breaking for the evening.

Alex rose and stretched, telling Peter he'd take him to the site in the morning. He spent a few minutes telling Peter how to dress and what to bring with him. Peter was grateful to the old man for his confidence and guidance. As he walked back to his room, he glanced down at the list of supplies Alex suggested, most of which were warm clothing. Excitement gripped him as he turned the corner to his room. He walked into the room, expecting to see Jake and the captain. To his surprise, his friends were no place to be found and he plopped down on his bunk to rest a moment.

He closed his eyes only to see a new vision. The image of a tall, stoic woman came into his mind. She was an elegant, strong woman and Peter recalled her briefly when he searched for Rebecca. Peter tried to speak but the woman raised her hand. She walked closer and whispered to him. At first, he couldn't hear anything she said until the words washed over him quietly.

"I'm Holly. You may remember me as Rebecca's companion. Peter, I only have a few seconds with you before they can track you! Rebecca has been taken by someone and we're searching for her as we speak. Be comforted by the fact I won't rest until she's back with me. I know this is frustrating for you to be so close but yet so far away. Please know I'm proud of the journey you've accomplished. Many lesser men would've been thwarted by now," she said, smiling.

Peter started, "Holly, you must find her! Something tells me I cannot finish my mission to enter the city without her."

Holly nodded. "Peter, you have everything you need to enter. You and you alone may enter. All you need is in you!"

"Holly, what do the constellations mean?"

Holly's eyebrows raised. "Peter, I'd love to help but if someone else is listening to this conversation, I cannot share much with you. Sorry."

Peter looked confused. "Holly, what if I cannot figure it out?"

"My dear boy, look at how far you've come. Do you really believe you won't go the last mile? No, my boy, you'll triumph, and we'll be waiting to embrace you! I have to go for now but remember all you need resides inside of you."

The image wavered and disappeared, leaving him to his thoughts. Once again, he was left with more questions than answers. How was he supposed to get into the city without the proper key? There was that word again and he thought about his revelation earlier, that he himself was the key. The runes were just meant to send people in the wrong direction. That couldn't be it though; the notes and journal had the runes all over it. He wrestled with the images of the runes until he was shaken awake.

Peter struggled to open his eyes and through a crack, he saw a distorted image of Jake looking down at him. He rubbed his eyes and focused more on his friend. With an effort, he propped himself up to talk to his friend. A serious face now subdued Jake's normal, boisterous nature. Peter sat up to take in his friend and he could tell something was off.

Jake sat on his bed and his lips curled. "Dude, listen, I know things are crazy and you're doing all you can to get into the city, but we need to do it like now!"

"What are you talking about, Jake? I just got here. I'm going to the site tomorrow."

Jake's expression worsened. "Man, I just spent all day with the captain in HQ. The enemy is on the move and they're bringing the big guns this time. It's literally a race against time now!"

"Jake, I can't very well go there in the middle of the night! Do you know how cold it is out there right now? I'll go at first light."

Again, Jake looked pleadingly at his friend but nodded. He went on to tell Peter about all the happenings of the day. Peter was shocked to learn about the buildup of military might on its way. It seemed to Peter that he was in serious danger of not finishing his task. The more Jake spoke of what the enemy now was moving their way, the more he knew why Jake was so freaked out. The captain showed Jake all the satellite pictures and he alerted Peter to the sheer size of the force.

After Jake briefed him on the total sum of their plight, Peter reevaluated his decision. Jake did tell Peter the force was still a few days off due to the size, but it was travelling quite fast. He looked down at his watch, three o'clock in the morning. Peter stopped Jake and asked where the captain was at that moment. Jake informed him, with everything going on, the captain needed to be in HQ. He told Peter the captain was mobilizing everything he could get his hands on. In the past, they were asked to stand down, but now they were being asked for help.

Peter told Jake to get his stuff ready and they'd go to the mess hall to load up on supplies. Neither of the boys checked in with the captain as they already knew what the answer would be. Once packed, they snuck over to supply and grabbed snow pants, coats, and boots. Jake also picked up goggles and facemasks for each of them. In the mess hall, they could see a few soldiers preparing for their day. They grabbed all they could carry and shoved it into their packs.

Once they were ready, Peter turned and wanted to know what they'd do with Alex but before Jake could answer, Alex came into the mess hall carrying all his gear. The boys couldn't help but smile as the little old man walked across the mess hall, slumped at the weight of his huge pack. When he stood before the boys, Peter couldn't help but reach out and bear-hug the old man. Alex allowed himself to be manhandled but laughed quite jovially.

The three companions stood looking to one another, waiting for the other to list travel options. Alex took control and told the boys he knew what to do and where to go. He did just that and led the boys to a loading dock. Alex brought them to a large vehicle that resembled a large snowmaking machine. He scrambled inside and told the boys to follow. Alex made short work of stowing their gear and they were underway through the now growing light. As the light became more pronounced, they could see the snow-covered landscape reaching out before them.

It took the companions thirty minutes to reach their destination. To the boys, the stark-white landscape didn't look much different from any of what they saw on the way here. Alex told them to get their gear and to make sure their skin was covered; it was still dangerously cold out now. The boys did as instructed, and felt like true soldiers as they walked down the open ramp, out into the hostile environment before them.

Despite the amount of gear they wore that made it difficult to move, the blast of cold air seeped in everywhere. Peter shook as the air went right up his spine, but he had little time to think as Alex was already fifty feet ahead of them. The boys struggled to keep up through the knee-high, newly fallen snow. The air was crisp, with little wind, and early sun. As they caught up to Alex around the corner, they saw the sky blazing with a myriad of beautiful orange, red, and yellow colors rising up to meet them. The site made all of them stop and enjoy the glory of the morning. Alex then urged them on and he then led them down into a crack in the ice.

At first, all Peter could see was walls of sheer ice that looked more like frozen waves rather than sheets of ice. The sunlight seeping onto the walls created a lighting effect one would see from a disco ball. The sparkling lights mesmerized the boys for a moment until Alex pushed them on. All three came to a halt before a large, white wall blocking their way. Peter eyed the wall with suspicion and Alex laughed. He told Peter to touch the wall. Peter did as instructed, and the white wall turned into a shimmering see-through force field. Peter stood in awe, not knowing what to do next.

Chapter 48

Holly and the general travelled through the night, coming closer to their home. The icy terrain made for quick travel and the general already alerted his men that they were coming. His men assured the general things would be ready upon his return. The general was quite upset at the report of the largest force to date marching on the main gate. He told the men what to do and he said he'd come in by one of the lesser known gates.

The general now changed direction slightly and made for a smoother terrain. As the miles sped by, each just felt an anxious energy building inside them, knowing they may have to fight their way into their own home. According to the general's sources, the main gate would be surrounded in a matter of hours. His people were quite sure they could repel another attack but the sheer numbers gathering on their doorstep would make things rather difficult.

General Giles looked out at the frozen land filled with nothingness and hoped Peter would soon find his way to them safely. A panicked thought filled his mind as he recalled the lovely Rebecca. He was filled with remorse at her loss and couldn't understand why Holly didn't go right after her protégé. All Holly would tell him was that she couldn't contact Rebecca, but she got the sense she was safe. The general knew the two ladies shared an uncanny connection with one another, so he let it rest.

Still, he couldn't help but feel very frustrated that he lost the young lady in his care. He wasn't used to losing a member of his crew, let alone a member of his extended family. For the time being, he'd let Holly remain mysterious but when they returned to their home, he'd approach her more on the matter. Now, his main focus was getting them both home safely and defending their home.

He guided the vehicle smoothly over the unblemished ice and snow. As they came closer to the little-known gate, Holly couldn't help but turn to her love and offer a glowing smile. An explosion then rocked the vehicle, causing it to flip over on its side. Holly and General Giles flew across the vehicle, smashing into the wall on the other side. The vehicle slid on the ice until it came to rest on the ledge of a large chasm at the edge of the ice. The wounded vehicle now teetered over the edge, threatening to fall over at any moment.

Stunned, both Holly and the general grabbed one another to make sure each was whole. When they were each satisfied that the other was sound, they scrambled to exit the fallen vehicle. Once outside, they couldn't see anyone or from where they may have been attacked. In all directions, they could see only ice and snow. The general ran back into the vehicle and grabbed their supplies, along with all the weapons he could carry.

When the general was back outside the vehicle, he did something unexpected and pushed the vehicle completely over the edge. He looked to his love and told her this may work in their favor, especially if they were indeed being followed. Holly offered little resistance and followed as the general led them back in the direction of the gate. According to the general, they should make the gate by nightfall. That would be none too soon as the temperature was now rapidly falling and even though they were properly clothed, they didn't want to chance it.

The two trudged through the knee-high snow and ice for a few miles, only to see a few odd-shaped lights before them. They then knew they weren't alone on their quest to enter the gate. Holly knew the gate wasn't far as the sun was now very low in the sky and the light grew dimmer. General Giles pushed ahead and quickened his pace, followed by Holly close behind. As the last remaining light of the sun disappeared in the horizon, they were attacked. Bolts of energy hit the snow around them, spraying ice and snow in every direction.

The general returned fire in the same direction the bolts came from. He and Holly dove behind an outcropping of protruding rocks. The general peered out, struggling in the dim light to see any of their attackers. Again, bolts struck the rocks near their heads, causing shards to cover their shoulders. This time, the general told Holly to stay right there and he'd move around to the other rock to lead them away from her. He crept over to another rock formation a few feet away and looked out.

From his current location, he could now see the shadows of oncoming soldiers. His eyes strained to pick up a small group comprising of six soldiers. The soldiers appeared to be on foot, which made the general feel good if he could dispose of these few. He raised his weapon and unloaded toward the lead soldier. The soldier never saw it coming and took the general's own bolt of energy right in his chest, killing him instantly.

The other soldiers hit the deck, staying low in the snow and ice. Again, the general spied the lead man crawling through the snow and took aim. He blasted the man right between the eyes and then did something completely unexpected. General Giles, feeling frustrated by everything that had befallen them, stood and rushed out at the rest of the soldiers with his weapon raised. He fired as he ran forward, blasting two other soldiers. That was until he was struck in the leg, sending him sprawling to the ground. Snow and ice filled his mouth while he struggled to get himself upright.

Pain from the wound shot up through his body but he was still in rage mode and continued forward, firing as he did so. The two remaining soldiers returned fire, missing as the general was now upon them. With one swift move, the general met the first soldier with a kick to the midsection, dropping the soldier where he stood. The other soldier raised his weapon to fire at close range but was thwarted by a punch to the side of his head. As his head snapped back, the other soldier was up now but couldn't find his weapon in the dark and was forced to face the general in hand-to-hand combat.

Both soldiers circled the general, waiting for him to attack. The general meanwhile used the time to save his energy as he felt his wound drain much-needed blood. The wetness ran down his leg as the stunning cold ripped through his now damaged clothing. He could feel the pins and needles of the shocking cold touching his now exposed skin.

While the closer of the two soldiers lashed out and tried to connect a punch to the general's head, he ducked out of the way. He responded in kind with a punch of his own to the soldier's sternum and dropped the man. The other soldier jumped on his back, pummeling his head. He flipped the man over using his own weight against him. Without waiting for another attack, he turned and faced the soldier rushing him. Thrusting out his open hand, he connected with the man's open throat, crushing his windpipe.

General Giles learned early in his career if his enemy couldn't breathe, they couldn't fight. With only one remaining soldier, he turned to end the attack. From behind the soldier though, he saw another figure appear. Long and lean, the figure came close to the soldier and waved a hand. The soldier lifted off the ground and snapped in half, falling lifeless to the ground. Out of the shadows came Holly.

The general went to meet his love. "My dear, could you not see I have things well in hand?"

"Yes, my love! I see you took good care of our attackers; however, I couldn't let you have all the fun!"

"Holly, that isn't funny! You could have been hurt."

Holly looked lovingly at him. "I was tired of them coming after you. Besides, you, my dear, are hurt. Do you not feel the wound on your leg or the freezing cold gushing onto your exposed skin?"

For the first time, the general strained through the dim light to see blood seeping through his clothing and the torn leg of his pants. Now the pain throbbed, and he looked to his love for help. Holly complied, and touching his wound, she sent a warm flow of energy into the damaged limb. The warmth flowed up his leg and within moments, the pain subsided, and the wound was closed. Holly told him it was only a temporary fix and the tissue was tender. She warned him the wound could reopen so he needed to be careful.

He reached up and cupped her chin with both hands, giving her a passionate kiss. She accepted the gesture and returned the favor with a kiss of her own. When they released one another, the general found a type of duct tape in his pack and wrapped up his leg to protect it from the elements. Once satisfied they could continue, he led the way, asking Holly to follow.

Within the next hour, they found evidence of life. After searching a little more, they followed vehicle tracks in the snow. Because the snow was so white, they could still follow the tracks with the rising sun, until they came to a crack in the ice. The general asked Holly to wait while he searched ahead. The tall, statuesque woman, unhappy with his decision, stayed put. He

319

stealthily walked into the opening in the ice. Within a few minutes, he heard voices and inched forward. From his vantage point, he could see three persons arguing about how to get into the city.

Rather than attack, he ran back to tell Holly what he knew. Holly told him they needed to be cautious and stay out here for now until they knew these people were alone. The general agreed and talked softly to Holly while looking to the horizon as the sun now snuck into view. As the warm light grazed their faces, they both looked longingly into one another's eyes. Many a time, they just wanted to go off on their own and start fresh by themselves, but always duty intervened.

Holding each other's hands, they searched all around them only to see nothing but the desolate, snowy landscape before them. The beautiful, warming sun sparkled on the ice, almost blinding them, until they looked away. They took deep breaths of the cold, crisp air and shut their eyes to enjoy it.

When satisfied they were alone, they turned to one another and discussed a plan to deal with the intruders. They decided the general would go in and immobilize them to find out what they knew. Holly agreed that a small group like this was just a probing to search for other ways into the city. Leading the way, the general once again snuck along the ice wall, careful not to alert the intruders to his presence. Holly, following close behind, could now also hear the argument over how to enter the city.

Both came within view of the intruders and to Holly's surprise, General Giles ran forward, tackling one of the younger people. The surprised young man jumped up to face his attacker while an older man and another younger man spun to face the threat. The general launched himself at the first young man, only to be taken down in a wrestling move. The general freed himself and stood to face the man again.

At this, Holly came into view and saw the trio before her, recognizing them all. Before she could stop her love, both men were interlocked in combat. She could tell the younger man was well versed in hand-to-hand combat, but her man was more seasoned. The younger man threw the general onto the ground but before he could attack again, the other young man came forward with hands raised and a look of rage in his eyes. She tried to cry out, but the words came too late. The other young man let out a scream and a huge bolt of energy came from him, sending the general and Holly souring through the air. They both crashed into the ice wall and were slow to get up.

Chapter 49

Colonel Whilhelm stood on the deck of his own assault vehicle and looked out at the sun rising on the frozen wasteland. He couldn't help but look around him at the sheer size of the force he now led toward his enemy's home. On either side of him, all he could see was a wall of vehicles. Commander Zosa alerted the colonel that General Giles would have to open the door to get in and then they'd breach the city. All reports stated they should arrive at the same time the general would enter the city.

The rumble of the huge vehicle made him feel superior and protected. Pride welled up within him as he thought of overtaking his enemies and finally entering the city, over which so much blood was spilt. News also came in the form of the field keeping the reptilian people prisoner was now all but down. The commander assured him he'd join shortly once the city was breached.

Although, the thought of the reptilian people free to run around everywhere didn't sit too well with him personally. He knew the real nature of these creatures and wasn't too keen on sharing this planet with such murderous creatures. Nonetheless, he peered out at his attack force and knew this time would be different. In the past, he'd led small probing forces only to be repelled time and time again. He definitely learned about the defenses of the city but until this point, he felt uncomfortable attacking with this large of a force.

The commander, with the reptilian people ready to pounce and the size of the force assembled, believed this was the time to attack. Colonel Whilhelm couldn't argue the logic behind this thought as he stood surrounded by metal and soldiers. Looking down at his watch, he tried to determine the time in which the actual attack might take place. According to his scouts, there was nothing between them and the main gate. This was the case most of the time they came up against the main gate, as his enemies always chose to stay cowering behind their magic gate.

This time would be different as they were bringing a secret weapon snuck out of the prison field by the reptilian people. This energy weapon should have little trouble leveling the magic gate. The colonel knew this time his enemy would have no choice but to come out and meet him head on. Excitement built within himself as this time he knew his success was all but assured. A smile crossed his cheeks, giving him an evil look.

The convoy rumbled forward at a furious pace as there was nothing in front of them to slow them. Mile after mile ticked away as they came quickly to their prearranged meeting area. He halted the vehicles a few miles away from the gate and checked in with all his officers, making sure everything was ready. He also called back to headquarters to make sure his air support would be ready and on time.

When satisfied all his plans were in place, he went into the vehicle, so he could report back to the commander. An image of High Commander Zosa came onto the screen and the colonel addressed him. He shared all the information he knew regarding the assault and waited for the commander's response.

The commander's face showed his anger. "Why have you stopped? Our force was rolling, never stop! Get them all going. The last thing we need is to be hit by our enemies like a flock of sitting ducks."

"Yes, sir. Right away! I just wanted to give you an update before the actual engagement began."

"You have, now get going!"

The image blackened, leaving the colonel fuming. He hated dealing with this smug ass. Once the city was taken, however, he could work on taking out this reptilian nuisance. He gave the order to continue forward and within a few minutes, the entire convoy moved forward. Again, the vehicles made their way toward their target and nothing hampered their approach.

As the gate approached, they slowed their speed but continued forward. The colonel gave the order for the first wave to move on the gate. This time, there were no troops yet, but he used all assault vehicles. They unleashed their own energy weapons on the gate, only to have them repelled by the protective shield covering the entrance. Then the Zarillion defenses kicked in and energy weapons appeared from the mountainside.

The Zarillion weapons pounded the colonel's vehicles, scattering them. At that time, the colonel's air support arrived, dropping all kinds of bunker-buster ordinance not on the gate itself but where the energy weapons came up from the mountain. This was a new strategy and paid dividends. The gate itself was impenetrable but the weapons themselves needed free reign. The bunker busters destroyed many of the weapons and created small windows into the mountain.

While the colonel continued to pound the gate with everything he had, the air strikes were very successful. Most of the weapons covering the entrance were now out of commission. The colonel ordered the vehicles to move forward and attack at will. The field still held but now there was little resistance around where the energy weapons once existed. He looked around and expected to see an air attack from his enemies but still nothing.

Then he ordered his troops to attack the breaches where the energy weapons once stood. Soldiers poured out of the vehicles and marched toward the mountainside. The enemy now answered and finally air support arrived, raining down on the exposed soldiers. Only because of the sheer numbers did the soldiers reach the holes left by the bunker busters. They were met by enemy troops and close quarters combat ensued. The colonel now kept a close watch on the air combat above him and then turned his attention to his troops making their way into the craters.

Blood stained the white of the snow-covered mountain. Fighting in the mountain reached a fever pitch. The colonel's soldiers swarmed up the mountain only to be met by enemy troops. The campaign seemed to be at a standstill until a few pockets of German troops broke into the craters and wormed their way inside. The enemy still repelled them, but they couldn't keep more soldiers from coming into the craters. Fighting now took place into the mountain itself and was slow since only small pockets could enter.

A few German soldiers were now inside the mountain but still not close enough to get the gate open. The colonel's idea was to wait for General Giles to show up, but Commander Zosa wanted it done now. The good news was the famous general wasn't there to defend his precious city. Now with a ground and air war, it would only be a matter of time before the gate fell this time. The mountain was now covered in soldiers from both sides and it was very difficult to see who now controlled the mountain.

At this time, the colonel ordered many vehicles to spread out around the mountain and surround it on all sides. He didn't want to leave anything to chance as he knew there were other ways to get into the mountain besides the main gate. While the soldiers continued their assault, and moved forward up the mountain, the colonel once again smiled. The battle went just as he planned. It seemed that the tide of battle would continue in his favor when huge bombers appeared overhead and bombed the colonel's front lines.

The bombs were devastating, and the entire front of the colonel's force was decimated in minutes. At this, the colonel's mood changed all at once and what seemed to be certain victory was now on the ropes. Again, his air support came to the rescue and ran the bombers off, but they served their purpose, making a mess of the colonel's front. He countered by moving more of his force up and concentrating fire on the main gate to probe for weaknesses. He ordered bunker busters to hit the sides of the gate rather than the actual gate itself. Hitting actual rock did have some effect but the shield still held.

A voice came over the intercom, "Sir, we're in!"

That was music to the colonel's ears. Years in the making, this moment was very sweet to him and wanted to savor it, but he knew the battle was far from over. He ordered more troops to the mountain and told air support to continue their assault on the main gate. The colonel couldn't help but think what happened to the general? There was still no word on his whereabouts. He called around to his officers for a report and to this point, everything seemed to be working in his favor. With a little luck, the gate would be his before nightfall.

Chapter 50

Rebecca's frustration overwhelmed her, and she raised her fists, pounding them on the table before her, smashing it to bits. In her rage, she stood and faced her Aunt Grace. The rage and energy threatened to subdue her, and she stood shaking. Her aunt came to comfort her, but Rebecca raised a hand in warning. The older woman stood in her place as if frozen in time. Unable to move, she tried to reach Rebecca in her mind.

She started, "My dear, stop! This is exactly why I've brought you here. You need to learn control. If you aren't taught properly, you could hurt innocents or even yourself. Peter, I cannot help right now but you I can teach, and you then can show Peter. You must stop!"

Her aunt's pleas came through her rage-filled barrier and she let her energy wane. When the rage subsided, she collapsed into a waiting chair. Her aunt came rushing to her side to comfort her. Grace caressed her cheek and told her it would be all right, but control was needed before she used her gifts again. Rebecca looked into her aunt's eyes only to see grave concern. With this much power, Rebecca knew she'd need a teacher and Holly spent many hours trying to teach her with little headway. She couldn't help but wonder if Holly's sister could be the one to help her discover her vast potential.

Fatigue ran through her entire body and she struggled to sit up straight. Every time she unleashed that much power, she used much too much of her very self to do so. Despite her expended muscles, her mind felt almost asleep. The feeling of mental fatigue scared her; usually, she could physically heal quickly. If this caused her mental anguish, then that would be something altogether different.

Once again, her aunt clasped her hands. "Rebecca, you must listen to me! I understand the attachment you have toward your loved ones, but until you're in control, they're all in danger, from you!"

"Aunt Grace, I'd never hurt any of my family members or anyone that meant anything to me!"

"I know, my dear!" Grace nodded.

Her aunt looked at her. "But, Rebecca, look at the table or what's left of it for a moment. That's but an object. Imagine what you'd do to another human being! Now imagine it were Peter."

Rebecca's eyes teared up. "I'd never hurt him!"

Her aunt engulfed her in a hug. The two held onto one another for a few moments. When they broke the embrace, her aunt told her the lessons needed to begin right away. Again, Rebecca asked if they shouldn't help Peter now. Grace assured her that Peter was now well beyond their reach and Holly was now with Peter. At this, she perked up hearing that Holly was there to help Peter. With a renewed vigor, she rose and told her aunt she was ready to begin. Grace turned to her new student and told her it would require her utmost attention. She reminded Rebecca if she couldn't concentrate, then all their efforts would be for not. Rebecca reassured her aunt of her commitment and faced her with steel in her eyes.

The look of grit seemed to satisfy her aunt who told her to have a seat. She told her niece they'd start small by sending some images into her mind, such as problems to solve. Grace explained that the smaller problem solving and critical thinking created a much more solid control over her emotions. Emotion was the greatest enemy, instructed her aunt.

The two women sat legs crossed facing one another on the floor. Rebecca closed her eyes and let her aunt into her thoughts. At first, she could see nothing, but then the image of the main gate of her city came into view. Rebecca couldn't help but think this wouldn't be one of Grace's small tasks. She focused on the mountain and could see the untold numbers of soldiers swarming the mountain. Rebecca could see the main shield held and the gate itself still stood, but she could also see the large blasted-out areas of the mountain open. Soldiers made their way into the openings, worming their way down into the mountain.

Not wanting to leave the scene, she focused more and worked her way into the mountain to see close-quarters, hand-to-hand combat before the inside of the gate. If the enemy won the day, the main gate would fall as would her city. Again, she felt the rage rise within her and once again, the power took over. She felt herself being shaken. Rebecca opened her eyes to see a frantic Grace looking concerned at her niece.

Rebecca shook her head and tried to focus on her aunt, but she could still feel the energy build up in her body, waiting for release. Her aunt took her by the shoulders and looked deep into her eyes, waiting for Rebecca to come back to her. It took a few moments, but Rebecca calmed her rage and looked questioningly in her aunt's direction. Grace then smiled and calmed herself. It seemed to Rebecca that Grace didn't expect this outcome.

She looked at her aunt. "Was this one of your problems I needed to solve?"

"No, my dear. I think you created that scenario on your own. Following your progress though, I was right there with you. I have a feeling, Rebecca, what you saw is actually happening right now!"

"Aunt Grace, then we must go! We cannot sit here playing games while my city falls!"

Her aunt looked sympathetically to her niece. "I feel for you. I truly do but, my dear, but your destiny isn't at the main gate. Your destiny will have far-reaching consequences for all humanity. If you leave now untrained, then you'll hurt someone you love. I can see that much!"

Rebecca's face struggled. "I cannot leave them to that fate! I must go to them!"

Her aunt looked to her. "Rebecca, by the time you reach them, the battle will be long gone. The best way to help your city is to finish your training and return to them with your full power ready to serve them."

The two sat looking at one another, each searching their thoughts for what to say to each other next. Rebecca knew her aunt was right, but still felt the tug of her friends and family. It really was Peter putting her over the top. She couldn't let Peter get to her city, only to see it overrun and his life put into danger. Peter shouldn't have been able to make the journey, but he faced unspeakable odds to reach her city.

Just thinking of Peter's bravery caused a warming in her heart. The thought of Peter with his friends coming into the city should be a cause for celebration but something told her their welcome would be anything but a happy one. Even though she couldn't help him, she knew others in the city would assist him and help him acclimate. Struggling to let go, she finally relented and looked to her aunt.

Grace, sensing her struggle again, comforted her. "It won't be long, my dear! You'll be with him soon. Trust me, the two of you are destined for greatness! Even the very wise don't yet understand the importance of the two of you together."

Rebecca peered to the floor. "Yes, but it seems as though I'm forsaking him! He needs my help and yet I'm here. Tell me, Aunt Grace, how is that not a betrayal?"

"Yes, it may seem that way. If you go in now, you may spend a few moments together, only to have them snuffed out. If you train, then you'll have the rest of your lives together. It's painful, yes, but in the end, this small amount of pain will lead to a life of joy and peace. A small price to pay, don't you think?"

Rebecca couldn't help but relent as she knew deep down her aunt was correct. If she hurt Peter by accident, she'd never forgive herself. When she saw him, she wanted to be her very best, inside and out. Again, she took her aunt's hand and nodded, telling her it was okay to begin again. This time, they sat and calmed their breathing. Her aunt told her to let go and clear her mind. Rebecca did as told and felt her body calm. She could feel her own breathing become regular and she closed her eyes.

This time, an image of Rebecca sitting at a gameboard with her aunt came to her. The two played several rounds of the strategy game. At first, Rebecca thought this was useless until Grace continued to win round after round and frustration set in. Rebecca could feel the rage begin as her competitive nature took over. At that moment, she remembered her aunt telling her everything was about control. Instead of lashing out, she refocused her efforts the next game. The results were shocking as she soundly beat her aunt time and time again until her aunt could no longer beat her.

Rebecca's eyes popped open to see a proud aunt staring back at her. She could tell by the smile on her aunt's face, the lesson went well. She rose to her feet, feeling not only confident but refreshed. Her aunt congratulated her on her victory and asked her to come with her for a moment. She followed closely behind until they came to a huge, ancient, oak tree. Rebecca couldn't help but be held in awe of the magnificent tree. What made the sight even more amazing was the tree was leagues under the sea.

Grace asked Rebecca to have a seat under the tree. Grace explained that this tree was descended from an ancient line of trees that grew hidden in Rebecca's own city. She went on to explain when this outpost was created, one of the first items grown was the great oak tree. Upon sitting on the ground, Rebecca could feel a great connection to the tree as it seemed to almost speak to her. Grace could feel this as well and told Rebecca the tree was an important part of their history.

She explained that would be a story for another day but today, she wanted to illustrate the connection between Rebecca's power and nature. Rather than question further, she relaxed under the eaves of the beautiful tree. Its branches seemed to reach out to protect her against any intruders. As she clasped hands with her aunt, the sheer peace she felt melted away all of her anxiety. The calm washed over her, and she once again let her aunt guide her.

This time, her aunt brought her to a very dark place surrounded by diseased and fallen trees. In an instant, her aunt disappeared, and she was left utterly alone. Walking in the dim light, she could hardly see where she was walking. Many times, she stumbled, almost falling forward until she came to a large clearing. As she walked forth in the clearing, she looked up to see the wonderful tree standing proud before her. She turned around to look at the devastation surrounding the beautiful tree. The clearing itself remained untouched as the green lush grass surrounding the tree offered a protection from the encroaching evil.

From behind the tree sneering at Rebecca appeared High Commander Zosa. He cackled at the sight of Rebecca and the two stood facing one another, leering. The commander came forward, threatening to strike the young lady. He hesitated for only a moment before sending a bolt of energy sailing at Rebecca, striking her square in the chest. The bolt sent her flying through the air as she crashed into one of the ruined trees on the edge of the clearing. The impact caused great pain and she could hardly breathe.

As she forced herself to her feet, she could hear the commander laughing at her and she rose to her full height, allowing the energy to fill her body. The rage again entered, and she could feel her strength returning. Once again, she walked into the clearing, stalking her prey. The commander stood before her, leaning slightly against the ancient tree, laughing. Her anger brimming over, she strode forward, ready to lash out at the commander.

The commander taunted her, "Come, my dear, let's see that famous temper! You know you want to strike me down. Do it! Come now, let loose, and let all that hatred flow. Give in to the destruction. Honestly, I could certainly use one of your talents. I still may have you yet!"

At this, Rebecca raised her hands to release the energy to destroy her enemy. Just as she was ready to release, she looked up to see the beautiful, ancient tree staring down at her, almost guiding her. With a sigh, she lowered her hands and walked away. If she unleashed all that energy, she wouldn't only destroy the commander but the tree along with it. She viewed the surrounding destruction and knew the beautiful oak was all that was left. Rebecca continued to walk back the way she came and as she entered the woods, she heard the laughing become louder.

The commander cackled. "I never took you for a coward! Is that it then, you cower and leave?"

She spun. "Destroy you, yes! Look at the devastation you cause. Look around you. This is to be your legacy, destruction in your wake! Well, not me! I'll create. Now be gone!"

With that, she flourished her hand toward her enemy, making him disappear into thin air. She turned to walk back the way she came; the blackness turned to light. Every step she took, the nature around her returned to its former, lush glory. When she returned to see her smiling aunt waiting for her, she turned to look from which she came. The sight took her breath away. The forest radiated life. Sunlight broke through the trees, creating intoxicating rays and the animals came out to meet her, stopping just before her, bowing.

Rebecca could feel the warming sun on her face as a new energy entered her body, which brought a great power, one of warmth and peace. She knelt to the ground to let the animals come to her. She played with each of them in kind and joy filled her heart. Then the sky turned dark and the animals scampered back into the woods.

A voice from the sky boomed, "This isn't over! I'll have you!"

The sky returned to its glory of oranges, reds, and yellows. She could feel the peace return and the fragrances of the golden woods reached her nose. Her aunt came to her and placed a comforting hand on her shoulder. Rebecca reached up and touched her aunt's hand lovingly. The two walked toward the sun sinking in the horizon. It seemed as though the sun just enveloped them with light and all of a sudden, they were back in the underwater city beneath the ancient oak tree.

A beaming Grace sat before her. "My dear, that was amazing! Control is exactly what was needed. You demonstrated remarkable control in the face of great evil. That, my dear, is what you'll be asked to do over and over again. Now that you're learning restraint, we can focus on your many gifts. Your power is the greatest any of our kind has ever seen. That's why it has fallen to me to instruct you as I, before you, needed to control my power. Unfortunately, I didn't have a teacher and was exiled by my people out of fear. I'll do all in my power to make sure this doesn't happen to you."

Chapter 51

Colonel Whilhelm screamed into his communicator, telling his officers to send every available man to the mountain. Now that his men were inside, he needed to get as many soldiers in the mountain as he could. The main gate still stood closed tight and no matter what he threw at the shield, it remained unbroken. His only chance at this point was to send as many men down the rabbit hole as possible and hope they could scatter the defenses enough to open the main gate. Once at the main gate, he could easily take the city as he still was surrounded with an overwhelming invading force.

Listening to his officer's responses, it sounded as though most of his remaining forces on foot made their way to the mountain. The fighting outside remained fierce as his air support lit up the skies with energy bolts, taking down much of the enemies' defenses. The bombers didn't return and things seemed to be well in hand. Colonel Whilhelm smiled inwardly knowing it was only a matter of time until the gate fell. Years upon years of failure now led to his ultimate triumph.

He stood on the deck of his vehicle, looking at the battle with immense pride. A commander's greatest pride was to see one's battle plans laid correctly in victory. To this point, everything the colonel expected was going to plan. He left most of his assault vehicles behind his main force, waiting for the gate to fall. According to his officers, the enemy was nowhere to be found. This was slightly concerning to the colonel as his enemy's secrets were still hidden behind the mountain. The colonel, quite aware they could be falling into a trap, told his men to be prepared for anything.

Again, an answer came over the communicator telling the colonel they were taking heavy losses inside the mountain. He peered toward the mountain with binoculars to see what transpired before him. From what he could see, his men were still streaming into the breaches in the mountainside. The numbers made him feel good as hey scanned the mountain to see little in the way of a defending force preventing his men from entering. Blood ran down the mountainside, leaving a gruesome site ruining the stark whiteness of a once unblemished snowfall.

Looking through the lenses, he could see the remainder of his men pouring into the mountain. He was certain that in a matter of minutes the gate would open, and he could roll his force into the mountain to take the city. With all the energy cannons destroyed or under his control, the defenses of the mountain remained none. The waiting kept him anxious. He spent many years waiting for this moment and as the last of his men slipped into the mountain, he smiled.

The colonel's wishes were granted as his ultimate goal took place before him. A once impenetrable gate rose slowly. Through the rubble and smoke, the colonel saw what he knew to be true. His enemy waited until now to enter the fray. Zarillion assault vehicles came out in droves to meet the colonel's forces. As the vehicles poured out, the colonel could still see his men in hand-to-hand combat by the gate. He gave the order to move forward.

His force met the Zarillion forces just before the gate and the impact was devastating. Torn, crumpled, and hot metal seemed to litter the battlefield. At first, the Zarillion forces looked overwhelmed but so many vehicles lay destroyed before the gate, it actually formed a barrier. The colonel, furious to get inside, ordered the way to be cleared. Larger vehicles came from the rear to clear the way, only to be met by the enemies' counter. Again, a large battle ensued before the gate.

Keeping an eye on his ground forces inside the gate, he now sensed a pit in his stomach. The large force that poured into the mountain now fought for their very lives. He could see his men fighting furiously but losing ground. Though the gate remained open, he couldn't get through the barrier of twisted metal and damaged vehicles. He reached up and yelled in the communicator, ordering air strikes to clear the way. Ordering the other vehicles to halt, he let the air power do its thing.

The air strike was extremely successful as they created a large path for the remaining vehicles to crawl through. The colonel pushed his force forward. Now finally came the Zarillion air response as the colonel moved into position to enter the mountain. The enemy air support stopped the colonel in his tracks. The sky became black with the enemy forces bearing down on his ground forces. His own air support now tried to save itself as the enemy sent a large air force to defend the gate.

Once again, the colonel couldn't believe his luck as it looked once again that victory would be snatched away from him. His mood changed as his own air force took control of the skies. The enemy fled off to lick their wounds and once again, the air was his. He moved his vehicles into position to enter the city and crawled through the crater created by the blasting of the battle. As his force came within a few feet of the gate, he heard massive explosions behind him.

He yelled into the communicator, only to find that their enemy was now attacking their rear. The air support that he thought had tucked tail and ran decided on a new target, his rear flank. He ordered them to hurry forward so they could get as many vehicles inside before the air force decimated them.

Explosions continued to rock the area behind the colonel as he inched forward. He ordered his own air support in to keep the enemy off them, so they could get inside. Once again, the air became a swarm of aircraft blotting out the sky. The vehicles crept forward.

As the colonel's first vehicles were to enter the city, he could see large, moveable cannons taking aim at the vehicles. He couldn't order them back in time and they were blasted to pieces in seconds. Furious, he ordered the cannons taken out. Weapons of his own pounded the cannons but with little effect for each cannon destroyed, another took its place. Again, the assault was at a standstill. The colonel watched as his forces on foot were all but destroyed. The only hope he had at this point was to get these vehicles into the gate and allow the rest of his force inside.

The aircraft continued to pound his vehicles while his own air force tried to gain control of the skies. He turned his energy towards the gate and ordered every vehicle within view to fire upon the opening. Within a few minutes, all the cannons were silenced and once again, he moved forward.

The once massive force that looked unstoppable now limped to the gate. His remaining vehicles rode into the open gate with little resistance. The colonel's own vehicle remained intact as he rolled into the gate. That was when the cannons once again fired upon the unsuspecting vehicles. These cannons came out of the walls and were unseen when they crawled into the gate. His vehicles were sitting ducks, and many were destroyed instantly. He ordered his own cannons to fire and returned his own barrage of destruction.

Once the last of the cannons were put down, the colonel pushed forward into a large, open cavern just inside the mountain. He could see no sign of the enemy as they hid ready to spring another trap. To this point, his victory was sorely paid for in blood. He assembled as many vehicles as he could fit in the cavern. The colonel sent scouts to find out which way they needed to go next.

One returned to him, saluting him. "Sir, we're still trying to gain our bearings but from what we can tell, we're in a large cavern. It will be a few minutes before we get a safe direction in which to travel. Also, sir, there's no sign of the enemy!"

"No doubt a trap! Keep your eyes open and report back to me as soon as possible!"

The man saluted and ran back into the cavern. Colonel Whilhelm knew the possibility of a trap, but also knew his enemies definitely suffered great losses. Quickly, he returned to his own vehicle until the soldier reported back to him. Once inside, he asked the driver to park along the opposite wall. The driver complied, and he sat waiting for word. It wasn't long before his answer came back to him.

Again, the man came over the communicator to talk to his superior. "Sir, we need to leave right now!"

"What, are you out of your mind? This is my finest hour! I'm triumphant. I'm the first to breach this gate within memory and I have our enemy on the run!"

The communicator crackled, "Sir, it's a trap! They allowed us to enter. This is a false gate! This isn't an actual entrance. We need to leave now! This is just a large cave."

At that moment, the colonel heard explosions rocking the cavern. The blast threw his vehicle into the wall, forcing him to crash to the ground. Explosion after explosion rang in his ears as he could feel concussion after concussion slamming into his vehicle. His man was right, this was definitely a trap. In his hour of triumph, his humiliation would be complete. The enemy allowed them to take the gate only as a ruse to trap his force. Explosions could still be heard as the colonel forced himself up. Looking around, he could see only one of his men in the vehicle was alive. Luckily, the colonel sat right near the wall when the explosion hit their vehicle. The rest of the crew wasn't quite so lucky.

He looked down to see his shoulder hurt where his body struck the wall. There was blood and it felt dislocated, but otherwise he was sound. The remaining crew member tried to sit up, but blood streamed from his head. Colonel Whilhelm knew from experience, with that much blood loss, the man would only live a few minutes longer. The man leaned against the wall and saluted the colonel before closing his eyes and died.

Colonel Whilhelm saluted the man back and made his way to the door of the transport. Everything looked mangled but the door itself seemed to be the only thing intact. He tried to open the door, but it seemed jammed shut. Next, he crawled over the dead bodies of his drivers to squeeze out of the smashed windshield. As he pried himself out of the broken window, he came to rest on top of a rubble pile.

Smoke, burning flesh, and the smell of burnt oil filled the air. He tried to look around, but the black smoke was so thick, he could only see a few feet in front on himself. Using his hands to grope in front of him, he worked his way down the pile of rubble. Once on the ground, he could see a little better in the dim, smoky light. The sight before him was gruesome.

Once a large cavern was now a blocked avalanche of broken rock and twisted metal. His entire ground force was all but destroyed. He looked to where the main gate once stood only to see the entire entrance blocked by fallen stone and destroyed vehicles. The only pocket of space unfilled by stone seemed to be just where he stood. Scanning the entire area, he tried desperately to find any signs of life. Nothing could he hear but the occasional fall of rock.

The deathly silence caused him to panic. This couldn't be how it ends. All his years of service come down to this, buried alive. The prospect of losing his life this way and not the battlefield offended him. Without thinking, he returned to his damaged vehicle to see what survival supplies he could find. To his great surprise, all he could find was a canteen of water and a few protein bars. He did find his own pack which did have some supplies, but overall rations would be meager.

Once outside the vehicle, he scrambled down to the stone floor and explored. His enemies knew the way out, therefore he could find his way out. That's if the enemy didn't block up everything. He wouldn't die down here.

Chapter 52

Peter stood, mesmerized by the clear sheen of the wall preventing their entrance into the city. He could see no markings of any kind on the wall itself or on the surrounding ice. Alex just shrugged his shoulders and told him this was as far as he had able to get and the rest would be up to him. This infuriated Peter, to come this far and be stuck before an impenetrable wall was too much to bear. Peter couldn't help but reach out again and touch the clear wall.

The wall itself felt cool to the touch but not freezing such as the ice walls surrounding it. To Peter, it seemed as if some unseen force powered the wall. Without thinking, he worked his way around, using his fingertips to feel his way. Much like the journal months ago, he felt small bumps resembling braille. The language invisible to the naked eye was right there for the right person.

Astonished, Peter continued frantically telling Alex and Jake of his discovery. Alex was beside himself and so full of excitement, he couldn't contain himself. He told Peter to continue and let him know everything as he'd record his progress in a journal of his own. Peter did as instructed and let his hand be guided by the invisible language. His fingertips picked up the bumps and his brain translated them.

At first, none of the words made sense to Peter. The message spoke of a Haven for just travelers. He didn't know what to make of this as this city was in such a remote, desolate area. How could a haven be in the middle of nowhere, so far from humanity? Also, who was the haven for if not his own people? The humans did have many places of refuge around the globe, but this was the first mention of such a place in a frozen wasteland. As he continued to decipher the message, it made more sense.

The message seemed to be geared toward off-world travelers or what Peter might consider aliens. It spoke of distant stars and travelling the cosmos. He was enthralled and sucked in by the message as he continued. Frustration continued to mount though as the message didn't speak about entering the city. The message was one of welcome and spoke of only those worthy to enter may pass. Peter was dumbfounded. How does one demonstrate how worthy they are before a clear, sealed door in an icebox cave?

When finished, he spoke to Alex and Jake, asking them what they thought, "All right, you two, this is nuts! How am I supposed to show my worth? There's nothing here. Nothing at all. I cannot find a puzzle, a clue, or anything to help us get into the city."

Alex added, "Yes, and we don't want to be out here when the sun goes down. You think it's cold now, well, it will be cold enough to freeze your blood. That's exactly why it has taken so long to figure any of this out. I couldn't exactly bring heaters in here to figure things out without melting the walls!"

Jake piped in, "Guys, we need to figure this out or go back until tomorrow!"

"No, way, Jake! We're getting in there today!" shouted Peter.

Once again, Peter moved forward and felt around on the smooth wall, reading the message, hoping he missed something before. When he was sure he read everything, he turned to his friends with his hands in the air. He asked Alex to take out the journal, so he could look at it. Alex did as asked, and placed the journal carefully on the pack so Peter could easily read the ancient text.

Again, Peter was faced with the constellation runes and no way to understand them. Peter once again went back to the wall to feel around. This time, near the middle of the wall, he felt lines and dots on his fingers. As he let his hands go over the lines, they formed pictures in his mind. They too were constellation runes. He was beyond excited and described this to his friends.

"Listen, guys, I think I have something here. The runes are here as well. So far, I've been able to feel all the runes I see in the journal."

Alex moved forward. "That's awesome, Peter! Are they in any pattern?"

Jake piped in, "Dude, just open the door!"

"Funny! What do you think I'm doing?"

Peter went back to his vigil on the wall with his hands. He worked his way around the entire wall until he walked backward. Staring at the wall, he just shook his head and walked over to the journal. He flipped through the pages, taking note of all he saw. When he was done, he closed the journal and paced. His friends could tell he wrestled with some inner turmoil and chose not to interfere. Peter mulled over what was in the journal and on the wall until he stopped.

He blurted out, "I have no idea what to do."

"It's okay. We'll figure it out. You did so much already. You have done more in this short time than I have with years of research!" the old man said.

Jake added, "Dude, you did awesome! No one would've figured out the braille except you! That was brilliant."

Peter thanked his friends, but he was in no mood to accept congratulations at this moment. They still sat on the wrong side of the wall and were no closer to getting into the city. He plopped down on the ice floor with his hands holding his head. So many people counted on him and it was overwhelming. The weight pressed down on him, threatening to overtake him. He couldn't let his friends down.

Once again, he stood. "I'm sorry, I just don't know what to do next!"

Jake came over. "You got this, man. Just take your time. Think about it. I'm sure you have everything you need here to get into the city."

Peter lashed out, "I don't! I don't know how to get in! All your badgering isn't going to help!"

"Okay, man! Don't get freaked out. I was just trying to help."

It was Alex's turn. "Peter, take it easy. I know this is stressful, but we're here to help."

Peter turned with an angry look on his face. "Help! What help are you! All these years of research and we're still no closer to getting in! What help can you offer?"

Alex retorted, "Young man, you don't have to be rude! Yes, this is difficult, but you don't have to undermine all that I've worked for over the years."

"I'm done listening to other people! I'm here in this god-forsaken place for what? A journal. My grandfather is gone. My mother is who knows where and I'm here in an icebox! Tell me, what am I doing here?"

The boy collapsed on the ground shaking his head. His mind was full of rage and frustration. Everything seemed to come at him all at once. Then, the image of Rebecca came into his mind. She didn't speak to him, but the warmth of her smile gave him new life. He tried to reach out to her with his own mind, but the image was quickly gone. The coldness of the ground brought him back to his current situation. Peter could hear Jake and Alex still arguing about what they should do next when it hit Peter.

He sat up straight and remembered he was the key. During his adventure, that sentiment was relayed to him multiple times. The runes weren't the key but he himself. Multiple times, he was told he had everything he needed to complete his mission right inside him. Still this puzzled him as to what exactly he needed to do to open the door. He may have what he needed in him, but it was still blocked from his view.

Peter stood just in time to see a large man running in and attack Jake. Jake, completely caught off guard, absorbed the brunt of the tackle in his midsection, causing him to sprawl on the ground. The fit young man rose quickly to face his attacker. Jake, a tall young man, stood eye to eye with his attacker and they danced around one another, waiting for the other to make a move. Jake sprung first and grappled with the attacker, tossing him down.

The older man hopped back up and looked at Jake with admiration, as if they were gladiators and now earned each other's respect in combat. The two turned to face off and the older man bested Jake, throwing him to the ground. Peter could feel the rage building in him as he watched his friend being attacked. He rose to his feet as he saw another tall figure coming into view.

With his emotions bubbling over, he walked forward with his hands raised, pointing toward the new threat. The older man and the tall person were now almost standing together.

Peter could see it was a woman but in his rage, he really didn't recognize anything but his own heightened emotions. He let the blast of energy go with a primal scream, sending it toward the attackers. The bolt of energy struck them both square in the chests, sending them crashing into the opposite wall. Both figures lay unmoving and Peter ran over to finish them.

His eyes still blazed with power as Jake came over and gripped his shoulder. Peter spun and almost released another bolt until he saw Jake's face. This brought him back to reality and Jake held him at arm's length, telling him everything was all right. Alex was now over checking on the fallen attackers. Peter shook off Jake and went to check for himself. When he arrived, the woman stirred.

As Peter knelt to look at his attackers, he couldn't help but look at the woman with some sense of recognition. He tried to search his thoughts, but he still could feel much of the rage still built up, blocking his mind. Without thinking, he reached down and helped the woman to her feet. She was quite tall, almost a head taller than Peter and very fit. Jake, meanwhile, tended to the man.

The man stood with assistance and looked at Jake, trying to get a measure of the young man before him. The tall woman did the same with Peter, but kept blinking her eyes, looking at him as if she didn't believe what they saw. Alex stood staring at everyone wondering what was going on. Neither party seemed ready to speak as they all continued to gawk at one another, hoping the other would speak first.

The statuesque woman spoke first, "Might I have the pleasure of addressing Peter Sullivan?"

Peter stood shocked. "How do you know me?"

"We've both traveled far and through terrible dangers to be here together! I'm Holly Cheric, companion to one very dear to you, Rebecca Beals."

He took a step back and things came back to him. This was the woman who was always on the edge of his visions as he tried to contact Rebecca. Peter strode forward and did something quite unexpected—he engulfed the woman in a hug. Her protector strode forward but stopped when she raised her hand to ward him off. She accepted the hug and returned one of her own.

She took his face in her hands. "I'm so glad to finally meet you in person, but we really must find a way out of here and get to the main gate."

Peter looked puzzled. "This is a gate. Can't we just go in here?"

With a concerned look, she started, "Peter, this is a very ancient back entrance. As far as I know, no one can enter here. The way I understand it, we can only exit the city from here. There are a few of these secret exits around the city once used to fool our enemies."

"Holly, I'm not so sure about that. There are runes and messages all over the door!"

It was Holly's turn to look surprised. "Tell me what you've found!"

Peter explained at length the things he discovered about the entrance. Holly listened intently and nodded when he was finished with his tale. She stood, thinking about Peter's discovery. Holly then took a moment to introduce General Giles. The general even went as far as to support Holly's claim about this being just an exit. He never came this way, but being responsible for the defense of the city, he was aware of these alternate exits.

Peter couldn't accept their explanations and again thought back to himself being the key. He searched his mind. Everyone kept telling him all he needed was inside him. Searching his mind, he created an image of the door using all the runes he felt with his fingers. A brilliant design of runes showed forth and he scoured the design to see if any pattern could help him in his quest. At first, there seemed to be nothing of value in his vision.

When he became frustrated, he glanced at his vision one last time. Something was missing but what? Peter took one last look and it hit him all at once. One thing was missing—the starburst cross! That was it. The starburst that became so important to him cracking the code back in his grandfather's study long ago. He was almost too excited to say anything as he came out of the trance.

Everyone just stood looking oddly at Peter as he ran to the door. Again, he let his hands run over the smooth surface. His friends could see the excitement in his eyes, but didn't interrupt his search. After a few more minutes, he backed away from the wall and spun to meet his friends. His companions waited for him to blurt out what was going on, but still Peter couldn't talk.

Peter paused. "There's something missing!"

Holly moved forward. "Peter, what is it? What's missing?"

"There's no starburst pattern. Look here at the journal. You see the large starburst cross? That's the only rune missing on the wall! We must find it."

Jake ran forward. "Maybe it isn't on the wall itself. What about the ice?"

They all searched around the clear wall on the ice, trying to find the starburst pattern. At first, the only thing they could see was the sheer, smooth, ice walls. Peter noticed the secret symbol hidden through a foot of smooth ice. To the naked eye, it was impossible to see but they knew exactly what they were looking for. Peter put his hand to the ice, rubbing just on the surface.

"I found it! Come here and look at this!"

They all ran over and surrounded Peter. Each member now wore a bright smile. Peter couldn't help but laugh. He knew there must be a way in, but how could he cut through a foot of thick ice. His companions patted him on the back and congratulated him. Thinking what to do next, he turned to Holly and looked at her longingly. She reached out and patted him on the shoulder.

Holly nodded. "You want to know how to get through the ice? Well, my boy, think for a minute."

Peter thought for a moment. "Holly, everyone keeps telling me all I need is in me!"

"That's right. You have everything you need. You're the key!"

Peter winced. "Again with I'm the key. Could someone just for once tell me how to open the door?"

"I'm sorry, Peter, but in this, I'm just as much a student as you. Like I said, I always thought these were just emergency exits. You found out they may also be entrances."

Peter pondered this for a moment and then walked back to the ice wall. The distorted image of the starburst cross stared back at him, taunting him. Frustration built, but this time, he embraced it and used the warmth of his aggression to build as well. He reached out and placed his hand on the ice, and released the warm energy. Before his very eyes, the ice melted, revealing the starburst cross built into the very rock of the hidden cavern.

He backed away to let each of his companions look at the starburst pattern. Again, Alex was just beside himself with excitement. Each person seemed ready to enter the city, but suddenly Holly's face grew concerned. This didn't go unnoticed by Peter, but he let it go; they were so close to their goal. Once everyone took a turn looking at the pattern on the wall, Peter moved over to the wall again.

Peter backed away. "Holly, would you like to do the honors?"

Holly strode forward and gave Peter a kiss on the cheek. "A true gentleman! Now I see what Rebecca fancies in you."

Holly reached in to place her hand on the starburst cross, but nothing happened. She tried again, this time pressing the image. Still nothing happened, and she pulled her hand out. Holly turned to her friends with sympathy in her eyes. All seemed very disappointed.

Holly turned to Peter. "You're the key, remember!"

Chapter 53

Peter looked up into the eyes of his companions as they looked back at him with a look of supreme confidence. All his trials through his journey brought him to this one moment. Taking his leave from his friends, he moved toward the hole in the ice and the starburst pattern within. Standing before the image, he again opened his mind, stretching it forth to the waiting pattern. In his mind, the pattern burned bright and he could feel the power enter his own body. The two powers melded together to create a blinding light.

The power of the light brought him back to reality as he opened his eyes to see Jake right next to him. Peter smiled at his best friend and reached in, touching the starburst cross. As soon as his fingers touched the raised pattern, he felt the energy melding with his own. The warm energy filled his mind and he could see the bright light moving his way. The light continued to grow as it moved toward him.

Peter let the energy into himself and it grew beyond anything he ever imagined. Even with this much energy filling him, he didn't seem in danger. As the energy continued to fill him, the brightness around him became so intense that his companions were no longer visible to him. When the brightness threatened to engulf him fully, he released it all into the starburst cross on the wall. All the energy flowed into the pattern and he heard a click.

When he opened his eyes, he stood on the opposite side of the clear wall, looking out at his companions. He reached forth and placed his hand on the starburst pattern on the wall and the sheer wall rose, allowing his friends to enter. They all looked in awe at Peter as he smiled at them as they entered.

When his companions were inside, he once again reached forward and locked the door, so no enemies could enter behind them.

Standing on the opposite side, they could feel warm air coming from the unknown corridor. Holly and the general now took the lead, walking forward a few feet before turning toward Peter and his friends. They all stopped and looked at Holly whose face now was extremely serious. Peter came forward to ask about the concern, but he could go no further as he bumped into another unseen field.

He looked up at Holly. "Holly, what happened? Why can't I go any further?"

A sad look came over her face. "Peter, you're one of us but your friends aren't. I'm sorry, Peter, you have a very important decision to make!"

"Decision! What decision? Everyone has made the decisions for me! Now I'm allowed to make decisions."

She started, "I cannot allow strangers to enter our city without council approval. Approval is something I cannot receive here in a remote corridor of some unremembered part of our ancient city."

"So, Holly, what does that mean?" said Peter.

"I'd have to treat them as though they were prisoners for now."

Peter jumped forward. "Prisoners! Are you kidding me! They risked their lives to come here to help you! This whole mission was to come here so we might help your people."

At this, the general came forward with a hand raised. Peter stopped but could feel the rage building in him again. The general put his hand on Peter's shoulder. The large hand felt comforting, so he allowed it to stay. Again, Holly looked at Peter through sad eyes.

She began, "Peter, this brings me no joy. If it were my decision alone, I'd transport you all to the council chambers right now, but it isn't just up to me. Here, we act together as a council and we don't act on our own accord."

Jake now chimed in, "What does that mean, we'd be prisoners?"

Holly turned. "Jake, please don't be upset. It's our law. No strangers are allowed into the city without leave of the council. What I propose is you allow me to arrest you briefly, so I may transport you directly to the council for trial."

Peter retorted, "Trial! Now, there's to be a trial!"

"Peter, it isn't an actual trial but to any civilian seeing us bring you in, they'd see we're following protocol. Our law is very important to our society. We live as one with our laws. Your friends won't be in danger, but we'd be following the rules put forth by our council."

"Holly, how can you ask this of me? I cannot allow my friends to be treated as criminals just because of some odd law. If you do this, they'll have the stigma of being a criminal on them in the eyes of your people."

Again, a sad look came over Holly's face. "Peter, I understand. I really do, and I sympathize. This is the only way they can enter the city without being branded as criminals. Believe it or not, if I bring them in, they'll be judged more fairly than if they trespassed on their own. With myself and the general as witnesses on their behalf, they'll be exonerated."

Peter looked at the faces of Alex and Jake. Each looked back at Peter, telling him it was okay. Jake knew Peter would never do anything to hurt him. Still Peter wrestled in his mind with how Holly could treat her friends this way after they traveled this far to help her city. What if Holly was lying and his friends were found guilty, remaining prisoners? Then what would he do? He knew nothing of this city or the people he'd be surrounded by.

He looked again at his friends. "What guarantee do I have that they'll be all right?"

Holly searched his eyes. "You have my word as a council member that your friends will be welcomed with open arms once brought before the council."

The general leaned forward. "You have my word as well as a council member they'll be taken care of. Peter, I know this is a lot to take in. I understand in your society you have the idea of innocent until proven guilty, but here in this case, we don't have that luxury. If we were on the surface, we may have been more apt to follow those ideas, but here in the underworld, we need extra caution."

"General, I appreciate your endorsement but again, you're asking me to allow my friends to be taken prisoner." He strode forward in rage. "I won't allow it! My friends go free or no one goes!"

The general stood protectively in front of Holly. Peter noticed this and raised his hand to release a bolt of energy, but Jake jumped in front of him. Peter tried to push Jake out of the way, but the muscular young man stood his ground. He looked at Peter, trying to calm him. Without letting the energy go, he dropped his hands by his side, but kept the energy ready to wield.

Jake stood in front of Peter. "Dude, it's okay, man. You got us here. I trust you. Do what you must do. Remember, this is about a lot more than just you and me. We came here to help. These council members will see that when we get there."

Holly came out from behind the general. "Jake, well said. Yes, Peter, we understand why you're all here. That doesn't make this any easier on any of us. As I said, it isn't just up to me. If I waltz into the council chamber with your friends, the other members will see it as a gross violation of protocol."

Chapter 54

An exasperated Peter leaned up against the hewn rock wall, trying to determine the wisest course of action. His friends, family, and even Holly's people counted on him. As a young man, his responsibilities amounted to doing well in school and picking up his room. Now, here he was faced with the ultimate of decisions regarding others' lives. Holly could see his internal struggle mounting and moved over to comfort him.

She clasped his hand. "Peter, you may not see this at this very moment, but you allowing logic to hand out your judgement is the very reason you'll make a wonderful leader one day."

Peter looked into her eyes. "It doesn't make the decision any easier, does it?"

"That's always the struggle for leaders. We're asked to put others' lives in our hands. It's an awesome responsibility, but look to your friends for counsel and don't make the decision on your own. That's why I told you rather than just place them in my custody, which is my right by law."

Peter walked over to his two friends and sat on the ground with them. Alex argued that they entered as free people and they should be allowed to be free going forward. Jake was quick to point out there was a lot more going on here than just a quick stint as a prisoner. Peter brought up the point he didn't want anyone becoming a prisoner and then the whole conversation started all over again.

Alex relented, "Listen, guys. I'm an old man and freedom is very important to me, but I'll follow whatever you decide. After all, it was you who found us a way in and I trusted your grandfather with my life. Why should I not trust his grandson with the same!"

Peter looked embarrassed. "Alex, I'm not my grandfather. He was a great man. I'm just a boy."

"From all I've seen, Peter, you're much like him and a natural leader. I'll follow you, my boy. Lead on!"

Jake started, "Dude, you know I'm with you to the end. Say the word and I'll be part of the chain gang."

Again, Peter couldn't decide what to do and thought of what his grandfather would say. He thought back to a time when he was really young at a birthday party and his friends all wanted to pin the tail on the donkey at once. His grandfather suggested they all get blindfolded and have at it together. Peter recalled how much fun they all had while bumping into one another and being silly. The lesson his grandfather told him was sometimes you must sacrifice what you want for the betterment of others. He thought for a moment and rose to face Holly.

Holly could see the seriousness on his face and waited for his response. Peter moved toward her and thought of the right words to say. He wanted to word it just right not to seem disrespectful. Peter peered over his shoulder at Jake and Alex before looking at Holly again.

Peter began, "Holly, I understand your position and I respect your authority, but I cannot have my friends as prisoners as I roam free. Therefore, I propose that you take us all prisoner."

Jake ran forward. "Pete, no way, man! I won't allow that! You're a leader, not a prisoner!"

He raised his hand to calm Jake. "This is the only way, Jake. Listen, we need to get to the council and we've spent too much time already arguing over what we're going to do. Our enemies, however, are on our doorstep and must be dealt with. If my being a temporary prisoner allows us to get to the council and help others, then so be it."

Peter felt a strong hand on his shoulder, only to look up and see the general looking at him in sheer admiration. Holly also came over and offered her congratulations. Jake just looked defeated and Alex still didn't know what to think. Peter again turned to his friends and nodded. They in return motioned their acceptance.

Peter faced Holly. "We'll all be brought to the council as prisoners. What do you need us to do?"

Holly gave Peter a look of immense pride. "You've grown a great deal today. This may be the first of your lessons as a leader, but mark my words, you're wiser than most twice your age. I'll make sure the council knows of your sacrifice here today! Your selflessness will be known throughout the entire city by day's end."

She came over to the three and looked at them as friends and not prisoners. "I may have to take you into custody, but know today, each one of you has a lifelong friend in me and I'll defend you to my last."

Alex, Jake, and Peter stood awaiting their fate. They really knew not what being taken prisoner by these people would entail. Each just looked at one another, waiting for the worst. Peter nodded and told them they'd be all right. Jake shook his best friend's hand and then punched him in the arm for good measure.

Holly stood before them. "Are you ready? You won't feel a thing. I'll basically put you to sleep and when you wake, you'll be with me in the council chambers."

Peter could feel the sleep already taking him. The last thing he saw before the darkness was the beautiful face of Rebecca. Her smile radiated and filled him with warmth. He'd find her if it was the last thing he ever did. The last thing he remembered was, "Rebecca, my love, I'm coming!"

Acknowledgements

My family and students are a great source of inspiration and drive for me as a teacher, as well as a writer. I continue to learn and thrive on the challenge this journey has provided me. My immediate family is my wellspring. I can only hope to continue to provide pages that they and many others will want to read. As an author, I will continue to give the reader reasons to want to turn the page.

As part of this continuing journey, I have been humbled by the readers of my words. They have been gracious and helpful in my growth process. As a lifelong learner, I am always looking for ways to improve and my readers have allowed me to grow. Independently publishing my works is a daunting task and I continue to fine tune my craft each day.

An independent author finds many friends along the way and I would be remiss if I did not acknowledge my friends at ARIA. The Association of Rhode Island Authors is a magnificent resource for myself as well as hundreds of other authors. My family is my rock for writing my stories but ARIA is my outlet to get my books to the world. With ARIA's help, I now have the support to turn my passion into a profession.

Thank you to all for believing in me. I will strive to create stories that inspire, mystify, and amaze. I hope you will continue to join me on my journey of discovery. The road may be long and winding, but begins with that first step. Though my journey has just begun, I am in awe of what the future looks like. Look for me over the horizon as you never know when I will arrive on your doorstep.

About The Author

Christopher Paniccia was born in Providence, RI. He grew up in East Providence, RI and Rehoboth, MA. For over twenty years he has been an educator at the elementary and college levels in the Boston area. As an author and illustrator his goal continues to be one of inspiring others to follow their dreams. His student's remain a huge inspiration to him and directly inspired his first book, "Gridiron Conspiracy." The Gridiron Conspiracy Trilogy continues to expand its reach to all types and ages of readers. He is a Veteran of the United States Air Force, where he was a Combat Medic. He lives with his family in the Boston area.

You can connect with Christopher online at:

https://www.facebook.com/authorcpaniccia/

https://cpaniccia.com/

cpaniccia@bridge-rayn.org

cpaniccio@bridge-rayn.org